HER
SHALLOW
GRAVE

BOOKS BY D.K. HOOD

Don't Tell a Soul
Bring Me Flowers
Follow Me Home
The Crying Season
Where Angels Fear
Whisper in the Night
Break the Silence
Her Broken Wings

D.K. HOOD

HER SHALLOW GRAVE

Bookouture

Published by Bookouture in 2020

An imprint of Storyfire Ltd.
Carmelite House
50 Victoria Embankment
London EC4Y 0DZ

www.bookouture.com

ISBN: 978-1-83888-040-8
eBook ISBN: 978-1-83888-039-2

To my wonderful readers.

PROLOGUE

Where am I? Evelyn Ross opened her eyes wide but only darkness pressed in on her. Had she lost her sight? Her head pounded and thirst had stuck her tongue to the roof of her mouth. Too afraid to move and heart pounding with fear, she touched her face, feeling to make sure her eyes were open. Her memory of last night was foggy, like reaching for an elusive dream. Where had she been? The memory of taking a ride into a town dusted with snow, filtered into her subconscious. She'd planned to look for a meal and a place to hole up until she found work. She searched her mind, grasping at ghosts, but the memory of what had happened after she'd arrived in town had vanished.

There was no valid explanation, nothing but a void existed, it was as if someone had stolen time from her. From the stale damp smell, perhaps, she'd crawled into someone's cellar or was in a shed but it was the middle of winter and although chilled, she should be freezing. Sudden moves could mean falling into the dark unknown. She took deep breaths of air that smelled like the bottom of her grandma's closet. Trembling with panic, she explored her surroundings with her fingers and found the unusual texture of rough blankets under her. The idea of someone locking her in a confined space was her biggest nightmare and she raised both arms above her in blind panic. As she stretched her fingers above and out to the sides, finding only air, she breathed a sigh of relief.

Darkness rose like a wall around her, she had to move and at least try to find a way out. She rolled onto one side, and examined what was under her, finding the distinct surrounds of a bed or perhaps bunk; more exploration found the head of the bed. She sat up and dropped her legs off the edge and her feet touched the floor. The next moment, she heard footsteps and the sound of a door closing. Whoever was upstairs had moved into another room. This was her chance to slip away unnoticed. She'd gotten in here somehow and there had to be a way out. She eased off the bed and dropping to her hands and knees, edged forward until she found the wall. In the darkness, she searched every inch of the cellar, running her hands over the walls until her fingernails bled before she found the staircase. At the top, a tiny line of light crept under the door. She fixed on it like a beacon and crept up the steps. At the top, she pressed her ear to the door. When no sound came from outside, she tried the knob, turning it slowly but the door didn't move.

As if someone was outside the door, listening, she heard a low chuckle and the jangle of keys.

"You're never leaving me." The voice was deep and masculine.

Angry, she hammered on the door. "Let me out!"

"I don't think so." He thumped on the door. "Are you thirsty? Hungry? You'll have to be nice if you want to eat. If you don't cooperate, you'll be punished." His voice changed, becoming hard. "I'm sick of playing games with you, you're no fun at all. Get back downstairs or I'll kill you—it's your choice."

She screamed for help until her throat ached and her voice came out in a whimper but it only seemed to amuse him.

"Yeah, scream. I like that and no one can hear you." He chuckled again. "No one is coming to save you, Delores."

"Who is Delores? My name is Evelyn. You have the wrong person." She shook her head in defiance, wishing her voice was more than a feeble croak.

"I know exactly who you are, Delores." He sounded self-assured and she could hear the excitement in his voice. "I control every breath you take. You belong to me."

"No! I'll never belong to you." She banged on the door. "Let me out!"

The door flew open, hitting her in the face. Her feet slipped and she fell backward into darkness. Agony ricocheted into her back as she slammed into the steps and then bounced down the stairs like a rag doll. Gasping to draw air into her bruised lungs, she closed her eyes. She'd broken one arm for sure and her hip hurt so bad, yet she'd survived. Nauseous from intolerable pain, she lay panting in a tangled mess on the cold cement floor. High above, the open door flooded the room with light. A man stood in the doorway, the backlight making his dark shadow menacing, but it was the glint of the weapon in his hand that petrified her. A light came on in the cellar and she made out his cold dark eyes. He was watching her without expression.

"You've been a very bad girl, Delores." He rubbed the muzzle of his Glock against his chin. "You've broken my rules and spoiled everything. We could've had so much fun."

Terrified, Evelyn stared at him. "We can still have fun. Please don't hurt me. I'll be good, I promise."

"It's too late." He chuckled as if at a private joke. "It always ends up like this, doesn't it, Delores? You begging for your life and offering me the world?" He aimed the pistol at her and smiled. "You already know the end to the story."

The steps creaked under his weight. He was enjoying her fear. In sheer terror, she tried to drag her battered body away and hide but the sound of heavy footsteps followed her, walking slow. There was no escape and he had all the time in the world. *I'm going to die.*

CHAPTER ONE

The Glacial Heights Ski Resort, Black Rock Falls

Monday

Sheriff Jenna Alton glanced at her reflection in the glass door as she made her way toward the brilliant white snowscape outside the ski lodge. She sure didn't resemble a sheriff at the moment, and the memory of her past life as DEA Agent Avril Parker was well hidden. Bundled up with all the resort shop had to offer in the latest ski gear, she slid on her UV sunglasses and pushed through the second set of doors, glad to be out of the overheated interior. She hadn't made up her mind if the two sets of doors created a chamber to prevent the heat from leaking out, or to give the guests a few seconds to acclimatize. If the latter was the case, it did little to stop the shock of the arctic blast hitting her the second she exited door number two. The icy chill of winter blasted her cheeks and the familiar smell she'd craved since the last melt, filled her nostrils. It was a fragrance only someone who'd been fortunate enough to visit an alpine region during snow season would recognize. She often thought it was like stepping inside a freezer but with a hint of fresh pine needles and a touch of woodsmoke. She inhaled and coughed as the air threatened to snap freeze her lungs. She stepped with caution onto the snow-covered path and made out Deputy Dave Kane, her close friend and ex-special-forces sniper and the best darn profiler she'd known. He stood six-five and in his big boots and fur trimmed hood, resembled a florescent blue sasquatch rather than a man. She blinked at him through the falling snow dusting the walkway. "Is that you, Dave?"

"Yeah." Kane turned away from the sets of ski equipment he had leaning against a pine tree, to look at her and grinned. "Ha, I love the new outfit. You look like the Easter Bunny, all pink and fluffy. Have you your GPS tracker and satellite phone with you? There's only a few people using the northern slopes and none have gone down today, so we'll need to be careful."

Not wanting to divulge what she'd thought he resembled, she smiled. "Yeah, nothing has changed since you last asked me."

She enjoyed Kane's company, they had an easy relationship and although she indulged in the odd girls' day out with her friends, she preferred to spend her downtime with him. As he lived in a cottage on her ranch, they'd become close but with Kane mourning the loss of his wife in a terrorist car bombing, being friends for now worked just fine. It was great to be away from the office, and over the weekend the slopes had been busy for so early in the season. They'd spent the weekend with her protégé Deputy Jake Rowley and his girlfriend, Sandy. The couple had returned home on Sunday night and Jenna had put Rowley in charge of the office. As the ski resort was only a short drive from town, Jenna and Kane planned to remain for the rest of the week unless a crime wave suddenly descended on the town of Black Rock Falls.

The fresh snow had given the entire village a powder finish and after getting their ski-legs over the weekend, they planned to tackle one of the advanced slopes. She took the skis he handed her and clicked in her boots. "Thanks." She looped the cords of the poles over her thick gloves and looked at her weird reflection in his sunglasses. She hoped he had the titanium plate in his skull—compliments of the car bombing—well-covered. The cold gave him incapacitating headaches and was the only Achilles heel of the strong capable man, well, unless she considered, his determination to jump in front of a bullet to protect her.

She followed Kane, sliding along the path to the northern slope and through the tall pine trees, their branches heavy with snow. The owners had used every care to blend in the resort so not to damage the environment, with no conspicuous buildings or bright colors. The main resort building and surrounding log cabin village seemed to grow out of the forest, and even the ski lift was unobtrusive and didn't ruin the majestic views. They ran the entire complex on solar- or water-generated power and the resort had become a beautiful addition to the county of Black Rock Falls. The slopes formed a natural break in the forest and the northern one ran parallel to one of the access roads to the resort. As they moved toward the top of the slope the trees cracked and groaned with the lowering temperature. Winter had come in a rush and taken nature by surprise.

When they reached the top of the slope Jenna stopped beside Kane to read the noticeboard. The prominent black diamond designated the slope for advanced skiers. It also gave the current weather report and listed any projected problems they might encounter on the way down and where to locate the ski lifts. The advice to stay in the middle was usual and Kane had already checked the conditions several times before they'd decided to ski. He took no chances of being out on the mountain during a blizzard. She moved up beside him. "You go first. I'll follow you down."

"I'd rather follow you, just in case." Kane inclined his head and looked at her but she couldn't see his eyes behind the blue reflective lenses.

Jenna laughed. "In case I fall? I won't. I'll be careful and if I did, you'd be back here in minutes." She grinned at him. "I like watching you. You go so fast it takes my breath away."

"Okay." Kane moved forward. "Meet you at the lift." In a swish of snow, he was away and heading down the slope.

She watched him for a few seconds and then followed. With a push of her poles and bending her knees, she tucked in her elbows, leaned forward, and surrendered herself to the thrill of the slopes. Glacial wind bit into her cheeks but the rush as she gained speed was exhilarating. As she entered a long sweeping bend, she noticed Kane jump to one side and come to a stop in a plume of white snow. He turned toward her and waved both arms. She zig-zagged to slow down and then mirrored his move in what she called a hockey stop and glided slowly to his side. "What's up?"

When he didn't answer, handed her his gloves, and then searched his jacket pocket for something, worry for his health churned her stomach. "Dave. What's wrong?"

"I'm not sure." Kane pulled out the small pair of binoculars he always seemed to have in a pocket and trained them along the trees growing alongside the road. "Oh, that's not good."

Following his line of sight, Jenna swallowed hard. "What the hell is going on?"

"Someone has decorated a pine sapling with what looks like body parts." Kane handed her the binoculars. "On the bend close to the road." He pointed in the direction and took back his gloves. "We'll have to go down, take the ski lift, and then go look. It might be a prank."

Jenna peered into the binoculars. "I can't imagine anyone doing that in this weather." She scanned the area. "Okay, I've found the bend."

"Move in slowly, I spotted them on the way down." Kane took her shoulders and turned her a couple of degrees to the left.

"I see it." The sight of discolored frozen arms and legs hanging from the snow-laden tree branches came into view and she gaped in astonishment. Some of the limbs had brightly colored tattoos and one of the frozen hands still wore a pinky ring. "That's no prank." She dropped the binoculars from her eyes and stared at him in disbelief. "Well, that's our vacation over. It's starting again. Another lunatic has arrived in Black Rock Falls."

CHAPTER TWO

The top of his truck, he'd discovered, made a fine place to rest his rifle and peer through the scope. From his position, he could make out the flashing lights of the deputy's black truck. He'd caught the expressions on their faces at his display and chuckled. Mouths turned down, the sheriff and her deputy had puffed out great clouds of steam and waved their arms around. Hampered by their thick winter clothes they resembled automatons. He glanced at his reflection in the side mirror and shuddered. The amount of clothes he had to wear in the mountains dragged him back to his memories of his time as a kid. He'd been the kid without a friend, more round than tall with zits covering his face in exploding masses. He'd hated himself and as he'd grown had taken steps to change his appearance, but the little boy, bullied or ignored, still cowered inside.

As the years went by, he often wondered why teachers, who professed to nurture their students, made two kids captains of opposing teams and allowed them to humiliate the other kids by choosing who was best and next best and so on to join their team. He'd always been the last pick, the boy nobody wanted. Did anyone understand what it was like to walk in his shoes or what it was like to feel worthless, unloved, and despised?

And then there was Delores. She'd made like she was his friend. He'd never forget her, the black fingernails, colorful tattoos, the ring through her nose, and her black hair. Most of the guys thought she was hideous but he'd loved her—until she'd humiliated him. The little boy hiding inside exploded into flames and a new man rose out of the ashes. He'd enjoyed killing her but it hadn't lasted long enough—he wanted more and had planned to spread her remains far and wide but when he'd returned to her shallow grave, he'd found it empty. Since then, he'd seen her in every town he visited. She just wouldn't stay dead.

He always gave Delores a choice. She could spend some quality time getting to know him before she died. He only wanted to talk and maybe a little company over dinner. He wasn't interested in sex but she always abused him, threatened him, and called him names. The screaming did something to his head, it turned on a buzzing sound that made him happy. At first, he waited for her to attack him and then he'd defend himself. It was the same as if a bear walked into his cabin and slashed out with its claws. It had been messy but he'd refined his skill as more Deloreses came into his life. Although, the last one had been a mite easier. He'd opened the door and set her free. She'd run through the snow, staggering like a wounded deer, and then he'd popped her.

He smiled. The sound of the chainsaw still rang in his ears. Left outside in the snow overnight, she'd made his work easy and then he'd hauled the smaller bits of her to a tree and added a few other touches and arranged them just so. It had become a skill he enjoyed. People would remember him for his frozen art but no one would recognize *her*, she'd become another statistic, another Jane Doe. He looked through his scope again and smiled. "You thought you were all that, huh, Delores, and now look at you, downgraded to bear popsicles."

CHAPTER THREE

Medical Examiner Shane Wolfe glanced at the desk over the shoulders of his two interns: Emily Wolfe, the eldest of his three daughters and Colt Webber, a badge-holding deputy at the Black Rock Falls Sheriff's Department. He nodded. They'd finished the tissue sampling exercise he'd given them and had achieved the same results. "Great job. You can finish up here. That's all for this semester. I want you to go back to school for the rest of the day and study for your exams. If anything interesting comes in, I'll call you." He smiled. "If you have any questions, drop by any time."

"I have to pick up some books from my locker." Webber stood. "But I can do that on the way home."

Wolfe looked at him. "Take what time you need. The exams take priority."

"I have everything we need here, so is it okay if we study in the front office, Dad?" Emily looked up at him. "It's as quiet as a morgue." She chuckled.

Wolfe smiled. "Sure, as long as you both study and don't waste time staring at your phones. The exams are important."

"I know, Dad." Emily tidied the bench.

Being ME had become his life now, but he still held the title of FBI handler for the man now known as David Kane. The quiet deputy remained a valuable operative and the office of POTUS required regular updates on his and Jenna's status. Wolfe had enjoyed a varied career in the military, starting as an IT specialist. He'd spent his deployment as a field medic, became an MD, and then while nursing his terminally ill wife, had studied forensic science. His arrival in Black Rock Falls hadn't been a fluke, it had been carefully engineered by the powers that be. After his wife passed, Wolfe found himself back on the payroll, with all the help the government could offer. Now he'd become part of a well-oiled team of professionals, which was just as well as Black Rock Falls attracted trouble. When his phone chimed a familiar ringtone, he sighed. If Jenna called him when she was on vacation, something was up. He strolled out the door and headed for his office. "Hi Jenna, what's up?"

"I'm staring at a pine sapling decorated with body parts. It's close to the backroad leading to the ski resort. We're on scene so you'll see Dave's truck. I need you out here now. I'll send you the coordinates." Jenna sounded all business. *"I'll get Rowley and Walters up here as well. We'll need to block off this road for a time."*

Wolfe turned back to the pathology lab. "Okay, I'm on my way."

He pushed open the door and Emily and Webber looked up at him. "Get your gear, we have a case in the mountains."

In less than ten minutes he had the ME's van packed and was heading out on the recently cleared roads. Clouds hung low in the gray sky and he could just make out the snow-covered mountains soaring out of the frozen forest. The van wasn't the best vehicle for traveling in the harsh conditions but he'd fitted snow tires and Webber had decided to follow him in his truck. As they reached Stanton Road and headed alongside the forest, the wind picked up and dislodged the snow piled up on the tall pines' branches. Ice-filled chunks of snow rained down on them. The wipers were no match for the frozen lumps and slowed down under the weight. "That's all we need." He pressed the water and jets sprayed the windshield. "Ah, that's better."

"Are you going to tell me about the case?" Emily had one hand locked into the handgrip above the door. "Jenna's on vacation, so who called us out?"

Wolfe didn't take his eyes off the slippery blacktop. "Jenna. Apparently, someone has decorated a small pine tree with body parts. She said it was on the backroad into the Glacial Heights Ski Resort." He slowed to move around a pile of snow that had spilled down onto the road. "I'd say Kane is working the scene with her now. If it's body parts the evidence on scene will likely be minimal."

"We may be lucky. I doubt the snowplow or brine spreader has been out there this morning or they'd have called it in." Emily turned in her seat to look at him. "If so, there may be tire tracks and footprints."

Wolfe glanced at her. All he could see was a strand of blonde hair escaping from her hood, wind blushed cheeks and a pink nose. With her sunglasses and scarf, she was barely recognizable. The GPS informed them to take the next left and they turned onto a side road that wound through the forest. Although the road was snow covered, it was minimal. The snowplow would have gone through in the last twenty-four hours, followed by the brine spreader. Snow tossed from the plow, along with leaves and other forest debris, formed a wall along each side of the blacktop. Snow dusted the gray piles but not enough to cover them completely. "We can assume whoever did this came by after the snowplow and up to the time Jenna arrived on scene." He cleared his throat. "Make a note to mention this to Jenna, she'll follow up and find out when they came through last."

"Okay." Emily pulled out a small book and made some notes.

As they took a sweeping bend, Wolfe made out Kane's unmarked black truck, his wig-wag lights flashing from inside. He drove up slowly, searching all around for any signs of disturbance. From inside his van, he couldn't see the crime scene at all. He pulled up behind

Kane's truck and Webber stopped behind him. He climbed out as Jenna appeared on the top of a bank of snow. He gave her a wave. "How far to the scene?"

"It's over here, a few yards from the road." Jenna pointed toward the front of Kane's truck. "There's a walkway cut through the snow. We believe the killer dug it out to gain access. We have checked all around, but the recent falls have covered any footprints or tire tracks, I'm afraid."

Wolfe jumped up beside Jenna and looked both ways. "Is it visible from the road coming down the mountain?"

"No and we were looking for it." She frowned. "We crawled down the hill and reversed back up and I scanned the trees with Dave's binoculars before we located the scene. It's just inside the tree line."

"Well, that shoots my timeline to hell. I thought the snowplow guy would've noticed it for sure." Wolfe jumped down to the road and offered Jenna his hand. "Show me what you've found." He turned to Emily and Webber chatting beside the van. "Grab our gear, the scene is a few yards inside the tree line. There's a cut-through in front of Kane's truck."

"I don't know how Dave spotted it on his downhill run, he must have the eyes of an eagle." Jenna's boots crunched on the icy blacktop. "He's photographing the scene. We thought the less time we spend out here in the freezing cold the better."

Wolfe followed her through a deep opening in the snowbank. "This would've taken some time. I don't know many killers who would go to this much trouble and it advertises the fact there's something through here."

"I thought the same." Jenna turned to him. "I'd say it wasn't done on the fly, he did this and then came back later to drop off the body parts." She waved a hand to where Kane was taking photographs. "This is new."

"Uh-huh." Wolfe stared at the ground, scanning for any scrap of evidence. He looked at Kane. "You found nothing, no footprints, drag marks, blood?"

"No, the snow was pristine, it's been snowing overnight and I doubt he'd try this in daylight." Kane walked to his side. "Although, as the tree is concealed from the road, it's possible."

Wolfe turned as Emily arrived with Webber carrying his forensics kit. "Okay, Kane has taken the crime scene images, we'll need to tag and bag the body parts." He glanced at Jenna. "From what I can see, it looks like we have the limbs of a female but what I'd like to know is where has he hidden the rest of her?"

"We have searched the immediate area but who knows what's lying under the snow?" Jenna frowned. "The rest of the remains could be anywhere." Her phone chimed. "I'd better take this, it's Rowley. He's up aways, stopping traffic." She walked away.

"Need any help?" Kane walked to his side.

"Nah." Wolfe examined a forearm hanging from the branch of a tree. "We might find some evidence on the twine he used. Cotton twine picks up fibers." He shook his head. "Look at the holes. I'll need to look closer but I'd say he drilled these when the limbs were frozen."

"That's not a good sign." Kane rubbed his chin and stared at the tree. "Maybe he keeps the rest of the body. I've read about cases where killers keep their victims in the fridge, so anything is possible."

"Dad." Emily walked over and held out two evidence bags. "Not one woman, two. These hands don't match, for one thing they're both left hands and the nails are different in shape."

Wolfe nodded. "We'll keep them frozen. Pack snow around the bags and I'll take a closer look when we get back to the lab." He turned at the sound of Jenna's voice. She was walking back toward his van with her protégé, Deputy Rowley, close behind.

"Rowley has some information. I figured you'd want to hear this in person." She smiled at him.

Wolfe looked at Rowley. "What have you got?"

"The cut-through was here before we arrived last Friday." Rowley puffed out great clouds of steam. "Someone had an accident on the slopes and the paramedics cut through the snowbank to get them out to the ambulance. I overheard someone talking about it at the front counter."

"Hmm, so the killer would have known about the cut-through." Kane stared into the distance. "That opens up a list of possible suspects."

"Yeah." Jenna nodded. "Someone working or staying at the resort, a paramedic, or someone who overheard another person talking about the accident." She snorted. "We've got this one in the bag."

"I wish." Wolfe stared at the tree. "One thing's for sure, we have another twisted SOB in Black Rock Falls."

CHAPTER FOUR

Kane's head hadn't touched the pillow when Duke's whine roused him from a deep sleep. The mountain air, exercise, and huge meal had tuckered him out. He'd been happy to remain at the ski resort for another night. Jenna wanted to speak to some of the guests who'd been in the vicinity of the murder scene the previous morning. They'd hunted down a few couples but by nine-thirty most had headed to their rooms and she'd decided to call it a night. He sat up and glanced at his phone; he'd been asleep less than half an hour. He looked at Duke. The dog whined and walked to the door, a signal he needed to go outside. At home, he had a doggy door, so Kane never needed to get up and walk him during the night. "It's really cold outside, you sure you can't hold it?"

Duke gave a low bark and scratched at the door. Kane sighed. "Okay, okay. We'll need to bundle up, it's way too cold to be going out for a stroll."

He dragged on clothes and then fitted Duke's coat. He pulled on his thick woolen hat and headed for the door. In the hallway, Duke let out two happy barks. "Hush, you'll wake everyone." He stared at Jenna's door and hurried down the hallway. They took the elevator to the lobby and he gave the sleepy guy on the front desk a wave before heading outside. They made it through the two main doors and a blast of wind hit him, pushing the hood from his head and stinging his cheeks with ice. He glanced around, deciding which way to go. Lights spilled a yellow glow over the track that led through the trees to the cabins. He walked in that direction. It would be the best place to give Duke a run, as they'd at least be out of the wind inside the thick forest. Icy patches shattered under his boots and the bitter cold seeped into every crack of his clothing as he set off. He'd walked about twenty yards before Duke had found a suitable spot and took off vanishing into the undergrowth. The moon was high but the lights on the pathway made the forest appear dark and foreboding. "Don't be too long."

Kane stamped his feet and pressed his hands under his arms but standing in one spot wasn't an option. He kept walking in the direction Duke had taken. Around the next bend the lights of a cabin burned in the distance about one hundred yards away. He frowned. This area of the resort was still under construction and as far as he was aware, the cabins weren't in use. Appliances had gone missing earlier in the year from the construction site, so he wondered if it was another burglary. He lifted the back of his jacket to search for his weapon. Even out skiing he'd worn the holster in the small of his back. It was a habit and yet he'd walked out without it. He shook his head in disbelief and picked up his pace. When he reached the road, he slipped into the forest. Frozen pine needles crunched under his boots and moving through the trees and dead ice-covered vegetation took longer than he'd imagined.

The sound of an engine broke the silence and he ducked behind a tree as the lights of a truck came around the corner and then stopped outside the cabin. He heard a muffled scream as two men climbed out the truck. One of them was dragging a tall young woman with long red flowing hair behind him.

"Let go of me." The young woman slapped at the man. "Have you gone bat shit crazy?"

"Shut up!" The second man grabbed her other arm and pushed her hard toward the cabin. "Get inside."

Kane took off at a sprint, bolting out of cover and startling both men. He stopped in front of them. "It's obvious she doesn't want to go with you. Let her go."

"Help me!" The woman struggled to get free. "They're kidnapping me."

"Take your hands off her and back up." Kane took a step closer. "She's not going anywhere with you."

"Let me go!" The woman stared at Kane. "Call 911."

"I said, get inside the cabin." The first man opened the door, gave her a shove and she stumbled inside. He gestured to someone inside. "We have trouble. She's not going anywhere. Get out here."

The next moment three men stepped out, closing the door behind them. Kane looked them over; they were all younger than he was, maybe under twenty-five, and in good shape. They ranged in size from five-ten to about six-two. He could take maybe four or even five of them down, no trouble, but six and whoever else might be inside could be a problem. "Yeah you do. I'm Deputy Kane from the Black Rock Falls Sheriff's Department." He straightened. In his snow boots he towered to at least six-seven. "Kidnapping is a federal offense. Let the woman leave with me and I'll walk away."

"Do we look like we care?" The first man grinned at him, stepped away from the others, and shaped up, lifting his fists to his face. "When they find you in the morning, we'll be gone and you'll freeze to death."

Kane inclined his head and smiled. "I don't think so. Do you boys really want to spend Christmas in the hospital?"

"Man, there's six of us and only one of you." The first man laughed. "Has the cold frozen your brain?"

So there are six of you, huh? Kane shrugged. "Nope, I'm giving you a choice. Give me the woman and walk away or suffer the consequences."

"You think you can take on all of us?" The first man snorted with laughter and looked around at his grinning companions before staring at him. "You won't make it to the hospital."

There's a fool in every group. Kane pushed his hands inside his pockets. "Do you really want to find out?"

Every group had a leader— he'd need to take him out first because the others would do one of two things. They would attack at once, or wait until their leader tried to knock him off his feet and then use their boots to cave in his skull. Kane took in the body language of each man. Only the first two had bundled up for the cold; the other four, although wearing thick sweaters, wouldn't last too long in the subzero temperature. Their muscles would become cold and slow down their reaction time. He on the other hand was warm from running, all warmed up and ready to fight.

His gaze flicked to the other men. They had fanned out and were making moves like brawlers; slapping fists into the palms of their hands, swiping at the ends of their noses, and looking at each other with over-confident expressions. The one thing that distinguished a person trained in hand-to-hand combat is they rarely moved during the showdown. Taking a step back to position his feet Kane dropped his hands to his sides and relaxed. In this position he had two choices: to strike with feet or fists. Brawlers would expect him to defend himself using his fists. He waited, relaxed and nonchalant, for them to make the first move. If they moved into his space and attacked, he would hurt them. He'd already planned his moves. Trained for one hit, one kill, he'd aim for disabling them unless they pulled a weapon on him and then all bets were off.

CHAPTER FIVE

Jenna stared at the ceiling unable to sleep after hearing Duke barking in the hallway. She'd gone to her door just in time to see Kane slip into the elevator. She glanced at the clock—in these temperatures, Kane wouldn't remain outside long and he'd been gone for some time. Concerned for him, she got up, dressed, and hurried to the elevator. In the foyer she spoke to the man at the desk. "Did you see a tall man with a bloodhound go out earlier?"

"Yes, ma'am. He headed out toward the new block of cabins. I'd say he took the dog into the forest to do his business."

Jenna waved at him, pulled her scarf up over her nose, and headed out the entrance. Using the light on her phone she could clearly make out Duke's pawprints in the fresh snow. As she walked toward the trail to the cabins, the trees cracked and groaned as they froze. Scattered pine needles made the snow look like a massive pincushion. In fact, under a full moon the snow-covered vista looked like another world. She hustled along, moving as fast as possible. If she met Kane on the way back, he'd probably laugh and tell her she worried too much but if something had happened, for instance, a branch had broken off and struck him, he'd be glad she'd come along. When Duke's tracks went off the trail and Kane's continued in the same direction, she followed but then stopped dead as his tracks disappeared into the trees. "Kane, are you there?" She turned the beam of her phone into the forest. Nothing moved. "Duke, Duke come here boy."

She heaved a sigh of relief when she heard a bark in the distance and moments later, her light picked up the red of Duke's eyes bounding toward her. She bent to rub his ears. "Good boy. Where's Kane? Seek Kane."

When Duke sniffed around the snow at her feet and then sat down looking up at her, she repeated the command with the same result. Then a memory filtered into her mind of something Wolfe had told her. It was very difficult for dogs to track in the snow. Her only choice was to continue along the pathway and hope she'd pick up Kane's footprints again. As they rounded the corner, she made out lights streaming from the windows of a cabin and a group of men outside. From the way they'd surrounded Kane, they didn't look friendly. "Oh, no."

She unzipped her jacket to access her weapon but things were escalating fast outside the cabin. She'd never seen Kane in full combat mode, or how good he was at defending himself. Their morning workouts aside, since receiving the plate in his head, she worried a head blow could cause significant damage. Panic caught in her throat and she hastened her step, aware of the slippery ice-covered trail underfoot. She could see them all now, two in snow gear, red and blue, three others in sweaters of various colors. Jenna took in the situation. From this distance, with everyone milling around, she could hit Kane if she used her weapon. The next moment, a man in a red ski jacket aimed a punch at Kane's head and all hell broke loose. She hadn't taken a breath before Kane lashed out with his foot and destroyed Red Jacket's knee. He turned and elbowed Blue Jacket in the face, shattering his nose. The man fell in a spray of crimson and lay motionless on the snow. Without breaking the flow, Kane pivoted and aimed a kick at one of the other men's heads, sending him crashing face first to the ground. Ignoring Red Jacket's screams of pain, Kane dropped into a fighting stance. His expression was deadly calm as he lifted one palm up and beckoned the other men with his fingers. Both roared and charged him, swinging wildly. Without seemingly exerting any energy, Kane ducked punches and struck like a snake. She heard the blows, the gasps of pain, and in seconds both men dropped into the icy drift waving their arms as if making snow angels. It was over so fast, if she'd blinked, she'd have missed it.

Jenna opened her mouth to call out but Kane had charged to the cabin, kicked in the door, and dashed inside. With Duke at her heels, she ran through the snow and skidded to a halt as Kane tossed a man out the door with such force, he slid past her face down in the snow and collided with Red Jacket who was howling like a banshee. She stuck her head inside the door, weapon raised. The cabin was empty but she heard voices. Moving with caution, she headed to an open door and found Kane inside a bedroom. "Dave, what's happening here?"

"Overdose." Kane appeared remarkably calm as he hauled up a woman and tried to make her walk up and down the room. "Those idiots kidnapped Kim here, to help." He indicated to a red-haired woman with a stunned expression.

"Kim?" Jenna stared at the pale young woman and holstered her weapon. "There's a Naloxone spray in our kit in the truck. Give me your keys, I'll go." She held out her hand for the keys but Kane laid the woman down on the floor and after ordering Duke to stay, sprinted out the door. She turned her attention to Kim. "Naloxone will reverse the effects of opioids."

"That's what I kept on telling them." Kim rolled her eyes. "I met them yesterday on the slopes and told them I was a nurse. The idiots must think I carry the spray on me." She kneeled beside the woman on the floor and slapped at her face. "Stay awake now, come on look at me. Sit up, yes that's right."

Jenna pulled out her phone, called the paramedics, and then contacted Rowley and Webber for backup. "If you can manage here, I'll go and see what I can do for the men outside."

"You should leave them to freeze." Kim had the woman sitting up. "The guy they left with me was rushing around like a lunatic flushing drugs down the toilet. These guys are doing more than partying." She pointed to a packet on the floor under the bed. "I kicked it out of sight when the deputy gave his name. I wanted to make sure the cops know who is responsible for this woman's overdose."

Jenna nodded. "Thanks, don't touch anything. I'll take some photos. Kane will be back with the kit soon and we'll get it into an evidence bag." She snapped a few shots and hustled outside pulling her weapon.

The men outside looked at her, dazed and confused, as they tried to get to their feet. Around them, blood stained the pristine snow and Red Jacket's continual screams of pain were upsetting. What had he done to make Kane inflict so much damage? From the angle of the man's leg Kane had shattered his kneecap. She had a duty of care to these men and cleared her throat. "I'm Sheriff Jenna Alton. Those of you who can walk, help the others inside the cabin before you all die of exposure." She waved her Glock at them. "Then maybe you'll be able to explain what is going on here and why you attacked my unarmed deputy."

"Trust me." One of the men staggered to his feet. "That guy don't need no weapon. He *is* a weapon."

CHAPTER SIX

By the time Kane waded through the snowdrifts to his truck and then turned back running with his medical kit in hand, sweat trickled down his back. In stark contrast, each breath of the subzero air sawed at his throat and the howling gale sent daggers of ice from the forest into his wind-burned cheeks. In the distance he could hear sirens—help was on the way. He reached the cabin, noting the injured men had vanished, and placed the medical kit on the floor before lifting the broken door away from the entrance. In the small room, Jenna held her weapon on the six men. They all seemed to shrink away from him as he gave her a nod and hurried into the bedroom. He dropped down beside the waxen-faced woman, located the Naloxone nasal spray from his kit, and administered the drug to the woman. He looked at Kim. "I hope we're not too late."

"She was awake before." Kim was staring at the woman. "There, look she's coming out of it now."

The woman's eyes fluttered and she dragged in a deep breath. Blinking, she stared at Kane. "Oh, I'm in trouble. You're Deputy Kane, huh? I recognize you from town."

Kane stood. "And you are?"

"Amy Fleming." Her mouth turned down. "I met Dean at the lodge, we came back here, had a few drinks and then his friends arrived. That's all I know."

Kane shook his head. "You'll be going to the ER. I won't be charging you with anything." He stood. "I have bigger fish to fry." He headed back to the other room.

"These men said you attacked them without provocation." Jenna had an expressionless face but her eyes danced. "Kim states one of these men flushed a large number of drugs but they've left enough behind to charge them with drug offenses."

Kane glanced around the room meeting each man's eye. "Well, the guy in the red jacket and the one in the blue kidnapped Kim and I caught them dragging her from their truck."

"He wouldn't let me go." Kim appeared at the door. "Deputy Kane identified himself and they threatened to hurt him so bad, he'd be found dead in the morning. They attacked him and he defended himself. If he hadn't intervened, Amy back there would be dead by now." She glanced over her shoulder. "I'll wait with her until the paramedics arrive." She turned back to the bedroom.

"Hmm." Jenna read them their rights. "You're all going to be held in custody in a secure hospital ward overnight. Once I have the arrest warrants, you'll be moved to the county jail."

"On what charges?" Blue Jacket held a rag to his broken nose.

"Kidnapping, drug offenses, and assaulting an officer will do for a start." Jenna glanced toward the door as sirens approached. "Ah, the paramedics have arrived and my deputies." She looked at Kane. "I'll go and give Rowley and Webber a rundown of the case and they can do a follow up at the hospital." She offered him her weapon. "Keep an eye on the prisoners."

Kane smiled at her and waved it away. "These boys aren't going anywhere. I'll see them safely onto the ambulances."

The first team of paramedics had Amy Fleming whisked away in seconds and to Kane's surprise, Wolfe appeared at the door with more paramedics close behind. "I didn't expect to see you here."

"I figured if Jenna called out Webber for backup, you'd need boots on the ground." Wolfe pulled a pile of flexicuffs from his pocket and handed them to him. "I'll prioritize the injuries for transport."

"Thanks." Kane followed him to each man. "We have a ton of people to interview on the other case. Jenna will get Rowley to process the paperwork and obtain the arrest warrants. She needed Webber to escort the prisoners to the hospital and get them tucked up in the secure ward."

"That sounds like a plan." Wolfe examined each man, spoke to the paramedics, and then walked back to Kane and lowered his voice. "You haven't lost your edge, I see."

"Not until I'm eighty, I hope." Kane secured the less injured men's hands behind their backs and Red Jacket—who'd given his name as Dean James—and Blue Jacket, he cuffed to the gurneys.

The prisoners fitted into two ambulances, which sped away with Webber in pursuit. Kane turned to Wolfe. "How did you find out we called for backup?"

"Webber called me." Wolfe shrugged. "He thought it was a need to know."

Kane nodded. "Well, he followed procedure. You are his superior." He turned as Jenna came back into the room.

"Ah Wolfe, I'm glad you came by." Jenna indicated to the bedroom. "Do you have an evidence bag? There's a quantity of drugs in there, under the bed. I'll need to know what we have here."

"I'm on it." Wolfe headed into the bedroom and returned in minutes waving an evidence bag. "I'll take this back to the lab and then head off home. I'll send you the results." He gave them a wave and hurried to his truck.

As Rowley walked through the door, Kane opened his mouth to speak to him when Kim grabbed his arm. He looked down at her.

She was quite beautiful and had to be close to five-ten. "Ah, is there something I can do for you?"

"Yeah, my head's a bit muddled. If I think of anything else, who do I call?" Kim frowned at him. "Do you have a card or anything?"

Kane always carried his cards and, pulling off a glove with his teeth, fished one out of his inside pocket and handed it to her. "The department is here and this is my private cell number."

"Okay and thanks for saving me." Kim's cheeks flushed. "Can you walk me to my room? Maybe stay for a drink? I just want to thank you for saving me."

Kane smiled at her. "Why thank you, ma'am, but I have to finish up here." He glanced at Rowley. "Deputy Rowley will take your statement and then give you a ride back to the resort before he heads back to town."

"I've seen you around." Kim was keeping a firm grip on his arm. "Maybe some other time, when you're not so busy?"

Kane flicked a glance at Rowley and didn't miss his snigger. He cleared his throat. "As you're a witness to the fight, it would be a conflict of interest but thanks for the offer." He stepped away. "Go with Deputy Rowley, ma'am."

"This way, ma'am." Rowley led her out the door. "I'll make sure you get back safely to your room."

Kane turned as Jenna appeared at his side. "Find anything interesting?"

"Nope. There's no personal belongings here at all." She pulled on her gloves and zipped up her coat. "I checked the men's jackets before they left. I have their cellphones and wallets but they weren't staying in this cabin. It's not fully furnished." She frowned. "I guess they broke in here to use it as a meeting place to sell drugs." She puffed out a cloud of steam in the cold room. "I'll talk to Rowley in the morning but I've handed him the case. We have gotten enough evidence to charge them, it's just paperwork and arranging transportation to county. We have a murder to solve and it takes priority." She shook her head. "I'll inform the management about the door."

Kane shrugged. "Sorry about that." He stared at her face and watched it change from concern to hilarity in a split second. "What?"

"One of the men we arrested called you a weapon." She grinned. "I haven't seen you in action before, well, not in full combat mode." She chuckled. "You *are* a weapon."

CHAPTER SEVEN

Winter had a special meaning for him. Delores didn't decay so fast in low temperatures and it gave him more time to arrange his most treasured pieces of her. The snow would cover his tracks and, in the melt, all traces of his existence would wash away. Only his creation would remain but he'd be long gone by then and looking for another town to hunt for her. He'd welcomed the first snow with a rush of enthusiasm, or was it anticipation making his hands tremble? Once Delores arrived in Black Rock Falls, more would follow and he'd be busy right through January. The snow-covered sidewalks had called to him, telling him the time had come to find her again. If he'd asked people to describe the season, most would mention the bitter cold and unforgivingly long freezing nights. For him, it was the steam rising from fresh blood, the excitement of luring her into his lair, and the surprise on her face when she realized he'd planned to immortalize her as part of his collection.

At this time of the year, most people lived in a world of gray but he'd always been special and seen things differently. His winter was an incredible shade of blue. Each touch of the full moon on the white-dusted town, enhanced rather than blurred his vision. Houses on every corner stood out in sharp lines and each shadow fell on the snow clearly defined. In the daylight, as his collections became visible, the panic would begin, the town would be running scared and yet they would continue to trust him. He smiled. Like Delores they always trusted him—at first.

Out driving and enjoying the solitude, he spotted her dark hair on the bus and followed. Through the window and highlighted by the bright interior, he witnessed her argument with the driver. From the man's expression, she'd used his kind nature to bully him into setting her down in the middle of town. He slowed as she stepped down from the bus. Slightly bedraggled, she turned to give the driver the finger and the ink on the back of her hand sealed her fate. She had an attitude in spades. With a tatty backpack slung over one shoulder, she moved along the brightly lit storefronts. He cruised by, watching her in his side mirror as she followed the passengers hurrying home from the bus and hustled them for money. He parked in a dark alley beside the church, slid out his truck, and followed her. Keeping a few paces behind, he could hear her stream of different excuses for being on the streets and by the time she paused at the entrance to the soup kitchen, he had the trap set.

The soup kitchen had finished serving meals for the night and Aunt Betty's Café would be taking last orders. He slipped inside the café, and purchased two coffees and two pulled pork sandwiches. As he dropped the sleeping pills into one of the to-go cups, he kept her in sight as she peered at the menu. Snow glistened off her dark blue hoodie. She had no place to go and not enough money to buy a meal. As she walked away toward the church, hunched against the cold, he collected his order and slipped outside. He followed her, walking a little faster, and then cleared his throat to say something but she spun around. "Oh, excuse me."

"Are you following me?" She glared at him with her chin stuck out in a belligerent attitude.

Hello, Delores, don't you recognize me? He smiled at her; it always put her off guard when he smiled. "Ah, no. Just making my way back to my truck." He indicated with his chin toward the dark alley. "If you're heading for the church, it's closed for the night. I have to get home to my wife."

"You close the church, what sort of a priest are you?" She wiped her red nose on her sleeve. "Well, open it. I need a pew to sleep on. I'll die out here."

"I can't do that, I'm sorry." He stepped into the alley. "I'm not a priest but I can help you. Are you hungry?" He offered her one of the sandwiches. "I have a spare coffee too."

"Yeah." She snatched it from him and ate like a dog, stuffing the food into her mouth. "I need a place to stay." She ignored the trash can close by and tossed the empty bag on the ground. She peered at him as she sipped the coffee. "You're a minister, or whatever, you're supposed to help me."

He'd set the bait and all he had to do was reel her in. He smiled again. "I'm sure my wife wouldn't mind if you took our spare bedroom for tonight—as it's an emergency. I'll be able to find you a place to stay in the morning." He waved a hand to his truck. "Our house is at the other end of town." He walked to the door pressing his key fob. "Unless you want to sleep on the church porch?" He opened the door and climbed inside, not looking at her, and started the engine.

The passenger door opened and she tossed her backpack on the floor and climbed inside. She sipped the coffee and yawned. "I sleep with a knife, so no funny business."

He backed out into the dark still night. She hadn't changed, her tongue was still as harsh as he remembered. The tattoos on her hands looked new and would enhance the design he had in mind. He nodded. "Once you're safely in your room, you won't see me until the morning."

No, she wouldn't see him coming—until it was too late.

CHAPTER EIGHT

Ava Price climbed into the truck, looked around at the pristine interior, and sipped her coffee. She'd gotten rides from all types. Some men had been fine and even offered her cash but she'd had her share of the predators. This guy, the minister or whoever, seemed okay. He had a wife at home and that was always a bonus. She watched him closely as he wasn't saying much. He was clean shaven, unusual in these alpine towns in winter, and plain-looking. Nothing about him, his manner, or speech made her wary. Heck, if she had landed a place to stay, she would be set. She cleared her throat. "Do you have kids?"

"Unfortunately, no, we don't." He flicked her a glance. "Don't worry, you're not taking anyone's room and my wife is used to me bringing home strangers. She will be more than happy to make you comfortable." He turned up the heat.

Warm air filled the cabin and Ava nodded, stifling a yawn. The idea of staying with this couple was getting better by the second. "I don't want charity; I'll work to pay for a room. I can get a job if I have a place to stay."

"Well, maybe we can come to some arrangement." He smiled at her. "There's always chores need doing on a ranch but it will be hard in this weather, chopping wood, cleaning out stables, and the like. Have you had experience working on a ranch?"

"I learn fast." Ava emptied her to-go cup and wished she had more. The sandwich had barely filled the chasm in her belly. "Is it far?"

"Not much longer." He looked at her. "What's your name?"

She waited a beat and then shrugged. "Ava."

"You can call me Preacher." He flashed her a grin. "Everybody who stays over knows me by that name."

Ava yawned. "Sure, nice to meet you, Preacher."

"Would you like me to contact your family in the morning, to let them know where you're staying?" Preacher sighed as if it was a chore to talk to her. "Although, I do understand if that's a problem. We have a ton of people who come to Black Rock Falls to disappear. You should know, there are quite a few homeless, addicts, and battered women and men just wanting to live off the grid here. We also have places to help you as well. You chose a great town to stop by."

She blinked at him, her eyelids so heavy she had to force them open. "That's good to know."

Tiredness engulfed her and she leaned her head against the window. Fighting against the sleepiness, she shook her head and looked at him but his attention had fixed on the snowy blacktop winding ahead of them into the night. Darkness surrounded them and the headlights lit up a forest, so dense she couldn't see any space between the tall pines. She'd close her eyes for just a few seconds, what could possibly happen?

CHAPTER NINE

Tuesday

Breakfast was just a pleasant memory by the time Jenna and Kane had finished canvassing the guests in the outlying cabins. The person who'd displayed the body parts on the tree must have been a phantom, as not one person they'd interviewed had seen anyone at all on the backroad at any time from Sunday to Monday afternoon. Exhausted from trudging through snowdrifts, Jenna stopped to catch her breath and scanned the sky. Although the snow had ceased for a while, the clouds promised more before long. She dragged her aching legs back to Kane's truck, creating a cloud of steam around her. The late night and early morning had taken its toll and right now all she wanted to do was get warm. Her feet had become way too cold inside the thick socks and her lips needed a coating of ChapStick. Of course, she'd left the latter in her other coat pocket, which was damp from the previous evening. The idea of returning to the resort was alluring but they'd checked out and thanks to another killer in town, their vacation was officially over. She stamped the snow from her boots and climbed into the passenger seat. Leaning back, she let out a long sigh. "Well, that was a complete waste of time."

"At least we left no stone unturned." As if reading her mind, Kane offered her a ChapStick from a packet in his console. "Need this?"

"Thanks." Jenna applied the balm and sighed with relief. "That's better. Let's get out of here."

"Where to? The office or do you want a ride home?" Kane turned up the heat.

Jenna smiled. "Home please. I need to get out of these clothes and eat. We don't have to rush into the office unless something comes up. We'll head back later. I called Rowley earlier, he has everything under control in the drug bust case. He obtained the warrants and statements. He's turned over everything to the DA. All the men apart from Dean James are going to county for processing. James is undergoing surgery on his knee this morning." She gave Kane a long look. "But he's not our problem anymore either, the DA is calling in the Feds to deal with him. The package under the bed was uncut cocaine and Wolfe said it weighed two pounds."

"Any comeback on me?" Kane started the engine and frowned when he turned to look at her. "I was expecting some noise about police brutality."

Jenna wondered why he'd been so distant all morning and shook her head. "No, the woman they kidnapped and my statement puts you in the clear." She smiled. "The DA couldn't believe you came out of a six-on-one fight with only a small bruise on your cheek."

"Hmm." Kane swung the truck around and headed down the mountain. "I'll have to practice ducking some more."

Jenna leaned over the back to rub Duke's ears. "Maybe, but your actions looked just fine to me. If you're that fast now, I can't imagine what you'd have been in your prime."

"I am in my prime." Kane chuckled. "Although the cold slowed me down some." He waved at the snow building up on the windshield. "It's snowing again and this makes it perfect for a killer. By the lack of evidence at the scene, I'd say it was snowing when he arranged the body parts."

"It seems so." Jenna turned back in her seat. "I wonder where he dumped the rest of the bodies. In this weather it won't show before the melt."

"We had a good look around the scene and didn't find a trace." Kane's lips flattened into a thin line.

Jenna stared at him. "Well, come on, put on your profiler hat. I can see this killer is different from the usual kill and dump. He is exhibiting his work. What do you think?"

"Yeah, but I would have thought he'd make a show of the torsos as well." Kane slowed to maneuver around a fallen branch. "He could be keeping them for another display. I agree, I figure this macabre presentation is a sculpture."

"The mind never ceases to intrigue me." Jenna leaned back in her seat. "All the psychopaths we have encountered are different, well, apart from being killers."

Her phone chimed. She looked at the caller ID. "It's Wolfe. I'll put him on speaker."

"Hi Jenna. I've examined the body parts, and they are from two different people. The killer severed the limbs post-mortem and from the pattern on the ice, the killer used a chainsaw or similar. I believe this points to the killer keeping the bodies frozen prior to dismemberment, rather than leaving them to freeze in situ. I'll have to wait for them to thaw and examine tissue samples to determine how long they've been frozen."

Jenna glanced at Kane and raised an eyebrow. "Any idea of the victims' sex? I noticed one had nail polish."

"Not yet. They are different blood types but nail polish doesn't necessarily mean a person is female. I'm running a DNA profile on each one and the chromosome analysis will give me gender. I'll get back to you in a couple of hours with the results."

"Okay thanks." Jenna disconnected and stared at the blinding white lowlands dropping away in the distance. It was so beautiful, and reminded her of the untouched frosting on a cake. "Two people murdered and not one call about a missing person." She cast a look at Kane. "Don't tell me Black Rock Falls has become a dumping ground for bodies now?"

"I sure hope not." Kane turned onto the highway. "Maybe we should call Jo? Having a behavioral analyst to consult would be an advantage. She might have heard about a similar case."

Jenna rubbed her temples. Her feet hurt as they warmed and her head throbbed from dehydration and hunger. "I will, if the killer shows himself again but we have handled worse cases than this one." She glanced at him. "Unless you need her help to profile this guy?"

"I figure, we need all the help we can get, Jenna." Kane shrugged and looked back at the road.

She liked Special Agent Jo Wells, formally Blake. Recently divorced, Jo had reverted to her maiden name. Jo had set up an FBI CSI field office in Snakeskin Gully, some three hours' drive from Black Rock Falls. After Wolfe had contacted her, she'd assisted Jenna with a recent case, along with detective, Agent Ty Carter. She'd gotten on with Jo and considered her a friend but didn't want to run to her with every problem she encountered. After all, she had Kane. His profiling skills hadn't let her down yet and it surprised her he'd mention calling Jo. It wasn't like him to be uncertain about a case. "Is there something about this killer that's worrying you?"

"Nope." Kane flicked her a glance. "It's that we have an FBI contact who would be sifting through bulletins daily and might have come across a similar case, is all. With no one apparently missing, we have zip to go on." He turned onto Stanton. "I can offer you a small insight into this type of behavior but without evidence it's difficult to profile."

Jenna nodded. "We have had no clues before and still caught the killer." She looked at the familiar buildings as they reached the outskirts of town. People milled around, clearing snow from their driveways. Woodsmoke curled upward from some of the houses adding to the picturesque scene. "Will you stop at Aunt Betty's Café please? The last thing I want to do when I get home is cook."

"I was going to go pick up the horses." Kane looked in her direction. "It's only a short detour."

Jenna huffed out a sigh. "That's not a good idea, Dave. We're both famished and cold but if you insist, we'll drop by on the way home from the office tomorrow." She glanced at him. "It really isn't a priority, is it? We're paid up until the end of the week and the horses are in a heated stable. We on the other hand have been working in subzero temperatures for hours and late into the night, we don't need to be getting up at five in the morning to feed the horses."

"Okay." Kane flicked her a worried glance. "I'm happy to leave them another day or so, it will give us more time to concentrate on the case." He pulled up a short distance from Aunt Betty's Café. "I'm ordering two stacks of pancakes. I need the carbs."

"If I survive the walk to the café, I'll do the same." Jenna wrapped her scarf around her face and pulled up the hood of her jacket.

The blast of icy wind cut through her clothes; the temperature had dropped so fast this year, her body hadn't had time to acclimatize. She slipped and slid along the sidewalk, frowning. The cleared path had a coating of ice but as they got closer to Aunt Betty's she noticed someone had sprinkled a liberal amount of salt and sand on the sidewalk. She turned to Kane. "I know murderers kill at any time but why would anyone come out willingly in this weather to decorate a tree with body parts?"

"This is one of the reasons I wanted to talk to Jo." Kane pushed open the door to the café and went inside. "She might have some insight into this kind of mind."

Jenna followed him to their reserved table at the back of the store. She sat down and looked at him with curiosity. "I trust your judgment, Dave, but if you want to speak to her, that's fine. It just seems a bit early into the investigation to be calling in the Feds."

"They won't be traveling here unless the weather breaks." Kane waved a hand toward the window. "I doubt Carter will risk taking the chopper out unless there is a break in the weather. I'm thinking maybe a conference call?"

"Sure, and I'll put out a carefully worded press release. Someone might recognize the tattoos?" Jenna moved the sugar bowl around on the table, thinking. "This crime is so unusual, I'd say if this guy has been working all over, they would've heard something although I don't recall anything in the news." A shudder of revulsion went through her. "Unless the bodies were never found. If the killer displayed them in remote areas, by the melt the wildlife could've cleaned up the evidence."

CHAPTER TEN

Restless, Preacher prowled his house. He moved from room to room hoping his heavy footsteps would be frightening Delores, or Ava as she wanted him to call her. She'd tried to hide behind a false name but he'd recognized her. She always played the same card by arriving in town homeless and hungry but the moment he'd gotten close, he'd seen through her disguises—seen the tattoos peeking out from the sleeve at her wrist. Although, no matter how many times he killed her, she came back and multiplied. Lately, Delores seemed to be everywhere. He had to collect them all—kill them all.

He'd locked her in the cellar, and hoped to make her compliant in the pitch black, but to his surprise she hadn't reacted as usual, screaming and hammering on the door. No, she'd remained on her bed as if waiting for him to make the next move. He liked that about her, it was as if she was learning to behave. He could use her new attitude to his advantage and if he found others, he'd add them to his cellar. She would explain how he expected them to behave.

There was everything she needed in the cellar: a bathroom, four beds, and a table and chairs. The latter he'd attached to the floor. In fact, he'd secured anything Delores could use as a weapon against him. She'd acted violently toward him last time and he'd broken her, spoiling the finish on his artwork. He wouldn't go into the cellar again if she was awake. Instead, he had fitted speakers inside, to allow her to communicate with him when he chose. He supplied

Delores with food and clean clothing daily via a dumbwaiter he ran from his kitchen.

He sat down before a bank of screens and watched her. His infrared cameras made sure he had her in full view, day or night. He liked to watch. He'd created his own private reality show and what he decided to do with Delores each day changed the outcome. Sometimes he'd feed her, sometimes not, sometimes he'd deprive her of light. He decided everything right down to her last breath. He would wait until her emotions changed from anger to despair, lift the dumbwaiter, and wait. She'd always try to escape and after climbing through the walls would find his special room. All he had to do was, watch and wait. By the time she came to him—and she always came to him, she'd beg for forgiveness and he'd ignore her pleas and kill her slowly.

He checked the time and excitement clenched his gut. He flicked on the TV to catch the news. Anger rolled over him in waves when the lead story didn't mention the cops had discovered his artwork in the forest. They'd found it, he'd seen them recoil in horror, but instead of showing the world, they'd kept the find to themselves. After the station break, he stared at the screen, waiting with growing anger. The newsreader looked at the camera and spoke, as if to him alone.

"The Black Rock Fall's Sheriff's Department is looking for anyone familiar with these tattoos." Two images, side by side, showed the colorful ink on the collage he'd used in his last creation. *"If you recognize any of these images, please contact Sheriff Alton at the office or call the hotline number displayed on your screen."* The newsreader frowned and looked at her notes. *"Now here is a strange request. Sheriff Alton has also asked you to call the hotline if any of your neighbors has been using a chainsaw in the last week or so. So, call in folks, and help out the Black Rock Falls Sheriff's Department."*

Preacher slammed his fist on the coffee table. "Is that it? No mention of my art? Nothing? How is the world going to remember me without media coverage?"

People didn't appreciate how much time he put into his creations. He'd worked long hours on each design. The precise way he displayed each part held a meaning—a secret meaning. He stood and paced again. If he wanted to gain recognition, he'd need a more striking display. He chuckled as his imagination took flight. It would be dark soon. He moved to the mirror and grinned at his reflection. His other self smiled back, confident and strong. No one could bully him now. His plan was set in his mind and the idea thrilled him. He met his own eyes in the mirror. "We'll just have to give Sheriff Alton something she'll never forget."

CHAPTER ELEVEN

Wednesday

Kane woke surprisingly early on Wednesday morning. He filled the coffee machine, waited impatiently for it to squeeze out a cup, and with no horses to tend to, sat at the kitchen table. He scanned the messages from Kim, the nurse he'd rescued from a group of men at the ski resort and shook his head. They were always the same: *Meet me for a drink* or *Come by and I'll cook dinner*. It had been amusing at first, in fact an ego booster that a beautiful young woman was interested in him but now she'd become a pest. His usual stone-faced expression to a woman hitting on him hadn't worked and she was behaving as if they were close. Ignoring her had been his best option but he'd caught Susie Hartwig's surprised expression when Kim launched herself at him at Aunt Betty's. She'd acted as if they were lovers. He'd left his takeout, disentangled himself, and dashed out the store. As luck would have it, Rowley was with him and had collected the food. Apart from giving him an amused look, Rowley hadn't mentioned the incident at the office—not that he had anything to explain.

Pushing Kim to the back of his mind, he perused his files on the case, sipping his coffee. There was no rush, sunup wasn't until around seven-forty-five and as Rowley lived close by, he opened the office at eight-thirty in winter. After the overnight blizzard they'd have to wait to follow the snowplow into town and he doubted they'd arrive before nine. As the first rays of the sun crept over the horizon, bathing the brilliant white landscape in gold, he peered through the window to view the conditions. Deep snowdrifts had evened out the view, softening the more dominant features as if covering the lowlands in a white comforter. Clouds hung heavy in the distance, promising more falls to come.

In the dawn light, Jenna's ranch house with the roof covered in snow and rows of icicles hanging from the gutters resembled the inside of a snow globe. Her cruiser, which she'd left outside her front porch had a covering of six to eight inches of snow. After feeding Duke, he'd pulled on his thick woolen hat and shrugged into his coat. Usually the heavy snowfalls gave a small rise in temperature but not this time. Under his boots the coating of ice on top of the snow crunched as he walked to the garage. His idea of buying his own snowplow, the type that attached to the front of his truck, would pay out in silver dollars this morning. Inside his garage, he attached the contraption and leaving the garage doors open, left his truck to idle.

He stared out the window at the stables. His body clock had woken him in time to tend the horses and he missed them. It was a time he enjoyed and never found tedious. He loved animals and the horses he counted as friends, same as Duke. Of late, Pumpkin, the black cat that had arrived at Jenna's house last Halloween, would join him and Duke in the barn each morning and night. She arrived in all weathers, jumping through the snow like a rabbit or dashing through rain, ears flattened against her head. She also enjoyed watching him exercise with Jenna, although the first time he'd aimed a kick at Jenna, Pumpkin had let out a snarl like a mountain lion. It seemed that Jenna had found herself a useful companion.

He checked his phone, scanning the files Wolfe had sent late last night. More images and blood work from the victims, both female and not related. There would be a lot to discuss with Jenna over breakfast.

He headed out into the cold again. At least it had stopped snowing and by his estimation, if he could clear the driveway, the snowplow man should be through by the time they left for the office. As he worked, he pondered over the results. Someone had murdered two young women and yet not a soul had gone missing from Black Rock Falls or either of the two neighboring towns, Louan and Blackwater. He'd read about killers who'd frozen their victims and one who came to mind was the notorious Richard Kuklinski, who allegedly froze his victims to confuse the time of death. But a killer who made a point of displaying body parts had another reason in his twisted mind—they just had to find out that reason and use it to catch him.

He'd parked his truck in the garage and was storing the snowplow when he heard Jenna calling his name. He brushed the snow from his hands and strolled out the garage. "Over here."

"Have you any Tylenol? I'm out and I have the headache from hell." Jenna's sheet-white face poked out from under her hoodie, a stark contrast to her cherry-red nose.

He hurried toward his cottage and used the keypad to gain entrance. "Yeah. You don't look so good."

"I'm dizzy and feel like my legs are made of lead." Jenna followed him into the kitchen and dropped into a chair. "Maybe I'm coming down with something?"

Kane took a bottle of Gatorade from the refrigerator and handed it to her. "More like dehydrated. We worked long hours in terrible conditions, we didn't drink water at all that I can remember. Try this but I'll get you something for the headache."

The one thing Kane understood was pain. He suffered agonizing headaches from the plate in his head and although he'd never admit it, the knee injury he'd suffered the year before had left him with significant discomfort, but he was working on it. He tossed her a box of Tylenol from the drawer in the kitchen and turned to the counter. "I'm making breakfast, it will make you feel better."

"I'll be fine." Jenna washed down the pills with the drink and stared at him. "Have you read over the files Wolfe sent overnight?"

Kane took eggs and bacon from the refrigerator. "Yeah, two women with ink, the killer dismembered the bodies post-mortem, and probably kept them frozen. They're not related to each other, so likely random thrill kills maybe?"

"With no missing persons in the neighboring counties that fit the description of the tattoos, we're looking for someone who has kidnapped these women from God knows where, killed them, and likely stored them in his freezer." Jenna gave a slight shudder. "He could be living anywhere and, in this weather, transporting the frozen body parts wouldn't be a problem. No smell, that's for sure."

Kane set about making breakfast. "Most use freezing to confuse the time of death but I don't think this killer believes time is an issue."

"How so?" Jenna stood and went to the counter. She checked the coffee maker and then added the fixings to the table. She turned back and pushed bread into the toaster. "Making it difficult to obtain a time of death throws our timeline into chaos. What other reason could he have?"

Giving her question some thought, Kane stirred the eggs and flipped the bacon. "I think he kills all year round and collects the bodies to display in winter. It's by choice he keeps them frozen for so long, and not as a ploy to confuse us. This guy could be so arrogant he believes he can't be caught." He loaded up the plates.

"Or the people he chooses are drifters?" Jenna took a strip of bacon from a plate and stared into space. "No one will report them missing but those types usually hole up somewhere warm in winter." She took the plate of toast and slid it on the table.

Kane carried the meals to the table and sat down. "That would make sense. You must remember if this isn't the killer's first dance, he might have a different slant on his victims. If he's planning on making another sculpture, I figure he's collecting what he needs to construct his next work."

"Hmm." Jenna buttered her toast and stared at her plate. "I think you're right. We should call Jo in on this case. I'd like to find out if she's seen anything like this before. I want to skip our workout today and leave after we have eaten, if that's okay?"

Kane poured coffee and examined her face as he added cream and sugar. Her cheeks had their normal pink glow again. He nodded. "Sure, we have had enough exercise lately. How's the headache?"

"Better, thanks." She glanced lovingly at his coffee cup and sighed. "I'll forgo the coffee this morning. I'll finish my drink. I'll be more aware of getting dehydrated from now on. It's something I didn't think about in the cold weather."

Kane chuckled. "Then I'll remind you and we'll keep a couple of bottles of Gatorade in the truck."

"How did I know you'd say that?" Jenna rolled her eyes and attacked her breakfast but Kane noticed the smile threatening at the corner of her lips.

As Kane had predicted it was close to nine by the time he turned into Main and headed to the office. They joined the line of vehicles crawling along behind the snowplow. Tempers were fraying and some of the drivers blasted their horns if another vehicle dared to cut in. Kane flicked on his wig-wag lights to keep order and just as well. As they got close to the local park two women dragging kids behind them threw themselves out onto the road, screaming in terror. When they spotted him and came slipping and stumbling toward them, he stopped in the middle of the road and turned to Jenna. "What's happened now?"

"Looks like we're going to find out. Pull over." Jenna zipped up her jacket with "Sheriff" across front and back and got out, beckoning to the women. "What is it? What's happened?"

As the women gestured madly behind them, Kane parked close to the mound of snow at the side of the road and climbed out. Of course, the people inside their cars had stopped to gawk and he waved at them to move on. Once the traffic was flowing again, he went to Jenna's side. The two women were talking so fast, he had trouble understanding them. The kids looked stunned or in shock. Unease crept over him. "What's going on?"

"There's a snowman in the park. They seem to believe it has a human head." Jenna gave him an incredulous look and then her face turned expressionless as she turned back to the women. "Okay, we'll deal with it, it's probably a store dummy. Take the kids to Aunt Betty's. We have a reserved table in the back, get some hot chocolate, put it on my tab. Please wait there until I can get to you. It's very important I speak with you again."

The women nodded in unison and Kane waved them toward him. "Come with me." He walked out onto the road to halt the traffic and they dashed across and hurried along the sidewalk to Aunt Betty's Café. He collected his crime scene bag from the back of his truck, patted Duke on the head, and then picked his way through the snowdrift to Jenna. "It's the missing heads and torsos, isn't it?"

"Well, one of them at least." Jenna glanced up at him, a frown creasing her brow. "I hope he's left a clue this time. We need to catch this sick SOB."

CHAPTER TWELVE

Jenna stared at the picturesque park surrounded by trees covered in snow. The pathways remained clear due to the copious amounts of salt the council had laid the previous day. The scene appeared so tranquil, she wondered if she'd wake up before the nightmare started to play out. Surely, only a dream could be so terrifying. Women dismembered and displayed in public places was beyond horrific and it pushed her flight or fight response off the chart. As she made out the snowman standing alongside the tree line, she clamped her jaw tight. She had to be professional and shut out the scene before her but as they got closer, the sight burned itself into her mind. This one she wouldn't forget.

Mindful of the area being a crime scene, she turned a full circle, looking for any other point of entry to the park. She surmised by the truck in the parking lot close by that the two women and their kids had entered from that direction. Thick snow covered the swings, slides, and carousel and she wondered why parents would bring kids here after a blizzard. She discovered why as she walked along the footpath. The kids had made snow angels just inside the gate and small footprints led away and came back in a loop. The young and innocent had seen the body, turned around, and hightailed it back to their mothers. One of the children had fallen in their haste but the other had kept on running. The idea of the children seeing a murder victim sickened her. The killer had sunk to a new low by leaving a corpse in a playground. She turned to look at Kane. He was scanning the scene with his cellphone, making a video of the area before they disturbed the snow. It was good to work with him; he had a professionally calming influence, and with him at her side she could face just about anything.

The moment Kane stopped filming she made her way from the pathway through the thick snow-covered playground to the snowman. She mentally steeled herself and almost laughed at her reaction to death. After so many murders in her county, she'd have thought she'd be blasé but unlike other cops she'd worked with, the victims in her cases had taken up permanent residence in her memory. As she moved closer to the corpse, she could hear Kane following, walking in her steps. She wondered how long the snowman had stood here undiscovered. There was no stench of death. Only the scent of pine trees, woodsmoke, and an alpine winter filled the air. The disturbing sight before her stopped her in her tracks.

Unsettled, she took a few deep breaths before moving closer. What loomed up before her out of the snowscape gave creepy a new meaning. The corpse was well-covered with snow but even the white dusting couldn't dampen the horror. Blue sightless eyes glistened with ice crystals and an open mouth smiled at her in a terrible blue lipped grin. The frozen hair poking out from under a red woolen cap, resembled a bunch of twigs. The killer had covered the body from the neck down with snow. No sign of injury was evident. Without saying a word to Kane, she called Wolfe. "We have located one of the bodies. We're on scene. We'll need a screen, it's in the kids' playground."

"Okay. I'm on my way." Wolfe disconnected.

Jenna turned to Kane. "Get all the shots we need and make a close-up video. I'll call Rowley and Walters to come down and secure the area. Is there any CCTV surveillance in this part of town?" She glanced around. "The one outside the bank might have picked up something, a vehicle perhaps?"

"I doubt it." Kane stared in the direction of the camera. "As far as I'm aware, that one is focused on the front door of the bank. We don't have anything near the park. If you remember, there was an outcry when Mayor Petersham suggested one for the park. Townsfolk didn't want people checking out their kids."

"Yeah, I do recall that." Jenna kicked at a clump of snow. "It wouldn't hurt to get Rowley to examine the footage we have from last night. He might spot a vehicle on Main near the park. We need something to go on, some small lead." She shivered. "It's so darn cold, I hope Wolfe gets here soon. We need to speak to the women who found the body. They won't wait around all day."

"We'd speed things up if we do a recon of the area." Kane moved around the body in a wide arc. "The killer could have dumped the other victim close by."

"Okay. You do that, I'll go and speak to the women." Jenna stared at the wide-eyed frozen stare of the corpse and imagined the terror the poor girl had suffered before her death. She had to catch this killer and the sooner the better. "I think I'll consult Jo when we get back to the office, I'll send the case files to her and see if she's seen anything like this before."

"Good idea. The more eyes on this case the better." Kane kept on working. "They'll probably be glad to hear from you. The blizzard will have them holed up in Snakeskin Gully twirling their thumbs."

Jenna called Rowley, as she walked toward Aunt Betty's. She asked him to round up old Deputy Walters to drop by for a couple of hours. They had calls on the hotline about people using chainsaws and he could check them out for her and call in if he found anything suspicious. A few people had stopped to stare at what Kane was doing and Jenna waved them away. "Nothing to see here, folks, move on now."

As the people dispersed, she made her way with care over the slippery blacktop to Aunt Betty's Café. She found the women at her table with the two children. Both little girls appeared white-faced and terrified. Jenna hated lying and preferred to tell the truth but this time she had to bend it a little to prevent the deathly images haunting the children for years. She forced her cold lips into a smile and sat down at the table. She looked at the kids. "It was a prank as we suspected, something left over from Halloween I gather. Nothing for you to worry about." She looked at the women and pulled out her notebook. "I'll need a statement from you. Can I have your names and details?" She scribbled the words "It's not a prank," and handed her book to one of the women. "If you could write them down for me please."

"I'm Libby Marshal and this is my sister Eliza Barratt." She took the book and her eyes widened. "Oh, I see." She held the notebook out for her sister. "You write down our details and I'll answer the questions."

Jenna nodded. "When did you arrive at the park?"

"Oh, about five minutes before we flagged you down." Libby frowned and looked at the children who now sipped their drinks, seemingly uninterested in their conversation. "We'd walked into the park and the kids made the snow angels then they ran off to see the snowman." She gave a strangled false laugh. "Gave us a fright. It must have been naughty kids playing a trick on everyone."

Jenna nodded. "See any other vehicles or people in or near the park?"

"Not that I recall. There were vehicles on the road but we came in from the other end of Main, the snowplow went through around eight, so we drove through okay." Libby smiled at her. "Since the council purchased more snowplows, our end of town is passable earlier than usual. It means the older kids can get to school on time after a blizzard."

Needing to get back to the crime scene, Jenna took the notebook Eliza handed her and stood. "It might be best if one of you walks back with me to collect your vehicle. No need to upset the kids again." She gave the women a meaningful look and stood.

"Yes, I'll come." Eliza jumped to her feet and looked at one of the girls. "Wait with Auntie Libby, Mommy will be back with the truck."

Jenna led the way out into the bitter cold. She could see Wolfe's van in the parking lot and he'd erected a screen around the victim. Crime scene tape stretched across the entrance to the park and Rowley was walking the perimeter, keeping the sightseers moving. She turned to Eliza. "I thought it would be better to hide the truth from the children."

"Yes, thanks, we appreciate it." Eliza fell into step beside her. "How do you cope with murders?"

Jenna shrugged. How could she tell the woman how the faces of the victims haunted her memories and often crept into her nightmares? She glanced at her. "Someone has to get justice for them and right now it's my job."

CHAPTER THIRTEEN

Hours earlier, Ava had woken dry-mouthed and disorientated in total darkness. Distressed, she'd called out but only the echo of her voice replied. It rattled around the room giving her the impression of being inside a large empty space. Where was she? The warm air surrounding her had a strange smell, musty and damp like a sack of potatoes. She had no idea where the man, Preacher, had taken her but he'd obviously planned to kidnap someone. Trust her to be his victim of choice. He'd somehow spiked her drink and she'd fallen into a deep sleep, for how long she had no idea. Afraid to move, she'd crept her fingers around the bed in slow careful movements. What did the stranger want with her? Alarmed, she'd checked her clothes, relieved when everything seemed to be in order. Apart from a blinding headache, and the desperate need to pee, she seemed okay. Time had moved slowly and she'd spent a long uncomfortable night, finally drifting off into an exhausted slumber.

It could've been moments or hours later when a bright light woke her. She blinked, looking around the neat room. It had no windows but she noticed steps leading up to a door. So, after he'd drugged her, he'd locked her in his cellar. A damp patch on one wall had discolored the paintwork leaving the unmistakable smell of mold. That was a weakness she could explore—damp made drywall easy to kick through—but first she had more urgent matters. She was about to look for a bathroom when a voice came from a speaker high in the wall.

"Good morning, Delores." She recognized the voice as Preacher but now it was almost sing-song. "Your breakfast is in the dumbwaiter. There are clean clothes in the closet. The bathroom is the door on the right. If you place your dirty clothes in the dumbwaiter, I'll return them to you in the morning. I've locked the cellar door. You know there's no escape. Behave and I'll treat you well."

Gripping her hands together in an effort to stop trembling, she stared at the speaker. She refused to let him know how much he'd frightened her. "My name is Ava. Why are you keeping me here, Preacher? If you think I'll willingly become your sex slave, you can think again."

"I don't want you for sex, Delores." Preacher chuckled low in his chest. His voice carried a confident swagger, and his next words made Ava's skin crawl. "But if I did you couldn't stop me, could you? Sooner or later, you'll have to eat and drink something and then... well, I could come down there and do whatever I wanted to you, couldn't I?"

CHAPTER FOURTEEN

Snakeskin Gully Montana

Behavioral analyst and FBI Agent Jo Wells looked over Bobby Kalo's shoulder to stare at her laptop screen. Kalo, a twenty-year-old Black Hat hacker known online as The Undertaker, had recently joined her team. The FBI had plucked Kalo off the streets at seventeen, after he'd come under investigation for hacking the Pentagon's mainframe. Following a long period of training they'd assigned him to work with Jo in the wild west out at the Snakeskin Gully field office. "Any luck?"

"Sure, I've set up our laptops with a list of links for direct access to the databases, one click is all you need." Kalo demonstrated. "You click on the link on the main screen and then use the icons."

Jo stared at the screen. "What about the passwords? Some of the sites are restricted."

"Ah, you don't need a password." Kalo gave her a smirk. "Once you've logged into your computer the databases are open to you."

"That's a mite dangerous." Agent Ty Carter pushed up the rim of his Stetson and dropped his boots from the desk. "Anyone can hack into a laptop, it's child's play."

"Not our laptops and phones." Kalo leaned back in his chair and pulled his shoulder-length fuzzy hair into a band. "It's kind of the same as I installed in the... ah... never mind." He grinned. "In simple terms it's kinda like a virus, if anyone hacks our systems, alarms go off everywhere, a little tracker seeks out the perpetrator, and we get their information but they get wiped out."

Jo chewed on her bottom lip. "How so?"

"Think of it like the stick of dynamite on *Road Runner*. If they light the fuse by hacking our stuff then—" Kalo opened his hands wide "—boom!" He stood and sauntered to his desk, took a candy bar from a jar, and dropped into a chair.

"I see." Jo had the mental image of a computer exploding then disintegrating into a pile of black dust. "Good job."

She glanced at her flashing email icon and sat down. "Carter, it's from Jenna. They have a killer freezing and dismembering bodies out of Black Rock Falls."

"Let me see." Carter moved a toothpick into the corner of his mouth and pulled his rolling office chair beside her. "Two bodies, both female." He enlarged the images and stared at the screen. "This killer likes ink. Something about it draws him to these women."

Jo flicked through Wolfe's preliminary report and scanned the crime scene photographs. "Yeah, seems so." She examined the images, trying to squash the shudder of revulsion. "How does he know they have ink? In this weather they'd be bundled up against the cold?"

"Beats me." Carter enlarged the image of the frozen head and leaned toward the screen. "This one has a tiny bluebird on her forehead just above her eyebrow." He shrugged. "They haven't found the other head yet, so we'll have to wait and see if the tattoos are visible."

She turned to Kalo. "See what you can find."

"I'm on it." Kalo tapped away at his keyboard, eyes flicking from side to side as he scanned the files.

The images confronting Jo reminded her of a case—but which one? "I've seen this before, I'm sure of it."

"I hope you're not planning on paying them a visit?" Carter rolled his green eyes to the ceiling. "We can't fly in this weather. I'll need three hours at least of clear skies before I'm taking that bird anywhere."

Jo lifted both arms in the air and dropped them to her sides. Bad weather had trapped them in town since the first falls. "I hadn't realized as this town isn't on any major routes to anywhere else, there would be no snowplow service past the local school."

"Uh-huh." Carter gave her a long considering stare. "That's why I rented a place in town for the winter. The road to my cabin is impassable." He scratched his cheek. "I've been trying to figure out why you agreed to set up a field office here? This town has a population of one hundred and most of them live off the grid."

Jo remembered the confrontation with Alexis, her boss and husband's lover. She'd had the choice: retire from the FBI or banishment to Snakeskin Gully. She stared at Carter. "It's a long story."

"Well, maybe you'll tell me sometime." He smiled around the toothpick between his teeth. "There's not much to do around here in winter."

"Oooweee, I have a match." Kalo grinned at her from across the room. "You gotta see this. It seems the psychopath named by the media as The Sculptor has been a busy boy. Sending the case files to your laptop now."

Jo looked over a few of the case files gathered from all over the country and shook her head. "If this guy is in Black Rock Falls, Jenna is going to need all the help she can get."

"She sure will and I wish I could be there for her." Carter stared at the screen. "I like Jenna."

Amused, Jo smiled at him. "I wouldn't mind having Kane here either." She chuckled. "Maybe we could swap. You and Jenna would make a nice couple."

"Call yourself a behavioral analyst and you can't see she's smitten by him?" Carter shrugged. "I don't make moves on another man's woman."

Jo hadn't seen this side of him before. "Smitten, huh? He's been working with her for years and he's still living in the cottage. I don't think so." She raised her eyebrows at him. "Can we get back to the case? What do you see, are there any specific similarities?"

"Yeah, some have different MOs but most are the same. It's too early in the investigation into the Black Rock Falls cases to say for certain if this is the same guy. We'll need to wait for Wolfe's autopsy report to be sure." He flicked back from the case file photographs to the ones from Black Rock Falls. "It's not a copycat, little information went out in the press releases."

Worried a delay might put Jenna and her team at risk, she leaned forward in her chair. "I'll forward these case files to Black Rock Falls and then I'll call Jenna. I'd be interested to find out Kane's slant on this killer as well."

After sending the files, she made a video call. "Hi, Jenna, we have the files and I've sent you what we have on similar cases. The killer in Black Rock Falls has the same MO as one the press named The Sculptor. He's been murdering women across the country for four or five years and from what I can see, we have likely only found the tip of the iceberg."

"Yeah, we thought this wasn't his first dance. He's too slick and leaves no evidence behind." Jenna shrugged. *"He's like most of the psychopaths we deal with lately. Does he do this in winter or all year round?"*

Jo turned to Kalo. "Can we give an answer on this, Kalo?"

"Yeah." Kalo glanced up from his screen. "All through winter."

Jo glanced at Carter. "Carter has a theory."

"Ink seems to be a link." Carter stared at the screen. "From what we're seeing they all had tattoos, they're all women around the same age, similar in build and hair color." He shrugged. "What gets me is he's doing this in winter. How is he choosing his victims? Most people are covered up."

"That's something we'll have to discover." Jenna glanced at Kane. *"Kane has some questions."*

"Hi, Jo." Kane's gaze was serious. *"From what we're seeing here, this guy is using these women as his art. I gather from the name given to him by the media, we're not alone in this assumption. We haven't found a cause of death, so am I right to assume he's getting no pleasure out of killing these women?"*

Jo pursed her lips thinking. "Oh, he gets pleasure out of killing them or he wouldn't be doing it." She waited a beat to gather her thoughts. "The type and the ink are representations of someone he wants to kill repeatedly, someone who caused him grief, maybe as a child. From what I've seen from his previous kills, at first he wanted to humiliate them. That phase changed."

"Why? It's unusual for this class of psychopath to change his MO mid-stream." Kane raised an eyebrow. *"Unless we're dealing with another multiple personality."*

"Not necessarily, because the last ten or so have been similar." Jo shrugged. "Maybe he found humiliating them didn't satisfy him, he needed to do more, hurt them more. I believe he uses the art excuse to validate his need to keep killing. He regards the women as the necessary pieces he requires to make his sculpture. Once he has decided how to use them, they're no longer people."

"That's disturbing." Jenna's eyes narrowed. *"How many have been identified? How many were reported missing?"*

"Kato, run the numbers, please." Jo smiled at Jenna across the miles. "It's real useful having a Black Hat, or should I say IT specialist, working in the office. He saves us hours of grunt work."

"There's been four out of twenty bodies identified. Six reported missing." Kalo lifted his gaze from his screen. "The identification came from dental records and DNA."

"Okay, thanks." Jenna cleared her throat. *"Carter, that's a ton of Jane Does. I'll go through the autopsy reports because I'm wondering if these women were prostitutes or the homeless?"*

"Yeah, that's an angle to chase down." Carter removed the toothpick and flicked it into the trash. "Although you don't have streetwalkers in town, do you? I'd start with the homeless—who has access to them?"

"We have shelters, the soup kitchen, churches, and the like." Jenna glanced at Kane and then back to the screen. *"We have had an influx of homeless people this year but the snow usually keeps them away. It is a good place to start."*

"Kane." Jo frowned. "If this is the same killer, he's delusional and lives in his own world. I'll go through the files some more but I'm thinking Caucasian, mid-thirties, unmarried who has a profession that allows him to move easily from place to place."

"Hmm. We'll have to narrow it down some more." Kane leaned back in his chair. *"Around these parts, that description fits many men. Truck or delivery drivers, doctors, dentists, casual labor to name a few. My money is on a trucker or delivery driver, he maybe gives a girl a ride into town, gets all her information and kills her."*

"It could be all of the above." Jenna shrugged. *"As no one seems to have logged any evidence against the killer, has anyone found where he kept the bodies?"*

"Nope, we assumed he used a hunting cabin, easily accessible in the snow, so not far from a main highway, and one that's cleared regular." Carter paused a beat and then frowned. "So in your case, just about anywhere along the entire length of Stanton Forest."

"Okay, we have a starting point." Jenna made a few notes on a notepad. *"I need to find out if any of the victims have been sexually assaulted."* She lifted her gaze to the screen. *"I consider it relevant to the case. Rape and murder are often part of the ritual, but I'm not seeing*

that here in the few cases I've scanned. I don't have an autopsy report on our victim, so can't rule it out. I'll need to investigate this aspect; with the humiliation and dismembering, if he's not raping them, he has a motive we have not come across before."

Jo nodded. "I'll ask Kalo to do the research to save time."

"Thanks, Jo." Jenna smiled at her and then turned to Kane. *"Do you have any other questions for Jo?"*

"Nope, but if it comes back none of the women were sexually assaulted, it's always a possibility the killer is impotent. If so, it puts a different slant on the revenge, doesn't it?" Kane turned to Jenna and frowned. *"This type he's killing, is the same every time—why?"*

"Revenge?" Jenna stared into the screen. *"They were close at one time and she humiliated him. He likely killed her and has been killing her ever since."*

Jo wanted to give Jenna a high five. "It would be a strong motive and that's further than anyone else has gotten on The Sculptor's case."

"Hmm…" Jenna shrugged. *"Now we just have to find him before he kills again. Not easy in the middle of winter with not one clue to go on."*

CHAPTER FIFTEEN

After four hours bumping along in the cab of an eighteen-wheeler with a man who smelled as if he'd missed out on the invention of deodorant, Zoe Henderson was glad when the truck stopped at a place lit up with flashing red lights that read, "Triple Z Bar". She turned to the driver. "Why are we stopping here?"

"I get a bed and a meal here. We're in Black Rock Falls. The town is in that direction but this place is cheap." He wouldn't meet her eyes. "You can join me if you like and I'll give you a ride into town first thing?"

The thought of a hot meal was tempting and she would find another ride before bedtime. "Yeah, sure." She grabbed her backpack and climbed down from the cab.

The icy chill seeped through her clothes and although the ground had a generous coating of salt and sand, ice glistened on the blacktop reflecting the bright lights in patches of flashing crimson. As she picked her way through the parking lot to the bar, she noticed the line of motorcycles outside. She'd fit in here just fine. Wearing a leather jacket, she looked like a biker's old lady and her ink and black fingernails alone would get her a ride into town. The last shelter had turned her away and pointed her in the direction of Black Rock Falls insisting they offered shelter for the homeless. Apparently, the town had long-term accommodation available and assistance to get a job. The bonus was a soup kitchen and a free clinic. She'd landed in paradise.

The dimly lit bar was hot and noisy. The smell of beer, sweat, and chili crawled up her nose as she followed the truck driver to a table. She glanced around—her entrance had gained the attention of a few members of the motorcycle club who'd pushed tables together and sat in a large group. Giving them her brightest smile, she dropped her backpack on the floor, peeled off her leather jacket, and rolled up her sleeves to display her tattoos. Sitting down, she stared at the sticky rings left behind from the last customer's drinks alongside a pile of dirty dishes. She looked at the driver. She hadn't asked his name, she didn't care, he served a purpose. "How do you order a meal here?"

"There's no fancy service here." He grinned a yellow-toothed smile at her. "I'll go up to the bar and get us the special." He collected the plates and looked down at her. "Be careful who you talk to, the Black Widow MC often drop by this bar."

"I'll be fine." Zoe crossed her legs and twirled a strand of black hair around one finger catching the eye of a member of the MC. The guy looked promising and she smiled at him. To her surprise, he stood and strutted toward her. He was tall and lean. She kept eye contact. *Here comes my ride into town.*

"Hey." The biker pulled out a chair, turned it around, and sat down, leaning his arms on the back. "I haven't seen you in here before, where did you come from?"

Zoe smiled. "All over, my man is on death row and I needed to get out of town. I jumped into the first eighteen-wheeler heading west." She indicated toward the bar with her chin. "The driver offered me a hot meal and a bed for the night."

"Honey, you don't want to stay here." He shook his head. "This place will give you cooties." He took a long look at the driver waiting at the bar and then nodded in his direction. "And he'll expect more than you're prepared to give."

"I don't really have a choice." Zoe let out a long sigh. "I'm broke and starving. I heard Black Rock Falls might take me in and help me find a job."

"Yeah, the town council don't like people sleeping on the streets hereabouts." He chuckled. "On account of the serial killers."

Zoe held up one finger and searched her backpack. She held up a book. "Yeah, I know all about the murders. It adds to the excitement of living here."

"You're one tough cookie. Why don't you eat your meal and then come over to see me?" He gave her a slow smile. "I'll give you a ride into town. I'll show you how to get a free meal and somewhere to stay without having to pay with sex."

"How do I know I'll be safe with you?" Zoe raised an eyebrow. "The driver seemed harmless enough."

"Because you can." He stood and walked away.

Intrigued, Zoe peered at his colors. In the dim light, she hadn't been able to read any of the jackets of the other members of his club. She heaved a sigh of relief at the name *Devout Sons* surrounding a silver cross on his back. Someone must be watching over her. It had to be a sign of better things to come. After traveling all this way, she'd walked into a biker bar and the first person she'd met belonged to a Christian MC. Grinning to herself, she stared after him. "Maybe for once in my life something is going to turn out right."

CHAPTER SIXTEEN

Thursday

It was a little after six when Jenna opened the front door to Kane. Snow was falling in a curtain and the white flakes had dusted Kane and Duke in their dash from the truck to her front porch. Outside, the winter wonderland cast an eerie light in the early morning dawn. "Come here, Duke."

Jenna toweled down Duke and dried his feet before he trekked snow all through the house. She turned to speak to Kane. "Morning."

"I noticed you didn't say, 'Good.'" Kane kicked off his boots in the mudroom by the front door and removed two layers of clothing before following her into the family room. "I bet this is going to be the coldest winter on record."

Jenna grinned at him. "You know if this was Scotland, they'd tell you, 'It isn't cold, you're just wearing the wrong clothes.'"

"If I bundled up any more, I wouldn't be able to bend my arms." He flashed her a white grin. "Haven't you noticed the people walking around town?" He held his arms out to the side and waddled a few steps to demonstrate. "We're all starting to look like penguins."

Jenna's gaze slid over his red nose and she nodded. "Yeah but you need to keep your beak warm. I have a spare scarf you can use." When he raised one eyebrow and just stared at her, she snorted in amusement. "It's black, Dave, and take it, you look frozen to the bone." He'd cleared the driveway and after collecting the horses the previous evening, had insisted he tend them alone this morning. "I'll help you with the horses in the mornings. It's way too much extra chores for you to do during an investigation. Did you get any sleep at all?"

"Yeah but I need a heavy workout to warm up my muscles." Kane's lips twitched up at the corners. "You planning on joining me today?" He bent to scratch the ears of Pumpkin, Jenna's black cat, curled up on the sofa.

Pleased to see his interaction with her latest pet, Jenna nodded. "Yeah, I'll meet you down there. I'll just put on a fresh pot of coffee and get changed."

Before Jenna opened the door to the gym, she heard the thwacks as Kane kicked and punched the bag. As usual, Kane warmed up with a routine that would have her exhausted before she started. She moved into the room and started her stretching routine, watching him spin and kick, punch and duck, sending the heavy sand-filled bag swinging violently. He moved fluidly and she recalled how he'd been when they first met. The blinding incapacitating headaches from the plate in his head had been his secret misery, but she'd been there to help him recover from a recent gunshot wound to the head and smashed kneecap. To see him fully recovered and moving so well make her eyes well up.

"What?" Kane turned and looked at her enquiringly. "Is there anything wrong?"

Jenna shook her head. "No, nothing's wrong."

"You look sad." Kane removed his gloves and tossed them onto a bench. "Remembering family?" He moved onto the mat and faced her.

"No, and I wasn't feeling sad." Jenna spun and aimed a kick at his chest, laughing when he deflected it. "I was just remembering you in a wheelchair and seeing you move so well now, it's kinda nice."

"I'm almost back to my peak is all." Kane shrugged. "It took more time to recover than I imagined."

"Good, then don't hold back today. I need a good workout." She ducked a punch and went to sweep his legs but he'd moved out of reach. "Dammit, stand still so I can hit you."

"Really?" Kane chuckled and in one slick move took her down to the mat and rolled over. "There. I'm flat on my back."

Winded, Jenna tried to suck air back into her lungs and rolled away jumping to her feet. Hands raised in combat stance, she moved toward him. "Get up."

"You come down here." Kane rolled toward her and took out her legs again.

Angry, Jenna glared at him. They'd never sparred like this before, usually it was practically non-contact—a punch and deflect, take each other down, disarm and restrain type of workout. This was different. "What is this, Dave? This isn't a workout—this is different."

"You told me not to hold back." Kane rolled over onto his elbows and smiled down at her, mischief sparkling in his blue eyes. "I've been spending a few hours a week over at Rowley's dojo with his sensei. I needed to bring my old skills back on line and increase my speed." He brushed a hair from her cheek and tucked it behind one ear.

The move had become so natural, in the same casual way he held her hand or put his arm around her when they were off-duty. The closeness they had often confused Jenna. The slow pace he wanted was nothing she'd experienced before but if friendship was all he had to give her right now, she could wait. She ignored the strange fluttering in her stomach and snorted. "Oh really?"

"Yes, really." He gave her a puzzled look. "Is that a problem?"

They all took a few hours from work each week to go down to the range to practice shooting and he had been going more often than usual between cases. "No, of course not, but you've never mentioned it before. So all those visits to the rifle range were really visits to the dojo?"

"Oh, I went to the range." Kane cleared his throat. "I know if my eye is in after a few shots. I don't need to use a box of ammo to correct my aim so I decided to use the time to improve my other skills. I've been worried about my agility since my knee surgery. You want me in top shape, don't you?"

"I sure do." Jenna pushed to her feet and offered him her hand. "I need to be in shape too and I could do with a few new moves. Teach me."

After breakfast they headed into the office. Jenna wiped the condensation off the frost covered window and took in the landscape. The spray from the snowplow had created a wall of gray glistening ice alongside the highway. All around, trees bent under the weight of the continuous snowfalls. The houses too had become white lumps in the scenery, with smoking chimneys and lacy gutters. Icicles hung from everything, signposts and mailboxes had transformed overnight and blended into the sidewalk. She frowned at the sight. Snow had come early this year and arrived with unprecedented force. She looked at Kane, who was humming along to a tune on the radio. "As Deputy Walters came up empty from the hotline calls about chainsaws and we have zip on the tattoos, I'm going to follow Carter's suggestion and show the photographs of the tattoos around the homeless shelters and soup kitchen today. If Rowley had hunted down a vehicle on the CCTV footage, we'd have had something to work with but from what he said, the snowfall was so dense, he had trouble making out anything at all. Without any leads, we really have no other place to start. I could put out another media report and see what happens."

"Yeah, some people wouldn't have seen the news and others wouldn't want to get involved." Kane pulled into his parking space outside the sheriff's department.

Jenna nodded. "I guess." She looked at Duke hiding under his blanket. "Duke doesn't look too keen to be out today."

"I think I'll leave him with Maggie." Kane frowned. "He was shivering so bad this morning when I was clearing the driveway his teeth were chattering."

"That new coat should be warm enough, maybe he needs boots?" Jenna chuckled at his aghast expression and followed him up the front steps and after giving Maggie a wave, hurried into the warmth of her office. Her phone chimed as she sat down at her desk. It was Wolfe. "Morning. Do you have an update on the snowman?"

"No. I'll do an autopsy tomorrow. It takes time to thaw out a corpse. I can't use heat or the body will desiccate. Before you ask, it's covered with a wet sheet to avoid that problem and it also must be kept in a sterile environment or I won't be able to trust the trace evidence."

Jenna stared at the wall, thinking. "I don't like your chances after finding it in the park. What about the limbs, any results at all?"

"It was fortunate it was covered by snow, that would've helped." Wolfe tapped at his keyboard. *"Yeah, I do have a few results for you. The snowman, as you call the victim, is female and I noticed a small hole under the hair at the base of the neck. It may or may not be a bullet wound but it's possible as there is a matching one just above the clavicle. It might be a through and through from a rifle, perhaps but I can't be sure until I've autopsied the body. If it is, it's likely the cause of death."*

Jenna made notes. "Dave was saying about how killers often freeze their victims to confuse the time of death. Is this the case with these victims?"

"It's doubtful I'll be able to determine TOD at all. Although—" Wolfe brightened *"—I do have some information gathered from the limbs.*

We know we have two different women but we also know they died at different times by the rate of decomposition in their cells. The samples I've taken indicate the killer froze them soon after death and thawed them at least once before he froze them again. The decomposition during the period of defrosting isn't the same. The cell damage isn't the same either. These women could have died at least a year apart."

CHAPTER SEVENTEEN

The sound of a woman's laughter in the hallway dragged Jenna away from making notes on the whiteboard. Since the first snow, the usual stream of people visiting the front counter had slowed to a trickle and rarely any of them laughed. Inquisitive, she walked into the main office and took in the scene. Kim Strickland, the woman Kane had rescued from the kidnappers, tossed her long red hair and looked up at Kane through her eyelashes. She had one hand resting on his forearm, and leaned toward him in an attitude of possession. Kane had his back against the counter with his arms crossed but gave the impression he was listening with interest to the woman's constant babbling. *So, this is the woman, Susie told me was hanging all over Kane at Aunt Betty's?* Jenna turned her attention to Rowley, who stood behind the counter, mouth open and watching the interaction between the pair goggle-eyed. Jenna frowned. Rowley had taken the woman's statement on the night of the incident and as far as she and the DA were concerned the case was in the hands of the court. *Why is she here?*

As she moved closer, she noticed a large gift basket on the counter and Maggie staring at it with distaste as if it contained poison. She ignored the couple and walked to the other end of the counter. "Where did this come from, Maggie?"

"Her." Maggie tipped her head toward Kim. "Said she'd sit right down here and wait until Deputy Kane would see her." She lowered her voice. "I told her, we don't allow none of the deputies to accept gifts but would she listen? No, she wouldn't. When she seen him coming out your office, she told me if I didn't go get him, she'd march right down and get him herself."

Astonished, Jenna patted Maggie's hand. "Next time come get me."

Jenna picked up the basket and walked toward Kane. In her periphery, she noticed Rowley move down the desk toward Maggie and busy himself with some paperwork. She plastered a smile on her face and looked at Kane's bemused expression. "Ah, Miss Strickland?" She held out the basket. "I believe this belongs to you?"

"No." Kim gave Jenna an exasperated glare, and not taking her hand from Kane's arm, turned to face her. "That's a little gift for Dave. He was so brave, fighting six men to save me. I owe him my life."

Dave? Jenna pushed the basket toward her. "That's very kind of you but I'm sure Deputy Kane has explained to you he isn't allowed to accept gifts for doing his job. That's what we pay him to do, Miss Strickland." She ignored the woman's haughty expression and turned to Kane. "My office, now!"

"Yes, ma'am." Kane's gaze searched her face for a second before turning to Kim. "I told you, I was just doing my job." He ushered her toward the front door.

"Dinner then or at least let me buy you a drink?" Kim pouted. "When you're off-duty and not under the glare of Dragon Lady."

"I have to go." Kane stepped away. "Thanks for dropping by."

"I'm not taking 'no' for an answer, Dave. I'll call you, tonight." She gave him a sweet smile, dropped the basket on a chair inside the door, and walked out into the snow.

The wave of jealousy at seeing Kane with another woman rushed over Jenna. She fought to keep it under control and went inside her office. She picked up the pen and added Wolfe's findings to the whiteboard alongside the notes from the files Jo had sent her. She'd set the other cases up as parallels to what they had so far. She'd been surprised at the wealth of information Jo and Carter had supplied. If this killer was The Sculptor, they would have the chance to take down a notorious murderer. When she placed the pen back in its holder and turned around, Kane was watching her with a puzzled expression. She grabbed her coat and shrugged it on. "We're going to visit the homeless shelters and show the photographs around, or did it slip your mind?"

"No, it didn't and I've printed up a pile of images of the tattoos to circulate." Kane crossed his arms. "Do we have a problem, Jenna?"

After waiting so long for him, the thought that he'd found someone else and not said a word had hurt her. Jenna couldn't meet his eyes. "We won't as long as you keep your personal life out of the office." She swallowed hard. "Maybe it's time for you to find your own place. I think we both need some space."

"If that's what you want." Kane turned to go.

Jenna watched him leave without a word of protest and gave herself a mental shake. She had a killer to catch and her personal feelings would have to be put on hold. After slipping a new statement book inside a waterproof folder, Jenna wrapped a scarf around her face, put on her shades, and pulled on her hat. She collected her things and headed out to Kane's truck, snagging the gift basket on the way. She'd drop it at the first homeless shelter. They'd appreciate the donation. Slipping and sliding through the snow, she waited for Kane to unlock the Beast and then climbed inside. Kane glanced at her as if gauging her mood and then started the engine but didn't drive away. She looked at him. "What's the hold up?"

"I need some answers." Kane huffed out a long sigh. "Are you really going to turn me out of the cottage in the middle of winter?"

A tightness clamped Jenna's gut. She kept her gaze straight ahead. He'd found someone to take his dead wife Annie's place in his heart and it wasn't her. The thought splashed over her in a tsunami of emotions. "Well, I think it's time you found a place of your own."

"But Jenna, it's my home." Kane turned in his seat and stared at her. "Why now?"

"Why now?" Jenna stared at the fabric lining of the truck's cab and shook her head. "It's all over town, you have an admirer. Having you living in the cottage, working out together, and you eating breakfast with me isn't appropriate any longer."

"I meant to tell you about Kim." Kane backed the truck out of the parking space. "I guess as she showed up at the office it's as good a time as any."

She fought for words. "It's really none of my business who you see on your downtime, Dave."

"I'm not seeing *her.*" Kane almost choked on the words. "*Jesus.* She's the last person I want to get involved with. It was funny at first but I figure she's kinda stalking me." He flashed her a concerned stare. "I should have mentioned it before but with the caseload, it slipped into the background."

Jenna caught the tick in his cheek. It always happened when he was concerned or angry and right now, she'd pick angry. "Okay, so you don't have to move out. How long has this been going on?"

"Since the incident with the men involved in the overdose and kidnap on the mountain." Kane parked outside the soup kitchen and turned to look at her. "Kim called me later that night—like at three in the morning. She said she was all wound up and couldn't sleep. She wanted to meet me in the bar for a nightcap. I refused and then all hell broke loose. I admit when she started crying, I caved. She'd been through an ordeal and I thought one drink wouldn't hurt." He rubbed his hands down his face. "Oh boy, was that a mistake. She's been calling or leaving messages since then, maybe ten or more a day. She keeps showing up, like if I drop by Aunt Betty's, she seems to appear from nowhere and we go through the same routine. She gets all familiar, grabs my arm, and leans against me like we're going together."

"You seemed a mite friendly toward her before, and I've seen you close down women who try to hit on you." Jenna shrugged. "Why not use the same tactic on her?"

"That works at first contact." Kane drummed his fingers on the steering wheel. "I usually ignore the question or change the subject. In this case, she assumes because I had a drink with her, I'm available."

Seeing how not handling something so simple was eating him up inside, Jenna considered her reply. "Women aren't so difficult, Dave. Just tell her plain and simple that you're not interested. Trust me, in the long run, it's the kindest thing to do."

"When she came by today, I made it clear I'm not interested. It didn't work." He looked at her. "You heard her."

Jenna snorted. "I heard you making an excuse for not seeing her. That never works, it feeds the flame of hope." She looked at him and smiled. "I never thought in a million years I'd see you confused about anything, let alone a woman's attention."

"It's not funny, Jenna. I think she might be dangerous." Kane let out a long sigh. "She's exhibiting obsessive behavior. It's not just the attraction to her rescuer some people develop. This is different, she showed me a side of her today that's worrying. Her eyes turned mean when you spoke to her."

"Okay." Jenna turned in her seat to look at him. "She's a nurse, so has to work. How come she seems to turn up when you're alone?"

"Not alone." Kane rubbed the back of his neck. "Just not with you, and if she's watching me all damn day, it's because she's on vacation."

"So she doesn't like you being with the 'Dragon Lady,' huh?" Jenna took in his serious expression. "This is really worrying you, isn't it?"

"Yeah." Kane's mouth turned down. "Especially now. I've upset you by not telling you." He cupped her cheek.

Jenna glanced around. Glad no one was walking by, she leaned into his leather-clad palm and stared at him. "Why didn't you trust me with this problem, Dave?"

"I'm so sorry. I'd never do anything to hurt you, Jenna." Kane bent and brushed a featherlike kiss over her lips. "Are we good?" He pulled back and dropped his hand.

Overwhelmed by his sudden show of affection, Jenna swallowed hard. "Yes, but now I'm confused."

"Trust me, not as much as I am right now." Kane gave her a wry smile.

Jenna squeezed his arm. "You're a complicated guy, Dave, but I'm starting to figure you out."

"I hope so." Kane blew out a relived breath. "One of us sure needs to."

With effort, Jenna gathered herself and concentrated on the problem at hand. "Now, show me the messages."

"Sure." Kane handed her his phone. "Check them out. I was going to block her number but if anything happened, I'd need them for evidence." He pressed his lips together. "It's not me, I'm concerned about, Jenna—it's you."

Jenna scanned the messages and sucked in a breath. The messages started nice enough and then turned to blaming her for being the reason Kane refused to meet with her. "How much do you know about stalkers?"

"Enough to know she's stalking me." Kane pulled his thick woolen cap down tighter over his ears. "They're people who exhibit obsessive behavior for example, following someone, sending unwanted gifts or messages, showing up at a person's workplace or uninvited to their homes. Following them, watching them. All these are obsessive traits associated with stalking. I can profile a killer but this is different. Whatever I'm doing it's making her worse and turning her aggression toward you." He met her gaze. "I don't know what she is capable of, Jenna."

CHAPTER EIGHTEEN

Elated, Preacher couldn't help smiling at his good fortune. Ignoring the biting wind and snowflakes brushing his cheeks, he pulled a woolen cap down over his ears and strolled down Main taking his time to peer into shop windows. He marveled at how clean and fresh Black Rock Falls appeared. Usually after the snowplow and brine spreader had been through, a mound of gray slush banked each road but as the snow fell it laid down a clean white surface. When the moon peeked through the clouds tonight the bright colors and snow-covered parked vehicles would exist in a world of gray and blue—his world.

He wanted so much to go by the park and see the crime scene tape flapping in the wind. It was as if the sheriff had hung the tape to advertise his artwork. A "Come and see" or "Look here," notice for any passersby but it wasn't the snowman he'd left in the park that amused him. As if staging his artwork hadn't been enough excitement for one day, last evening, a young woman had walked into his life—a perfect example of what he craved. Dark hair and small with an attitude he would love to tame. Her black fingernails and tattoos had drawn him to her like a magnet. Everything was perfect, Zoe was new in town, homeless—she needed him and now she was fast asleep in his cellar. He'd found two perfect examples of Delores—which one would come to him first?

He rubbed his hands together and peered at a display of chainsaws. He loved chainsaws and had a mind to buy another. They gave him a surge of creativity with such intensity, he could almost compare it to lust. He moved along the visually tantalizing display. New and glossy, the machines lined up with price tags and cards explaining their many virtues. He read each one, savoring the features. There were so many different types to choose from with different blade widths, engine size, or run by electric or gas. Preacher inhaled. He could almost smell the oily slickness of the chain and hear the noise they made. His hands trembled with excitement as he visualized the blade cutting through a frozen body like butter.

CHAPTER NINETEEN

Black Rock Falls had three homeless shelters and a soup kitchen. The soup kitchen received funding from a local charity and the local Catholic church ran one of the shelters. Overseen by Father Derry, the volunteers came mainly from his congregation, and he rarely turned anyone away from Our Lady's Sanctuary. The homeless didn't get the same automatic pass into the council-run shelters. The town council had converted the abandoned sawmill into two. New Start for men and New Hope for women. They offered a different solution to homelessness and people who wanted to turn their lives around, received assistance to find work but in return did chores and gave a portion of their salary to keep their bed. The latter received funding from a charity overseen by the town council. Apart from the live-in managers, all other assistance to run New Start and New Hope came in the form of volunteers.

Jenna had helped on many occasions and found giving a couple of hours serving food in the shelters or soup kitchen, fit into her busy schedule. She made her way to Our Lady's Sanctuary, heartened to see many of the Black Rock Falls community giving their time to assist the less fortunate. She edged through the line crowding the front door and waved at the woman sitting at the check-in counter. The front of the building held an area for serving meals. The stark room with its tile floors and plain white walls buzzed with low conversation and the clatter of plates and cutlery. A long line of bedraggled exhausted looking people waited with trays to collect a hot meal and beverage. Volunteers worked in a production line wearing brightly colored aprons and hair nets. They seemed to avoid eye contact as they dished out the food, a stark contrast to Father Derry's calm voice welcoming everyone and the cheery old man chatting as he wiped down tables and collected dishes.

Jenna tried to ignore the pungent smell wafting from inside and making her slightly nauseous. The food cooking in huge steaming pots in the kitchen, mingled with body odor, cigarette smoke and bleach. She made her way around the trestle tables and headed for the main hall. In the walkway hidden beside a vending machine, she found the bulletin board and moved a few notices to make room for one of Kane's flyers. She plucked one from his hand and attached it with a pin. Across the top of the images of the tattoos he'd printed in bold:

Do you recognize these tattoos? Call the sheriff's department hotline on the number below or drop by.

"These are great." Jenna made her way into the main hall and stopped at the door. "Oh, this isn't good."

Her heart ached for the sea of miserable faces packed inside the room. People spilled out of the sleeping areas and crowded around the main hall. Many had squashed onto old sofas and beanbags. Others sat on mattresses pushed hard against the wall. Most looked bewildered and clutched plastic bags or duffels to their chests as if terrified someone would take them. Some sat on the cold floor, backs propped against the wall, staring with empty vacant eyes as if not believing their situation. Although a TV tuned to a local channel chatted away in one corner and the room was brighter with pictures on the wall, this part of the shelter had the feeling of hopelessness. "I wonder if those people have eaten today? They look too scared to move."

"Unless they have a buddy, I doubt it." Kane's mouth turned down at the corners. "They'd figure a bed was better than a meal." He scanned the room. "I had no idea we had so many homeless."

Jenna wrinkled her nose at the smell of boiled cabbage wafting from the kitchen and shifted her gaze to him. "I blame Mayor Petersham. He had to crow about this being a town where we cared about people's wellbeing and the fact he'd built two shelters. Since the news hit the media, the down and out have been coming here in droves."

"Is it okay if I go grab them some food?" Kane gave her a pleading look. "There are children here and everyone is so busy in the kitchen. I can't just stand by and see them go without."

Jenna nodded. "Sure, go talk to Father Derry. He'll have a ton of sandwiches in the kitchen." She glanced at the two women with young ones huddled together. "I'll call New Hope and insist they take them."

She made the call and after a heated discussion made some headway. The manager agreed to find room and would be sending a bus along shortly to collect them. Jenna had no idea why the women had fallen on hard times but New Hope had five rooms set aside for emergency accommodation for battered women and their kids. As they were empty at present, she insisted he spare two of them. Next year would be different with ten rooms available when *Her Broken Wings Foundation* opened its doors out of a refurbished plant on the other side of town.

Jenna moved from person to person, showing the images and asking if they'd seen a woman with tattoos like them. Most just shook their heads but a volunteer with the name *Claude* printed on a nametag, looked at them with interest. She took in the lean muscular man. Acne scars spoiled a once handsome face and when he moved closer, she pushed the photograph under his nose. "Do you recognize these?"

"Maybe." Claude took the photograph and peered at it closely. He ran the tip of his finger over the design in almost a caress. "Could be I've seen it on a missing persons flyer in the office." He looked back at Jenna and his expression hardened. "We get quite a few young women with ink come by here." He crinkled his nose as if he'd smelled something bad. "They think they're all that until they have no food in their bellies or a place to sleep and then they become passive real fast."

Astonished Father Derry would have someone so callous working with these unfortunate people, she bit back a stinging retort and lifted her chin. He had information and she needed it. "Show me the flyer."

"It could still be at the front counter." Claude handed her back the flyer. "Follow me and we'll go see."

On her way to the office, she passed Kane carrying a tray piled high with sandwiches. Three people followed behind, with food and drinks. She smiled at him. It was so like him to care for the wellbeing of people. "I'll be back in a minute."

She followed Claude in the back door to the office at the front counter. The room smelled of coffee and she could see a fresh pot brewing on a counter. She looked at the forlorn faces waiting in the line to register. The smell must be driving them crazy. She shook her head to stay in the game and went to the noticeboard.

"It was here somewhere." Claude lifted the notices and peered underneath and then tugged at one. "Here you go. Evelyn Ross, nineteen, out of Colorado Springs and reported missing last winter." He pointed to the rose on the young woman's arm. "Looks the same."

Recognizing more than the rose, Jenna scanned the image and composed her expression. The butterfly on the hand was identical in color and design. She looked at Claude. "Do you have many missing persons flyers here?"

"Some." Claude looked interested and opened a drawer. He pulled out a bunch of papers. "Father Derry asks us to pick them up if we see them on our travels. Most folks here aren't too forthcoming on where they came from or where they've been."

Peering at the ten or so faces staring out from the flyers, Jenna pulled out her phone, laid them out on the table, and copied them. She glanced at Claude, who looked excited as he gazed at the images. "Have any of these people dropped by here?" She collected up the flyers tapped them into a neat pile and handed them to him.

"Not that I know about." Claude sifted through the flyers and then pointed to a young woman with dark hair and tattoos. "I did see this one in a paper when I was traveling through Colorado. They found her under the ice in a lake. She must have fallen in and drowned." He gave Jenna a slow smile and chuckled deep in his chest. "Although, I can't imagine why anyone would go skinny dipping with snow on the ground."

Jenna pulled out her notebook to record the woman's name. "Can you remember where they found her?"

"Nope." He shuffled his feet. "But it was around March after the melt."

"What were you doing in Colorado?" Jenna raised her pen. "On vacation?"

"I wish." Claude shook his head. "I'm a long-haul trucker. I deliver and collect goods from all over. I drive for Jim Foxx Trucking out of the industrial area south of town." He glanced behind him. "I gotta go. I have chores to do."

Jenna nodded. Many long-haul truckers worked as a two-man team. One sleeping while the other drove. "Sure, just one more thing. Do you drive alone or do you have a partner?" She shifted her weight from one foot to the other, bending one knee to give a more casual pose.

"It depends on where they send me." Claude lifted one shoulder as if reluctant to give her any more information. "I sometimes drive with Jo… ah, Josiah Brock. He was with me on that haul. He lives out on Snowberry Way. He's a good guy and helps out at the soup kitchen a couple of times a week, when the weather causes road closures."

"And where do you live?"

"Stanton Road, near town." Claude flicked his eyes over her. "I'm not in any trouble am I, Sheriff?"

"No, but I need the details of the people I speak to. I'm sure you understand?" Jenna made a note of the man's address. "Okay, thanks for your help." She turned and headed back to the hall.

"I've asked everyone here. No luck." Kane folded the flyers and pushed them inside his jacket.

"Okay, we'll split up and show them around to everyone in the dining area." Jenna looked at him. "You go ahead, I'll inform the women with kids that they have a place to stay tonight."

"More will be coming." Kane scanned the room. "This place is bursting at the seams."

Jenna pulled off her woolen cap and pushed a hand through her hair tucking it behind her ear. "I'll speak to the media. I'll ask them if they'll do a follow-up story and make sure they make it clear we have no room here."

"Father Derry will have them sleeping in the church before he turns anyone away." Kane's brow furrowed. "I'm not sure how long his supplies will last. Maybe ask the reporter to add that donations to the church are needed urgently."

Jenna nodded. "I'll call them when I get back to the office. I need to send copies of the missing persons flyers to Wolfe. We may have found the snowman victim. Go. I'll catch up with you in a minute."

She watched him go and, in her periphery, caught sight of Claude peering at her from a doorway. The hairs on the back of her neck raised in warning. Had she missed something? She ran the conversation through her mind and remembered the way he'd almost caressed the images of the tattoos, as if he had a connection to them. He drove a long-haul truck, traveled from state to state, and worked with the homeless. She sent the files to Wolfe with a brief message and then walked casually toward the women with children to give them the news but kept one eye on Claude Grady. *Are you my first suspect?*

CHAPTER TWENTY

Snakeskin Gulley

It was late in the afternoon when Ty Carter picked up the phone on Jo's desk and peered at the ID. "It's Dave Kane, want me to take it?"

"Yeah thanks." Jo covered the mouthpiece on the landline and then went back to her heated conversation with the FBI Director.

"Dave, it's Ty Carter. Jo's tied up on the other line. Do you have information on the frozen ladies?"

"No, Wolfe will be conducting the autopsy tomorrow. It takes time for the bodies to thaw. I've sent you all his findings to date." Kane cleared his throat. *"The investigation is underway on the search for the killer, we have visited all the homeless shelters and asked about the tattoos. We got one possible and Jenna is hunting down that lead and we have a possible suspect. Rowley is on that now, but that's not why I called. I needed to get Jo's take on stalkers."*

Surprised, Ty raised his eyebrows. "Stalkers? They follow people around, man. Show up and cause trouble. Threaten to kill you or your family. You know that, right?"

"I know enough to charge one but this is personal. I'm wondering if I'm overreacting to a come on."

Finding it difficult to understand Kane's concern. Ty dropped into Jo's office chair, leaned back, and crossed his booted feet on her desk. "How so?"

He listened with interest at Kane's description of the kidnapping and drug arrest at the ski resort. "So what made you buckle and have a drink with her? You don't seem the type to fall for a woman's charms." He bit back a grin. "She's a babe, right?"

"Yeah, but it wasn't about her looks. She was in shock after the fight. Her eyes were so wide I thought they'd pop right out of her head. When she called my room, crying, I considered it duty of care—she thought it was a date."

Ty stared at the ceiling as Kane detailed his previous few days' encounters with Kim. He dropped his feet from the desk as Jo walked over and stood beside him. "Jo's here, I'll bring her up to speed and then put her on." He covered the mouthpiece and gave Jo the details. "So what do you think?"

"Harassment for sure and maybe a stalker in progress. Put the phone on speaker. I'll talk to him." Jo placed a cup of coffee on the table, pulled up another chair, and sat down. "Hi, Dave. As you suspected this is a classic obsession case but she's escalating. The fact you shut her down in public and she completely discounted what you'd said and mentioned she'd call you later, was the flashing red light—making an excuse for your denial of her advances by bringing in Jenna might be a problem. If she threatens her, that's lights and sirens."

"She hasn't threatened anyone yet. I admit, her attention was an ego stroke at first and I figured I was overreacting." Kane let out a long sigh. *"I don't want to be rude to her but if I don't put a stop to Kim's infatuation it will as sure as hell cause problems between Jenna and me. She wasn't impressed with her coming by the office bearing gifts."*

"Are you and Jenna in a relationship?" Jo raised one eyebrow at Ty.

"Not at the moment." Kane lowered his voice. *"We're close friends is all."*

Ty wrote, "*He wouldn't care what Jenna thinks if he didn't like her.*" in Jo's notebook and grinned. Dave and Jenna lived separate lives. *Go figure?*

Jo shot him an exasperated look and lifted one shoulder. "I see." She flipped the page on her notebook. "The problem I see, Dave, is that Kim is directing her frustration toward Jenna. She sees her as an obstacle to the relationship she wants with you. Of course, it's all in her mind. She believes she has a claim on you."

"*Okay, but apart from the messages, I don't have enough to charge her with stalking.*" Kane sounded tired. "*The fact I had a drink with her in the middle of the night will be damning.*"

Ty rolled his eyes upward. He just knew where this was leading. "Don't tell me, you walked her back to her room and somebody saw you?"

"*Yeah. I wasn't thinking, her room was on the way to mine and I just wanted to go get some sleep.*"

"Uh-huh, if you got a judge to sign the harassment warrant, the DA wouldn't take it to court." Ty removed his Stetson and studied it before pushing it back on his head. "He'd say she's a spurned lover. Problem is, the defense will have the CCTV footage of you going back to her room in the early hours of the morning. Since then, she has an excuse to pursue you. She now can say you've shown interest in her."

"*Yeah, I understand the implications and this is why I called, Jo.*" Kane's voice had become concerned. "*I need to know more about the personality I'm dealing with and how to get myself out of this mess.*"

"What you've done so far is good." Jo blew on her hot coffee and then took a sip. "The problem is recognizing any psychotic behavior before it gets out of hand. Not all people with obsessive behavior escalate into stalkers but some can cause major problems. It seems Kim is aware of your closeness to Jenna, so she's a potential threat."

She sipped again. "Maybe suggest Kim does something in her spare time to keep her occupied and away from you. She may not have any interests outside her work at the hospital."

Ty exchanged a meaningful glance with Jo and nodded. Right this moment, Kane was walking on a knife's edge. He stared at the phone. "Well, I guess you could ask her to dinner and act like a complete ass. It might put her off."

"That's not going to happen." Kane's voice was like ice.

Jo's eyes flashed with anger as she looked at Ty and then depressed the mute button on the phone. "Have you lost your mind?"

Ty shrugged. "It might have worked."

Jo released the mute button and her lips flattened. "Dave, just keep deflecting her advances and try my other suggestions."

"Okay, I'll try that angle." Kane blew out a breath. *"I'm concerned she might go after Jenna."*

Ty had seen stalkers turn to murder in the blink of an eye. "Yeah, it's possible but if she makes any threats toward you or Jenna, you'll get her on stalking. You'll have to watch Jenna's back."

"I always do."

CHAPTER TWENTY-ONE

Black Rock Falls

Friday

It was just after nine by the time Wolfe had finished explaining the procedure for autopsying victims who'd been subject to freezing to his daughter Emily and Colt Webber, both interns studying forensic science at the local college. "The need for a complete sterile environment to avoid cross contamination is crucial during the thawing process. This is why I'll be restricting Jenna and Kane to the viewing area."

He glanced up as Jenna led Kane into the glass-partitioned section of the room. He pressed his mic button. "Morning. I'll be starting soon. I'll pause at the end of each section for questions."

"Okay." Jenna's voice sounded scratchy through the intercom.

Wolfe uncovered the torso of the woman with the severed limbs set out around her. The ghostly bluish-white skin and open staring eyes looked ghoulish even to him. He did a cursory examination. "We have a Caucasian female, approximately twenty years old, well-nourished, five-five, dark hair, blue eyes. I've documented tattoos of various designs on arms, small of back, and face. The fingernails are dirty and broken. I'm running a soil comparison analysis on the samples from under her fingernails to discover where she was at the time of death. I can tell the samples from under the nails contain a decaying vegetation mixture usually found in wooded areas but it will take more investigation to determine if it is Scobey soil, which is found in Stanton Forest." He glanced up at Jenna's tap on the glass.

"Any sign of sexual assault?" Jenna frowned. "Cause of death?"

Wolfe examined the body and took swabs. He handed the swabs to Emily, who made the slides and stood to one side while he peered into the microscope. He walked back to the gurney. "No sign of sexual assault, no semen in the vaginal cavity. We have no clothing to test for trace evidence and the killer packed her in snow. All the external swabs I've taken during the thawing have yielded no foreign human DNA." He moved to the head of the torso. "There is an exit wound below the clavicle consistent with a gunshot wound. The entry wound is in the back at C5. If she was running away, I estimate the shooter is at least five-ten, as the bullet trajectory is in a downward motion, although the damage to the nails could indicate she fell or was crawling through a forest at the time of death. I will complete a full autopsy to confirm, but this injury has likely severed the spinal cord resulting in immediate paralysis. If this assumption is accurate, she couldn't have crawled away after receiving the injury. The cause of death in this case would be asphyxiation from the paralysis caused by a gunshot wound." He glanced back up at Jenna.

"Does the pathology on the victim's torso indicate she could have been frozen and thawed like the limbs we found?" Jenna's gaze sharpened. "I'm wondering if he kept the limbs and torsos together?"

Wolfe turned to his interns. "Colt, tell Jenna what we discovered."

"We evaluated the samples by microscope and an electronic image analyzer. In both victims we found extended extracellular spaces and shrunken cells resulting from the freeze-thaw cycle. In the body parts without the torso, the findings were more pronounced, which would indicate the second victim was frozen for a longer period."

"Something else significant." Emily looked up at Jenna. "The flesh on both victims has burns consistent with the use of dry ice."

Wolfe smiled at her and then turned back to Jenna. "This strongly indicates the burns happened during a thaw cycle. The bodies had started to thaw and the killer used dry ice to re-freeze them. Perhaps he wanted to move them to another area. The burns are consistent with the result of dry ice on uncovered decomposing flesh."

"Ah, that information is gold." Kane peered through the glass at him. "If this is The Sculptor, we have just discovered how he moves his victims interstate."

"Well, the information we have would indicate he was moving the bodies. Why else use the dry ice, a chest freezer would work better?" Wolfe leaned against the counter and looked at them. "If he's been killing all over, it would make sense why these women aren't showing up on any missing persons files in Montana. Of course, once I have the dental records or a DNA match, we'll know if the victim is Evelyn Ross, out of Colorado Springs."

"She fits the preferred type of The Sculptor and would make it two for two in Colorado Springs. The frozen woman in the lake was identified as Connie Sandford." Kane's gaze drifted over the body. "Both women are the same type as her. Dark hair, five-five, around twenty, and with ink. Add the freeze and thaw cycle in the majority of victims and it's too much of a coincidence not to be him."

"And we have a long-haul trucker waving a red flag at me." Jenna had a satisfied expression. "I think we need to pay a visit to Claude Grady's boss and find out where he's been."

CHAPTER TWENTY-TWO

"Hey, wake up." A female voice dragged Zoe from a deep dreamless sleep.

She opened her eyes and a lightbulb hanging from a long cord in the middle of a darkened room went in and out of focus. Nauseous, she shut them again and sucked in a breath of stale, rank air. Where the hell had she slept last night and why did she feel as if she'd been eating sand? Her head throbbed as if she'd been drinking heavily. From the angry voice, she must have fallen asleep in somebody's spot. It had happened before and she didn't intend to cower to anyone. On the streets and homeless, she had gotten used to defending herself. Sliding one hand down to her leg, she fumbled for the blade strapped to her ankle and came up empty. Realization, that she wasn't wearing her jeans or boots slammed into her. She opened her eyes, slowly peering through the lashes at the dark-haired young woman looking down at her. Forcing words from her parched throat, she tried to sit up but the room spun and she fell back into the pillows. "Where the hell am I?" The croaky voice coming from her lips was unrecognizable. Taking it slowly, she eased into a sitting position and peered under the covers. "Where are my clothes?"

"I don't know, mine are missing too. I'm Ava and I don't have a clue where we are, but we're locked in a cellar. Here, drink this, it will help." Ava thrust a glass of water into her hands and sat on the bed next to her. "I woke up and you were here. Did Preacher bring you?"

I'm locked in a cellar? Zoe's heart pounded but she needed to evaluate the situation. She sipped and looked around the room. Beds, tables, and chairs—it resembled a survival shelter. The cool fresh water slid down her dry throat in a calming balm. "I'm Zoe, I don't know anyone by the name of Preacher. The last thing I remember was getting a ride into Black Rock Falls with a biker."

"Did he tell you he had a place for you to stay for the night?" Ava picked at her nails. "Tall, lean, muscular, with a soft voice?"

It was as if a wall in her head had blocked the memories. Zoe allowed the images of the two men she'd met previously to percolate into her mind. Not the trucker but maybe the biker was Preacher. "Yeah, he did. I guess that description fits the biker but for some reason, I can't remember what happened after we got into town."

"I'm sure Preacher, the guy keeping us here, uses a date-rape drug. That's why you can't remember what happened." Ava gave her a solemn look. "I don't sleep much, I've been too scared to shut my eyes but last night after dinner, I fell asleep and woke up this morning without my clothes."

Panic gripped Zoe and the glass tumbled from her fingers but it didn't smash, it bounced across the floor. "Are we his sex slaves?"

"He hasn't touched me yet." Ava pushed her hair into a ponytail and secured it with a band from around her wrist. "I'm pretty sure I've been here a few days. It's hard to tell. I think he drugs our food when he wants to come down here. Preacher hasn't threatened me at all. He supplies clean clothing and three meals a day but won't say why he's keeping me prisoner."

The hairs on the back of Zoe's neck prickled in a warning. She'd read about men like this man, Preacher. She turned to look at Ava and wondered just how naive she was. "Haven't you heard about men kidnapping women and selling them to the highest bidder?" She looked into Ava's eyes. "To him it's not about using us for sex—"

she held up her hand and rubbed her thumb on the pad of her first finger in a circular motion "—it's about money." She shuddered. "If he undressed us, how do we know he didn't film us or pose us for photographs? If he did, he'd likely post them on his secret club page and wait for the highest bid."

"You think?" Ava chewed on her fingernails.

Zoe slipped out of bed, testing her balance before moving around the room. "Have you tried to escape?"

"Of course I have." A flash of annoyance crossed Ava's face. "There's no way out. The door at the top of the steps is locked and would be hard to force because it opens inward." She sighed. "There's nothing in here to use as a weapon, food comes on paper plates with plastic utensils, the glasses are plastic, same with the cups. All the chairs are bolted to the floor."

Zoe squared her shoulders and turned to face her. "I don't give up too easy. Give me five minutes to get my head on and we'll work on a solution." She glanced around. "Where's the bathroom?"

"Over there." Ava went to a closet and threw open the doors to reveal a rack of clothes and shelves containing underwear. Below sat a neat row of boots of various design and sizes. "Grab something to wear. There are toiletries in the bathroom. Don't be too long, I'd say he was waiting for you to wake up before he feeds us and I'm famished."

Zoe took a few seconds to look at Ava. If she'd only been here a few days, why was she already showing the resignation of Stockholm Syndrome. She'd soon have her snapping out of that and she'd start over breakfast. Heading to the bathroom, she took in the structure of the cellar and nodded to herself. *There is always a way out.*

CHAPTER TWENTY-THREE

Snowflakes piled up on the windowsills as Jenna glanced out the window, hoping they'd make it home this afternoon before another blizzard hit the town. She glanced at the clock and calculated what she needed to do for the rest of the day. Waiting for a positive ID of the snowman victim, slowed the investigation but she had plenty of time to follow up with Jim Foxx, the owner of the trucking company, before the snowplow made its last trip of the day from town at five-thirty. As it went right past her front gate it would sure make life easier. In fact, if they gave the driver a call and followed the snowplow home, all she had to do was open the gate and her friendly neighbor would cut a path straight to her front door.

She tried the office and a recorded message gave her a list of numbers of people to contact. She called Mr. Foxx and he answered on the third ring. "Mr. Fox this is Sheriff Alton, I wonder if you could give me some information on a couple of your drivers?"

"I'm not inclined to give out such information, Sheriff. Privacy laws and all that." Foxx sounded defensive.

Jenna pulled a face. "Ah, well one of the men in question has already admitted working for you and where he went on his last trip, but as I'm conducting an investigation, I would appreciate your assistance." She cleared her throat at the stony silence at the other end of the line. "The man in question is Claude Grady. He stated he made a trip to Colorado recently with a man by the name of Josiah Brock. Could you confirm that please?"

"Okay, this question is easy. You already know Grady went to Colorado last trip. Josiah Brock no longer works for me. I believe he's working out of Blackwater. My competitor, Blackwater Trucking, came by here offering my drivers more than I could pay them and I lost a few good men."

Jenna made a few notes. "Did Brock ever ride with Grady?"

"Yeah, I believe so." Foxx sighed. *"If you need any more information, you'll have to ask Brock."*

Jenna twirled her pen in her fingers, she had to ask but somehow knew the reply. "Would you be willing to give me the routes Grady took in the past twelve months or so?"

"I'm afraid not, Sheriff. You'd need a search warrant for that information." The line went dead.

Jenna snorted. "Well, thank you so much for your cooperation." She dropped her phone on the desk, leaned back in her seat, and looked up just as Kane entered the room bringing with him the smell of winter and loaded up with takeout. He was wearing a grim expression. Jenna patted her knee and Duke laid his head on her lap, clearly upset as well. "Anything wrong? Duke looks sad."

"Uh-huh." Kane arranged the food on her desk. "Duke's just fine but I had another run-in with Kim at Aunt Betty's." He pulled off his coat and hung it on the peg behind the door.

"Oh man, you should have been there." Rowley followed him close behind carrying to-go cups of coffee. "That woman is a siren. She had every guy in the store drooling over her and Kane pushed her away as cold as ice—you should've seen his face, he looked like a hired killer." He placed the cups on the desk, moved one over toward Jenna, and then straightened to remove his jacket.

If you only knew. Jenna's stomach growled with hunger as she peered into the bags. "What did she do this time?"

"Same, she hung all over me. Made like we were going together." Kane dropped into a chair and pulled off his woolen cap. He ran a hand through his tousled hair and looked at her. "She invited me to spend the weekend with her at her secluded hunting cabin out at Blackwater."

"Ha." Rowley flashed a wide grin. "She said she would make him real cozy and—"

"Enough!" Kane's look was dangerous. "You have a report to discuss. Sit down and tell us what you've found."

"That can wait." Jenna slipped her gaze over Kane. His tight jaw, ticking cheek, and murderous expression told her Kim was getting way out of hand. She turned her attention to Rowley. "Do you mind giving me a few moments alone with Kane?"

"Yes, ma'am." Rowley grabbed his lunch and left the room.

Jenna stood and pushed the door shut behind him and then went to lean against her desk in front of Kane. "Okay, it's just you and me. What happened?"

"Like I said." Kane looked up at her and narrowed his eyes. "Kim's not listening to anything I say and I've been blunt. I can't charge her for stalking me. She doesn't pose a physical threat to me and being annoying doesn't make her a stalker but we may have a case for harassment. Carter believes the DA wouldn't touch the case after I had a drink with her and then went back to her room. He'd say I encouraged her attention."

Shocked Jenna gaped at him. "You did what?" She swallowed hard and avoided his stubborn gaze. "You never mentioned that before."

"No because I knew you'd react like you are now." Kane looked at her with an annoyed expression. "Her room was on the way back to mine is all but I would have been captured by the CCTV cameras in the elevator." Clearly agitated, he rubbed the back of his neck. "Do you honestly believe, after all we have been through together, I'd start chasing after women?"

"I have no claim on you, Dave." Jenna looked at her hands, not sure what to say to him.

"I don't want to lose your friendship, Jenna." Kane stared at the ceiling for some moments before looking at her again. "You know I care for you. I'm just not going to make a commitment until I'm sure I'm able. I don't want us living with Annie's ghost and I can't let her go yet."

He rarely mentioned his dead wife and his confession stunned her. "Okay. I understand about Annie but as Miss Strickland is harassing you, I would've thought you'd discuss her with me before calling Carter."

"I called Jo." Kane folded and unfolded the woolen cap in his hands. "I wanted her expertise on how to deal with Kim." He sighed. "Nothing she mentioned has worked so far."

"The first mistake is calling her Kim." Jenna tapped her pen on the desk. "It's way too personal. You should call her Miss Strickland." She cleared her throat. "You can tell her to leave you alone, she won't break."

"I know that and today I told her to step away or I'd arrest her for assaulting an officer of the law." Kane snorted. "She laughed at me."

Jenna dropped her pen into a chipped mug on the desk with a picture of Hawaii on one side. "So your 'back off or I'll kill you' face didn't work?"

"Obviously." Kane held up his phone and rolled his eyes. "Twenty messages today and I can't step outside without her appearing out of thin air. She must be following me." His ringtone filled the room and he glanced at the screen. "This will be her fourth call since I walked out of Aunt Betty's."

Jenna plucked the phone from his hand as he went to decline the call. "Let me speak to her."

"It will only make things worse." Kane's lips thinned and turned down at the corners.

Jenna had never seen anyone outwit Kane. She had to step in and deal with Kim Strickland. "We'll see about that." She accepted the call and listened to the suggestive promises the caller was making. "This is Sheriff Alton. I'm monitoring and recording all calls to this number. I do not tolerate private conversations of this nature to my deputies. Please disconnect now as no further warnings will be issued." Not waiting for a reply, she disconnected and handed him back the phone. "Block her calls."

"Okay." Kane scanned his screen and then looked up at her. His expression was wary. "You need to be aware that she might turn aggressive toward you. Right now, she sees you as an obstacle preventing me from dating her."

"The moment she threatens either of us, we'll arrest her for stalking." Jenna rounded her desk. If Miss Strickland kept hassling Kane, she'd try a face-to face and if that didn't work, she'd get an arrest warrant for harassment and let the DA sort it out.

"Copy that." Kane stared at his hands. "I didn't want to add to the caseload. It seems such a stupid thing to be worrying you about."

"Not really. It's just another day in the office, Dave." Jenna pushed a hand through her hair. "No different from the drug bust, chasing down Jones's missing bull, and the wreck on the highway. We deal with multiple cases at the same time. We're a small team, that's life."

She wanted to push Kim Strickland from her mind because right now, she had more important things to do. "Put her out of your mind for now and concentrate on the murders. Call Rowley back in. I want to hear what he's found on Grady. That guy at the shelter is up to something and I need to know if he's involved."

When Rowley came in with a half-eaten sandwich in one hand, coffee in the other, and an iPad tucked under one arm, Jenna waved him to a seat. "To bring you both up to date, I struck out speaking with the Foxx trucking company. They won't give us anything without a search warrant. Okay, Rowley what did you find on Grady?"

"No priors, he has a clean driving record but he does have a sealed juvenile jacket." Rowley sipped his coffee. "I hunted down the other man in your report as well, Josiah Brock. Now this guy did time upstate for animal cruelty some years back. Since then he comes up squeaky clean." He placed his cup on the desk. "Both men are long-haul truckers and active on social media. In fact, Grady posts selfies from most of the places he's traveled."

Jenna swallowed a mouthful of turkey on rye. "What about Brock?"

"I didn't speak to anyone at Blackwater Trucking but I found the company's web page and it gives a list of all the places they go to and when. If we can link any of these journeys to murders, we'd have enough probable cause for a search warrant to view the company's logs." Rowley looked at her with a satisfied expression.

Inspired by Rowley's enthusiasm, Jenna looked at Kane. "Anything of use from the hotline?"

"I followed up a few leads and found nothing." Kane hadn't touched his food. "I've been sending copies of the tattoo images to as many tattoo artists I can find, and there are thousands, maybe millions in the country. I've been concentrating on Montana but we'll need to cover as many states as possible, at least all major cities. As Grady mentioned a body in a frozen lake out of Colorado, I've requested information on that case and the email has gone out to all law enforcement offices in the state."

"So we have a wait and see situation right now." Jenna stared at the whiteboard. "We need Wolfe's results and information on the death in Colorado. It will be interesting to see if the cases are similar."

"I doubt it; from what I found out about the case, the body wasn't dismembered. Unless the killer was using the pond to freeze the corpse and someone found her before he had time to collect her." Kane lifted his coffee and eyed her over the rim. "The only similarities I can see here are the basic descriptions of The Sculptor's victims. One of our victims could be a match—and as we don't have that crucial part of victim two's body, we can't assume the cases are connected and it's going to take more evidence to convince me our guy is The Sculptor."

CHAPTER TWENTY-FOUR

"Sheriff." Maggie knocked on Jenna's office door and clung to the frame for support, her eyes wide.

Jenna shot to her feet at Maggie's alarmed expression. "What's happened?"

"It's the rest of the body of that poor girl—they found her." Maggie pressed a hand to her heart. "Mayor Petersham thought it might be a prank but his wife insists it's real."

"Sit down." Kane pushed to his feet and offered her his chair. "Now take a few deep breaths and tell us what happened."

"Oh, it's terrible. I can't bear to speak about it." Maggie's hand trembled as she pressed it to her mouth.

Jenna moved around the desk and patted her on the shoulder. "I need to know what the mayor said to you, Maggie."

"His wife dropped by their cabin in Stanton Forest and found a body stuck in his chimney—she'd been... oh Lord, I can't say." Maggie dragged in a long breath and looked at Jenna. "I've been here a long time and thought I'd become hardened to the awful things people do to each other, but this madman is involving everyone in his crimes." She took a shuddering breath. "Poor Mrs. Petersham. She was so distraught the mayor had to call in Doc Brown."

It was obvious they wouldn't be getting more information from Maggie. Jenna leaned against her desk to look at her. "Why didn't you let me speak to the mayor?"

"He said he had to go and tend to his wife and to tell you." Maggie pressed both hands on the desk and stood. "You'd better hightail it out there."

Jenna nodded. She had no idea the mayor even owned a cabin in Stanton Forest. "Okay. Do you want to take the rest of the day?"

"No. I'll be fine in a minute or two." Maggie gave her a small smile. "You'll be needing me here." She stood shakily and headed out the door, using the wall for support.

"I've never seen her react like that before." Kane stared after her.

"Me either, it must be bad." Jenna considered what she needed and walked back around her desk. "Okay, I'll need both of you so grab your gear. Call Wolfe for me, Kane." As Kane headed to the main office, she picked up the phone to call the mayor for more details and then changed her mind. She looked at Rowley; as a local, he was her go-to person for information. "Do *you* happen to know where the mayor has his cabin?"

"Yeah. He's had that old cabin since before he became mayor. My pa and him used to go hunting up there." Rowley stood and gathered his things. "It's past the ski resort and set right snug against the mountain. I'll get the coordinates."

"Thanks." Jenna glanced at the snow piling outside the window in drifts. "It will be snowed in for sure."

"The road must be clear for Mrs. Petersham to have driven there but it's not a place I'd visit in winter." Rowley scratched his cheek as if thinking. "Maybe the mayor had the snowplow do a special run."

"Hmm." Jenna pulled on her coat. "There's been extensive upgrading of the roads in that area for the resort, maybe the mayor extended them to his property as well." She thought for a moment. "Follow us in your truck and go tell Kane about the road. Wolfe will need to use his truck today. If it's as bad as you say, he won't get the van up there in this weather."

"Yes, ma'am." Rowley hurried out the door.

Jenna went into the main office and filled the Thermos flasks with hot coffee. She collected sugar, cream sachets, and to-go cups, and stacked everything in a container. She considered taking the huge jar of cookies on the counter. Worried a blizzard might trap them on the mountain, she added the cookies and a box of energy bars. When Kane walked toward her, bundled up for the trip, she pointed to a carton of bottled water. "We'd better take those with us. I have a few supplies in case we get snowed in."

"I have water in my truck, Jenna." Kane smiled at her and grabbed the jar of cookies from the top of her pile. "Hmm, cookies."

Unable to stop the smile from twitching at the corner of her mouth, she pulled Kane's woolen hat down over his ears. "I need you on the ball up there, Dave. No risking headaches okay?"

"It gets better every winter." Suddenly serious, Kane brushed his knuckles down her cheek. "Thanks for caring."

"A-hem." Rowley walked up beside Jenna. "I've messaged the coordinates to everyone."

Mentally shaking her mind into action, Jenna nodded at him. "Thanks."

"The weather isn't looking good and we have about three hours before sunset." Kane stared out the window and then back at Jenna. "I asked Wolfe to meet us at the park. I suggest we head up the mountain in a convoy."

"You read my mind." Jenna pulled on her gloves and handed Rowley the carton of supplies. "Okay, head out."

"I'll leave Duke with Maggie." Kane called the dog to follow him to the front counter. "Do you mind? Just in case we get stuck on the mountain?"

"He'll be fine here." Maggie patted Duke's head.

Jenna smiled as Duke obediently climbed into his basket under the front counter, turned a few times and then flopped down with a sigh. "Be a good boy for Maggie."

"Don't you worry about him." Maggie, seemingly recovered from her shock, beamed at the dog. "I'll take him home with me if needs be."

Jenna gave her a wave and headed for the door pulling on her sunglasses. "We'll be checking in every half-hour."

The cold smacked Jenna in the face the moment she stepped outside. Glad her sunglasses prevented the glare, she blinked into the bright light. She'd never gotten acclimatized to the freezing temperatures in Montana and living in an alpine region meant every winter was the same. She moved carefully. Underfoot, the ground was slippery and although the local council spent all day trying to keep the sidewalk clear, the constant snow soon washed away the salt mixture. She climbed into Kane's truck and with Rowley following close behind, they made their way to the park. As they drove by, Wolfe—with Emily and Webber inside his truck—tucked in behind them. They made it through town and soon hit the highway alongside Stanton Forest. The few people Jenna noticed along the way trudged along bent over against the cold and bundled up in brightly colored coats, hats and boots.

When the GPS indicated they take a road into the forest, Jenna turned to Kane. "That road has been cleared this morning, most of the others are snowed over. It would seem being mayor has its benefits."

"Maybe not." Kane slowed to take the bend and glanced at her. "The killer wouldn't have been able to get anywhere else, would he?"

They climbed a steep windy dirt road, both sides flanked with huge snowdrifts, the once pristine snow was gray and filled with pine needles and other debris. The snow made the road so narrow, if they met another vehicle coming the other way, there would be no room for it to pass. On one side, the road dropped away to a deep gulley, and if they accidently went through the wall of snow thrown up by the snowplow, they'd fall to their deaths. As the wheels spun and slid around a steep turn, Jenna gripped the seat. "One thing is for sure. The killer has a good all-weather vehicle to get up here." She looked behind at Rowley and Wolfe. "It looks as if everyone is okay behind us."

"Our vehicles are the best available." Kane smiled at her. "Don't worry, we'll be fine getting up the mountain. The road isn't that bad and the Beast can handle just about anything." He stared ahead. "Although coming back down in the dark will be slippery if the snow keeps up. I hope recovering the body won't take too long."

Jenna scanned ahead, searching the snow-laden trees for any sign of a cabin but all around was dazzling white and black tree trunks. "I'll hand it over to Wolfe. If we do the grunt work, we should be out of here within the hour. I had hoped to follow the snowplow home tonight."

An open gate with the name "Petersham" painted on a wooden board on the fence, came into view. As Kane drove through and they took a switchback through the trees, Jenna picked out the small cabin nestled in against the mountain. Snow had spilled off the slope covering the roof. "It looks like the cabin has grown out of the rock."

"I'm surprised the roof hasn't collapsed under the weight of the snow." Kane crept the truck forward, his head moving from side to side as he scanned the area. "No sign of another vehicle. One set of tire tracks in and out as far as I can see."

Jenna searched the area. "I guess when she saw the body she didn't hang around."

"No wonder. Now that's just plain nasty." Kane pulled up some ways from the cabin and stared out the window.

A shiver of horror crept over Jenna. She blinked at the sight before her and her mind refused to make sense of it. Sticking out of the chimney was a frozen naked torso. The killer had trimmed the sides of the body to make it fit neatly into the flue. On the head sat a red Santa hat with fur trim. Speechless, she stared at the macabre scene for some moments before the closing of Kane's door dragged her back to action. She pulled off her warm gloves and slid on a pair of surgical ones in their place. In this weather, she and the others would suffer frostbite if they didn't hurry. As she slid down from the seat, Wolfe came to her side and she turned to him. "How are you planning on getting up there?"

"Same way as the killer, I guess." Wolfe's sunglasses reflected the scene before him as he scanned the area. "I'd say he took the path up the side of the mountain and from the drag marks in the snow, he had a sled of some type and dragged it behind him. Let's take a look." He headed in long strides to where Kane and Rowley stared at the cabin.

"Morning, Sheriff." Colt Webber, forensics kit in hand, touched his hat and followed Wolfe.

Jenna took a deep breath of the pristine mountain air and cold stung her lungs. She found it strange walking onto a crime scene without the usual smell of death, it made everything seem surreal, dreamlike. The cabin was well-loved and in excellent shape. Curtains of bright red and white gingham graced every window and a swing seat sat on the porch. Alongside, was a woodshed with an ax buried in an upturned stump as if the owner had just walked away. Everything apart from the body appeared untouched and normal. She noticed Emily beside her but couldn't gauge her reaction with the wraparound sunglasses blocking her eyes. "You okay, Em?"

"Sure." Emily turned to her. "He's carved her like an ice sculpture. Everything inside is going to fall out when she thaws." Her mouth turned down. "I bet Dad gives me the job of cleaning her up for the identification. What we need on the team is a mortician."

"Maybe ask Mr. Weems to drop by." Jenna watched her retreating back.

"Nah." Emily turned and walked backward. "He likes them all stitched back together. This week the morgue is going to look like Frankenstein's workshop."

"Emily." Wolfe spun around and dropping his glasses, gave his daughter a look to freeze Niagara Falls. "The death of a young woman is not a joke. If you plan to work with me, you'll need to treat the victims with respect."

"I do, Dad." Emily's back straightened. "I wasn't being disrespectful. I was stating a fact. We have been reassembling the first victim and it was the easiest way of explaining it to Jenna is all." She looked up at the frozen remains. "She looks the same type as the last victim. Dark hair, tattoos, earrings, and I'd say she's under twenty. Both victims seem to match the others murdered by The Sculptor." She looked at Kane. "Do you agree, Dave?"

"Maybe." Kane's attention was fixed on the body. "I think making a decision before an autopsy is a mistake but I do agree the hair color and tattoos are a match."

"At least we won't have to wait too long to know if this torso and the spare limbs belong together." Wolfe peered over his sunglasses at Jenna. "I'll do a DNA profile when I get back to the lab. You'll have it before you leave this afternoon."

"That would be great, thank you." Jenna glanced around the scene. "Wolfe, I'll take Rowley and we'll do a recon of the area."

"Sure. Webber, take a video of the scene." Wolfe handed him a camera. "Emily, you take the stills. I want them from every direction, close-up and don't forget the entire area around the cabin. Start over by the trail leading up the mountain." He turned to look at Kane. "If you'll come with me, we'll try and get the remains down."

"I'm glad I'm not doing Kane's job." Rowley walked beside Jenna. "I can see straight through to that poor woman's lungs."

Jenna glanced at him. "We have to stop this killer." She looked around the vast forest, deadly beautiful, and sighed. "This is no out-of-towner. This maniac is living here right among us."

CHAPTER TWENTY-FIVE

It never ceased to amaze Preacher how fate played a part in his life. It was as if the things he needed arrived by simply thinking about them. He'd required a chimney to present his artwork and the next moment had overheard Mrs. Petersham mentioning a trip to her cabin in the forest to retrieve a suitcase filled with winter clothes, that she planned to donate to the homeless. The snowplow would clear the road for her trip, and right at that moment, fate had given him not only a place to present his work but the opportunity to make the news once the mayor's wife had viewed it.

The snowplows ran to a schedule, for people to follow or avoid them, and it took him less than two minutes scrolling his phone for the information. Less time again to call about the extended road clearing and what roads were on the daily route. He smiled into the dazzling white surroundings. Dressed all in white, he blended into the background and from his perch hidden above the cabin, he could admire Delores. He'd used his own special technique to keep her eyes open. One drop of glue to each lid once life escaped her, had given him the wide-eyed effect he required. He wanted her to know where he'd left her, naked for all to see. She'd become his tribute to silence and each time he cut and formed her to his own design, the memory of her taunts faded. He wished he could get closer, just one more time, to see the dusting of snow covering her glistening flesh—each perfect flake a creation of nature.

A rush of excitement gripped him. They'd be here soon to search for a hint, any little clue to find and stop him but it would never happen. He hadn't driven to the Petershams' cabin—he wasn't that stupid. He'd taken the main road to the parking lot alongside Bear Ridge about one hundred feet above it, and using a sled to carry Delores, had made his way down the mountain trail to the cabin. On leaving, he'd been careful not to leave his footprints behind, and if the sled hadn't slid down the narrow trail after he'd removed her body, no one would have known he'd used a sled at all. Snow made it so easy to cover his tracks—a pine branch dragged behind him obscured even the deepest footprints and nature had done the rest.

Nothing came close to the thrill of someone almost discovering him. He'd been adding the final touches to his creation when he'd heard Mrs. Petersham's SUV coming toward the cabin. She'd been early. She'd mentioned to a friend that she planned to leave at twelve to give the snowplow time to clear the road but had arrived just before twelve at the cabin. With no time to cover his tracks, he'd scrambled up the rock face, to hide and watch.

Preacher chuckled with glee at the memory. He'd been close enough to see her stare out the window, eyes wide and mouth gaping open in shock. Her gasp of fear had made his pulse race. In her hurry to leave, she'd fishtailed in the snow and scraped the side of her vehicle against the pines, scarring their majestic trunks. He'd waited for the sound of her engine to disappear into the distance and then gone back down and tidied up some. He'd brushed away his footprints and then made his way back up the mountain to his hideout to wait. The snow fell thick and fast obscuring his path as if he'd never been there. Only the mark cut into the ice from the sled would betray him but it gave little away. How many people in Black

Rock Falls had sleds? Hundreds, maybe thousands. He swept his binoculars from left to right and listened for the sound of vehicles. They would come—they always came to admire his creations.

The snow muffled sound but the roar of powerful vehicles soon rumbled up the mountain. Heart thumping fast with anticipation, Preacher stretched out on the snow, binoculars aimed at Sheriff Alton and her team. If he had a mind, he could shoot them but that would be no fun at all. He watched the movement below with interest. The sheriff's posse had arrived with engines roaring, making no effort to be quiet. The unmarked black truck that chauffeured her, led a marked pickup with a uniformed deputy behind the wheel and following him, a large white truck bearing the insignia of the medical examiner. As the people emerged, their reactions to his art were varied. The sheriff had a look of hopelessness, the younger deputy glanced and looked away, but the others moved closer and examined it without expression. The sheriff acted like a general issuing orders to her troops but then spent her time searching around the outside of the cabin. She'd find nothing. He hadn't gone further than the end of the rockface.

As the Medical Examiner and the big deputy eased their way toward Delores, their voices carried to his position. They worked together as if they'd been doing so all their lives. Speaking in hushed tones, they spent a deal of time testing the roof before the ME slid over to Delores on a rescue stretcher, took some photographs, and then removed her. He wrapped her in silver foil like leftover takeout before they carried her back to his truck.

Images of inside the mortuary danced in his mind. He wished he could be there, listening to the discussion as they admired his work and discussed the finer points of his technique. They must surely admire his creativity. He could visualize the autopsy and the ME sorting through the parts of her like a jigsaw puzzle. How fine she'd look with his neat stitches crossing her chest. Would he reattach her limbs? It was a shame they'd bury her or turn her to ashes. In his world of ice, she'd be with him forever—but he didn't mind, there would always be another Delores.

CHAPTER TWENTY-SIX

At last they had secured the crime scene and the torso of the young woman was in safe hands. Jenna kicked the snow from her boots and trudged inside the sheriff's department. The office had a homely smell of new books, freshly brewed coffee and the vanilla air freshener in the foyer. She walked to the counter. Maggie looked at her with apprehension and she smiled at her. "Everything is taken care of, Maggie. Did Duke behave himself, no howling at the door after we left without him?"

"No, he was too busy eating to notice you'd gone." Maggie wrinkled her nose. "Although, he was a mite interested in the delivery. I must say, it doesn't smell so good." She pointed to a large manilla envelope on the counter. "It's for you."

Jenna picked up the envelope. It was heavy and bulky with just her name printed on the front. "Did it come by courier?"

"That I can't say." Maggie shuffled some paperwork. "It was here when I came back from the bathroom. With you all gone, I had no one to watch the counter but I did lock the cashbox in the drawer."

"That's fine." Jenna chuckled. "You can't be in two places at the same time." She walked into her office, removed her gloves, and then tore open the envelope.

A plastic bag slid out onto her desk. Inside, the mutilated body of a rat lay in a pool of blood. Jenna stepped away and swallowed hard. She moved swiftly to the door. "Kane, get in here."

It seemed to take ages for Kane to amble into her office. Jenna indicated to the rat. "Mail call."

"That can't be from the killer." Kane stood hands on hips. "He wouldn't risk leaving any traceable evidence and he's never mailed anything before. If he did it would be part of a body not a rat."

Jenna had already decided who had sent the rat. She nodded. "Oh, it's not from the killer. It's been sent to scare me off. The only person I've upset lately is Kim Strickland. She's escalated. This has to be from her." She rounded her desk, dropped into her chair, and went straight to her computer to hunt down Kim's address from the Motor Vehicles Division database. "If it's her, this is a threat and we'll have her for stalking. Go check for prints."

"Copy that." Kane pulled surgical gloves from his pocket and gloved up.

Anger rising, Jenna wrote down Miss Strickland's address. "It's her, I know it." She looked up at him. "Are you aware she lives in an apartment opposite the bank? She can keep you under surveillance from her darn window."

"I didn't know. I'm sorry, Jenna. I'll deal with her." Kane slid the rat back into the envelope and picked it up between thumb and finger. "I'll go see her."

Snorting, Jenna stood. "You're not going anywhere near her. On your way to the evidence room ask Rowley to write a generic media release for the current case and after that I want you to update the files." She met his gaze. "We have a full caseload and this can be put on the back burner for now."

"Okay." Kane examined her face. "If it is her, we'll need her set for comparison. We could send Rowley?"

"Leave that to me." Jenna waved him away.

Blood boiling, she returned to her desk and printed a photograph of the tattoos they'd been showing around town. Careful not to touch more than the very corner, she slid it inside a manilla folder, pulled on her gloves, and headed out the door. As if she didn't have enough to deal with, she had a stupid obsessive woman on her case. Solving the dead rat mystery and getting Kim Strickland out of her hair would be a quick fix and then she could concentrate on solving the murders. That was life in Black Rock Falls. There was never just one crime to solve but a myriad of different problems, which as sheriff, she was expected to deal with daily.

She tucked the folder under one arm and trudged along Main. Keeping in mind the woman was probably watching her as well, she stopped by a few stores along the way asking if the folks were happy with the condition of the sidewalk—using any excuse to be in the store. She crossed the slippery blacktop to the gap in the snow left from the snowplow and continued along the other side of the road. When she came to the small building housing four apartments, she made her way round back to the parking lot under the building. To her surprise, Kim Strickland was heading for her vehicle carrying a medical kit balanced on top of a box of supplies. Jenna strolled toward her. "Afternoon, I'm speaking to the townsfolks about these tattoos. Could you look and see if you recognize them at all?" She pulled the photograph from the folder.

"As soon as I have a free hand. If you could open the door for me, I'd appreciate it." Kim raised one eyebrow and her red lips curled into a satisfied smile. "I'm planning a romantic weekend away with Dave and I'm all packed and ready to go. I'm sure he told you all about our plans?" She rested the carton on the hood of her large SUV. "I just have to make sure my kit is up to date and pay a visit to the pharmacy. He'll be by after he's given you a ride home." She gave Jenna a stricken look. "Oh, he didn't tell you about us yet, did he?"

Did Kim really believe Kane would go to her cabin with her? The woman was delusional but she'd play along to get the prints. Trying to keep her expression neutral, Jenna opened the passenger door as directed. "Deputy Kane doesn't discuss his private life with me. I'm surprised he'd plan to go anywhere this weekend. It's not safe to travel in this weather and we have a huge caseload." She stepped back as Kim lowered the carton into the back seat.

"Oh, the road between here and Blackwater is open and my place is on the edge of town, so we'll be fine." Kim removed her gloves to fumble inside the medical kit and then straightened. "What did you want me to see?" She pushed something into her pocket and stepped to one side.

Jenna thrust the photograph into her hand. She couldn't believe her luck. Kim held the image up to the light leaving latent prints.

"I can't see, it's too dark in here." Kim stared at the image and shook her head. "Could you reach in the passenger door and turn on the headlights for me?"

"Sure." Jenna had what she wanted and would play along.

As she bent inside the door, something sharp jabbed her in the thigh. She fumbled for the headlights but Kim pushed her hard in the back and she fell across the seat banging her head on the steering wheel. "Ouch! What are you doing?"

"We are going for a little ride, Sheriff." Kim leaned her weight on Jenna's back, holding her down with remarkable strength. "You're in my way."

Another sharp sting in her thigh and her limbs became like Jell-O. Confused, Jenna wriggled to get free in the constricted area but her strength had deserted her. Mouth suddenly dry, Jenna turned her head and stared into Kim's wild eyes. The effects of a powerful drug had her in its grip and she fought hard to keep her eyes open but the empty floating feeling was dragging her down. She pawed at her weapon only to have it dragged from its holster. Her fingers refused to move and not one sound came from her cry for help.

"You think you're all that, ordering Dave around, but you fell into my trap. I knew you'd come alone. The rat was too much for you to resist, wasn't it? You just had to confront me. I knew you were jealous but you can't have him. He's mine." Kim dragged her into a sitting position and gripped her face looking into her eyes. "I'll make sure you'll never see him again."

Panic gripped Jenna but the drug was taking control, dragging her into unconsciousness. *I'm in the hands of a lunatic.* Her head fell forward and her eyelids grew heavy as darkness surrounded her.

CHAPTER TWENTY-SEVEN

Preacher waited almost an hour before he headed back to his truck, pulling his sled behind him. He took in the scenery, enjoying the way the cold bit into his cheeks. The ice falling from the tall pines stung his face but he enjoyed it. He'd been suitably impressed by his genius and smiled all the way down the mountain roads. He'd planned to drop by the Triple Z Bar to celebrate when fate took a hand once more. As he headed down the highway a woman came into view and he did a double take thinking for a moment he'd imagined her but there she was, as plain as day. She stood on the side of the road, thumb out and waiting for him to give her a ride. He pulled up beside Delores and she opened the door and looked at him. Snowflakes dusted her raven hair and made her more desirable. His heart missed a beat as he scanned her eager face and his attention came to rest on the tattoo of a black tear at the corner of one eye. He heaved in a deep breath, almost overcome with emotion. She was so perfect, he had to school his features to appear less eager. "You look, cold, tired, and hungry. Where are you heading?"

"I hear Black Rock Falls has places for the homeless, so I'm heading there." She looked at him with a hopeful expression in her eyes.

Preacher smiled. "This is your lucky day." He pulled his special Thermos from the console and waved it at her. "The shelters are full but my wife and I have two women around your age staying with us. We offer a room and three meals a day for help with the animals. I only have room for one more, if you're interested?"

"Sure, beats freezing my ass to death out here. Count me in."
She climbed into the truck and took the Thermos with a smile.
"Thanks. My name is Isabella." She poured hot chocolate into the
cup and sipped greedily.

He smiled at her, marveling how fate had delivered Delores to
him once again. "They call me Preacher."

CHAPTER TWENTY-EIGHT

Kane had scanned the prints on the parcel and sent the rat's remains over to Wolfe. He'd updated the files and strolled into Jenna's office. Surprised to see the chair empty, he headed back to his desk. He'd given Rowley the task of sending the crime scene images of the girl in the chimney to all agencies. Although frozen, her features were distinctive. The snake tattoo curling around her neck and down around her breast, a distinguishing mark. He set about sending the description to the list of tattoo artists across the country. Someone must recognize the young woman.

It was after five when Duke whined and rested his head on Kane's knee. "Oh, is that the time? Okay, come on, I'll get you something to eat."

He stood and walked to the kitchenette, filled Duke's bowl, and went about making a fresh pot of coffee. He leaned against the counter and stared at the practically empty office. Rowley was chatting on his phone to his girlfriend, Sandy, explaining why he would be late. Kane smiled to himself. Rowley would propose to her at Christmas. It was good to see Jake so happy. With all the murders happening in Black Rock Falls, this small piece of normality was comforting.

"Where are you, Jenna?" Kane pushed his hands into the front pockets of his jeans to stop himself reaching for his phone. He'd looked at it so many times since she left, expecting her to call. He'd pushed away the temptation to call her several times but when she'd left, she'd given him his orders and made it clear she didn't want him involved. Sure, she'd been angry but was probably down at Aunt Betty's Café chatting with Susie to get her head straight.

"Has Jenna called in since she left?" Rowley spun his chair around to look at him. "It's getting late and you'll miss the snowplow, if she doesn't get back soon."

Kane pulled out his phone. "I hope she's just cooling off; she wasn't very happy when she left." He shrugged. "I guess a message wouldn't hurt."

We'll need to leave soon to follow the snowplow, what's your ETA?

He waited some minutes before the message notification chimed on his phone.

Not sure.

Kane read the message and sighed. He tried again.

If you plan on working the case this evening, I'll have to go home to feed the horses.

He waited again for what seemed like ten minutes.

Don't whine to me about your chores, Deputy. Head off and feed your precious horses. I'll find my own ride home.

Kane read the message and shook his head in disbelief. Jenna had never been darn right nasty. He called her and from the recorded message, he knew she'd refused to take his call. His first instinct was to go and find her but she'd see that as being overprotective. Maybe she just needed some alone time. Perplexed and torn between what he wanted to do and giving Jenna some space, he stared at Rowley. "Seems like Jenna has taken some personal time. We might as well shut up shop. She's finding her own way home." He showed Rowley the messages.

"Okay." Rowley's eyebrows rose and he cleared his throat. "You know her better than I do but she's never nasty." He turned off his computer and stood. "You sure she's okay? There's not a cry for help in those messages, is there?"

"I don't think so, but I'm sure this has to do with Kim Strickland." Kane rubbed the back of his neck. "There was a dead rat waiting for Jenna when we got back, and she was convinced Kim had sent it to her. She went to Kim's apartment to straighten out a few things."

"Alone?" Rowley's eyes opened wide. "Why didn't you go with her?"

"It's complicated." Kane leaned one hip on the edge of his desk. "Jenna insisted I stay away from Kim, she wanted to handle her alone. I don't believe she considers Kim a threat and we both know Jenna can take care of herself."

"Why would Kim hurt Jenna?"

Kane threw both hands in the air. "The woman is harassing me and Jenna would arrest her in a heartbeat but because I walked Kim back to her room after we had a drink the night of the drug bust, Carter's advice is to work it out. He believes her defense would make her out to be a spurned lover, especially after they call witnesses from Aunt Betty's and view the CCTV footage from the ski resort." He sighed. "I can only imagine what trash talking she's doing to Jenna. I can't rush down there and see what's happening. Kim will take it to mean I'm protecting Jenna and Jenna will figure I'm being overprotective. I can't win either way."

"Hmm, it must be a bad situation for Jenna not to talk it out with you." Rowley frowned. "Give her some time before you message her again." He pulled on his coat. "Give me Kim's address and I'll drop by her apartment before I head home and see if Jenna is still there. If not, I'll drive by Aunt Betty's. She's on foot and can't have gotten far." He glanced out the window. "Snow's stopped and at least the road will be clear for you for a time."

Concern gnawed at Kane's guts but he straightened. "Call me if you see her. I'll send Maggie home and go and feed the horses. I'll come back when I'm done and see if I can locate Jenna." He sighed. "She has her keys if she needs to get back in here."

All the way back to the ranch, Kane allowed the messages to run through his mind. Although Jenna hadn't added a hidden message to say she was in trouble, her attitude toward him gnawed at him. It was so uncharacteristic for Jenna to be rude. Something was up and he needed to check on her fast. He did his chores with speed and, taking Duke with him, headed back into town. He hadn't heard from Rowley and called Wolfe to bring him up to date with the situation. "Can you ask Em if Jenna's called her?"

"Sure." Wolfe's voice came through the car radio via the Bluetooth phone connection. He came back immediately. *"Nope. Which is unusual. Jenna usually calls Em when she needs some girl talk, and this problem sounds like something they'd discuss. Maybe she called Jo but if she did you won't get much out of her—Jo, I mean. She keeps confidences. Jenna might just be dealing with the problem. If she hadn't replied to your messages, I'd be worried."*

Unconvinced, Kane drove into the night. "I can't help feeling something is wrong. I upset Jenna by not explaining the situation about Kim earlier but we're good now. What if the killer has kidnapped her or Kim is working with the killer and using this to distract us all, so he can kill again? Or to give him time to set up another display?"

"Jenna would press her tracker ring if she was in trouble." Wolfe said nothing for a beat as if thinking. *"If you're concerned this Kim*

person or the killer has Jenna, why not send her a fake message? In the meantime, I'll track her phone—but that's between us, I don't want to be hauled over the coals by her if she finds out."

"Thanks, man." Kane pulled to the side of the road and messaged Jenna a blatant lie.

I figure you need to check on your foal. I think it has a fever. It could die in this weather. I'm not experienced enough with horses to know what to do. Please advise.

Kane waited and nothing happened. No reply came. He pulled back onto the road and turned into Main, scanning the stores and all around. His phone chimed and he pressed the green phone button on his car's screen. It was Rowley. "Did you locate Jenna?"

"No, I went by Kim's apartment and no one is home, her parking space is empty. I've been hanging out at Aunt Betty's with Sandy. We both thought Jenna would come by for a meal but she's a no show. She hasn't been by at all and as its after seven now, I'm thinking she could be at the Cattleman's Hotel?" He heaved a sigh. *"We've both tried calling her and she's not picking up."*

"Okay thanks." Kane pulled up outside the sheriff's department but the place was in darkness. "She's not at the office either. I'll call the Cattleman's Hotel and ask if she's there. Someone would have noticed her in uniform. If she's not, I'll come by Aunt Betty's. If Jenna sees my truck outside, she might drop by."

"Okay." Rowley seemed concerned. *"I'll call the cab company and see if she took a ride anywhere. She might be at home."*

"Not likely, she hasn't got the control to open the gate and if she triggered the boundary alarm, I'd get a notification on my phone." Kane drummed his fingertips on the steering wheel. "I'm worried about her."

He made the call to the Cattleman's Hotel and the woman at the counter rang through to the bar and restaurant but no one had seen Jenna there either. Alarm bells went off in his head. This behavior was so out of character. "Something is wrong, Duke, we have to find her."

The air was still and the moon had finally managed to force its way through the snow clouds. The world had changed into shades of blue and gray, deep shadows filled the alleyways. Kane looked up and down the street. It was quiet with only one other person driving along Main but a few vehicles lined up at the curb outside Aunt Betty's Café. He found a space and parked.

"Come on, Duke. It's just as well Montana law allows police dogs into restaurants. I wouldn't want to risk leaving you in my truck in these temperatures." He let the dog jump down and they climbed over the mound of snow and hurried into Aunt Betty's.

He found Rowley and Sandy sitting at the table reserved for the sheriff's department and sat down. Although the cramping in his stomach from worrying about Jenna had diminished his appetite, his disciplined training pushed him to eat. He had no idea how long it would take him to find Jenna and it might be some time before he had the chance to eat again. In subzero temperatures, eating meant the difference between survival and death. He ordered at the counter—coffee and a bowl of chili—and asked them to fill his Thermos before adding a stack of sandwiches to go.

"You're planning on staying out as long as it takes to find her, aren't you?" Rowley peered at him over the rim of his cup.

Kane attacked the chili the moment it arrived and nodded. "Yeah, something is wrong if Jenna is not responding to calls. Wolfe is tracking her phone. It's the only option I have. If she's safe and needs some alone time that's fine but I need to know."

"She would've called me." Sandy's eyes searched his face. "We talk a lot lately and she mentioned someone called Jo. The FBI agent I think, so she might have called her too." She sighed. "We're close friends. I'm worried. She knows I work nearby and she'd only have to walk inside my office if she needed a ride. Jenna is way too sensible to just run off without telling anyone especially after what happened to her the last time."

A vivid memory of Jenna's kidnapping flashed across Kane's mind. Her ordeal so terrifying, it had caused PTSD. "No, she wouldn't just take off."

His phone chimed a message and he swore under his breath the moment he read it.

If my foal is ill, call the vet. I'm busy.

Kane held out the phone to Rowley. "Someone has Jenna and is using her phone."

Before Rowley could reply, Kane heard the soft voice of Kim Strickland behind him. He turned to glower at her.

"Hello, Dave, can I join you all? I'm here all on my lonesome." Kim ran a hand down his back.

Kane shook his head. "No! I'm sorry, Miss Strickland but I'm on duty. Please leave me alone."

His phone chimed again. It was Wolfe. "I have to take this." He turned his back on Kim and took the call. "Do you have anything for me, Shane?"

"Sure do, Jenna is in Aunt Betty's Café."

CHAPTER TWENTY-NINE

The hairs on the back of Kane's neck stood to attention. He gripped his phone. "She's not but I am. I'll call you back." He disconnected and dialed Jenna's number.

Behind him Jenna's ringtone filled the café. Kane leapt to his feet and in three strides had grasped Kim's arms behind her back, cuffed her, and pushed her over a table. As she screamed abuse at him, he emptied her pockets and found Jenna's phone. He dragged Kim to her feet, spun her around, and eyeballed her. "Where's the sheriff? What have you done with her?"

"Didn't you want her out of your life?" Kim's astonished expression said volumes. "She treated you like garbage. I threw out the trash."

Kane's mind slowed dropping into combat mode. He could see everything clearly and what moves to make. The fob on her car keys was brand new. He stared through the café window and spotted a late model SUV. "That your vehicle out there, the blue one?"

"Yes." Kim's eyes filled with tears. "I did it for you, Dave—for us."

"There is no *us*. There never was and never will be." Kane curled his lip in disgust. He'd had enough, and her obsession was going to stop right here and right now. "I'm not interested in you, Miss Strickland. You were in trouble and I helped is all. I did my job and I'd do the same for a dog."

Seeing the fear in her eyes, he took a step back. Twice now, he'd allowed her to see a side of him he usually kept under wraps. The agent sent to take out targets was a man devoid of emotion, a killing machine. He could have killed the men attacking Kim but he'd made the choice to disable. In the past he hadn't had that option. Now that Jenna was in danger, he'd allow the machine to take control until he found her.

People in the café were staring open-mouthed at him. The place had become silent, and nobody as much as flinched. Dragging up every last ounce of professionalism he lowered his voice. "Tell me where she is or I'll throw you in jail tonight."

"No! She can die for all I care." Kim's eyes flashed. "You'll want me when she's gone."

Kane slammed his fist into the table, sending the salt and pepper crashing to the floor. "Who else is involved? Tell me!"

When Kim shook her head, Kane moved up so close to her, he could smell the cigarettes on her breath. His nose wrinkled at the smell. "Provoking me is a real bad move. Tell me where you have the sheriff. Who else is in this with you?"

Ice-cold control slipped over him and he stood a breath away from her. The move was made to intimidate not harm. No matter what the provocation, he'd never resort to hitting a woman—not ever. Beside him, Duke growled deep and menacingly. His floppy skin pulled back to show sharp teeth and his hackles stood up. Gentle old Duke was ready to attack. In his peripheral he could see Rowley rushing forward and he took a step back, his mouth dry. He glanced down at Duke and hardly recognized him by his aggressive stance. "Down Duke, it's okay." He patted the dog on the head. *He knows Kim has hurt Jenna.*

Taking a deep breath, he pulled out his phone and called Wolfe. "Jenna's been kidnapped. I have the woman responsible but she's not saying if anyone else is involved. The Sculptor might have her, Shane. I'll need you to track the GPS in her vehicle. Jenna is out there somewhere and hasn't activated her tracker. She's in trouble."

"I'm on my way." Wolfe disconnected.

The next moment Rowley was at his side, his face pale. Kane turned to look at him. "Read her her rights and then book her for kidnapping. Throw her in a cell and see if you can get someone from county to pick her up tonight."

"Without a warrant?" Rowley took hold of Kim's arm. "Want me to call the DA?"

"No." Kane snorted. "She confessed in front of the entire room. I don't need an arrest warrant."

"Yeah, I heard her confess." Rowley turned to Kim and read her her rights.

"Go to hell." Kim glared at Rowley.

"Tell us where you have the sheriff. If you cooperate the judge will go easy on you." Rowley sounded sincere. "You're digging a deep hole for yourself, ma'am."

"No." Kim shook her head. "I know the law and you can't take me anywhere without a female officer. I'll tell everyone you tried to rape me."

"That's not the law but if you're planning on falsely accusing Deputy Rowley, I'll arrange for a female deputy to go with you." Kane turned to where Sandy stood watching, wide-eyed. "I need your help to transport this suspect to the cells. I'm deputizing you."

"Okay." Sandy pulled on her coat. "Don't worry about her. Go find Jenna."

Anxious to find Jenna, Kane looked at Rowley. "You have your orders. Get her out of my sight."

"Do you want me to call in Deputy Walters to watch over her until county arrives?" Rowley looked at Kane. "I'll come with you as backup."

Kane shook his head. "No time and I need you here, Jake. I'll ask Wolfe to come with me in case Jenna needs medical assistance."

"Copy that." Rowley took his coat from Sandy and shrugged into it. He handed her Kim's possessions. "Let's go." He took hold of Kim's arm and dragged the abusive woman outside to his truck with Sandy close behind.

Kane went back to the table to grab his coat. He dropped a wad of bills on the table, gave the waitress an apologetic stare, and scooping up Kim's keys, headed outside to wait for Wolfe.

He didn't have to wait long, Wolfe's white truck slid into the space behind the Beast and Kane rushed to Kim's SUV to open the hood. He paced up and down as Wolfe used his magic to trace Kim's movements.

"Got it." Wolfe closed his laptop and shut the hood. "She did a turnaround outside Blackwater. I have the coordinates." He handed the laptop to Kane. "I'll grab my bag."

"I'll warm up the Beast." Kane hustled to his truck, secured Duke, and started the engine.

"Wait!" Susie, came to his door. "You forgot these." She handed him his Thermos and sandwiches. "Go find Jenna."

Seconds later, with Wolfe at his side, Kane sped through town and out into the pale moonlight. He glanced at the glistening blacktop, the recent wash from the brine spreader holding back the ice. "What's the latest on the road conditions? Can we get through at speed?"

"Checking now." Wolfe scrolled through his phone. "Yeah, the brine spreader went through at seven. Road is clear to Blackwater, maybe ice patches before dawn. We're good to go. No snow forecast until late tomorrow."

"Roger that." Kane flicked on lights and sirens and stepped on the gas. "ETA?"

"Forty minutes at sixty." Wolfe turned to look at him. "So I'm guessing twenty." He cleared his throat. "Don't hold back on my account."

"Good to know." Kane blew through town in seconds. "But tighten your seatbelt, the ice patches are unpredictable."

Stanton Forest and the houses scattered along the opposite side of the road flashed by in a blur of light and dark. He slowed to take the on-ramp to the highway and hit the blacktop doing seventy. Ahead it seemed as if every eighteen-wheeler trucker had the same idea as them, getting to the next town before the next snowstorm. He'd been in law enforcement for some time and he'd never yet had an eighteen-wheeler give way to lights and sirens. Looking ahead down the straightaway, he pushed the Beast to one hundred and ten to overtake the convoy of vehicles. His truck picked up at once, engine roaring like an angry lion, and they passed six vehicles before the next sweeping bend came rushing up.

Kane said nothing and kept his eyes fixed on the road as the miles ticked by, but his mind was playing and replaying different scenarios of finding Jenna. Would she be alive, badly injured, or bleeding out? "How much longer?"

"Ten." Wolfe held up his phone as calm as if he were at home sitting in his armchair. "Show me what you've got, Dave. We need to get to her fast. We don't know what shape she's in and it's below zero out there."

Remembering Wolfe would have executed hair-raising stunts as a combat chopper pilot, Kane glanced at him and focused back on the road. Another convoy was moving at speed ahead, nose to tail like elephants in a circus, headlights piercing the darkness in a tunnel of light. He slowed a little but kept a good distance from the last truck to enable the burst of speed he needed to pass seven eighteen-wheelers at once. "When the road straightens out again, I'll pass them. I hope the road is clear."

Of course, headlights came around the bend in the distance but as the trucks turned, he spotted a gap. "Hang on."

He slammed his foot on the gas and the truck's engine roared. He waited until the last second before pulling out. Flying past one truck, two, three as the lights on the other side of the road grew larger and horns blared, he kept his foot flat to the floor. As he passed the fourth truck, he hit the brakes and in a scream of tires the Beast drifted sideways into the gap. He hit the gas again and wheels spinning leapt forward almost rear-ending the vehicle in front of him. Horns blasted all around him as the eighteen-wheeler in the other lane sped by in a rush of wind. Kane eased out to look, and finding the way clear, pulled out again. The Beast's hood seemed to lift as the tires gained traction and they shot past the remaining three vehicles.

Ahead, the glistening blacktop snaked out before him, a black line through snow-covered lowlands. The moonlight shone intermittent between the gathering clouds changing the snow packed scenery into every shade of gray. Traffic coming in the other direction blinded him with their headlights but he followed the road, watching the signposts flash by. "How much longer?"

"There should be a sweeping bend ahead. At the end look out for a wooded area and a road on the right. That was where Kim stopped for about ten minutes before returning home." Wolfe turned to look at him. "I can't see Kim overpowering Jenna. She's a tall, strong woman but Jenna was armed and can handle herself."

Kane slowed as they hit the sweeping bend and spotted the trees. He switched off lights and sirens before turning down the snow-covered road and following the deep grooves made by other vehicles. There was no need to advertise the fact they were there—just in case someone was standing guard over Jenna. "I'm not ruling out an accomplice. I wouldn't put anything past that woman."

"You may be right." Wolfe was looking ahead. "I see a truck outside that cabin."

Kane shook his head in dismay. "Kim told me she had a cabin but that one is posted as a hunting cabin. One of many in this designated hunting area no doubt."

"So, we may be dealing with a hunter sheltering from the weather." Wolfe raised one eyebrow. "Maybe we go in silent?"

Kane turned off the headlights as they rounded the bend and the small hunting cabin came into view. He turned off the engine and the truck coasted down the hill and came to rest not ten feet from a silver pickup. "Stay here." He patted Duke on the head and slid from behind the wheel.

He edged around the other vehicle running one hand over the hood and turned to Wolfe. "It's still warm. He must have just gotten here."

Pressed against the rough log wall, Kane turkey-peeked through a window and it was as if he couldn't breathe. Jenna lay on her back on a mattress on the floor, eyes closed and not moving. A man on his knees was bending over her and easing down her jeans. He heard Wolfe grunt behind him and they both ran at the door. He tried the handle. Locked. Without hesitation, he aimed a kick beside the handle and followed the shriek of splintering wood into the cabin. In two steps, his fingers closed around the man's coat and he hurled him into the wall. He heard Wolfe crashing in behind him and the sound of fists hitting flesh but Kane's focus was on one person—Jenna. He fell to his knees and pushed the raven hair from Jenna's ashen face. He dragged off his gloves and searched her neck for a pulse with trembling fingers. His ice-cold fingers should have gotten a response from her. "Jenna, Jenna."

No sign of life pulsed against his cold fingertips. Blind fury smashed into him. He stood and turned slowly to stare down at the unconscious man lying in a pile against the wall. He wanted to destroy him and started toward him fists clenched.

"Dave, forget him." Wolfe headed toward Jenna. "Help me here."

Kane stared after him, empty, drained of emotion. The machine had taken over again to deaden the pain. "It's too late, she's gone."

CHAPTER THIRTY

Kane paced up and down the cabin staring at the inert body of the crumpled man. He wanted him to regain consciousness so he could shake the truth out of him. He swallowed the waves of emotion crashing down over him. It was his fault Jenna had died. It was no different to when Annie died in the car bomb. Two innocents dragged into his world. If Kim hadn't seen him fight those men or the terrorists hadn't blown up his car, both women would be alive. He roared and punched at the cabin walls.

"Dave, get over here and help me. Now!" Wolfe had dropped to his knees and was feeling for Jenna's pulse. He ripped open the front of her shirt. "She's warm." He pressed his ear to her chest. "Thank God! She's alive but only just. Her heart is failing. What did they give you, Jenna?" He checked her eyes. "Opiate overdose. It's not too late to reverse it. Get my bag." He tapped Jenna's face and gave her a shake. "Jenna, wake up. Come on, fight."

Kane turned and stared at her in disbelief. "She's alive? But I couldn't find a pulse." He fumbled in his pockets for the drug reversal nasal spray. "I have Naloxone." He thrust it into Wolfe's hand and heart racing with anticipation, waited as he administered the drug. "It's too late, isn't it?"

"I don't think so." Wolfe administered a second dose. "Breathe, Jenna. That's it." His fingers pressed against her throat. "I can feel a pulse."

Heart thumping in anticipation. Kane stared at him. He needed to do something to help. "I'll get your bag."

"Not yet, just wait." Wolfe sat Jenna up and propped her against his knees. "Come on, Jenna, deep breaths." He flicked a glance at him. "Talk to her. We must bring her back. The drug will kick in faster if she breathes."

Kane stared at him, unsure what to say. He raised his voice. "Dammit, Jenna, suck in some air before it's too late."

As if in slow motion, Kane stood frozen in time, waiting a lifetime for her to respond but it was only a minute or so before Jenna took a deep breath and another minute or so before her eyes fluttered open. Relief flooded over him as time slipped back to normal. He stared at her pale face and squatted beside her. He took her ice-cold hand and rubbed it between his own. "Jenna, stay awake, keep looking at me." When she moaned something inaudible, he leaned closer. "You okay?"

"I need water." Jenna's voice came out in a whisper and then she frowned. "What happened to your hands?"

Kane glanced down at his skinned knuckles and shrugged. "I had to get through the door."

"Okay." She was recovering fast and looked down at her torn shirt and then up at him searching his face. "Have I been…?"

"No, that was me, sorry." Wolfe frowned and eased out from behind her. "We couldn't find a pulse. Someone drugged you."

"That bit I know." She looked from one to the other. "I'm so cold. Where's my coat?" She tried to get up.

"You just stay there and take deep breaths." Wolfe was reaching for his phone. "I'll call the paramedics. You'll need to go to the hospital for observation."

"No way." Jenna held her head in her hands. "Take blood and do what you do, Shane, but no hospital. I have a string of murders to solve." She looked up at him. "I'm fine and I'll get back to solving the murders but right now, I want to get back into town and drag Kim Strickland to jail."

Kane stared at her, trying to hide his emotions. He swallowed a few times and forced out words from his parched throat. "She's in custody. I'll go get you some water." He stood and searched the cabin, located her coat and tossed it to Wolfe.

Built as a haven for stranded hunters, the cabins had a supply of essentials. He found a carton of bottled water, cracked one open, and handed it to her. She looked better already and color was coming back into her cheeks. "I'll call the Blackwater Sheriff's Department and get them to take our prisoner into custody. We're out of jurisdiction here."

"What prisoner?" Jenna peered around the cabin. "Oh! I've never seen him before. Did *you* beat him up, Dave?"

Kane looked at his boots. "Ah, well I tossed him into the wall." He glanced at Wolfe, who gave him a very subtle shake of the head. In that second, he decided not to inform Jenna he'd disturbed the prisoner's obvious intent to rape her. He didn't want to trigger a PTSD episode. "He was going through your pockets and had removed your coat."

"I put him down." Wolfe shrugged. "He was resisting arrest. You can see Dave's point. You were down, a guy was leaning over you. Trust me, he deserved a beating."

"And he tried to remove my jeans, didn't he?" Jenna sipped the water and looked straight into Kane's eyes. "You can stop using your combat face on me, Dave. I'm not going to break. Oh, boy. He thought I was dead too." She pushed a shaky hand through her hair. "Nice to know they have sick freaks in Blackwater as well."

"We thought Kim might have had an accomplice and didn't discount the possibility she was working with The Sculptor. I'll run his prints but I'm guessing he just came across you. His truck motor was still warm when we arrived and Kim was in town when we left to find you." Kane touched her cheek and pushed a strand of hair behind one ear. "I have coffee in the truck and I'll need to bring Duke inside before he freezes to death out there." He straightened. "I won't be long."

Once outside, he made the call to the Blackwater sheriff and ran the prints. The man was out of Blackwater and had a sheet. He collected his Thermos, the takeout bags of sandwiches, and Wolfe's bag then headed back inside with Duke at his feet. Jenna was in a chair, in front of an old wood stove, which Wolfe was attempting to light. Kane placed everything on the table beside Jenna and poured her a cup of coffee. "I have sandwiches. I guess you haven't eaten for some time."

"I somehow knew you'd have a stash of food." Jenna looked at him. "Can't we just leave and drop the prisoner into the Blackwater sheriff? I want to go home and get some sleep."

"You're sure not sleeping or going anywhere yet." Wolfe checked her blood pressure. "Not until I say so. You nearly died, Jenna. I'd like to take blood and find out what she used on you."

"Go right ahead." Jenna sipped her coffee and smiled when Duke rested his head on her knee. "Is there something you're not telling me? Duke's giving me his sad face and Dave looks like he wants to kill someone."

Kane didn't respond. Instead, he wedged a chair against the broken door, checked the prisoner, who was out cold, and went back to sit with her. How could he explain the rage, the need to tear apart the man who wanted to hurt her? His feeling of emptiness when he thought she'd died, came back in a rush. He schooled his expression. "You were down, I reacted with necessary force but I'm always in control." He smiled at her. "He's alive, isn't he? Mind you, Shane lost it there for a second or two."

"Basic restraining tactics." Wolfe stored the blood samples and then poured himself a coffee. "And to answer your next question, we can leave as soon as someone arrives to pick up that pile of garbage, you should be able to travel by then."

"Something else." Jenna lifted her chin. "I want to take some swabs and make sure you test me for all the nasties."

Kane took her hand. "He didn't rape you, Jenna. He didn't get the chance."

"It's late." Jenna's hand trembled. "Kim gave me the first hit of whatever around two, maybe three, I don't remember. She obviously kept me under all the time and then hit me up before she left me here to die. You caught Necrophiliac Man but who else came by in the hours I was out cold?"

"You were dressed." Wolfe narrowed his gaze. "Few rapists dress their victims after an attack, they get away as fast as possible."

Kane cleared his throat. "Not so often in date-rape cases when the victim is unconscious. Often the rapist replaces the clothing and acts as if nothing happened."

"See." Jenna looked from one to the other. "It was possible but I'm not allowing any of this to leave this room. If we make a big issue of it, then as sure as the sun rises in the morning, Kim will find out and I'd never give her the satisfaction."

"Okay, we'll do all the tests but I'm not comfortable taking the swabs, Jenna." Wolfe swallowed hard and looked at Kane.

"Oh, stop it both of you. I'll do it myself." Jenna straightened her clothing and refusing Wolfe's hand, pushed to her feet. "Let's get out of here."

CHAPTER THIRTY-ONE

Saturday

It was a good day and if Preacher's latest creation made the news it would be perfect, although to date, the coverage of his art had been sadly missing. What must he do to get media attention— send the sheriff a head on a stick? He grinned and munched on toast, his feet resting on the coffee table as he watched the array of screens. His girls had woken to a pot of fresh coffee, orange juice and a selection of cereals. They couldn't complain he didn't feed them well, that's for sure. He had his reasons. His art would suffer if he displayed emaciated damaged specimens and he always made a point of making sure they'd showered before he used them. He supplied the best toiletries, to keep their hair and skin smooth. They'd never gotten cold. He kept the heat up and filled a closet with coats boots and sweaters. On waking they'd spoken in hushed tones, not understanding how Delores number three had arrived without a sound. He liked that Delores number one, or Ava as she insisted they call her, explained the situation to the others. How they must behave and act under his care. They'd all eaten and sent back the dumbwaiter and he'd sent it straight back. They understood the rules. To eat again, they must shower and change and then deposit their laundry into the dumbwaiter. He liked to watch them shower and see how the water highlighted their tattoos. It helped him decide how best to display them.

He'd sent down fresh clothes for them to wear, articles from the other Deloreses. Seeing the new girls wearing the same clothes gave him wonderful memories, flashing technicolor visions of their last moments, or where he'd placed them in his artwork. He crossed his legs and sighed. It had been an eventful evening and a thrill to meet another Delores so willing to join him. It was just as well he'd added a little something to the other girls' food last night and once asleep, he'd been able to carry Delores number three downstairs, removed her smelly clothes, and after taking photographs of her beautifully inked flesh to study later, he'd tucked her into bed. He'd moved around the cellar, checking everything was okay and collecting a strand of hair from each girl. He preferred to tug out a strand when life still flowed through their veins. With the root still attached, it remained alive, long, silky, and luxurious. He kept the strands with his girls' IDs, to remember every little detail of their last moments. His heart picked up a beat as a creation formed in his mind. His fingers tingled with the memory of ice-cold flesh. He needed one to come to him soon—he couldn't wait much longer.

CHAPTER THIRTY-TWO

Dragging herself into work after the longest Friday she'd ever lived in her life was an effort for Jenna. Although Wolfe and Kane had insisted she work from home, she'd refused. They'd clucked over her like mother hens. Deep down she appreciated their care but it wasn't necessary. She didn't have any serious injuries, apart from a headache from hell and no appetite whatsoever. By noon, she'd been ready to scream and Kane, being his usual diplomatic self, had driven her to the office.

The night before had gone on forever. After the Blackwater deputies had hauled away their prisoner, Kane, face pale and still in combat mode, with his lips turned down at the corners in a permanent scowl, had reluctantly taken her to Wolfe's office. Once there, she'd bagged up her clothes and collected the necessary swabs. After completing Wolfe's check list and including allowing him to take samples from under her fingernails, she'd sat with her back to the tile under a hot shower for a very long time trying to piece together the sequence of events.

The day came back to her in random thoughts but she clearly remembered Kim Strickland sticking her with something and then nothing before she woke, freezing cold, with Wolfe calling her name. She would never forget the expression on Kane's face. She had seen the same expression, as his target would have seen during his time in combat. The way he'd turned off his emotion and became cold, hard, and determined was disturbing. If he'd been in a blind rage, she'd have understood him better, but she knew at that moment, if someone ever hurt her, he would hunt them down and bring them to justice.

Eventually, she'd crawled out the shower and dressed in the spare set of clothes Kane had collected from the office. They'd headed home, saying nothing, but he'd refused to leave her alone. She'd woken at six with Pumpkin curled on the end of her bed and Duke beside the bed on the rug. As Kane had checked her throughout the night, she doubted he'd slept at all. After sending him home, she'd sat in the hot tub for half an hour before examining every inch of her body in a full-length mirror. She had a bruised elbow and a lump on her forehead but found nothing else and then climbed back into bed and slept until ten.

Leaning back in her office chair, she tried to concentrate on The Sculptor cases, scanning the notes on the screen but couldn't concentrate. The wait for Wolfe to complete the tests was agonizing. When her phone rang, Jenna stared at it for a moment. Wolfe, no doubt had finished examining the swabs from her and her clothes. A part of her didn't want to know. She just wanted to make like nothing had happened. As she hesitated to answer, she felt rather than saw Kane slip into her office and close the door. Kane, her rock, had her back as usual but she couldn't look at him, not yet. Taking a deep breath, she answered the call. "Hi Shane, what did you find?"

"*The swabs are clear, no seminal fluid or foreign DNA in you or on your clothes. No residue from a condom.*" Wolfe heaved a deep breath. "*I haven't done a full tox screen, that will take a few weeks, but as Kim is a nurse, I tested for morphine and it came back positive. The blood is under analysis for STDs but I can't imagine I'll find anything. I'm sure you're okay.*"

Jenna looked up at Kane's anxious face and gave him the thumbs up sign. He seemed to sag against the wall and then gave her a brilliant smile. She turned her attention back to Wolfe. "Thank you!"

"That's okay. I have information on the first victim. The dental records are a match for Evelyn Ross, nineteen out of Colorado Springs and reported missing last winter." Wolfe paused for a beat. *"I'll be performing the autopsy on the second victim at three. I've taken all the necessary swabs, so you'll be able to be inside the room with me this time, no worries about cross contamination at this stage but I have Webber here if you'd rather rest up a bit."*

"I'm fine." Jenna wanted to punch the air. "We'll be there." She disconnected and looked at Kane. "We have confirmation on the first victim. As we suspected she is Evelyn Ross and Wolfe is conducting the autopsy on the second victim at three. It will be real stinky. We get to be in with Wolfe this time."

"Oh, goodie." Kane pulled a disgusted face and then straightened. "Did I mention, we have received a ton of emails from other states on the tattoos. I've split the list with Rowley."

No one had mentioned Kim Strickland's name since her arrival. Jenna wondered if Kane was being overprotective again. She fingered the pens in her old chipped cup. "Why are you keeping me out of the loop on the Kim Strickland case?" She looked up at him. "I'm still the sheriff, I need to know."

"Sure. The fingerprints on the envelope carrying the dead rat are a match and she's being held in county. She's been charged with kidnapping and attempted murder of a law officer. The DA is waiting for a statement from you about the kidnapping." Kane pushed both his hands inside the front pockets of his jeans. "I've given a statement and Wolfe too." He lifted his chin. "We have to stay out of it, Jenna, Rowley is taking the lead, he's the only one of us not involved. Once he turns everything over to the DA, it will be out of our hands. She won't get away with kidnapping you, we have too much evidence. You don't need to worry, Jenna, the court will decide what happens to her. I'm sure she wasn't involved with The Sculptor."

Jenna nodded. "Okay and what about the man in the cabin?"

"He's in the hospital in Blackwater, broken nose, ribs, and a concussion." Kane looked chagrined. "He has a string of sexual assault charges against him. The sheriff wanted to charge him with assault but their judge is having none of it, says Wolfe and me assaulted him. The guy isn't pressing charges, so unless you want to accuse him of attempted rape, he's gonna walk."

"It looks like you arrived just in time, doesn't it? The disgusting animal." Jenna shuddered and then thought for a moment as the vivid image of the beaten man drifted back into her mind. "None of The Sculptor's victims have been sexually assaulted, so he can't be involved. You must agree he doesn't fit the profile? I agree with you, what happened to me was Kim Strickland acting alone. I'm going to let him slide with the proviso the sheriff keeps him in his sights."

"Oh, I'm sure he will. He mentioned making him wear an ankle bracelet to keep track of him, so he'll know if he leaves his house." Kane straightened. "If that's all, I'll get back to the emails."

Jenna held up a hand. "You can sleep anywhere, right?"

"Yeah, it was part of my training." His brow furrowed. "Why?"

"I want you to forward me all the emails on your list and then go down to the cells and sleep for a couple of hours. I'll take you to grab something to eat before we attend the autopsy at three." Jenna noticed the slight upturn of his lips and a flash of amusement in his eyes. "Don't tell me you don't need sleep. I'm surprised you can see out of your eyes they're so bloodshot. That's an order, Deputy."

"Yes, ma'am." Kane touched his woolen cap and smiling headed out the door.

Jenna set about writing the statement for the DA. Once she'd finished, she sent it by attachment to his office with a note saying that she'd have Rowley drop by before two. It would be months before Kim Strickland went to trial for kidnapping and attempted murder.

It would be unlikely she'd be granted bail. When her trial date came around Jenna would be called as a witness but for now, she could put her out of her mind. She glanced out the window. Snow had started to fall, turning the gray slush on the side of the road to white again. She loved a winter wonderland and had to admit, the picturesque town did look amazing covered with snow, but the bitter cold brought so many accidents and often the elderly perished in the harsh conditions. She shook her head trying to concentrate on the contents of the emails. As she went through the list, she found nothing of significance and then she came across an email from a tattoo artist out of Colorado. He believed he could be the artist of the snake tattoo on victim number two and vaguely recalled the ink on victim number one. He'd left a number and Jenna called him, giving her name and why she had contacted him. "Do you record any of your artwork?"

"Yeah, and since I wrote that email, I've been searching through the shots. I inked both of those women last year but not both at my shop." He cleared his throat. *"The snake, yeah, but the butterfly was at a convention. I remember the girl was young-looking and I had to ask for ID. The butterfly is not my usual, it's a red admiral from the UK. She said it would remind her of her grandma. I wrote their names and the amount I charged them in my records."*

Excited, Jenna made notes. "That's great news. Can you give me the details?"

"Sure. The snake one was Charlotte Barnes out of Denver and the butterfly, Evelyn Ross out of Colorado Springs." He sighed. *"No addresses, I'm afraid, but I can send through copies of the photographs? I have headshots of these two as well."*

Jenna grinned into the empty room. "Yes, please that would be great. Send them directly to me." She rattled off her email address. "Thank you for your help."

"My pleasure." He disconnected.

She waited impatiently for the images of the two smiling young women to drop into her inbox. She scanned the faces and compared the images on file. There was no doubt, they'd found the names of the victims. She called Wolfe. "I think I have the identity of victim number two, the possible is Charlotte Barnes out of Denver. I'll forward you the images I received from the tattoo artist. They look like a match. I'll have to hunt down where they're from and notify their families."

"That's great news." Wolfe cleared his throat. *"If they're both out of Colorado, it might save a ton of grunt work if you contact Jo and ask her IT whizz kid to see if he can chase down the victims' last known addresses and then you'll be able to deal with the correct law enforcement agency."*

Concerned, Jenna stared out the window. "We have spoken to her already and I don't want Jo thinking I need to run to her for help every time I have a case."

"As soon as the victims' hometown law enforcement know you've found their missing persons, you'll be working with them to solve the murders. The sooner this happens the better. You're just using available resources."

She pushed her bangs out of her eyes. "You're right, a good leader delegates and uses all resources to hand. I'll call her and then contact the victims' local law enforcement. They might be able to lean on the local dentists to get you Charlotte Barnes' dental records. I know you won't give a positive ID without them."

"You know me so well." Wolfe chuckled. *"Ask them to contact me."*

Jenna smiled. "Leave it with me, if we have the IDs, all I need now is the killer. See you at the autopsy." She disconnected.

Standing, Jenna entered the current information onto the whiteboard. She printed the images and attached them. Looking into the fresh, young faces, she frowned. "Who killed you?"

CHAPTER THIRTY-THREE

Not having any viable suspects, Jenna stared at the whiteboard. With all the information to date laid out, still nothing gave her a clue where to find the killer. She had one person of interest, the strange man helping at the shelter, Claude Grady, and could include any number of long-haul truckers living in town. She tapped her bottom lip, considering the conversation they'd had with Jo and Carter. Although Grady didn't appear to have a motive and being odd didn't make him a killer, it had to be someone who moved around. She palm-smacked her head. Or usually went on vacation each winter to parts unknown. Now that would make sense. The killer maybe worked in a plant that closed over the holidays—some of them closed for six weeks or more once the snow came. If he went to another state to collect his victims and then brought them back to Black Rock Falls, he likely stored them for the entire year, taking them with him the following year to display in another town. It made perfect sense. The girls wouldn't be missing in the town and classed as a Jane Doe. She needed more background information on the two frozen women they'd found. What were their circumstances? How did they become victims?

She leaned against her desk. With no leads and nothing of use coming in from the media releases, she had no choice but to wait and hope some information about the movements of the two victims became known via the investigations in their hometowns. Someone must have seen something. Right now, she was flying in a holding position waiting for The Sculptor, if he was their killer, to make his next move. Grabbing her statement for the DA, she headed out to Rowley's desk and cleared her throat. "I heard from a tattoo artist we have a match on one woman and a possible on the other. I'm going to give Jo a call and see what information they can find for us." She gave him the women's names. "We'll need to know more about them and how they met their killer."

"Well, we already know their hometowns from the tattoo artist. While we're waiting, I'll hunt down their photo IDs and do a search of the Colorado databases." Rowley glanced at her. "If I can find out where they went to school or where they last worked, we might be able to locate some of their friends."

Impressed by Rowley's enthusiasm, Jenna nodded in agreement. "Okay, I'll contact Jo and see what information she can add to what we have already. I guess the more of us working on this the better." She glanced at the clock. "Before you start your research, do you mind taking my statement into the DA's office and then taking your break? I'll be going to Aunt Betty's when Kane gets back and then we're going to attend the Charlotte Barnes autopsy, so we'll be gone awhile." She handed him the document.

"Yes, ma'am." Rowley pushed to his feet. "Right away."

Jenna walked back to her office, went to her coffee machine and poured a cup, adding sugar and cream. The horrible nagging doubt she'd had about someone raping her and the worry of infection had gone and her stomach was telling her it was way past her time to eat. She glanced at the clock. Not much longer and she would be ordering a meal with Kane at Aunt Betty's Café.

Returning to her table, she made the call to Agent Jo Wells. After explaining what she needed, she waited for Jo to pass the information to Bobby Kalo, their reformed Black Hat hacker, to do his magic. She sipped her coffee and heard Jo pick up the phone again. "Any interesting cases on your desk?"

"Nothing. We're snowed in, have been for a few days so we couldn't help if someone called. Trust me, Snakeskin Gully isn't the end of the earth but you can see it from here." Jo chuckled. *"We'd have been better opening an office in Black Rock Falls for all the good we're doing here. Hey, how is Dave handling his stalker?"*

Jenna brought her up to date with her kidnapping. "So, the stalking charge is off the table and I went straight to kidnapping an officer of the law with intent to kill."

"That will keep her busy for some time. At least she's out of your hair." Jo sounded distracted. *"You sure the guy in the cabin isn't involved?"*

"Pretty sure." Jenna put her phone on speaker and rubbed her temples. "The Blackwater Sheriff is hunting down any known associates. If he knew Miss Strickland, we'll find out and take it from there."

"Ah Bobby has a hit on your victims, he is emailing the info to you now." Jo sighed. *"It's pretty isolated here, I'm starting to go stir crazy. We need a Cattleman's Hotel big time. Apart from a couple of bars, there isn't anywhere to go for entertainment and trust me, an FBI agent isn't that welcome in local bars."* She snorted. *"Although, Carter is in his home away from home here. They accepted him when he moved into the forest but not me. They all look at me as if I have two heads and then dash across the road to avoid eye contact."*

Jenna frowned. "They'll like you soon enough once they're in trouble. Any progress with the local sheriff?"

"No." Jo barked out a laugh. *"He is very nice but having Carter with me all the time makes life difficult. Are all these ex-military so overprotective?"*

"I'm afraid so." Jenna smiled into the empty room. "It's in their genes." She heard a phone ringing in the background and Carter's deep voice.

"I've gotta go and speak to someone on the other line. Let me know if you need any more help with The Sculptor case." Jo disconnected.

Jenna read the information Kalo had emailed her and made the calls to the appropriate law enforcement in Colorado. After explaining the murders likely happened in their state, she advised them to contact Wolfe for more details. The fact that both girls had come from another state, confirmed Wolfe's theory of the freeze and thaw cycle. If the killer had frozen them and transported them to Black Rock Falls, her town was probably his home, but why risk capture by displaying his victims in his hometown? She could hear Kane's voice in her mind explaining how psychopaths considered themselves invincible and smarter than anyone else. "Hmm, well Sculptor, you're in my town now and your killing days are numbered."

Snowflakes stung Jenna's cheeks as she hustled inside Wolfe's office door. Using her card to gain entrance into the morgue she led the way with Kane close behind. All during their meal she'd discussed her theories about the possible killer and he'd agreed. "The problem is, how many people leave Black Rock Falls in winter to go on vacation?" She walked backward along the hallway looking at him.

"Too many." Kane unzipped his coat and pulled off his hat. "I've been following normal procedure and running down possible suspects but I can't point the finger at anyone just yet." He stuffed his hat and gloves into his pockets then shucked his coat as he walked. "I can place all the sex offenders in town over winter last year. I've compiled a list of anyone involved in art including those who arrange the local festivals and work in industries that shut down over winter."

Jenna shrugged out of her coat. "So you're convinced this lunatic is using women's bodies to form his sculptures."

"Yeah, from what I've seen that's the case." Kane paused in the hallway and hung up his coat on one of the pegs on a row outside Wolfe's office. "The women he chooses are the same type, they mean something important to him. I'm guessing something happened to him by someone with similar features to trigger this behavior. The fact the women are naked, tells me he wants to degrade them but as he's using them as his art, the woman meant something to him at one time."

"So why move them around and why freeze them?" Jenna unwound her scarf and added it to her coat on the peg. "What are we dealing with here, Dave?"

"This is way above my paygrade but he could be killing for a number of reasons." Kane went to a bench, opened a jar of mentholated salve, and spread it under his nose. "He takes women from other states, so they are more difficult to identify once found, and as a visitor to another state he's incognito, no one knows him." He pushed a face mask on his nose. "Or like you said, he can only get away to kill people during his winter vacation."

Jenna pulled a paper gown over her clothes to keep the stink out and handed one to Kane. "Why keep them frozen?"

"I'd say he likes to spend time with them or he's looking for the perfect place to display his art. Keeping them frozen is convenient and they don't stink up the place." He handed her the salve. "A person who does this isn't exactly logical, he could be doing it for one or all of those reasons. Problem is, nothing I've told you really leads to our killer, does it?"

Jenna fitted her face mask. "No, it doesn't." She sighed. "He has to be local because he knew how to avoid the CCTV cameras and the backroad to the ski resort." She looked at him. "How did he know the mayor's wife would be heading for her cabin? He's close, I can almost feel him."

CHAPTER THIRTY-FOUR

Wolfe smiled at the sight of Jenna and Kane coming through the door of the examination room. They looked as if they'd prepared for brain surgery, with their gowns, caps, and gloves. He caught a whiff of the mentholated salve and went to greet them. "Before we begin, I'd like you to look at the X-rays." He indicated to the screen. "As you can see, Charlotte Barnes' cause of death was asphyxiation due to strangulation. There is a fracture of the hyoid bone and the killer crushed the larynx. This would have taken a considerable amount of strength and it was a slow death. Like I've mentioned before, killing like this is up close and personal.

"Did he use a chainsaw like before to dismember the body?" Jenna nodded at Emily and Colt Webber then turned to Wolfe. "The damage to her torso was extreme."

"Yeah, look." Kane pointed at the X-ray and ran a finger across the marks on the damaged ribcage. "That sure looks like chainsaw marks to me."

Wolfe nodded. "He used the same chainsaw on both victims. I matched the grooves and they're identical. You'll see when Colt gets the body, the flesh has the same uneven marks." He looked at Jenna. "Emily is going to conduct the preliminary examination, as I mentioned on the phone, I've taken all the necessary swabs. There is no indication of sexual activity prior to death."

"Nervous about conducting your first autopsy?" Jenna peered over her mask at Emily.

"No, I wouldn't say nervous. Determined more like." Emily helped Colt pull out the gurney and they slid it beneath the overhead light. "I want to help solve a crime. If we prove this is Charlotte Barnes, she needs justice and I mean to find it for her." She pulled back the sheet with a flourish and one hand went to the mic. "We have a female, approximately eighteen to twenty years old, Caucasian, brown hair, and blue eyes. As we have a torso and the limbs are separate, we estimate her height to be five feet, five inches. Before death, we consider her body weight and condition to be normal for her age. She has a tattoo of a snake around her neck extending to one breast and down to her navel. There is extensive laceration to both sides of her torso, displaying clear sight to her lungs and intestines."

"Have you discovered any blunt force trauma to the head?" Kane moved closer, peering down at the lush black hair. "Any gunshot wounds?"

"No." Emily lifted the head to display the neck. "There are substantial hematomas in the neck region and distinct thumb prints over the larynx. This would indicate a substantial and prolonged struggle before asphyxiation."

Wolfe nodded. "What does the position of the marks on the neck tell us?"

"She was strangled face to face and most likely lifted off her feet." Emily looked at him. "This is typical for the killer to use the victim's weight to increase the pressure on the neck. He wanted to see her die and would have lifted her eye to eye with him."

"If I can butt in here?" Colt Webber pulled back the sheet to display the missing limbs. "I found something unusual. Look at the limbs and the victim's torso. Apart from the damage inflicted by the killer, there are no injuries on the torso. On the hands, the nails are fine. She has no ligature marks, no damage."

"Did you find the same on the first victim?" Jenna turned to Wolfe. "You thought she was shot running away?"

Wolfe went to the body storage and pulled out a drawer. "Look for yourself. Apart from a few scratches, consistent with running through a wooded area, and dirt under her nails, this woman displayed no signs of mistreatment. The soil sample from the first victim came from Colorado. I have tested both victims for various drugs, although a full tox screen is underway. Both tested positive for the date-rape drug, Rohypnol."

"So, he's picking them up, drugging them before he kills them, and then puts them on ice. He's not keeping them alive as sex slaves or whatever." Kane shook his head. "Hmm, so thrill kills? Can you tell if they were dead before he froze them?"

Wolfe nodded. "Yeah they were dead." He turned to Emily. "Go on, what else did you find?"

"In both victims, their expressions have been posed. He used glue on the eyelids to keep them open and to hold the lips in a smile on both women. I found traces of toothpicks in the teeth, which I believe he used to hold the face in the desired expression." Emily frowned. "He wanted them laughing." She looked at Jenna. "Both had traces of the same body lotion on their skin. It's not a common one either. I found it in one place in Montana, one of those hippie shops. I think that's too much of a coincidence."

"So, the evidence suggests he drugged, killed. and froze them and then transported them here from another state before exhibiting them." Jenna's brow furrowed. "But finding the same body lotion would suggest both women had been together at some time?"

"Or he's taking them home and keeping them prisoner before he decides to kill them? There's no evidence to prove he had them at the same time but maybe he held them at the same place." Kane leaned back on the counter. "He's not having sex with them as far as we know and he's not abusing them. In fact, from the condition of the bodies, he's caring for them." He threw both hands in the air. "Yet, he murders them, cuts them up, and displays them. Wow! This guy is breaking new ground when it comes to exhibiting an unusual psychosis. We'll be able to re-write the book on psychopathy with this one."

CHAPTER THIRTY-FIVE

Sunday

Ava paced up and down the basement, feeling the eyes of the other captives on her. She stared at the dumbwaiter and turned to Zoe. "We have to escape. There's three of us, we should be able to overpower him."

"How?" Zoe picked at a thread from her sweater, curling it around one finger. "He never comes down here."

"He knows nobody is looking for us, so is taking his time, I guess." Isabella pushed both hands through her hair and her mouth turned down. "I'd like to know what he wants. He keeps us warm, feeds us and we have clean clothes. What is he getting out of it?"

Unable to offer an explanation, Ava shrugged. "Unless he has cameras down here and he's watching us like his own reality show. The sick freak."

"Do you really think so?" Zoe looked at her, wide-eyed. "I don't see any cameras."

"Cameras are so small these days, we wouldn't notice them. Jeez you're so naive, I can't believe you survived on the streets." Ava stood before the two girls sitting on the bed. "I've been wondering if we can use the dumbwaiter to escape. There must be a gap between the walls, right?"

"I guess so." Zoe shrugged. "Why? We can't go up in it, it's too small and he's up there, I can hear him walking around. There's no way of making it move anyway, it's controlled from above."

Unconvinced, Ava walked to the dumbwaiter and opened the sliding hatch. "Just as I thought. When the dumbwaiter goes up, it leaves a gap. There's nothing in here just the cables."

"What are you getting at?" Isabella pulled her long black hair up into a ponytail, secured it with a band, and then walked to her side. "It's dark and filled with cobwebs, shut it before something runs out of there."

"Can't you feel that?" Ava leaned in closer to the hole in the wall. "There's a cold wind blowing in from somewhere. The passageway between the walls must lead to the outside. I think we should go and see where it comes out."

"I'm not sure risking climbing in there to look is a good idea." Isabella frowned. "Which way would we go? What if he's watching us? You know the penalty for noncompliance. I'm not sitting in the dark, starving to death again."

"I'll go. Critters don't frighten me. I've slept rough too many times to worry about them anymore." Zoe blinked at Ava through her pink streaked black bangs and shrugged. "I'll take the right and you the left."

Ava nodded and shivered. "It's freezing in there, we'll need extra clothes but not too many, we don't want to get stuck."

"What do I do if he comes to the door?" Isabella's expression turned fearful. "What do I say?"

"Let me think." Ava looked around frantically for inspiration. "Say nothing. Make up our beds to look as if we're in them and then go to bed. He'll only look down from the top of the stairs and he'll think we're asleep." She waved her away. "Do it now. Zoe, get ready; we haven't got much time. We'll have to get out and back before he sends down our next meal or we'll be stuck in here. You know he leaves the dumbwaiter down until we send back the dishes."

"Okay." Isabella handed her a thick hoodie. "But if you find a way out, don't come back. Go for help. The highway is east of here.

I remember turning left onto a bumpy road before I fell asleep. If you make it to the highway, you'll be able to get a ride into town."

Ava pulled on a second pair of socks and pushed her feet into her boots. "Okay." She took the coat and helped Zoe through the small hole. Using a chair, she climbed up and lowered herself inside the wall. To her right, she could just make out Zoe's white sweater moving slowly away from her. The girl had walked away without any sign of fear. The unemotional response worried her. It was as if Zoe had become complacent, being a prisoner. She lowered her voice. "Be careful."

Swiping at cobwebs heavy with dust, she swallowed the lump in her throat, and taking small steps, moved toward the breeze. The walls smelled bad, as if an animal had dragged its dinner inside to eat and left bits of it to rot. Underfoot, the boards creaked and when her foot sank into more than a few soft spots, panic had her by the throat. If the floor gave way, she could fall through at any moment and be stuck inside the walls forever. Taking a few breaths to steady her nerves, she ran her fingers along the gritty, rough wooden beams that crisscrossed the wall. In the dim light, she tried to ignore the unidentified objects brushing her cheeks and kept going. The need to get away far outweighed her fear of confined spaces. Ahead, she made out the corner of the house. A beam of light streamed through a manhole in the floor above, no doubt to give access to maintain the dumbwaiter. A makeshift ladder formed from the corner house beams led to the open hole. She'd have to risk Preacher detecting her and climb up to reach ground level.

The ladder wasn't in the best of shape and nails stuck out all over hanging loose in the rotting wood. She swallowed hard at the thought of falling and lying injured inside the walls but grit her teeth, tied the arms of the coat around her waist, and pulled herself up. Breathing heavily, she climbed. The crumbling steps disintegrated at her touch but she kept going. The next moment her feet slipped and chunks of the ladder fell away. Hanging by her fingertips, she stifled a cry, and spread her feet looking for the logs that made up the cabin walls. Terrified, she hung like a bat trying to regain enough strength to go on. It seemed like hours had passed by the time Ava reached the main level of the house. Filthy and dying of thirst, she poked her head through the manhole and peered around. A door was directly in front of her and the double-walled passage went both ways. Gasping for breath and arms burning from exertion, she clambered out the hole and sat for some moments to gain her breath. Conscious Preacher might hear her, Ava pushed down the waves of panic making her hands shake and moving as swiftly as possible, headed toward the light streaming through a gap in the floor a few yards away.

Crawling on hands and knees, she edged closer, wishing she had gloves to avoid the splinters from the rough floor. Blackened wooden boards had rotted away leaving a jagged gap. With one hand on either side of the hole, she poked her head through and stared at the confined space under the cabin. Sliding like a snake, she dropped through the hole and belly crawled over rocks and dirt to the snow-covered ground surrounding the house. She bit her bottom lip. It would be easy to follow her trail in the snow but she had no choice. She made her way to the edge of the house and stared with relief at the tall pines surrounding the cabin. If she could make it into the forest, she would be harder to find. Finally free, she stood on trembling legs and dragged on her coat. The icy chill bit into her skin and snowflakes melted on her hot cheeks. She took one look behind her and crept into the forest. Before she'd made cover, she heard a door creak open.

"You'll be sorry." Preacher elongated the words in a sing-song fashion as if taunting her but it was his chuckle that made her blood run cold.

CHAPTER THIRTY-SIX

Inside the wall of the cabin, an icy breeze brushed Zoe Henderson's cheeks like the cold breath of a grave. The torture of indecision threatened to crush her as she edged her way forward. How much time did she have before Preacher sent down the dumbwaiter and sealed her inside the coffin-like walls? She moved as fast as possible, batting away cobwebs carrying fat spiders and searching for a way to escape. Ahead of her the only light came through a few tiny gaps between the logs. There had to be another room in the cellar. Above, she could clearly make out footsteps. Was he coming down the stairs? Had he heard them inside the walls? Surely Ava had gotten away by now. She'd headed toward the breeze, there must be a break in the rotting wooden floor somewhere.

The footsteps stopped and Zoe held her breath. No voice came from behind her, Isabella was playing her part and pretending to be asleep. Edging forward, her hand brushed against something metal. Frantically she searched the wall. Her fingers closed around a doorknob. A pulse thumped in her ears. It was now or never. Turning the handle gently, she almost cried out with joy as the door opened. She peered into a dark room and listened. Not one sound came from inside. Fear gripped her as she pushed open the door and stepped into the room. The air had a strange smell, like the meat department in a store. She ran her hand over the wall and frowned at the unmistakable slide of thick plastic under her fingers. Before she had time to think, a bright light blinded her. She staggered back, fumbling for the door handle. Then she heard a voice.

"Ah, so it's you." Preacher sounded calm. "I wondered which one of you would come first."

Zoe turned and looked into his cold soulless eyes and dread washed over her. A bench carried a bloody chainsaw and chest freezers lined the walls. She stumbled over her words. "I'm sorry, I'll go back to my room."

"No, that's not possible." Preacher was slowly pulling on a pair of leather gloves as he walked toward her. "I need you for my art."

CHAPTER THIRTY-SEVEN

It was anything but a lazy Sunday morning for Jenna. After helping with the horses and a brisk workout with Kane, she had just packed the dishwasher when the phone rang. It wasn't the assigned ringtone of anyone in her team or a 911 emergency. She glanced at the time. Who was calling on a Sunday at seven in the morning? The caller ID said "private number" and a cold chill trickled down her spine. She glanced at Kane who sat at the kitchen table staring at his laptop. "Private number, maybe a burner. I'll put it on speaker." She answered the call. "Sheriff Alton."

"Morning Sheriff, this is Bobby Kalo from the FBI field office, out of Snakeskin Gully." Kalo waited a beat. *"Sorry to bother you so early but Jo asked me to call you. We have found a match on both sets of fingerprints from the victims found in Black Rock Falls. They confirm the identities, both had juvi rap sheets in Colorado."*

Jenna heaved a sigh of relief. "That's great, Bobby, can you send me the details and a copy to Wolfe? How come we missed them?"

"Ah, records of nonserious juvenile offenses are accessible only at the state and local levels but were recently incorporated into the FBI database." Kalo cleared his throat. *"I'll send these now and hand you over to Jo."*

"Hi Jenna, is Kane with you?" Jo sounded all business this morning.

Jenna glanced at Kane and shrugged. "Yeah, he's here. What's up, Jo?"

"From Shane's report and what we have established since yesterday, both victims were last seen in Colorado at a homeless shelter, over one year ago. The information I have is that both planned to hitchhike in different directions, neither were heading for Montana. It's reasonable to believe the victims died in Colorado and as we have no specific location, it would be better if we took over the case."

It was a blow and Jenna didn't reply, allowing the implications to run through her mind. "Jo, we can't be sure the women died in Colorado. If they were hitchhiking, the killer could've brought them here and then killed them."

"Unlikely from Shane's findings. He has evidence to suggest the victims were thawed and then refrozen." Jo lowered her voice. *"I'm not taking the case away from you, Jenna, but you have no authority in Colorado, and we do. There are reports of similar crimes coming into my office and I'll need to use the FBI's resources to hunt them down. It makes sense for you to concentrate on Black Rock Falls and leave the Colorado cases to us. We have the resources to hunt down the information on the victims. Together we can catch this killer, for as sure as the sun is rising tomorrow, The Sculptor is in Black Rock Falls."*

Jenna shrugged and her gaze fixed on the table. "Okay. We originally thought maybe a long-haul trucker was involved and we have one person of interest. If you believe The Sculptor is targeting homeless women with tattoos who hitchhike then we need to dig a bit deeper."

"Carter here. We're still snowed in, so useless right now but it's usual for hitchhikers to hang around truck stops looking for a ride. Problem is after a year, nobody is gonna remember one of a hundred or so passing through. I'll send out 'Have you seen these women' flyers but after so long the chances of anyone remembering them is slim."

"Can we trace where the victims holed up?" Kane raised an eyebrow at Jenna. "If they were homeless as you say, they may have visited shelters."

"The problem with that, Dave—" Carter sounded amused *"—is that the majority of homeless are incognito, they don't want to be found."*

"Well, you should know all about that, Carter." Kane flashed Jenna a grin. "So we'll need their last known point of contact for information? Can you hunt them down?"

"That's what I do." Carter snorted. *"We have been working on this since five this morning."*

Jenna sat at the kitchen table and poured herself a coffee, she held up a hand to Kane. "Okay, so we'll concentrate on possible persons of interest here. If The Sculptor is here in town, it's logical to believe if he murdered, froze, and transported the victims to Black Rock Falls, he must have a residence in Colorado or here. He'd need privacy for storing and dismembering bodies, or keeping women prisoner, so we're looking for a needle in a haystack. He could be living anywhere in Stanton Forest or in the Rocky Mountains."

"Yeah, it will be a huge task to locate him, those off the grid are like ghosts, but I'd still be inclined to look at anyone involved with the homeless." Jo yawned. *"Sorry, I haven't been getting much sleep and getting up every morning to dig out my vehicle is a nightmare. As soon as the melt comes, I'm building a garage."*

Jenna frowned. "There are usually people looking for work at this time of year, why not hire someone to help you? High-school kids needing a few extra bucks might be willing to dig out your vehicle."

"Ha, when you visit us, you'll understand. Those not on ranches run the stores in town. There aren't too many kids looking for work here." Jo chuckled. *"I'm heading home now to spend some time with Jaime before she forgets she has a mother. We have done everything we can for today. We'll pick up the investigation again in the morning. Let me know if you need anything."*

"Okay, thanks." Jenna disconnected and looked at Kane. "What do you think?"

"One, the killer moves around, but he doesn't have to be a trucker." Kane turned his coffee cup in his large hands. "He could fit a woman in the trunk of his vehicle. Most truckers are drivers, they don't own their eighteen or whatever wheelers. I can't imagine them risking carrying a body along with their load—and they run on tight schedules, so wouldn't have time to stop and dump a body." He lifted his gaze to her. "Secondly, I agree with Jo, he could work with the homeless in some capacity and be able to gain his victim's trust. A woman would most likely go with him if he offered her a ride. So we're looking for a white male, maybe in his forties, who comes across as friendly but nonthreatening. We know he drugs them, so once they are asleep, he has free range to do what he wants and as they are as Carter put it 'incognito', when they vanish nobody cares." He sipped his drink. "The biggest problem we have, is unless he kills someone here, we don't have a starting point. So far, we have victims from Colorado with no clue to where they died or how they arrived here. This Sculptor guy could be just passing through town. He could be anywhere by now. We're chasing shadows, Jenna."

CHAPTER THIRTY-EIGHT

Gripped with terror, Ava Price stumbled through the dense undergrowth and squeezed between black trunks packed so close together, no trail was evident. The snow-laden pines surrounded her as far as her eye could see. With each step, the heavy branches dripped icy water down her collar. Exhausted, she stopped to look behind her, but could see nothing but trees and snow. The temperature was so low each breath cut painfully into her lungs but she had to keep going. Stopping in this weather meant freezing to death. If she could just find her bearings or a trail leading to a road, she might have a chance to get help.

She peered all around and listened intently for any sound. The forest was deceptive; the trees creaked and groaned as the wind whistled through the branches. Every noise set her nerves on edge. Preacher could be right behind her and she wouldn't know until it was too late. To her left she could hear water, perhaps the famous Black Rock Falls was close by. Surely there would be a trail leading out of the forest if she could make it there. The falls were a tourist attraction and she may even find a cabin in the forest close by.

Heart racing, she took another furtive glance behind her. If Preacher was following her, the trees could easily conceal him and he would know the forest. Running on adrenalin and determined to survive, Ava dragged her frozen feet onward toward the sound of the falls. A loud bang startled her and a whooshing sound came close by. Had someone shot at her? Panic cramped her stomach and she ducked down, scanning the forest in all directions. The next moment, a massive bough came crashing through the branches, splintering on the way down and sending shards of wood in all directions. She covered her head and ducked away. It must be colder outside the protection of the forest than she'd imagined. The loud noise was frozen branches, snapping away from the trees. She had to keep going, and dragged her painful legs through the dead bushes, stopping only to grab a handful of snow to quench her thirst.

Hands and feet numb and cheeks frozen, she stumbled out the forest. In front of her was the edge of a waterfall. The falls had frozen in parts and didn't come close to the expanse of the impressive Black Rock Falls she'd seen on the net, but it didn't matter. People visited waterfalls all over the county and she might find help close by. Standing on the edge of a boulder, she made out a trail alongside the falls that led to the top. Without a second thought, she pushed her ice-cold fingers inside her pockets and made for the pathway.

Muscles aching, she climbed to the top of the trail and looked behind her. There was no sign of Preacher. Heaving a sigh of relief, she followed a narrow path. At the sight of a hunting cabin in a small clearing, she whooped with joy. She dragged herself to the front porch to find its front door padlocked for the winter and all the windows had shutters locked tight. A locked metal meat locker, dusted with snow, sat under a tree. It was big enough to hold a full elk. She sat on the porch steps to rest, staring into the distance, but as the sweat from climbing the fall's trail turned to ice, she stood and searched around. The dirt road at the back had to be the way back to town.

Lifting her knees, she trekked through the thick snow to the road. Snow piled on each side, a sign a snowplow had gone through recently. Cold bit into her cheeks but keeping moving had warmed her a little. Making her way around the first bend, she caught a glimpse of the lowlands, which put her position at the top of the mountain range, many miles from town. The small road ended in a T-junction with a wider road leading in both directions. She headed down the mountain and, in the distance, heard an engine moving slowly in her direction. She ran slipping and sliding down the road until a truck with a snowplow attached to the front came into view. Standing in the middle of the road, she waved her arms to get the driver's attention. As the snowplow slowed to a stop, the door swung open. Without a second thought, she jumped inside and closed the door behind her. She turned to the driver. "Thank you. I need help. Do you have a cellphone? I need to call the cops."

The man was bundled up against the cold and wearing sunglasses with only a small patch of his cheeks visible. He turned and looked at her and shook his head but said nothing. Uncertainty crawled into Ava's belly. She gripped the door handle ready to leap out and run away. Had she gone from one bad situation to another?

"Hot chocolate?" He startled her when he spoke in almost a whisper. The stranger took a Thermos from between the seats and handed it to her. "Drink it before I go. I don't want you to spill it on the seats." His voice was raspy and gruff. "I'll call the cops from home. Back there." He indicated behind him with his thumb.

"Thanks." Fingers numb with cold, Ava fumbled with the top but managed to pour the meager contents into the cup. It was warm and very strong but she drank it down and then handed him the Thermos. "Can you take me there now?"

"Soon as I visit the meat locker." The man headed the truck toward the old hunting cabin.

The warmth inside the truck was delicious and Ava leaned back in the seat, trying to ignore the pain in her defrosting limbs. As the truck made its way slowly up the mountain, Ava had trouble keeping her eyes open. She sat up straight but the heavy feeling of impending sleep had her in its clutches. As they drove along the road to the cabin, she pinched herself to keep awake. The truck stopped alongside the meat locker and the man climbed out. He unlocked the padlock and threw back the lid, making a loud clanging noise that echoed through the forest. Too exhausted to move, Ava followed him with her eyes as he opened the back door of the truck and lifted out something wrapped in a blanket.

Ava stared as he dropped the heavy bundle, a pig maybe, into the locker. She made out a flash of pale flesh as he pulled the blanket away and the carcass thumped to the floor. As he stepped away gathering up the blanket, his scarf fell away from his face. Terror gripped her as she recognized Preacher. Shaking her head in denial, she stared at him—surely, exhaustion was playing tricks on her. She squeezed her eyes shut and then opened them and blinked wildly. Trying desperately to focus, she gaped in horror at the opening to the meat locker. A human arm—a woman's arm—hung over the edge.

Realization slapped her in the face. Preacher had killed someone. Panic closed the scream in her throat. She had to get away from him but couldn't lift her arms. Pushing feebly at the truck door with her shoulder, she tried to open the door but it was as if her body had quit responding. She stared at Preacher. He was speaking, so softly she couldn't make out the words, and leaning in the locker as if arranging the body. Her attention fixed on the arm he was tucking inside. She recognized the tattoo of a rose on the back of the hand and the black nail polish. Her heart pounded in disbelief. He'd murdered Zoe.

CHAPTER THIRTY-NINE

Monday, Week 2

Kane sat bolt upright in bed at the sound of the 911 ringtone on his phone. His internal body clock that woke him at five each morning never failed. He turned on the bedside lamp and stared at the clock; it was four-forty-five. Grabbing his phone, he pushed back the blankets and sat on the edge of the bed. He took a pen and writing pad from his bedside table before accepting the call. "911 what is your emergency?"

"There's a body." A man gasped. *"Oh, my Lord. A naked woman on the steps of the* Black Rock Falls Daily.*"* He gave a moan of despair. *"She's smiling and her eyes… Oh sweet Jesus, they're wide open."*

Making notes, Kane cleared his throat. "What is your name, sir, and I'll need your details?"

"Barry Lynch. I'm the editor of the newspaper." He was breathing hard as he reeled off his phone number and address. *"This is the scoop of the century. I called the photographer and I'm getting a camera crew down here."*

Kane winced. "Please don't do that, Mr. Lynch. I appreciate this being an important new story for you but if this woman is a victim of a crime, we'll need to discover who hurt her. If you disturb the crime scene, valuable information will be lost. Tampering with a crime scene is an offense. I'll have the ME on scene as soon as possible and I'll notify the sheriff." He sighed. "Please don't touch anything. Hold the line for a minute, please."

Kane dialed the landline, woke Rowley, and explained the emergency. "Get there now. You'll need to prevent the media from disturbing the scene. I'll contact Wolfe."

"Copy that." Rowley yawned. *"I'm on my way."*

Kane made the call. With both Wolfe and Rowley living in town, they'd handle the situation until he arrived with Jenna. "Ah Mr. Lynch. The ME is on his way and Deputy Rowley. Please stay where you are and do not disturb the scene."

"You can't stop the press but I will keep my people a good distance away." Mr. Lynch disconnected.

Kane called Jenna and with the phone on speaker, dashed around dressing. "I'm dressed. I'll drop some hay into the horses before we leave. It will take me five minutes, max."

"Sure, but have you looked outside? We won't be going anywhere unless you clear the driveway first. Let's hope the road into town is passable." Jenna sounded wide awake. *"Rowley can handle the media if they show and Wolfe is only five minutes away. By the time we get there, Wolfe will have processed the scene. I'll go and feed the horses. You go out and clear the snow. I'm glad you purchased that attachment for your truck. I told you it would come in useful."* She disconnected.

"Uh-huh." Kane stared at the phone and then at Duke in his basket, snoring softly. He shook his head. "Black Rock Falls, perfect one day, deadly snowscape the next."

It was slow going into town and Kane was glad he'd rigged out his truck in the latest snow gear. He'd left Duke curled up asleep in his basket, his dog bowl filled and the heat on. The dog had shown little interest at the chance of leaving with him and buried his nose under his blanket. He'd be fine at home in the warm today. As they approached the newspaper office, he spotted a small crowd of people on the sidewalk, bathed in the glow of Wolfe's powerful halogen lights. Yellow crime scene tape fluttered in the breeze and he made out Deputy Rowley's cruiser in front of the stairs leading to the newspaper office with Wolfe's van blocking the view of the body. He drove past and then mounted the sidewalk from the opposite end and parked. "It looks like they have everything under control." He indicated to a silver Jeep Cherokee. "Emily is here as well."

"No doubt Webber will be on scene soon. They are dedicated." Jenna slipped from her seat and headed toward Rowley. "Check out the scene. I'll speak to the witness."

Kane followed and made his way between the vehicles. Wolfe had erected a screen in front of the victim and shadows moved around speaking in hushed tones. He peered around the screen and stopped dead. The young woman was posed. She sat on the steps, her elbows resting on one step and reclining as if enjoying the sun. Her mouth was turned up in a horrific grin and her wide eyes seemed to hold an astonished expression. Her skin was as if she'd been carved in marble, smooth and glistening with ice. Long snow-dusted black hair hung down to cover her breasts. Tattoos stood out against her pale skin. By her size, coloring, and ink, she had to be another victim of The Sculptor.

He did a visual scan of the area but all he could make out to the perimeter of the light was a thick coating of snow. He turned to look at the group of reporters, taking in the features of each one. Did they all belong with the media or was The Sculptor among them watching for a reaction to his latest work? He took out his phone to take a photograph and waved his arm. "Hey over here."

As expected, they all turned as one to look at him and he captured the image. He stared at the photograph and all the faces shone back at him in the beam of Wolfe's light. If The Sculptor was here, he had his picture and Jenna and Rowley would have taken all their names and contact details on arrival. An odd man out would be easy to check. He pocketed the phone and stood at the edge of the crime scene. "What have we got, Shane?"

"This one is different to the others in a number of ways." Wolfe headed toward him. "At first I thought maybe a copycat but we didn't release any crucial details and this one follows the killer's MO to some degree. Once I get her back to the lab, I'll be able to confirm my suspicions."

Kane pushed his hands into the pockets of his jacket as a stinging cold breeze brought with it a flurry of snow. "That's good to know." He frowned. "What are your suspicions?"

"The body appears to be fresh." Wolfe looked at him over his face mask. "As if someone snap froze her minutes after death, or before she died." He shrugged. "It wouldn't take long to freeze a woman with her body mass in this temperature. Faster still in the mountains. Anything from twenty minutes to a couple of hours."

Kane looked at the victim and slowly back to Wolfe. "Did he use glue again?"

"It sure looks that way." Wolfe frowned. "She was posed before rigor set in. The pinpoint hemorrhages in the conjunctiva of the eyes would indicate strangulation and hand marks are evident but again, I'd say he used gloves. I'll be interested to see if she has a broken neck. The head isn't sitting quite right." He walked toward the body. "I'm just about finished here. Do you want to take a look at her in situ?"

"Yeah." Kane followed him and examined the body. "She put up a fight. Her nails are broken."

"Yeah, Wolfe squatted down beside the body. "See here, the marks on her neck? I'll check for skin under her nails but we see this when a victim tries to pry the killer's hands from around her neck. He has large hands and would have cut off the supply of blood to her brain. She could've died from asphyxiation or even a cardiac arrest. I'll know more later today."

Kane nodded. "Okay, how long will it take to discover if she died here? I mean if she doesn't follow the pattern of thaw and freeze like before?"

"As soon as I take a tissue sample, I'll know for sure." Wolfe stood. "It will take a couple of days for her to thaw but once I remove the glue, we should be able to get a reasonable photograph of her. She must be someone's daughter."

Kane glanced behind him as Jenna came around the screen. She stopped and stared in horror. He glanced back at Wolfe. "I hope someone has reported her missing."

"How long before you can remove the body?" Jenna indicated over her shoulder with her thumb. "The vultures are circling. The TV crew followed the snowplow from Louan and I gave a 'no-comment' statement."

"Now, if you've seen enough?" Wolfe turned to Kane. "I'll leave you to bring Jenna up to speed." He waved is interns over and they placed the body on a gurney and covered her with foil.

Kane gave Jenna the details as they helped dismantle the screens and lights. Once the ME's van was loaded, he waited with Jenna for Emily to drive away. They turned into the full blare of the TV cameras. Questions flew and he could feel Jenna tense beside him. He glanced at her. "May I?"

"Yeah, give them both barrels." Jenna headed for his truck and then turned and walked backward to continue the conversation. "Rowley is meeting us at Aunt Betty's for breakfast, we can hunt down missing persons from there on our phones while we're eating."

"Copy that." Kane turned and almost collided with a blonde-haired woman with ruby lips, wearing a stylish winter coat and expensive boots. As she opened her mouth to speak to him, he side-stepped her. "I'm sorry, the sheriff doesn't have a statement for you at this time."

"We could all see it was a body of a woman, Deputy Kane." The reporter stepped in front of him again and stuck a microphone in his face. "Is she another murder victim?"

Kane gave her his best "back off" stare. "The sheriff's department hasn't issued any statements pertaining to murder victims. The previous deaths are still under investigation by the medical examiner." He straightened. "I can confirm we discovered a body of a female approximately eighteen to twenty years old with dark hair and blue eyes. Cause of death is undetermined and we'll be issuing a statement later today. If anyone knows of a missing woman fitting the description, please call the sheriff's department. You can be assured if any of these deaths are homicides, the sheriff will be working around the clock to find the person responsible." He turned and marched back to his truck and climbed inside.

"It looks like The Sculptor again." Jenna turned in her seat to look at him.

"Yeah, but this time Wolfe believes the victim died here." Kane started the engine. "This murder was rushed. He hasn't mutilated the body, just posed her, which takes it to a new dimension. What he did to her is power and humiliation. He wanted to make a statement and by placing her on the newspaper's front steps, he's gotten the media coverage he craves."

"Maybe now he's been on TV, he'll move on?" Jenna frowned.

Kane shook his head. "No, he won't. He's enjoying himself too much."

Jenna stared out the window. "If you're right, I figure he's just gotten started."

CHAPTER FORTY

Preacher stared at the TV and gave a growl of satisfaction. His art had made the news this time and although the media coverage had blocked out the view of Delores, the description given by the reporter had made him smile. He'd enjoyed seeing her wide-eyed shocked expression, the way she stumbled her words as she explained the threat now hanging over Black Rock Falls and how the sheriff was working around the clock to catch him. He snorted. "She couldn't find her nose in the dark."

The thumping on the bedroom door came again and he rubbed his temples. He would regret bringing Ava, as Delores insisted he call her, back to the house. He should have finished her and placed her in the meat locker but he'd needed to keep her around for a time. Problem was, she'd contaminate the girl in the cellar by telling her about the one they called Zoe, and he couldn't have that. He had big plans for Isabella or Delores number three—big plans. He swiveled his chair and looked at the screen. Ava stood in front of the camera, draped in a blanket, her mouth turned down making her ugly. As she'd slept, he'd nailed the shutters closed and rigged a camera in the spare room. He could talk to her, via a speaker. "What is wrong with you, now?"

"You can't keep me in here without clothes, I'll freeze to death." Ava thumped on the door. "I know you killed Zoe. You are one sick SOB."

He'd turned up the heat and it was as warm as toast inside the cabin. She was lying to him and it made him angry. He flicked on the mic. "You broke the rules. Zoe, as you called her, broke her neck and I put her on ice so she didn't stink up the place."

"I don't believe you." Ava shook her head. "You should have called the paramedics."

Preacher smiled at the memory of squeezing the life out of Zoe, feeling her tremble against him as her life drained away. The look in her eyes, the pleading for forgiveness as his fingers closed around her soft neck. He'd used his skill to make her smile and when he'd set her out for all to see, she was happy to be part of his exhibition. "Now why would I want to do that?"

"Okay, okay. You don't want anyone else here, I guess, but why did you take my clothes? Do you get off seeing me in my underwear?" Ava glared at the camera. "Or are you selling photos of me to your friends?"

Preacher leaned back in his seat and stared at the ceiling. "I don't see you like that anymore, Delores. You stopped being anything of significance to me the moment you climbed into my truck."

"What the hell do you mean by that?" Ava stuck out her chin. "And my name is Ava, not Delores."

He narrowed his gaze on her, feeling nothing but a surge of power. He controlled her and could laugh at her now. He allowed his gaze to move over the scratches on her cheek and untidy hair from running through the forest and sighed. Hadn't he given her every comfort to preserve her skin? Now he had no choice, he wouldn't present a damaged piece of artwork again. He would keep her until she was perfect. "You are the means to an end, nothing more. Your complaints mean nothing, your comfort means nothing. I offered you a warm bed, good food, clean clothes and yet you preferred to run into the woods."

"I'm sorry, okay?" Ava's eyes brimmed with tears. "I'll be good and do anything you say but give me back my clothes."

Tears made him angry, they spoiled Delores' eyes. He pushed down the urge to strangle her and clenched and unclenched his fists. Conversation with the items in his collection was redundant, although he enjoyed seeing her grovel. "You can't escape if you have no clothes. If you try again, you'll die out there before you get to the forest. Now, if you're planning on eating and drinking sometime today, follow the rules."

"I need to pee." Ava paced up and down the room. "There isn't even a bucket in here. If you want my cooperation then allow me to go to the bathroom." She looked in the camera lens. "As you say, I can't escape without clothes, can I?"

Preacher had taken everything into consideration but had wanted her to ask him. Withholding bathroom visits could become another tool in his arsenal. His bathroom could be accessed from either bedroom but he'd locked the door to her side. He stood and walked through his bedroom to the bathroom. After removing all his things, he left small single-use toiletries on the shelf. He sniffed the body lotion and then added a hairbrush. On the towels he placed a set of clean underwear and summer weight PJs. He checked the bars on the window and unlocked the door before moving into his room and locking the door behind him. He went back to his office and stared into the screen. "I'll allow you to use the bathroom. Clean yourself up and change your clothes. Disrespect me again by breaking the rules and you'll die slowly in your own filth." He chuckled. "Do you know how long it takes to die of thirst, Delores?"

"No." Ava sniffed and stared into the camera, red-eyed.

Preacher grinned. "I do."

CHAPTER FORTY-ONE

It was turning out to be an exhausting morning for Jenna. Wolfe had confirmed the body was indeed fresh. Decomposition was virtually non-existent, which meant the victim had only been frozen recently and within minutes of her death. The killer was active in Black Rock Falls but who was his victim and who might be next on his macabre list? With people arriving daily, regardless of the freezing temperatures and snowfall, the victim could have been one of many. The media had broadcast the victim's description and as no one had reported anyone missing, she doubted the victim was one of the townsfolk but it was still early.

Now aware the young woman died in her county, it was like déjà vu on steroids as she went over the casebooks from the previous Sculptor cases and compared them with what she had now. What she had now was zip. Nothing had come through from Jo or Carter, and she wondered if they were still "in the loop" with the Colorado investigation. Starting over and hunting down clues and suspects was like walking in quicksand, as although there were many consistencies between the cases, she had little hard evidence, apart from a frozen corpse of similar type and age.

After exhausting the local databases, Jenna had put her team to work hunting down possible missing persons from other states. The day seemed to be lasting forever. The hands on the clock had dragged themselves to eleven by the time Kane and Rowley came into her office and sat down. She looked at them. "What do you have for me?"

"We have three possible." Kane placed three printouts on the desk and pushed them toward her. "Ava Price, Isabella Bennett, and Zoe Henderson. They all fit the general description and the first two went missing over two years ago. Zoe is a runaway from a string of foster homes but they gave up the search when she turned eighteen. She's been on the streets since she was fifteen."

"Three, huh? Let's hope he hasn't got the other two on ice somewhere." Mind reeling with possibilities, Jenna leaned on her desk. "It's a long shot but did these women have cellphones? We could just call them?"

"We thought of that too and no. They don't." Rowley shook his head. "I found nothing in their names. I guess they could be using burners. If they're homeless having a plan might be beyond their means."

Jenna stared at her notes. Three possible victims and a killer who had decided her town was the place to be this winter. She had little choice but to work the case with only one person of interest, Claude Grady, and he was little more than a gut feeling. She had no evidence against him, none at all. Who was the girl in the morgue? She lifted her gaze. "If we assume the victim is one of the three women you mentioned, we at least have a starting point. Right now, we have zip."

"You do have Jo and Carter working the case for the other victims found here." Kane looked at her. "They might find something we missed—a connection between the victims perhaps?"

Jenna shook her head. "We didn't miss anything and I hope they're keeping us in the loop. I haven't heard back from them. Let's move on. Anything else I need to know?"

"There have been sightings." Rowley looked down at his iPad. "A couple of homeless shelters out of Wyoming and another in Salt Lake City. Isabella was born in Utah, the other two hail from Wyoming. Kane has the details."

Jenna twirled her pen in her fingers, thinking. "Hmm. Any vehicles?"

"Nope. Nothing on record. No fingerprints for Zoe but we have copies for Isabella." Kane rested one boot on the other knee.

"What else did you find?" Jenna looked at Kane's relaxed pose. He always seemed to take everything in his stride. For him, a horrific murder was just like any other crime to solve.

"I had a long list of towns in Wyoming with shelters. I called a few of the receptionists and was lucky and hit pay dirt after the third call. One of them recalled a girl named Ava staying a few weeks. From what they remember, Ava was a hitchhiker, and got rides with truckers mostly. It's what they do to get around."

Jenna nodded in agreement. "I called Father Derry earlier and he seems to think hitchhiking is their favorite mode of transport as well. Few homeless waste their money on a bus ticket. Many just stay in the same town for years. What about the others, Kane?"

"Salt Lake City was easier and I had a hit for Isabella. Nothing for Zoe yet, but I'll keep searching." Kane stretched out his long legs. "I figure we'll have more luck identifying the victim by her tattoos."

"Not if they got them after they left home." Jenna stood and entered the information on the whiteboard. "We'll need to nail down who is in the morgue. Have you hunted down any relatives?"

"Yeah and I've sent all the info and images of the tattoos on the victim to the local law enforcement in the victims' hometowns. Wolfe was able to get some clear shots. They'll pay the relatives a visit and get back to us as soon as possible." Kane glanced at his notes. "Wolfe has already sent an image of the newspaper office victim to Jo and asked if she can get a facial composite of the victim completed today, rather than waiting for the corpse to thaw. Once Wolfe has an ID and a relative, he'll be able to back it up with either mitochondrial DNA or dental records."

Jenna wrote on the whiteboard. "That's great! With their help to identify the victim, we can turn our attention to finding the killer. If I recall, Carter advised us to look at truckers and Jo wondered if the victims were homeless."

Kane leaned back in his chair. "It would be a perfect scenario for a serial killer. He picks up a girl in his rig, asks her a few questions and if she's far away from home, she becomes a victim. He can take his time because it's unlikely anyone will miss her." He met Jenna's gaze. "Or be hurrying to identify her body when he's finished with her."

Jenna's mind went back to Claude Grady, the volunteer at the homeless shelter. His attitude and behavior had worried her. If the killer was murdering the homeless in her town, he would be on the top of her list of suspects. "Yeah, a trucker might be feasible but so would anyone who works with the homeless. With the number of long-haul truckers in town and the volunteers giving their time in Black Rock Falls this winter, plus the usual staff, we'll need to compile a list." She slipped behind her desk and sat down.

"The killer must own a hunting cabin or live in an isolated ranch hereabouts." Kane stood and went to the bubbling coffee maker. "I know we're talking hundreds of people, maybe thousands, who have cabins in the forest but we're talking about a place they have access to even in winter. So maybe a place adjacent to a road that's cleared by the snowplow."

"So anywhere from here to the highway and beyond bordering Stanton Forest." Rowley looked skeptical. "The forest has many passable trails in winter, the elk and deer move from place to place and keep them clear. Many people living in the forest clear the trails as well. We'd have more luck finding a four-leaf clover."

Jenna shook her head. "No, Kane is right. We have a ton of people to consider. Removing those living in town would be a start."

"I'm not convinced a killer couldn't keep a frozen woman here in town." Rowley took the cup Kane offered him and placed it on the desk. "Live women would be a problem but frozen women aren't going to make much noise, are they?"

"Agreed." Kane placed a cup before Jenna and then took his coffee and sat down. "But we gave out a press release when we discovered the severed limbs at the ski resort. We specifically asked if anyone had heard someone using a chainsaw. All the reports that came in checked out as legitimate. I'm sure the hotline would be buzzing if someone around town was using a chainsaw now it's all over the news there's a murderer in town."

Jenna sipped her coffee, savoring the rich brew and mulling over what everyone had said. "Okay, I have a plan." She held her cup in her palms enjoying the heat flowing through the porcelain and looked at her deputies. "We have to start somewhere. We have two trucking depots in town and a truck stop out at the Triple Z. Rowley, you head out to the truck depots and go straight to the manager. See if he'll cooperate. I didn't have much luck over the phone when I called. Find out if they have regular hauls to Colorado, Utah, and Wyoming. That information should be public knowledge. If so, try and persuade them to give you the names of the truckers who regularly drive that route and if any own their own rigs. Especially anyone transporting frozen goods. Maybe have a chat with any other truckers you run across. Show them the pictures of the three missing girls and see if you get a reaction."

"Copy that." Rowley made a few notes.

"I'll jump onto the Motor Vehicles Division database and search for the vehicles and then cross reference the owners with the county property records and see what comes out." Kane smiled. "Too easy."

Jenna smiled at his enthusiasm. "I'll ask Maggie to do that for us. I'm thinking out of the box. If our killer is just passing through town, he might have stopped by the Triple Z Bar. I'll head out there with Kane. It's a well-known truck stop. Some long-haul truckers stay there and I figure it's a good place to ask questions and show around the photographs."

"Yeah, I know hitchhikers wait there for a ride." Rowley frowned.

A shiver ran down Jenna's spine. "Only to end up in the hands of a madman."

CHAPTER FORTY-TWO

The cold crept in through the cracks in the walls and Ava shivered as she paced barefoot across the creaky wooden floor. An emptiness had replaced the anger raging against Preacher. There was no way out. She had become his prisoner. She smothered a distraught sob. It was as if a void of hopelessness had seeped inside her and set up camp. She glared at the camera. On the other side of the locked door, Preacher would be watching her every move. It was as if his eyes had burned into her skin as she'd taken a shower. She'd bathed wearing her underwear and then dressed hiding under a towel. He hadn't said a word to her but she could hear him breathing through the speakers. He made her skin crawl.

She'd dried her hair and rubbed the fragrant body lotion he'd supplied into her skin before waiting to be allowed back into the bedroom. This was another new rule. She went into the bathroom and the door locked behind her. When she'd finished, he expected her to ask him to open the door. She had to admit, apart from being his prisoner, Preacher had catered to her needs but now things had changed. Like when she'd first arrived, she'd become a rat in an experiment. Do the deed and get the reward. She'd showered as he'd asked and when she left the bathroom, he'd left a meal for her.

His rules had been simple enough:

No crying, screaming or hammering on doors.

Keep clean and change clothes daily.

Use the body lotion.

Do not attempt to escape.

All simple rules that guaranteed food and light until she realized he planned to kill her. He'd murdered Zoe, she had no doubt—and was Isabella alive, still locked in the cellar? She hadn't heard her and Preacher hadn't mentioned her at all. When his voice came over the speakers, she turned and looked at the camera. He called her Delores again as if in his deluded mind, she was someone else. She refused to allow him to see how miserable she felt and lifted her chin. "What is it now?"

"The tattoos, what meaning do they have to you?" Preacher's voice was conversational. *"Why did you select those designs?"*

Ava wrinkled her nose and turned away. She didn't want to cooperate but if she planned to survive another night, she needed to eat. "They mean different things to me. The poppy on the back of my hand, is to remember a friend who died of a heroin overdose. The bluebird on my shoulder is to remind me of the times I was happy as a kid."

"Would you like to come and sit in the kitchen with me and tell me about being happy?" Preacher sighed. *"I have never had that feeling before and it sounds nice."*

Ava swallowed the fear in her throat. If she could gain his trust, she might be able to escape. He couldn't stay home all the time and as he'd often provided them with fresh bread, he'd have to make trips to the local store. Heart threatening to leap from her chest, she nodded. "Sure, I'd like that, thank you."

"Tell me you won't break my rules." Preacher sounded excited. *"I want you to promise me."*

Ava would do anything to get out of the room. "Sure, I promise."

Moments later the door opened and Preacher stood there with a Glock sticking out of the belt around his jeans. Ava swallowed hard. Before her stood a tall, lean, but muscular man. She took a hesitant step toward the door but he moved like lightning, clasping her wrist and spinning her back against his chest. His forearm pressed against her windpipe. In sheer panic she squirmed. "What are you doing?"

"I'm being careful." Preacher's voice held a smile. "I have knives in the kitchen but they're for my use only."

Ava sagged against his chest. She had no chance against him and going along with him might keep her alive for another day. "Okay."

Panting with fear, she looked around as he walked her backward down a narrow hallway and into a kitchen. The place was rustic, and old mixed with new seemed to be his decorating style of choice. The kitchen was surprisingly clean and somewhere nearby a dryer tumbled clothes. The room smelled of fresh laundry and heat radiated from a wood stove. A large scrubbed wooden table took up most of the room. At one end sat two metal rings with handcuffs attached. Opposite the table a TV screen hung on the wall.

"Sit at the table." He edged her forward. "I'm going to cuff you so you don't try to escape and then we'll talk some."

Ava tried to keep the tremble out of her voice. "I'm not going to try and escape again. Like you said, I'd die outside in this weather." She sat and spread her arms wide allowing him to cuff her.

She heard him chuckle and then he showed her a hunting knife. She swallowed the scream threatening to spill out of her mouth and said nothing. If he wanted her terrified, he'd won but she wasn't going to give him the satisfaction of seeing her frightened. She'd read about men like him on a power trip. They fed off fear and she'd die before she cowered before him. "Nice knife. Is it new?"

He answered her by slicing the top of her PJs from wrist to neck and by the time he'd finished she sat in her underwear. Trembling, Ava grit her teeth and looked him straight in the eye. "I thought you didn't want me for sex?"

"I don't. I want to admire your skin is all." Preacher bent and sniffed her then traced her poppy tattoo with his tongue. He lifted his gaze and stared at her, his face only a few inches away from hers. "I'm saving you for something special."

Ice-cold fingers of terror walked down Ava's spine. He was so close she could smell what he'd eaten for breakfast. She didn't turn her head away. He'd said that to scare her and was waiting for her to react. She'd studied criminal psychology for a year before dropping out and remembered reading something about not being able to reason with a psychopath. *I must think about every word I say.* This guy was beyond creepy and his dead eyes held not one ounce of compassion. To him she'd become someone he could dominate—an object. She wanted to pull away, struggle and cry out, but that's what he'd expect from her.

She swallowed hard. In the past, she'd been able to talk her way out of bad situations and now would be no different. "That sounds like fun." She stared into his eyes. "I see you like my ink? Do you have any tattoos?"

"No." Preacher sat down beside her and looked at his hands as if stymied by her reply. "I just like them for my art."

The image of Zoe's pale hand slid into her mind and realization swamped Ava in a tsunami of horror. Her knees shook and she squeezed her legs together. "I love art. How did you get started?"

"I watched a show on TV about making art out of trash." He leaned back in his chair. "Some of the artists are famous for their trash art. At the time I was dumping my trash and then I figured, people should see how I rose like a phoenix and went from a boy to a man."

Ava noted the acne scars on his face. He was likely bullied at school and something must have happened to trigger him. She nodded. "Yeah, same. I gave the finger to the world and I do what I want now too."

"I can't walk away." Preacher held his head. "Delores won't let me. She keeps coming back so I create a sculpture to forget her."

She had to make him believe she was not his Delores. Ava nodded. "Good idea. I like your style." She smiled at him but fear gripped her insides. "Can you show me your art?"

"Not my art but I'll show you photos of their tattoos. I like their hair too and I keep strands but I wouldn't want anyone touching them. I'm sure you understand?" Preacher chuckled deep in his chest and pulled out his phone. He held out the phone to her and scrolled through so many images it made her head spin. He became animated and excited looking at them. "I found these Deloreses in Colorado."

Biting hard on her cheek to keep her expression bland, Ava turned her attention to the images on the screen. Her pulse raced so fast her head spun but she remained calm on the outside. He was watching her so closely that she could feel his breath on her cheek. Finally, he placed the phone on the table and looked at her as if waiting for a comment. She nodded unable to form words for a beat. Apart from Zoe and Isabella, she recognized herself among the images, drugged, naked and posed like all the rest. It made her sick to her stomach. Forcing herself to look at him, she pushed words from her suddenly dry throat. "Impressive ink. You have an eye for design, I see. Your sculptures will make you famous."

"I am already." Preacher played with his phone turning it over in his hands. "Delores was on the news. She looked so fine on the newspaper office steps."

Ava tried to swallow the bad taste in her mouth as the truth dawned on her. "You turn Delores into art?"

"Yeah. It's the only way I can get her to smile at me again." He ran a finger down her arm. "I thought you were Delores but maybe I'm wrong. You smile all the time."

Ava shivered at his touch. The touch of a sadistic serial killer. She decided to play her hand. It was likely he planned to kill her anyway but every day she remained alive gave her a chance to escape. "I'm not Delores, my name is Ava and I think your idea of turning Delores into art is spectacular."

He made no reply and for long minutes only the sound of the clock ticking on the wall filled the room. Ava held her head high and fixed her gaze on him. She had to be strong or he'd kill her for sure.

"You're a strange woman." Preacher shook his head as if finding it hard to understand. "I have never met anyone that appreciates my art before. I made a snowman and left it in the park recently." He frowned. "When a couple of women walked by, they ran screaming to the sheriff."

Why would people be frightened of a snowman? Ava shrugged, clanking her cuffs. "Some people have no taste. I bet the snowman was brilliant. I wish I'd seen it." She shivered and he noticed.

"You're cold. I'll make you a hot drink." Preacher stood and pulled out the fixings to make hot chocolate. "We are going to have so much fun together, Ava."

CHAPTER FORTY-THREE

The phone rang on Jenna's desk as she headed for the door. She picked up the receiver. "Sheriff Alton."

"Jenna, this is Ty Carter. We have the facial composite of the victim. I emailed it to you. We ran it through a facial recognition program using your three possible suspects and it came back as a match for Zoe Henderson. I passed the information onto Wolfe and Miss Henderson's hometown law enforcement office and they are moving on it as we speak. They'll contact you, once they've notified next of kin. I asked the cops to obtain permission for the release of dental records as well."

Relieved they had a name at last, Jenna made a note in her book. "Thanks, Ty. I really appreciate your help with this case."

"My pleasure." Carter cleared his throat. *"It's a tough one and spread over at least two states. This killer has been busy. I'll contact you if we get a breakthrough and if you want to brainstorm anything, call me any time."*

Jenna looked up as Kane peered in the doorway. She met his gaze and then looked away. "Okay, thanks, Ty. I'll be in touch." She returned the phone to the cradle and looked back at Kane. "We have a positive on our victim. Zoe Henderson. I'll forward the email to you and Rowley and then we'll hunt down when she arrived in town. She would've had to hitchhike, so we'll start at the Triple Z as planned. It's the logical put down place for any local truckers."

"Why would you think that?" Kane leaned against the doorframe pulling on his gloves.

After sending the mail, Jenna led the way outside before answering him. She stepped with caution onto the slippery sidewalk and pulled up the hood of her coat against the chill. "Most trucking companies frown on their drivers giving people rides. It's an insurance issue." She led Kane to his truck and waited for him to brush the snow from the hood and windshield before jumping in the passenger side and turning to him. "They drop people at the Triple Z. There they can get a ride with someone passing through."

"It seems a bit far from town to leave someone in this weather." Kane frowned. "It wouldn't be too difficult to drop them in town." He backed the truck out with care and took off at a snail's pace. "If I was new in town, the first place I'd go is Aunt Betty's but if I was broke, I'd hunt down a soup kitchen or the homeless shelter. No one would risk sleeping rough in this weather."

Jenna stared out the window at the relentless snowfall as Kane negotiated the truck through snowdrifts and onto the brine-covered strip of blacktop. It never ceased to amaze her how people adapted to harsh weather conditions. No matter, rain, snow, or shine, the townsfolk continued with their day-to-day tasks as normal. The wonderful smells drifting from the bakery had wafted past her on the way out making her stomach growl. The cold had returned her appetite with a vengeance. They drove past one of the churches and Jenna dragged her thoughts away from food and turned to Kane. "If someone was homeless or in need of assistance they might go to a church."

"Yeah." Kane headed along Stanton Road. "No questions asked and they often have spare clothes available as well. Some of them run charity shops and have a place for emergency accommodation in their halls. It would be worth checking them out as well."

Jenna stared at the forest in all its wild beauty. The snow-covered branches hung low over blackened trunks. The trails leading inside seemed to vanish into darkness. The stillness broken only by the loud crack of frozen branches tumbling to the ground. She rubbed her hands together. "I think this is going to be the coldest winter yet. It's still a couple of weeks until Christmas and when I first arrived here, the temperature usually dropped to its lowest in February."

"I hope the mayor has the resources to keep the roads clear. We don't want to be snowed in like Jo and Carter." Kane turned onto the on-ramp to the highway. "In this town, the moment we're not around, all hell will break loose."

Jenna looked at him. "If it gets to that stage, we'll get the horses cared for here in town and take up residence at the Cattleman's Hotel. In fact, I might mention the possibility to Mayor Petersham, it would be less expensive to hire more men to drive the snowplows."

"I'd make the call sooner than later." Kane shook his head. "The snow is relentless this year."

The Triple Z lights flashed in the distance turning the stark white patches of snow to red. The parking lot was clear and a line of trucks sat in a neat row at the far end of the lot. Many had no doubt stopped for a meal. Kane parked close to the entrance and Jenna followed him inside. The usual smell of food, beer, and sweat crawled up her nostrils. As they walked through the tables and made their way to the bar, people nudged each other and conversations stopped. She glanced at Kane. "We'll need to blend in slow here and not charge in and start asking questions. The chili is pretty good. We could eat and then speak to people as we leave and make it look like an afterthought. We might get more answers that way and seem less aggressive?"

"You don't have to ask me twice. I'll order." Kane leaned on the bar as the barkeeper came toward them looking anxious. "Coffee and we'll take the chili. We'll sit at the bar."

"Sure." The man relayed the order returning with mugs, cream, and sugar. "It won't be long." He gave them a wary stare. "Anything else I can help you with, Sheriff?"

Jenna slid onto a barstool and pulled off her gloves and hat. "Well, yes there is." She lowered her voice to a conspiratorial whisper. "Have you seen this girl?"

She pulled her phone out of her pocket, scanned the files, and laid the phone down inconspicuously on the counter facing him. "I'll be honest with you. She's the dead girl they found outside the Black Rock Falls newspaper office. She arrived here from Colorado and we'd like to know how she got here. If you've seen her or know who gave her a ride, we need to speak to them. Her killer is a very dangerous man and has been murdering people all over the country." She looked him dead in the eye. "Do the right thing and we'll keep your name out of it."

"I've seen her. She came with a trucker but left with someone else." The barkeeper's eyes flicked from side to side as he wiped the bar. A bell rung and he turned and walked away.

Jenna looked at Kane. "Think we'll get anything else out of him?"

"Maybe, he just doesn't want to be seen talking to us." Kane poured them both a glass of water from a jug on the bar. "Wait and see."

When the barkeeper returned with a tray containing their food and a full coffee pot, Jenna noticed writing on one of the paper napkins. She pulled the small pile toward her and then slid the napkin into her pocket. They ate their meal. It was filling but not as good as Aunt Betty's. She surveyed the room, picking out a table with men conversing over a meal. She turned to Kane. "Those guys look like truckers. We'll go over nice and casual and show them the photo before we leave."

"That was the plan unless you came all this way to eat chili?" Kane chuckled. "Not that I'm complaining but at Aunt Betty's I can have the apple pie as well." He finished his coffee and sighed.

Jenna rolled her eyes. "I'll buy you a whole pie on the way home." She slipped from the seat and pulled bills out of her pocket and dropped them on the counter. "My treat."

She glanced at the men staring at her. "What's wrong now?"

"Now they'll think I'm a very lucky man." Kane grinned at her. "A meal with the boss and she pays. Promise of a pie as well. Now that will make the gossips' tongues wag."

Ignoring Kane's chuckle, she headed for the truckers and pulled out her phone to display the image. "We're looking for anyone who gave a ride to this woman from Colorado. We're not here to arrest anyone, we just need some background on why she was here and where she was heading. Please take a look."

She moved from man to man showing them the image. They shook their heads and then one man shrugged and asked for another look. "I gave her a ride. She said her name was Zoe and she was heading into Black Rock Falls to the women's shelter. She planned to get a job and work there."

Jenna didn't ask for his name in case she spooked him. The company he worked for and his first name were on his jacket. "Did you give her a ride into town?" She pulled out her notebook and took down the details.

"Nope. It was getting late and I was heading to Blackwater and not due in until the morning." The man scratched his head. "I took a room here for the night and bought her a meal but when I headed for the bathroom she'd gone when I returned." He cleared his throat. "She was young, maybe too young to be in here."

"So, you don't know what happened to her?" Kane moved beside Jenna.

"Nope." He shrugged again. "I spent the rest of the evening with one of the boys here and then went to bed."

"He was with me." One of the other men with the name *Jerry* on his jacket looked at Jenna. "I'm Jerry Tonks, we work over at Blackwater. I didn't see the girl but I saw Pete here sitting alone at the bar."

Jenna made notes. "Okay thanks." She handed them both a card. "If you think of anything else, please give me a call."

"The girl, is she in trouble?" Pete looked up at her. "She seemed to be running from something."

After exchanging a glance with Kane, Jenna sighed. "We found her dead this morning. We're trying to trace her next of kin."

She watched the man's surprised expression and then led the way out to Kane's truck. She climbed inside and pulled the napkin from her pocket. She stared at the message. "She left with a member of Devout Sons."

"The motorcycle club out of Blackwater?" Kane started the engine. "They sound like a Christian MC. Maybe she asked them for help?"

Jenna looked at him in disbelief. "Do you honestly believe an eighteen-year-old girl would go up to a gang of bikers and ask for help? In Black Rock Falls—where no one is who he seems? I don't think so."

CHAPTER FORTY-FOUR

Tuesday, Week 2

After an exhausting evening hunting down the clubhouse of the elusive Devout Sons MC, Jenna, Kane and Duke set out for the roadhouse on the highway toward Blackwater. After making a few calls they discovered the president of the club owned the roadhouse. Concerned the club president would close in around his members, Jenna spent the time on the road checking into the background of Oliver Morgan, known as Mad Dog Morgan and everything she could find on the Devout Sons.

She leaned back in her seat and pushed her phone back inside her pocket. "Oliver Morgan served time for rape of a minor. Apparently, he found God in prison and joined the Devout Sons six years ago and worked his way up to president. As far as we know, he hasn't offended again."

"More like he's not been caught." Kane returned his concentration to the highway. "We have investigated pedophiles and a leopard doesn't usually change his spots. Rather he'd join a like-minded pack to keep his activities secret and share his trophies."

Jenna nodded. "That might be why it was so hard to track them down. So if you're correct, we're unlikely to get any cooperation from him at all?"

"On the contrary, he'll be as nice as pie." Kane's mouth turned down. "Don't forget they can't see anything wrong with what they do, they 'love' children." He snorted. "He'll likely give us a name but will make sure the guy knows we're coming and provide him with a rock-solid alibi. It's what they do."

"Will you be able to read him?" Jenna had faith in his skill as a profiler, he hadn't failed her yet. "You usually know if someone is lying."

"Maybe but as I said, they believe they do no harm, so the usual body language I use to tell when they're lying doesn't apply. They're not psychopaths, well, not usually. A psychopath's type of deception is different and they usually run to certain types so are easier for me to understand. Pedophiles have so many faces of evil, they can be loners, run in groups, or any number of small cells. There are some that fall into certain categories but the number of possibilities is endless." Kane flicked her a glance. "I studied the old case files and notes Jo sent me to hone my skills but I have watched her in action. The way she manipulated our last killer to get answers was incredible. She has skills I could only dream about but then she is one of the top FBI behavioral analysts in the country. She'd be able to tear someone like him to shreds."

Jenna sighed. "Then if we believe this biker is a suspect, we pray for a break in the weather. I'm sure the moment it's possible, she'll come and help out."

They turned into the roadhouse and Jenna headed inside as Kane took the opportunity to fill the truck with gas. The parking lot was encircled by a wall of snow and crammed with a variety of vehicles including a bus. Inside the place smelled of hot donuts and coffee. Booth-type seating lined one wall and regular tables and plastic chairs filled the rest of the room. It was surprisingly busy with a variety of people all talking at once. She walked up to the counter and smiled at the gum-chewing sixteen-year-old. "Morning, is Oliver Morgan here today?"

"Yeah, he's in the office." She pointed to a door marked "Private" on the other side of the eating area.

"Thanks." Jenna waited for Kane to walk through the door with Duke on his heels. "He's in the office." She rolled her eyes as she noticed him sniffing the air. The bitter cold had stimulated his appetite to another level of unbelievable and she'd been finding cookies squirrelled away everywhere in the office of late. "We really don't have time to stop to eat here. We'll go by Aunt Betty's for takeout on the way back to the office. We don't know how long the road will be open."

"Sure." Kane shrugged. "I get hungry more often in winter, but with the workouts and the cold weather, I need to eat or I burn muscle."

Jenna stopped in the middle of the restaurant and looked at him. Six-five and at least two hundred and fifty pounds of muscle without one ounce of fat. She'd become so accustomed to his size, and working alongside Wolfe at six-three and Rowley six-two, he seemed normal to her. Until she'd seen him in action at the ski-resort she'd almost forgotten she had a man capable of unarmed deadly force working beside her. She cleared her throat. "Well then, I guess we'd better grab something to go?"

She knocked on the office door and then turned the doorknob, only to find it locked. She heard a gruff voice from inside and long moments passed before the door flew open and a man in his forties, with a tattoo of barbed wire around his neck, glared at them.

"I'm interviewing here." The man seemed to register the "sheriff" logo emblazoned across the front of Jenna's winter jacket and swung his gaze to Kane and then back to her. "Ah... Sheriff, is there a problem?"

Jenna peered past the man to the young girl sitting in a chair before his desk, her face beet-red. Beside her, Kane tensed and she turned to the man. "Oliver Morgan?"

"Yeah. I own this place." Morgan turned to the girl. "Wait outside. Tell Sally to give you a drink. I'll finished the interview when I have spoken to the cops."

The girl hurried out the door and Jenna exchanged a meaningful look with Kane. "Why don't you go and order some takeout? I won't be long."

"Sure." Kane turned slowly and followed the girl toward the counter.

The urge to ask Morgan why he thought it necessary to interview an underage girl with the door locked raged in Jenna, but that could wait. She needed information and alienating him at the get-go would get her nowhere. "I believe your MC was at the Triple Z the other evening and one of your members gave a ride to a young woman? I need to speak to him."

"What makes you think it was one of my boys?" Morgan leaned against his desk and folded his arms across his chest in a typical defensive move.

Jenna shook her head. "I didn't just pluck the name of your MC out of my imagination, Mr. Morgan. We have a ton of witnesses who saw him leave with the girl." She lifted her chin. "I need to know where he set her down. She turned up dead." She sighed. "As the last people to see her alive, you automatically come under my radar. I want a name or I'll have to take you and your boys downtown. I'll do such thorough background checks on the lot of you, I'll know what you ate for breakfast this morning."

"Okay, okay." Morgan held up his hands. "I don't know where he took her. He didn't say, probably the soup kitchen or the shelter. He left then came back sometime later."

Jenna took out her notepad. "What's his name and where do I find him?"

"Axel Reed." He smiled. "He's our minister. Holds a service in our clubhouse every Sunday like clockwork. He lives in Black Rock Falls." He gave out Reed's details. "He's at the soup kitchen today. He works for the charity that runs the place, tomorrow you'll find him hauling donations from the local stores."

"Okay, thanks for your cooperation. There is just one other thing." Jenna made notes and then looked back at him. "The girl is underage. It's inappropriate to have her inside a locked office with you for an interview, especially with your record. Have I made myself clear, Mr. Morgan?"

"You have indeed, Sheriff." Morgan gave her a hard, almost threatening stare. "Perfectly clear."

Jenna pocketed her notebook and turned as Kane moved to her side. "Are we good to go?"

"Yeah. I ordered." Kane was wearing his combat face again. "I need to have a private word with Mad Dog here while the girl is filling my order. Will you take Duke and meet me at the counter?"

"Sure." Jenna turned and noticed the girl from the interview sipping a soda and looking at a business card. She wanted to see what Kane had to discuss with Morgan but he'd stepped inside and the door shut in her face.

She heard a scuffle and a screech as the desk scraped across the floor. Morgan's voice sounded alarmed and Kane's low and deadly. She moved closer and listened.

"If you think you can hide your dirty little secrets from me, you're mistaken. I know what you are and if you lay one finger on that child out there or any others, I'll find out and hunt you down like the dog you are." Kane opened the door but didn't appear and his voice lowered to a whisper. "You won't be able to breathe from now on without me knowing." He moved to the doorway about to leave when Jenna heard Morgan's voice from behind him.

"You won't find nothing to hold up in court." Morgan was breathless and his voice a little too high.

"You won't make it to court." Kane was deathly calm as he turned back.

Jenna heard a body hitting the wall and a moan. She turned and hurried to the counter and although the law enforcement officer in her gnawed at her insides to intervene, she figured Kane had his reasons to threaten Morgan. By the time she'd collected the takeout, Kane was beside her. "Ready?"

"Nope." Kane shrugged. "I have to wash my hands." He headed for the men's restrooms.

As they walked back to his truck, she turned to him. "What did the girl say?"

"You don't want to know, Jenna." Kane opened his truck door for her so she could set the takeout down, and then helped Duke into the back seat.

Jenna climbed in and waited for him to slide behind the wheel. "I need to know and why you roughed up a witness. You don't get cooperation by threatening people."

"He asked that child to, let's say *pleasure* him, to get a couple of hours of work a week." Kane's eyes flashed dangerously. "If she'd agreed to stand up in court and testify against him, I'd have hauled his ass in but she refused. She was barely able to speak to me but I gave her my card and my word to deal with him. She promised to call me if he touches her or anyone else inappropriately." He started the engine. "Sometimes as cops we give warnings rather than tickets. I just gave him a warning is all."

He'd likely scared the man to within an inch of his life but rather than criticize his ethics, Jenna nodded. "Okay. When we get back to the office, I'll send everything we have on Morgan and his MC to Agent Josh Martin. His team is in the Sex Crimes Against Children program. They might place an agent in the MC undercover to find out how deep this goes."

"Martin is a good agent but they have a massive caseload." Kane turned onto the highway. "Where to?"

Jenna dropped a few cookies on the blanket for Duke and then turned to him. "The soup kitchen, to speak to Axel Reed. He's the biker who gave Zoe a ride into Black Rock Falls last Wednesday night. He might be able to tell us where she's been living since then. He is employed by the local charity who runs the soup kitchen and lives in town." She opened the bag of donuts and placed then within Kane's reach. "He's the minister for the MC."

"Do you want me to question him?" Kane bit into a donut and sighed with delight.

Jenna bit back a grin. "No. You show the photograph of Zoe around and see if anyone recognizes her." She stared out the window. "If she made it into town, someone has to have seen her."

CHAPTER FORTY-FIVE

Preacher had seen the girl with the peaches and cream complexion in town many times. He couldn't fathom his attraction toward her but the sight of her stirred something deep inside of him, a hunger no food could satisfy. Maybe it was her faultless symmetry. Her face as perfect as if created from the mind of a great artist. The shape, with high cheekbones and *retroussé* nose, made her look like an earthbound goddess. As he walked from his truck, she slipped from her silver Jeep Cherokee and picked her way across the snow-covered sidewalk, looking almost ethereal in the swirling snow. A strand of blonde hair had escaped from her hood and curled enticingly around one glowing cheek. He loved her eyes—they were as gray as a winter sky. He could imagine her frozen in time, those pretty eyes staring into forever.

He had to have her. She'd never abuse him or leave him and never grow old. He'd keep her in a block of ice and admire her. All he needed was a freezer with a glass door and she would be the centerpiece in his home. She would become a piece of his art he would never share with another soul—not even Ava.

He made his way across the glistening blacktop. The smell of brine and chemicals had tainted the fresh mountain air and he coughed in disgust. He approached her vehicle, then slowed as an eighteen-wheeler came toward him. He dropped his newspaper, slipped out his hunting knife, and using the truck for cover, bent and stabbed the tire. The noise from the rig drowned the hiss of air as the tire deflated. He retrieved his newspaper and followed the girl into Aunt Betty's. She stood at the counter waiting for her order. He stood beside her and smiled when she looked at him. "Have you tried the apple pie?"

"Yeah, it's the best in town." The girl turned back to collect her order and then without a backward glance left the café.

He ordered the pie and a to-go coffee. By the time he'd collected his order, the girl was staring at her vehicle in dismay, her phone in one hand. He placed the takeout in his truck. After wrapping his scarf around his face, he pulled his hood down low and pushed on his sunglasses. He now resembled most of the men in town and crossed the road to her. "Is there a problem?"

"My dad is busy and isn't picking up his phone and neither is my colleague." She pointed to the tire. "I have a flat."

Preacher smiled. Young women were so impatient, and he'd often used that fact to tempt them into his truck. With the digital age, they wanted instant satisfaction and not waiting for a relative or the auto club to help them was usually their downfall. "I'd change it for you but I have a bad back. Where were you heading?"

"Only to the medical examiner's office, not far." She frowned. "I can walk, I guess, but the food will get cold."

Preacher shrugged. "I'm going that way. I'll give you a ride. You can trust me, I'm a minister. What's your name?"

"Emily Wolfe." She smiled. "I—"

"What's happened, Em?" A huge deputy came up behind him.

"Oh, Dave, am I glad to see you." Emily beamed at him. "I have a flat. This man just offered me a ride."

"I see. If you give me your keys, I'll fix it for you. Do you want to grab your things and wait in my truck?" Dave the deputy indicated to a black truck parked a few spots away ahead of her. "Jenna is there. I won't be long."

"Okay." Emily handed over the keys.

As Emily scurried away, Preacher took in the man with an expression carved in stone. He was one of the few people Preacher couldn't read and the deputy's eyes held no clue to his inner thoughts like most people. "Just being neighborly and offering my help to change her tire is all."

"Thanks, but I can handle it from here." The deputy bent to examine the tire and then nodded slowly. He straightened. "Where are you heading?"

Preacher waved a hand to the center of town. "To the library."

"Okay." The deputy examined his face. "Thanks for your concern."

Glad he had his face well-covered, Preacher headed across the blacktop but didn't go back to his truck, he walked slowly up the sidewalk in the direction of the library. He'd missed an opportunity but there would be others. He'd made a connection with Emily Wolfe and the next time they met he'd use the familiarity to gain her trust. He walked on in the snow, changing his stride and leaning a little to the left. Making himself recognizable to a trained law enforcement officer and going straight back to his truck would be a mistake. Deputy Dave would take down his license plate and he was way smarter than that. He glanced over his shoulder to see him still staring after him and gave him a wave. He'd double back and go pick up his truck the moment the deputy turned away. "I'm one step ahead of you, Deputy, and I always will be."

CHAPTER FORTY-SIX

Perplexed, Jenna turned in her seat but couldn't see why Kane had pulled in and dashed off without explanation. She moved to follow him and then noticed Emily heading toward her, looking upset. When she climbed into the back seat, dropped bags of takeout, and hugged Duke, Jenna looked at her. "What's going on?"

"I got a flat." Emily shook the snow off her hat and looked forlorn. "A guy offered me a ride and I was just going to refuse when Dave stepped in. I guess he's going to call Miller's Garage and get someone out to change it." She blew out a long sigh. "Poor man, Dave frightened him to death and he said he was a minister."

Jenna frowned. "Minister or not, with a possible serial killer in town you wouldn't be stupid enough to get a ride with a stranger, would you?"

"Oh, doh!" Emily rolled her eyes in an exaggerated manner. "I do autopsies on murder victims; do you honestly believe I'd be that dumb?"

"I guess not." Jenna changed the subject. "Is the autopsy on the latest victim on schedule for this afternoon?"

"If I ever get back with the food, it will be." Emily sighed. "I guess I can reheat it in the microwave."

"Yes, that would work." Jenna leaned back in her seat. "Anything interesting happening in the world of forensic science lately?"

They chatted for a while about the new sample-testing equipment Wolfe had purchased for the lab and the different techniques she had learned over the past month.

"It's very intensive most of the time." Emily suddenly smiled. "Did you know, Dad has a real neat coffee machine in his office now? It makes a real nice cappuccino. When you drop by later, I'll make you one."

Jenna laughed. "I'll look forward to it." She glanced up as Kane tapped on Emily's window and then opened the door.

"I changed the tire." He reached in and collected the takeout bags. "Come on, I'll walk you back to your Jeep."

"Catch you later." Emily smiled at her and followed Kane into the swirling snow and out of view.

Duke whined and Jenna laughed at him and rubbed his ears. "Did smelling that takeout make you hungry? You're as bad as Kane."

It was some time before Kane got back to the truck and dropped something heavy in the back. Inquisitive, Jenna looked at him. "You could've called Miller's to send someone out."

"To change a tire?" Kane shook his head. "It took no time at all but I'm taking the tire to Wolfe. It looks like it's been slashed."

Concerned, she turned in her seat. "Who would do that?"

"I'm not sure but some guy was hanging around." Kane shrugged. "Maybe he was just being neighborly but these days it's hard to trust a stranger approaching a young woman alone and offering her a ride." He gave her a long look. "It's not because I don't believe Em is capable of taking care of herself, I do, but when I saw that guy hanging all over her, I did get a little overprotective." He sighed. "I just care about Wolfe's kids, you know."

Jenna smiled at him. "She is your best friend's daughter and part of our family. Of course, you're protective. She's still a little girl in your eyes but you must remember, she's a grown woman now and she's seen her fair share of murder. Trust me, she'd never climb into a stranger's vehicle."

"That's the problem, they don't necessarily have to agree to take a ride with our current killer." Kane frowned. "From the evidence of drugs in the victim's blood, he could have them subdued and inside his vehicle before anyone noticed."

"Well, if he was up to no good, he's using a trick to put people at ease." Jenna raised one eyebrow as she looked at him. "He told Em he is a minister."

"She didn't mention that to me." The nerve in Kane's cheek twitched. "You mean that could've been Reed?"

"Maybe. I'll pull up his driver's license." She went to work on her phone and then held up the screen. "Well?"

"I couldn't say, he had his face covered." Kane examined the image. "He's the right height at least but he was bundled up against the cold and wearing sunglasses. He said he was heading for the library but he'd go right past the soup kitchen."

Jenna took back her phone. "Let's go see if Reed is there. As far as we know he's the last person to have seen Zoe alive. He could easily be our man but Em isn't the killer's usual type so maybe we're worrying about nothing." She peered out the window at the swirling snow. "The soup kitchen isn't far and we could walk from here."

"Nah." Kane looked over one shoulder and then moved the truck onto Main. "I can't leave Duke in the truck without the heat on. We'll get closer and take him with us." He smiled at her. "The great thing about being with the sheriff is that I can park anywhere and never get a ticket."

They drove about a hundred yards down Main and Kane pulled into a service alleyway beside the building. Jenna pulled up her hood and ducked outside into the cold, pulling on her gloves. The sidewalk was dusted with snow and although a good coating of salt had been scattered around, the blizzard-like conditions were making the slippery pavers treacherous underfoot. Narrowly avoiding a collision with two women carrying overflowing shopping bags, she reached the soup kitchen and pushed open the door. Duke sped inside past her. The dog shook himself vigorously, ears spinning like a windmill and sending snow flying in all directions.

It seemed that no matter what time of day she walked into the place, there was a line of people waiting to be fed. The food smelled delicious and made her stomach growl. Soup kitchen was a misnomer for this charity. Hot meals were available from six in the morning until eleven at night. They included soup, a hearty chili or casserole made from donated meat, usually from elk or deer hunters, a selection of vegetables, pies, and cookies from the Women's Association. She stamped her feet on the hessian sacks at the front door and turned to Kane. "I'll speak to Axel Reed. You go and talk to everyone. See if anyone recognized Zoe. She had to be staying around here somewhere."

"Or the killer had her holed up in his house." Kane shrugged. "I hope not." He turned away.

Jenna scanned the cafeteria for one of the supervisors. Noticing a woman she recognized, she eased her way through the people milling around or sitting at the rows of tables. "Hey, Jenny, nice to see you." She pulled out her phone. "Have you seen this girl?"

"No, I don't think so but with everyone bundled up against the cold, everyone looks the same of late." She smiled at Jenna.

"Do you keep a list of who works here or helps out?" Jenna pulled out her notebook. "I assume you work in shifts?"

"I can tell you who is on salary but not the volunteers, they sometimes come for an hour or two and leave. They're in and out all the time. Do you have a day in mind? I could ask the office to email you a copy."

Behind her, she could hear Kane asking in a clear loud voice if anyone had seen Zoe. She nodded. "Yes please. Last Wednesday evening between say nine and closing would help." Jenna kept her voice conversational. "Is Axel Reed in today?"

"Yeah. Is there a problem?" Jenny frowned. "He is employed here and a good worker."

Jenna shook her head. "He's not in any trouble. What does he do here?"

"He collects food donations and enters them into our stock list. He'll be in the storeroom out back." She turned to a man carrying a large steaming pot to the people serving. "Josiah, when you've put that down, can you take the sheriff back and introduce her to Axel?"

"Sure." Josiah placed the pot into the serving area, wiped his hands on his apron and smiled. "He came in just before, he's out back."

The man's name, seemed familiar and then dropped into place. He was the driver working for the trucking company out of Blackwater. She couldn't believe her luck. "Are you Josiah Brock?"

"That's me." Josiah gave her a slow smile. "Am I in trouble, Sheriff?"

"Not at all but you can clear up something for me." Jenna took out her notebook. "I know you work out of Blackwater but do you recall driving a rig with Claude Grady any time in the last year?"

"Maybe, I'd have to check the logs. We have driven to Colorado, Utah, and Wyoming, so it's hard to remember. I've driven with him in the past a few times but I own my own rig now, so I go where they pay me the best rates." He glanced away for a beat and then turned his attention back to her. "Why?"

Jenna stared at him. "We have been looking into truckers who drive to all those places regular, and with refrigerated trucks. Your name came up in a conversation."

"I don't know why. I don't own a reefer." Josiah pushed a hand through his hair. "Claude drives one regular but he'll be on downtime like me at the moment until the roads clear."

Jenna made a few notes and then looked back at him. "Are you employed here too?"

"Nope, I just help out from time to time." Josiah shrugged. "I like the company."

Jenna showed him the image of Zoe on her phone and watched his face carefully. "Do you know her or have you seen her in here at any time?"

"Can't say that I have but we have a ton of young people in here lately. I could've missed her." He lifted his gaze back to her. "Do you want me to take you to Axel now?"

Jenna nodded. "Yeah thanks." She had another thought. "Where do you live?"

"I have a cabin out Snowberry Way. It's only a small place but it's home." Josiah led the way through the kitchen to a storeroom, where a man was checking boxes and making notes on a clipboard. "Axel, the sheriff wants a word with you." He turned to leave. "Nice to meet you." He gave them a wave and went back to the kitchen.

When Axel turned around, he tried unsuccessfully to hide his concerned expression at the sight of her and leaned casually against the wall. Jenna lifted her chin and took in the tall, lean, muscular man wearing a leather jacket with his MC's colors on the back. "Axel Reed? I'm Sheriff Alton. I spoke to Mr. Morgan this morning and he mentioned last Wednesday night you were at the Triple Z Bar. You gave a ride to a young woman by the name of Zoe Henderson. Do you remember her?" She took out her phone and accessed the file with Zoe's photograph and showed it to him.

"Yeah, I gave her a ride." He swiped the back of his hand over his nose. "She was hitchhiking with a trucker who planned to stay overnight. I figure he wanted her to stay with him and stepped in to offer her an alternative."

"And exactly what was your alternative?" Jenna eyeballed him. "We'd like to know where she's been living since last Wednesday night."

"I dropped her here at the service alleyway and told her to go inside and ask one of the supervisors to call the women's shelter, so she'd have a bed for the night." Axel frowned. "I haven't seen her since. She hasn't been by for a meal so I assumed she'd moved in there."

Jenna slid her phone inside her pocket. "We found her body outside the newspaper office on Monday morning."

"She's dead?" Axel shook his head. "So young."

It seemed a strange reaction from him. Most people would ask how she died and be inquisitive. She gave him a direct stare. "Where were you on Sunday night?"

"I went out to Mad Dog's Roadhouse for dinner and played cards most of the night." He shrugged. "Why don't you ask him?"

Jenna watched him closely, noting his folded arms and defensive stance. He was hiding something. "When you dropped Zoe in town, what direction was she heading when you last saw her?"

"I don't recall." Axel lifted his gaze to her. "She climbed off my bike, handed me the helmet, and I stowed it in my saddlebags. When I looked back, she'd gone. I assumed she'd walked in here."

"I see." Jenna stared at her notebook and then back at him. "Do you own a hunting cabin?"

"No, I don't own a cabin but I do go hunting and sometimes use a cabin from time to time, like most folks around here."

Jenna turned as Kane walked back into the room and beckoned her. "Okay thanks, Mr. Reed. I'll be on my way."

She walked to Kane's side. "What have you got for me?"

"Two of the men I spoke to remember seeing Zoe on Wednesday night just before this place closed." Kane pulled her into the hallway. "They didn't see her getting off a motorcycle but recall her speaking to a man—tall is all they remembered and perhaps, white. They said she walked with him in the direction of the church."

"Which church?" Jenna looked up at him. "The Evangelical Center would've been closed at that hour. Maybe she headed to the Catholic church?"

"The EC." Kane turned his woolen cap around in his hands. "She was heading right and the Catholic church is to the left." He frowned. "The men I spoke to were inside until closing and then headed in the same direction to sleep."

Surprised, Jenna shook her head. "There's nowhere to sleep up there. Most head in the other direction."

"I asked them the same question." Kane pulled his woolen cap down over his red-tipped ears. "They bunk down out back of the town hall. There's an outbuilding out there, Mayor Petersham arranged to leave it open and supplies mattresses and blankets. There're a few necessities in there and heat. Apparently, it's not well-known and a few of the regulars here use it when the shelters are full."

Jenna met his gaze. "They would've walked right past the EC?"

"Yeah, they said they left a few minutes after she went past. It was snowing bad but they didn't see her or the man but they did see taillights." Kane glanced at the door to the storeroom and signaled with a finger over his lips for her to be quiet.

Jenna followed his gaze and picked out the shadow of someone eavesdropping in the doorway. She nodded and raised her voice but held up a hand for Kane to wait. She needed to find out if Reed was listening. "Okay then we're done here. We'll head up to the women's shelter and see if she arrived there."

She made a walking motion with her fingers and then grabbed her throat to tell Kane to surprise Reed, or whoever was listening so intently to their conversation. At Kane's nod, they turned back and moved silently toward the storeroom. There was a slight scuffle as Kane pounced. Jenna peered into the storeroom to see Reed up against the wall, hands firmly behind his back. She looked at him.

"Okay, Mr. Reed. Why the interest in our conversation? Is there something you're not telling us?"

"Ouch! No, I've told you everything I know." Reed looked over his shoulder at her. "I'm a preacher. I wouldn't hurt her. I was trying to help her. Let go of me, I haven't done anything wrong."

Jenna shot a look at Kane's hard expression and then back to Reed. "Was that you on Main earlier helping a young woman with a flat tire?"

"I was on Main earlier, yeah, but I didn't see no woman with a flat tire." Reed looked at her. "But I would've stopped if I'd seen her. Why?"

"Never mind. Where's your coat?" Kane released his grip and stepped away. "Show me."

"Okay, okay. It's in the locker room drying out." Reed rubbed his arms as he led the way to a steamy locker room and indicated to a row of coats, some still glistening with snow. "That's mine." He pointed to a dark coat and scarf much the same as the other four hanging on pegs dripping puddles on the floor.

"Do you wear sunglasses?" Kane was examining the coats.

"Yeah, like just about everyone in town who doesn't want snow blindness." He shook his head. "It's hard to drive without them."

Jenna looked at Kane and he gave the slightest shrug. It was obvious he couldn't ID the man who'd spoken to Emily. She turned her attention back to Reed. "The supervisor mentioned you collect donations. How do you do that on your motorcycle?"

"I have a truck." Reed turned and led the way back to the storeroom and then pulled up a roller door. A gush of freezing air and snowflakes rushed in making the storeroom resemble a snow globe. Outside, parked in front of Kane's truck, was a white pickup with a hard tonneau cover.

"How do you transport perishables?" Kane stared at the truck.

"It's not a problem in winter but in summer, I have a refrigerator that slides right in there. The power connection is at the back." Reed looked at him and shook his head. "Take a look, I don't have anything to hide. Do you mind if I get back to work now?"

Jenna nodded. "Sure, thank you for your time." She led the way out into the cafeteria section and looked at Kane. "Was it him with Emily?"

"Same height and the voices are similar, both men are locals." He glanced at her. "He seems a little too cooperative, maybe you can sweet talk him into allowing Wolfe to take a few swabs from inside his refrigerator?"

"Me?" Jenna looked at him in disbelief. "It wasn't my charm that made him talk, you almost popped his arms out the sockets."

"Well, I could if I'd wanted to but I didn't. It was well within the guidelines of restraint; I can assure you. It worked, didn't it?" Kane snorted. "I hope he's on our list. I don't trust him."

Jenna nodded. "Me either and he's one to watch for sure."

CHAPTER FORTY-SEVEN

After making a short visit to the shelters and showing Zoe's photograph with no result, Jenna discovered that after leaving Axel Reed, the young woman had apparently vanished into thin air. She hunted down Claud Grady again to establish his whereabouts on the previous Wednesday night, the last time Zoe was seen alive. He seemed vague and uncooperative. "Mr. Grady, it was only last Wednesday, surely you remember where you were?"

"I wasn't here, I dropped some donated coats to the soup kitchen and then went home, I think?" Grady looked at his hands. "I'm not sure."

Jenna made some notes. "Okay, where were you on Sunday night?"

"Here, helping out, and then I went home." Grady shrugged. "I live alone, Sheriff, you'll have to take my word for it."

"When you drive to Utah or Wyoming do you often give hitchhikers a ride?" Kane looked down his nose at him.

"Yeah, we all do. They're good company." Grady shrugged. "Anyone who tells you otherwise is a liar."

Jenna nodded. "Okay, thank you for your time." She looked at Kane. "Let's go. I need to drop by Aunt Betty's before we head back to the office."

Despondent and not looking forward to witnessing Zoe's autopsy in a couple of hours, Jenna purchased a pile of takeout from Aunt

Betty's, climbed into Kane's truck, and they headed back to the sheriff's department. It was good to be inside out of the cold. They shucked their coats and Kane waved Rowley into her office. In a few minutes, Jenna had brought him up to speed with their investigation. She took a bite of her hotdog and stood to enter information on the whiteboard. After adding Axel Reed to her persons of interest list, she sat back down and sipped her coffee. "We have no proof that either of these men are involved." She picked up the hotdog, viewed it with dislike, removed the sausage from the bun, and tossed it to Duke. "But we have made a case on circumstantial evidence before, and so far, Reed was the last person to see her alive."

"He could easily be the same man who asked Em to take a ride with him." Kane pushed a slice of peach pie toward Jenna. "If I'd seen his eyes, I would've been able to make a positive ID."

"It is suspicious but people do help out each other here." Rowley scratched his cheek. "It may be innocent enough."

Jenna took a bite of the pie and sighed. She had some idea why Kane was addicted to fruit pies. Fresh and warm from the oven, they were delicious. She dragged her mind away from pies and swallowed. "Ah, we're attending an autopsy this afternoon. Do you want to come or are you still hunting down truckers?"

"No thanks. I have a ton of work here." Rowley grimaced. "I did look into the routes used by the long-haul trucking companies and all in the surrounding counties cover Wyoming, Utah, and Colorado, which makes life a little more complicated. I've also been hunting down truckers with cabins or ranches in the area. There are over a hundred and most of them are snowed in but I drove out to two of them. Both were locked up tight for the winter. There're quite a few truckers with ranches. I planned to check some of them out this afternoon unless you need me here?"

"Do the owners fit the profile?" Kane looked at him. "White male, late thirties to early forties, travels out of the state for work or pleasure?" He shrugged. "Well, that's my take on him. We'll contact Jo and see what else she has to offer on the profile of The Sculptor but I figure checking out those over fifty is a waste of time. I know it's a myth that all serial killers are loners but due to the nature of the crimes, I figure this guy lives alone in an isolated area."

Jenna looked across the desk. "He'd be nonthreatening and look like an ordinary Joe. Or he has an angle that makes women trust him from the get-go. He must speak to the women he kills to get their confidence. It looks like Zoe got a ride to her death willingly. The men from the soup kitchen were minutes away from her and if she'd screamed, they'd have heard her."

"We have time. I'll run this past Jo now, if she's in the office. I'll put my phone on speaker." Kane pulled out his phone and made the call. She answered on the third ring.

"Agent Wells."

"Hey Jo, it's Dave Kane. Do you have time to run through the profile of The Sculptor with me? The gang's all here sans Shane."

"Sure, I've worked up a victimology as well that might help. I've only just received the final search results." Jo tapped away on her computer keyboard. *"Okay, we compared appearance of the victims across all of the kills we assume can be attributed to The Sculptor, including Zoe Henderson. The database picked up a ton of similar victims. From what I'm seeing, we may have underestimated the number of women he's murdered."*

"How so?" Kane raised one dark eyebrow and looked at Jenna.

"I'll explain in a moment but first, we need to discuss the killer's MO. I've collected all the data of similar cases going back over ten years, and factored in your conclusions and observations. I have a list. I'll email you a copy now.

All their cellphones chimed an incoming message at the same time.

1. *He kills to type. Dark hair, five-five, slim build, and all have tattoos of some description.*
2. *The women are all loners, runaways, and either on the streets or living in shelters. Very few have been listed as missing persons which would confirm this.*
3. *I believe the kills are opportunistic, or very close to it. He sees the woman that fits his need and then strikes soon after.*
4. *Strangulation, from the front, eye-to eye up and personal is favored but he will shoot them in the back, if they try to escape.*
5. *No sexual assault.*
6. *From the autopsy reports, all the women were well-nourished. Seeing as they were homeless, this suggests they were held for a time before he murdered them.*
7. *No torture evident.*
8. *Freezing, winter or ice is evident in all the cases.*
9. *Posing the frozen victim at first and then escalating to displaying body parts, as Dave suggested as his art.*
10. *All victims are naked, clean, and without any trace evidence.*
11. *He uses a chainsaw.*
12. *He uses Super Glue on all his victims to create an expression.*
13. *Traces of Rohypnol, the date-rape drug found in all victims over the last five years.*

Jenna scanned the list Jo had sent and nodded. "Yeah, these are the same conclusions we had but how many victims and when did this start?"

"I'll hand you over to Carter." Jo cleared her throat. *"He has that info."*

"Hi Jenna, we're talking hundreds across the country but I believe we have found a starting point out at Blackwater. I went back a bit

*further just in case. Eighteen years ago, Delores Garcia, seventeen, went
missing early December. She was found the following March after the
melt. Naked and posed, her eyes pulled open with duct tape and her
mouth pulled back in a smile. Apart from using the glue, it was the
same as the Zoe Henderson case. In fact when I send you the crime scene
photographs, you'll be surprised at the resemblance."*

A tingle slid down Jenna's spine. If the killer started in Blackwater,
he could be close by and not passing through as she'd hoped. "And
the others?"

"There seemed to be a hiatus for about four years." Jo's voice came
through the speaker. *"Which, for a psychopath, isn't unusual. They
can start slow and escalate or stop altogether. Most times, once they
start escalating, they find it difficult to stop unless they have something
to take its place. In this case I would assume something substantial
intervened to put his need to kill on hold. An event could have triggered it again or whatever was preventing him killing, ended."* She
sucked in a breath. *"So, include this data when you're hunting down
suspects. Getting back to the victims, Kalo is entering the updated data
into the computer and we'll have a more accurate list soon. The main
concentration of victims have been discovered in Utah and Wyoming,
so you can leave them to us."*

Jenna nodded. "If he's using the snow to cover his tracks, those
would be the places to go." She lifted her cup and sipped the now
tepid coffee. "If he's been living in Utah or Wyoming, perhaps the
current cold spell here drew him to Black Rock Falls?"

"Just a minute." Kane cleared his throat. "Four years—that could
be a jail term or he could've enlisted in the military."

*"Exactly, and something we'll look into. If he's active in Black Rock
Falls now, that is your priority. We're handling the cases of the last two
victims, so you don't have to worry about them."* Jo took a breath.
"Okay, now getting back to his profile. We discussed age. Kane and I

both agree the killer must be in good shape and mid to late thirties. I figure he started early, maybe at high school. He knew his victim and she was the first trigger to his psychopathy. Something happened between them, maybe he loved her and she didn't see him as a friend or lover. This would be why he's gluing their eyes open. He's making her see him. The smile is what he craves from her. I believe every kill is Delores Garcia."

"So why is he killing all over the country? Most serial killers operate within certain boundaries. They have a comfort zone." Kane leaned on the desk and stared at the phone. "He had that in Blackwater, so what made him start killing all over?"

"We don't know where he lived after the four-year break but we're searching everything we have to find men from Blackwater who lived in Utah or Wyoming. Their comfort zone extends around their home or work, and is their anchor point. They usually kill in familiar areas and only extend if they haven't been caught. In their minds they likely believe they are doing the world a favor and they'll never get caught. On the other hand, if this man travels extensively, his comfort zone expands accordingly."

Jenna nodded in agreement. "Yes, we have dealt with that type before. Kane suggests a white male who lives alone, do you agree?"

"That is a stereotype that doesn't apply to all psychopathic serial killers but in this case, I agree with Kane. If he has a wife and children or lives with his folks, he'd require a separate place to keep his victims and wouldn't risk allowing his family to see the other side of him. People like this usually lead a double life, the killer side and the family side. Very few families are aware of a killer in their midst." Jo sighed. *"I know you're both mindful of the other traits: he slides unnoticed into his environment, has a good job, gets on with everyone. That seems to be a given with most of them."*

"Yeah, we came up with the same profile." Kane smiled at Jenna. "Thank you for your time. I'll send you our updates as they occur."

"Hey guys before you go, it's Carter again." Ty Carter sounded excited. *"We're trying to clean up the CCTV footage from outside the newspaper office. I'll call you if we find anything."*

Jenna smiled. "Great, thanks." She waited a beat. "You still there, Jo?"

"Yeah. It's been great speaking to you all." Jo cleared her throat. *"There is one other thing. The posing of Zoe Henderson the same as Delores Garcia marked the beginning of a new cycle. He posed her at the newspaper office because he craves notoriety. If he isn't satisfied by the response, he'll commit an atrocity."*

Jenna gripped her cup so tight it groaned. "Worse than he has already?"

"Yeah, and it's going to happen in the next forty-eight hours."

CHAPTER FORTY-EIGHT

Preacher had gotten hot food from Aunt Betty's and now sat opposite Ava at the kitchen table. He'd take it slow with her as he needed to test her trust. He'd started by giving her clothes and then as she showed her loyalty to him had released both her hands during meals with him. He wasn't anyone's fool and kept his Glock on the table and her feet securely chained to the floor. "Eat your burger."

"It's delicious, thank you, Preacher." Ava nibbled at the bun, her long fingers caressing it in her small hands. "You're very kind to me."

Preacher liked it when she held eye contact and smiled at him. He hadn't cared to become involved with a woman since Delores but Ava seemed different somehow. She greeted him when he came home as if she genuinely was glad to see him. The problem was, he couldn't push away the need to strangle her. Every time she displayed her long white neck, his fingers tingled to enclose it and squeeze. Yet he enjoyed the company. It had been good to have someone to talk to, someone who didn't scream or beg. He wanted her to be free but she'd run away again. If he became bored with her, he'd let her go just for the sport. The thought of hunting her down and killing her excited him but he pushed it down and ate his meal.

"You went down to the cellar before, is Isabella still down there?" Ava nibbled on one of her fries.

"You mean Delores." Preacher picked up a remote control and accessed the split screen to find his last Delores, zooming in on her.

He indicated to the screen. "Yeah, it looks like she hasn't attempted to escape. She follows the rules and gets the privileges."

"I'm sorry I tried to escape." Ava looked at him from below her lashes. "I thought you were going to rape me or sell me into slavery."

His gaze moved over her, examining her eyes. He could tell when people were telling the truth. "I don't rape women. I think rape is disgusting and I wouldn't sell a woman. I love women." At her sigh of relief and relaxing of posture, he changed the subject and gave her a slow smile. "Did you know, I use a chainsaw to create ice sculptures and then display them all over. One of my pieces was mentioned on TV just the other night."

"Ice sculptures as well as making Delores into a snowman?" Ava smiled at him. "You must be very talented. I'd love to watch you sometime."

Preacher contemplated Ava's request. He needed to make a statement piece, a showstopper with Delores but he didn't have too much time to arrange things and scope out a suitable site to display her. The blizzard-like conditions wouldn't last more than another couple of days. The weather forecast predicted a lull in the snowfall for next week. He needed the snow to cover his tracks and confuse any CCTV cameras he may have missed. In the nighttime, during heavy snowfall, any footage picked up by CCTV cameras distorted and appeared more like background radiation. To speed things along so Ava could watch him, he'd have to start with Delores alive. Maybe fix her eyes and her mouth before he silenced her screams. He nodded absently. "Okay, I'll allow you to watch me create my next piece but first you have to do something to prove your loyalty to me."

"Sure." Ava met his gaze. "Anything you want. I like being here with you."

Preacher chuckled. "That's nice."

"What do you want me to do?" Ava leaned forward, obviously interested.

Preacher would need time to think of a special test for her. "I'll tell you later."

CHAPTER FORTY-NINE

"Will we ever catch this maniac?" Jenna unclipped her seatbelt and turned to Kane. The tip of his nose was red from the cold and he looked tired. "He's eluded law enforcement all over and we have circumstantial evidence and only two potential suspects."

"Two potentials are good." Kane pulled up his hood over his woolen cap. "More would be a problem. We can keep eyes on two far easier than ten or so." He sighed. "I just wish the sketchy CCTV footage from the newspaper office had yielded more than a shadow but at least we have the time the killer dumped the body."

Jenna pulled on her gloves. "Yeah, which makes me wonder if he lives somewhere as isolated as you imagine. How did he get her into town at five in the morning? The roads would've been impassable." She blinked as a thought occurred to her. "Oh, don't tell me he's a snowplow driver?"

"Or he drives a powerful truck with a snowplow attachment like mine?" Kane shrugged. "That's possible but hundreds of guys have those in Black Rock Falls and if anyone had seen him, they wouldn't have taken much notice." He looked at her. "As he seems to move around so easily in the snow, I'd say we add that possibility to our list. I'll check out the snowplow route times, they've been running twelve hours a day lately. He might have just followed one through town."

"Good idea." Jenna stared at the ME's office door and sighed. "Let's get this over with. I want to get home before I drop from exhaustion. It's been a very long day."

The thought of attending another autopsy of a young woman soured Jenna's belly. She climbed out the truck and headed for the cleared and well salted pathway to Wolfe's office. She scanned her card on the door to the morgue. Inside, the sadly familiar smell of antiseptic, menthol and death greeted her. As they headed down the long, tiled corridor their footsteps sounded irreverently loud. The morgue wasn't like a hospital. It was so quiet and she found herself dropping her voice in respect to the dead. This part of the building unlike the pathology labs and Wolfe's office area, gave Jenna a feeling of hopelessness, as if all was lost.

Jenna removed her coat and hung it on a peg outside the morgue. She stuffed her gloves and hat inside her pockets. An inexorable feeling of helplessness drifted over her as she took gloves and a mask from Kane.

"What is it?" Kane turned to her and grabbed her shoulders. "Are you coming down with something?"

Jenna shook her head. "No, I'm fine." She tried to smile but her lips quivered. "It's just all the people who have died on my watch. I feel responsible is all."

"You didn't kill them, Jenna." Kane rubbed her arms but his eyes held a sorrow she hadn't seen before. "You nearly died a few days ago and you've been going hell for leather since without a break. Most people would take days to recover from an overdose and you went back to work the next day. I'm not surprised you're stressed."

"I wasn't in a coma." Jenna didn't want an excuse. "Kim was a nurse and she just kept me under. I figure she planned to let me freeze to death. Wolfe used two doses of Naloxone and I was fully alert before I left the cabin."

"You had no pulse." Kane looked distraught. "I thought you'd died. Thank God Wolfe was there. I made a mistake, Jenna, that could've cost you your life."

Unable to understand the emotion moving through him, she swallowed hard. "What mistake?"

"When that guy was leaning over you, I just picked him up and threw him at the wall. I felt for a pulse in your neck and found nothing, not even a flicker. You were cold and limp. I wanted to kill the man who'd hurt you but before I could do anything, Wolfe ripped open your coat and listened to your chest. Only then, he gave you the Naloxone." A nerve in Kane's cheek twitched. "My fingers were numb from the cold. I missed your pulse and should have administered the spray. You nearly died because of me."

"It wasn't your fault. You didn't drug me. I—"

There was a whoosh as a door slid open.

"When you two have finished gazing into each other's eyes. I have an autopsy to perform." Wolfe looked from one to the other with his eyebrows raised in question. "It's getting late and if you're planning on following the snowplow home we'd better get started."

Jenna followed Wolfe into the room, pulling on her mask as she went. She nodded to Emily and Colt before stopping at the undraped body of Zoe Henderson. She pushed all doubts from her mind. She'd find her killer if it was the last thing she'd do. "Okay, what can you tell me about Zoe Henderson?" She waited patiently for Wolfe to start the recorder.

"Caucasian female, five-five, of average weight for her age, and in good physical condition." He glanced at her over his mask. "She has pierced ears and tattoos all of which have been photographed and catalogued. All internal organs are normal weight and size, she ate a meal of eggs, toast, and coffee approximately two hours before death. I found traces of Rohypnol the date-rape drug in her system. I tested specifically for this drug as it was found in the other victims but have completed a full tox screen." He indicated to the X-rays on a screen. "From the X-rays no head trauma is evident but there is damage to the hyoid bone and bruising consistent to strangulation from the front. Thumb prints are evident over the larynx and there is a stretching of the tendons in the region to suggest the killer lifted the victim off her feet during the attack. I found slight bruising on the forearms consistent with defense wounds. I would suggest Miss Henderson fought back, although I found nothing under her nails."

The idea her killer might be injured would eliminate both her suspects. "So what are we looking for here? How much damage did she inflict?"

"She wouldn't have been able to make many hits. Let me demonstrate." Kane turned to Jenna and grabbed her shirtfront. "If I keep my elbows out, it would be hard to get a punch in especially if you can't breathe and your feet are off the floor." He glanced at Wolfe. "Do you agree?"

"Yeah." Wolfe indicated to the bruising on the neck. "The killer has above-average-sized hands and exerted pressure on both carotid arteries. It only takes eleven pounds of pressure for ten seconds to render a person unconscious, so she wouldn't have had time to fight for long." He sighed. "He would have needed to hold the grip for four to five minutes to assure brain death. This type of strangulation is very personal, most who use it don't realize that unless the pressure is continued a person will revive in ten seconds. Most killers prefer to use a cord and from behind so they can perhaps use a knee in the back to increase the pressure and completely close off the trachea but, whatever method, brain death would still occur in the same time."

Jenna looked with compassion at Zoe's staring eyes and gruesome twisted smile. "Will you be able to remove the glue before her parents see her?"

"No need." Wolfe shook his head.

"They're not coming." Emily's eyes flashed. "Pigs. They don't even want to ship her body home. They just sent a check to cover the funeral expenses."

A wave of sadness flowed over Jenna. "I'll make the arrangements." She gathered herself and looked at Wolfe. "Any signs of sexual assault?"

"No, and no recent activity." Wolfe looked at Jenna. "My conclusions are Zoe Henderson died of cardiac arrest due to asphyxiation. She was murdered approximately last Saturday, posed, and frozen within half an hour of her death. This murder is different from the others. No mutilation or severing of limbs. I think he was in a hurry and wanted her out there on Monday morning for all to see. He wanted the press involved."

"He's craving attention and getting clumsy." Kane glanced at Jenna. "The media played down the murder, so if he follows the pattern of behavior Jo suggested, he's going to go all out next time."

Who would be next? Would it be someone from her town, a friend or neighbor's child? Jenna couldn't stand the thought and shook her head in dismay. "We have to stop him, Kane. We have to stop him now!"

CHAPTER FIFTY

Wednesday, Week 2

After eating breakfast sitting on her bed, Ava listened intently to the roar of a truck engine returning to the ranch house. Preacher hadn't been gone for long this time, maybe an hour or so. She had no clock in her room, which made life difficult. Often, he fed her and went out for hours at a time. She never knew when he would return. At first, she'd searched for a way out of her room but there was no escape, Preacher had her room locked up tight. She'd screamed out for Isabella but heard nothing. Heck, she didn't even know if she was still alive. Preacher never mentioned her at all. The time alone was driving her crazy, no books, nothing to read, nothing to do so she'd spent the time exercising. If she built up her stamina, she'd have a better chance against him—if she ever escaped.

Trembling with fear as the key turned in the lock, she moved away from the bed and tried to compose herself. Preacher was a man of many moods and the slightest thing could set him off. Images of Zoe's dangling arm as he placed her in the meat locker played in her mind in a loop. To stay alive, Preacher would have to see her as a person and so far, she'd achieved one small step in the right direction. He was at least using her name now. The more she could gain his confidence, the more chance she had of escaping.

As the door swung open, he stood some ways back, holding a gun on her, his black eyes cold and expressionless. Under his gaze, fear like she'd never experienced before strangled her. If she appeared to be afraid, he would feed on it and want more. It took every ounce of willpower not to cower in his presence. Fixing a smile on her face, she looked at him bundled up in his winter gear with snowflakes melting on his heavy hoodie. The smell of winter drifted in the room and she suddenly craved fresh air. "It's still snowing, I see."

"Yeah." Preacher looked at her as if assessing her. "I have a test for you. If you pass, I'll allow you to watch me create my next artwork. If you enjoy it as much as I do, you'll be free to roam the house." His mouth twitched into a smile. "I may even take you out hunting with me."

Unnerved by his overenthusiasm, Ava nodded, but inside she knew there'd be a catch. "Okay, what do you want me to do?"

"I want you to ride into town with me." Preacher brought up his gun and aimed it at her face. "Be mindful that I'll have this trained on you the entire time. I'll fit a suppressor on it, so if you try to escape my truck, I'll kill you and then drop your body down a mineshaft for the rats to eat. No one will hear, no one will care."

The way his eyes had changed unnerved Ava. It was as if he was daring her to escape just so he could kill her. She swallowed her fear and nodded. "That sounds like a fair bargain. I won't try to escape, Preacher. Is there anything else I can do to prove it to you?"

"Maybe." He gave a curt nod as if making a decision. "Come into Aunt Betty's with me and make like we're friends."

Ava frowned. "Where does Aunt Betty live?"

"It's a café in town." Preacher tilted his head, observing her. "Well?"

Good heavens, in a store, she could yell and scream that he had a gun on her. Excitement shuddered through her. She'd be able to escape. Nodding furiously, she smiled at him. "I'd love that, thank you."

"Okay but you say one word or make one strange gesture or eye movement and I'll come back and cut Delores into little pieces. Fingers first and then toes. I'll make her suffer and tell her it's your fault." He smiled at her. "No one knows about this place and I can keep her alive for a very long time, Ava. Only you will hear her screams."

Stifling the gasp from the waves of horror that engulfed her, Ava stared at the floor. Isabella was still alive but he'd kill her if she didn't comply. Looking into his dead eyes made her want to scream but getting hysterical would break a rule and she'd be back to square one. Her only hope of survival was to make like she was part of his world. Trying to reason with him would get her killed. Wracking her brain and pulling up anything she could remember about psychos from books she'd read, she forced her mouth into a grin and lifted her chin but didn't meet his eyes. Her only option was to play him at his own game. She laughed albeit on the edge of panic but it took him off guard.

"You think it's funny?" Preacher moved closer and stared into her eyes so close his breath brushed her cheek. "Look at me?"

Heart thumping so loud, and afraid he might be able to hear it, Ava looked him in the eye. "She's a pain. And maybe I'd like to see her chopped into pieces."

"Really? But that won't stop me killing you if you misbehave." Preacher shook his head slowly and then stepped back and waved his gun at her. "Get bundled up against the cold." He indicated to a closet in the hallway. "I'm leaving in five. Hurry I've left the truck running."

After Ava had dragged on a heavy coat, boots, and gloves, she waited for Preacher to unlock the front door. When he waved her in front of him, the wonderful smell of the pine forest, greeted her, cold seeped through her clothes. She stepped outside and blinded by the brilliant white surroundings, stumbled down the front steps. Cold burned her lungs and she couldn't see. Squinting, she stopped walking and conscious of his Glock pointed at her, turned toward him. "It's too bright, I can't see. Remember, I've been in the dark for ages."

"There are sunglasses in the truck." Preacher grabbed her arm, pressed the gun into her ribs and dragged her to the truck. He shoved her against the door. "Get in."

Once inside, she took the sunglasses from the dashboard and slipped them on. She clicked in the seatbelt and then cried out in alarm when he slid a zip-tie around one wrist and attached it to a metal ring screwed into the console. She looked at him. He'd covered his face with a scarf and pushed on sunglasses. Under his hood he was unrecognizable. "Sorry. You startled me, I thought it was a snake."

"No snakes about in the snow. They're cold-blooded and would move so slow they'd freeze." Preacher grasped the steering wheel and the truck moved along a cleared track with snow piled up high each side. "I love winter."

Ava glanced at him. "Me too."

As they drove along a track, Ava took note of her surroundings. Behind her, the forest stretched out forever and she recalled following a path to a small waterfall. Where was she? As the road continued downward and the trees thinned, she could see for miles. Below was a vast snow-covered lowland with buildings in small clumps peeking out from a blanket of white. The road they traveled on stopped at a wide ranch gate with an open padlock hanging from a chain. Huge signs sat on both sides warning people not to trespass and of dangerous rockslides ahead. They continued down the mountainside, and after negotiating switchbacks too many to count, the road ran into a highway recently cleared and brined. "You're lucky the snowplow guy comes up to your house."

"He doesn't." Preacher glanced at her. "I clear my own roads. Nobody comes here." He turned onto the highway and accelerated.

It wasn't long before they drove past houses and then into a very busy town. "Is this Black Rock Falls?"

"Yeah." Preacher glanced at her. "I guess you don't remember it, seeing as you arrived here at night."

Ava looked out the window, memorizing where the sheriff's department was situated. She hadn't realized the town would be so big. People milled about everywhere, bundled up and chatting with each other in huge clouds of steam. It was like looking at a comic book and she kept expecting words to appear in the cloud bubbles so she could read their conversations. When Preacher pulled into a parking space and reached for the knife in his belt, she held her breath as he cut her free.

"Remember." Preacher stared at her. "I have my gun in my pocket. Be nice, Ava and we'll have some fun later. You and me, we could be good together."

Terrified at becoming his partner in murder, Ava forced her body to relax. He was so smart he'd pick up any change in her mood. She rubbed her wrist and then looked at him. "Yeah, I think we could. I'll be so good you'll want me to come out with you every day."

"Wait here." Preacher slipped from the seat and walked around the hood. He pulled open her door and helped her down. With his arm firmly around her waist, he led her toward a store with a sign saying, "Aunt Betty's Café." He looked down at her. "Smile at me, Ava, I want people to see how happy we are together."

Aware he could kill her in seconds, Ava forced her lips into a smile. "Okay."

Inside the café, as they waited for their order, Ava stared at the plates with samples of Aunt Betty's newest delights. She pulled off her glove and took a piece of cake and pushed it into her mouth. "Oh, that's wonderful."

Against her, Preacher stiffened as the sheriff moved beside her. Ava took in the woman, with the bright yellow banner across her chest and back, with the word *Sheriff* printed in bold letters. She glanced at Ava with intelligent eyes as if taking her in with one quick scan. Wanting to cry out, run away, do something to make her notice her, Ava drew a breath and then pictured Isabela alone in the cellar and what Preacher would do to her if she made a sound. She dragged her eyes away from the sheriff's inquisitive stare and moved her attention to the other samples. She selected a cookie but noticed how the sheriff had stared at the red poppy tattoo on her hand.

"Anything else you want, honey?" Preacher squeezed her so tight, Ava had to bite back a gasp of pain.

She looked up at him. "No thanks. We have everything I need."

"Put on your glove and let's go." Preacher picked up the bag and led the way out. On the footpath he turned to her. "You did good."

Heart sinking at having to return to the house with him, she climbed into the truck and stared at the sheriff walking toward a black vehicle. The next moment, as if she'd felt her cry for help, the sheriff turned slowly and looked at her. Their eyes held for a second and then the sheriff turned and climbed into the black truck. Ava turned to see Preacher staring at her. She looked at him and lifted her chin, thinking wildly of something to say. She had to convince him it would be a big mistake to kill her. "Now will you believe I like being with you? We'll be like Bonnie and Clyde."

"They died in a hail of bullets." Preacher stared after the sheriff. "Don't worry. That woman is too stupid to catch me. Many have tried but I'm still here and I ain't going nowhere."

CHAPTER FIFTY-ONE

Jenna and Kane had dropped by a long list of cabins owned by truckers and people working at homeless shelters but after a long morning of traveling roads more suitable to ice skating than vehicles, they'd come up empty. Claude Grady's hunting cabin was inaccessible, so was removed from their list. When Kane stopped to refuel, Jenna had grabbed takeout from Aunt Betty's to eat on the way to their next stop. With Rowley feeding them information at a steady rate, they'd traveled miles and then came a breakthrough. Just by chance, Rowley had discovered the whereabouts of a hunting cabin used frequently by biker Axel Reed. High up in Stanton Forest, it was one of two remaining on their list. Josiah Brock, the trucker who volunteered at the soup kitchen, owned the last one.

Since Black Rock Falls had suffered its share of serial killers, Jenna had developed a suspicious nature. In fact, her suspicion radar was on full alert and had flashed like wig-wag lights the moment she set eyes on the girl in Aunt Betty's. The man accompanying her was so bundled up, his own mother wouldn't have recognized him, and when he'd driven off with the girl in his truck, snow and frost had obscured his plate. She sat in Kane's truck staring at the vehicle as it blended into the traffic and vanished in the persistent heavy snowfall.

"What is it?" Kane was staring at her one hand under the carboard tray carrying to-go cups of coffee.

"I saw a girl in Aunt Betty's with a tattoo on her hand. I'm sure I recognize it from one of the missing persons' files we have received but we have looked at so many." Jenna pushed the coffee toward him and dropped the takeout on the console. "I need to check." She pulled out her phone and scrolled the images. "I've found it! Ava Price out of Wyoming. She's the same height and has black hair. It could've been her."

"If she's alive and well, and eating at Aunt Betty's, why are you concerned?" Kane picked up the bag of takeout and pulled out a sandwich. "Did she give you a wink or mouth, 'help me' or anything?"

Jenna shook her head. "She was wearing sunglasses and no, she didn't mouth anything but the guy with her had his arm around her waist. He could've been holding her against her will. I had this gut reaction something wasn't right with her."

"Ah, let me think." Kane waited a beat. "If you were in trouble and standing beside a sheriff, wouldn't you at least mouth the word, 'help'?"

Allowing the scene to run through her mind, Jenna sighed. "Yeah, I guess so. Unless she removed her glove to allow me to see the tattoo. That might have been a call for help."

"We only know the girl is missing." Kane finished his sandwich and sighed. "She may be holed up with her boyfriend and doesn't want to be found. It happens all the time but if you're worried about her safety, we should go and check her out. Did you get the plate?"

Jenna shook her head. "Only a partial. Montana plate ending in six, eight or nine. White Ford pickup." She glanced at him. "It's like looking for a needle in a haystack, but we can try." She entered her password and then the information on the mobile digital terminal screen in Kane's truck. "I'm glad we have all databases including the FBI's at our fingertips. Wolfe certainly can charm Mayor Petersham when it comes to obtaining new equipment."

"Ha." Kane grinned at her. "The updated MDT didn't come from the mayor. That was Wolfe with a little help from Bobby Kalo."

He winked. "We can access the FBI databanks without a separate password and thanks to Kalo, we're untraceable."

Jenna gaped at him. "That's illegal… are you saying we're hacking the FBI databases? We're committing a federal offense?"

"No, technically we're not." Kane looked at her over the rim of his to-go cup. "Have you formally resigned from the FBI?"

Jenna shook her head. "No."

"Me either and are we to protect our new identities at all cost?" Kane reached in the bag for another sandwich. "We took an oath, right?"

"Yes… but…" Jenna stared at him and sighed.

"So, we are following orders by remaining invisible." Kane took another bite of his sandwich and chewed slowly. He waved at the MDT. "And we are allowed to use any available resources at our disposal." He smiled at her. "Where were they heading?"

Jenna fastened her seatbelt. "Toward Stanton Forest." She glanced at the coordinates of Axel Reed's cabin. "We're heading that way."

"You said she was with a guy." Kane placed his cup into the console and pulled out into the traffic. "Did he resemble Axel Reed or Claude Grady?"

Jenna opened the bag of sandwiches and pulled out one. She didn't feel hungry but working at this pace, she ate when she could. "It was hard to tell. He was wearing a hoodie, sunglasses, and a scarf much like the man you described who offered Emily a ride."

"Hmm, like about another hundred men walking through town." Kane turned onto Stanton Road and glanced at the GPS. "How did Rowley discover Reed had a cabin?"

Swallowing a sip of coffee, Jenna turned to him. "He called Bobby Kalo. Asked him if he could help. Bobby discovered Reed was gifted a cabin owned by his uncle, on his mother's side. He found an old post on Facebook, mentioning Reed and his MC going up there for a weekend."

"How come it didn't show on our search?" Kane slowed to take a cleared dirt road into the forest. "I searched all the property records for his name specifically. I only came up with his place in town, no hunting cabin."

"That's because the deed is still in his uncle's name. The family name is Simpson." Jenna stared at the forest flashing by. "Pretty smart if you don't want to be found."

"Yet you said he denied owning a cabin?" Kane picked up speed as they hit the cleared road. "An out and out lie."

A strange twist of excitement gripped Jenna. "Yeah, and Reed fits the profile. It will be interesting to see if the road to his cabin is clear and he's holding a girl with a red poppy tattoo against her will." She looked ahead. "Although, I can't see a white pickup on this road. I think that's just wishful thinking."

The GPS instructed them to take a left down a narrow but cleared road through the forest. Snow lined the sides of the road in a white wall, prickly with an abundance of pine needles and gray in places from the tainted slush. They climbed slowly and steadily winding upward. They passed a few gates on the way, all with signposts warning that trespassers would be shot. After following some confusing switchbacks, they came to a gate with similar warnings but with the name *Simpson* written on a mailbox tipped at a jaunty angle. Jenna looked at Kane. "Now we know why the road is clear—they get mail service up here. We should walk in, if it's innocent we don't appear so threatening and we can call out."

"Hmm, in normal circumstances I'd agree with you but I'm not so sure it would be the best tactic." Kane stared at the gate. "If we're dealing with The Sculptor, which is more than likely, he'll shoot us. He'd be within his right to do so. We'd be better driving in lights flashing, so he knows who we are from the get-go. The Beast is reinforced steel with bulletproof windows but I'm still wearing a vest before I set one foot inside his property."

Saying a silent 'Thank you' to Wolfe for supplying her department with liquid Kevlar vests, Jenna slid out the door and met Kane at the back of his truck. Inside, Kane was fully equipped for any situation. Jenna removed her coat and shivered as the bitter cold bit into her in seconds. She pulled her vest over her head and fitted it securely before shrugging into her coat. The vest was the latest technology and unlike the old style, it was light and comfortable to wear. It didn't impede movement. The liquid Kevlar not only solidified on impact from anything but also absorbed the shock as well. She'd heard a rumor from Wolfe that full suits were available and a person could be protected from neck to ankle and yet still be able to execute a full range of movements.

"I'll have one of those." She indicated at the helmet in Kane's hand. "We'll look like a SWAT team."

"Good choice. We have established this guy could be ex-military." Kane pushed the helmet onto her head and then pushed one over his black woolen cap. "If he is, he'll use a headshot to take us out." He opened a metal box containing his rifle and assembled it in seconds. His face had set in combat mode. "I'm taking this as well, just in case he tries to run."

A chill, not from the cold mountain air, slid down Jenna's spine. Here was the sniper, the tactical and professional Kane. She respected his expertise and nodded. "Okay." She tightened the straps on her helmet and checked her weapon. "I'm good to go."

Jenna opened the gate and climbed back into the truck. With the blue and red wig-wag lights reflecting in the snow, they drove up the winding road. A white pickup sat in the driveway. Jenna's heart picked up a beat at the sight of Axel Reed walking across their path carrying something in his arms. As they moved closer, he ignored them and kept moving. "Oh, that doesn't look good."

Unease cramped Jenna's gut as she pulled her weapon and slid from the truck taking aim at Reed's chest. She blinked twice to make sense of the gruesome scene before her. Blood dripped from the biker as he struggled to drop a bloody plastic bag into the open door of a meat locker.

CHAPTER FIFTY-TWO

In a millisecond, Kane took in the threat and scanned the immediate area searching for any movement. The man, dripping with blood, turned slowly to look at them with a surprised expression. Kane had rolled into his yard but with the lights flashing they were more than a little visible. He had his Glock trained on Reed's head and he wouldn't miss.

"Sheriff's department." Jenna stood behind the door aiming her weapon. "Hands on your head."

"What the hell is going on here?" Axel Reed wiped his hands on his blood-soaked jeans and lifted them shoulder-high.

"I said, hands on your head. Link your fingers." Jenna moved out from the safety of the door. "Now."

"Sure, but I'll make my hair all bloody." Axel Reed glared at them. "Can't a man butcher a bison on his own land anymore? Since when has that been an offense. I have a hunting license and the beast was on my land."

Kane moved closer and peered into the meat locker. He couldn't tell the origin of the meat but pieces that size meant it wasn't human. He turned and gave Jenna a nod. "How did you shoot and move a beast that size on your own?"

"Who said I did it on my own?" Reed looked from one to the other. "I'm unarmed and pose no threat. Would you mind not pointing your weapons at me?"

Kane holstered his weapon. He could draw down on a man in a split second if necessary. "So who helped you butcher the beast? There's no way one man could've carted a bison from the forest to here in the snow."

"I shot it and friends helped me field dress it but we had to transport it here in the bed of an old pickup." Reed wiped the back of his hand across his nose leaving a bloody streak. "When I heard your truck, I thought it was Josiah coming by to help me carve up the meat. I need to get it finished and packed before it freezes."

After peering around the trees, Kane spotted what was left of the bison, hanging from an A-frame. Beside it sat a long bench scattered with knives and saws commonly used in butchering. "That's a lot of meat for one man."

"Yeah, and my friends have already taken some for helping me." Reed looked pleased with himself. "It's mighty fine eating and will keep me going for some time. I'm giving some to Josiah and I'll take what I don't need to the soup kitchen." He looked from one to the other. "Unless you'd like some?"

Kane and Jenna both shook their heads. Kane cleared his throat. He preferred his meat from a store and without the risk of parasites. "Thanks, but no thanks."

"We're looking for a girl by the name of Ava Price, she has a tattoo of a red poppy on one hand. Have you seen her around town?" Jenna moved closer to him and held up her phone.

"Nope, can't say that I have." Reed looked agitated. "Mind if I keep going?"

Kane pulled out a pair of latex gloves and exchanged them for his leather ones. "Mind if we take a look around? If I recall when you spoke to the sheriff, you said you didn't own a hunting cabin or land up here. You mentioned before about shooting the bison on your land. Why lie to the sheriff?"

"It's not my land, it's my uncle's land until the deed changes hands." Reed waved a bloody hand at the cabin. "Look all you want. The door is open."

"Thanks." Kane followed Jenna to the cabin steps and then paused when another truck rumbled into the yard. He turned and stared at the driver. "That must be Josiah."

"Yeah, I've met him. He helps at the soup kitchen and came to my attention after interviewing Claude Grady. I figure Grady wanted him for an alibi and as luck would have it, Josiah Brock was at the soup kitchen the other day when we stopped by. He knows Grady but can't say for sure when he last drove with him." Jenna frowned. "He's on our list of cabin owners to check. I'll go inside and look around. I want you to speak to Brock, see if he's willing for us to toss his cabin as well."

Kane removed his gloves and handed them to her. "I'm on it."

He watched Jenna take out her Maglite to enter the small cabin and waited for Brock to climb out of his truck. A tall lean muscular man, Josiah Brock was the same build and height as Reed and was dressed the same as many of the men in Black Rock Falls. He walked toward him, waiting for a reaction to seeing the sheriff and her deputy at his friend's cabin but he only noticed Brock's forehead wrinkle into a frown over his sunglasses. He moved in front of him, "Ah, you must be Josiah Brock. Haven't I've seen you at the soup kitchen?"

"Yeah, I help out. I like the company." Brock indicated to Reed with his thumb. "It's isolated out this way and Axel is my closest neighbor but he doesn't drop by often."

Kane nodded and pulled out his phone. "Have you seen this girl?" He held up the screen to display Ava's image.

"No and I think I'd remember her." Brock removed his sunglasses and peered at the image. "Has something happened to her?"

Kane shook his head. "Not that I'm aware, we just want to speak to her and we're asking people who help out at the shelters if they've seen her. She's homeless. And last reports said she was seen up this way." He shrugged and leaned against a tree. His relaxed manner might put Brock at ease. "We planned to stop by Snowberry Way after leaving here. Do you mind coming back with us so we can take a look around? We're looking for tracks to see if the girl came by that way."

"Knock yourself out but you don't need me there. I figure I'd remember if a beautiful girl dropped by and I haven't noticed any footprints in the snow lately." Brock smiled at him. "I don't lock my doors and have nothing to steal. Although, the bears have been known to raid my meat locker if I don't keep it locked down tight."

Kane nodded. "No dogs?"

"Nope." Brock shrugged. "I had a cat once but never replaced her because I'm away so much."

"Okay, thanks." Kane headed toward the cabin as Jenna was walking out. He lowered his voice but behind him Brock and Reed were talking up a storm. "Find anything?"

"No." She snapped off her gloves. "No one is living there. There's no cellar. It's very small inside. If he is keeping anyone against their will, he's doing it in town—or he has an accomplice." She indicated with her chin toward the men. "They look like close friends."

"Maybe, but killing takes a dominant and submissive. I'm not seeing that here. I think it would be more likely to be one of Reed's MC buddies, like Mad Dog Morgan. My understanding is that Reed doesn't come up here often, so I figure he does most of his interacting with Brock at the soup kitchen."

"That's not a place most people would risk planning murders." Jenna looked downhearted. "I'm sure Reed is involved. He fits the profile and so does Grady... well, come to think of it, Brock does as well. My money is on Reed. We have found him out to be a liar and he was the last person to see Zoe alive."

Kane shrugged. "We haven't found any solid evidence against any of them yet but on the bright side, Brock gave us permission to search his cabin." He gave the men a wave and led the way back to his truck.

"That's good. Although I think it's a waste of time. He wouldn't give us the run of the place if he had anything to hide." Jenna removed her gloves and followed him. "How far is it?"

Kane climbed behind the wheel and consulted his GPS. "Not far."

The cabin was about a mile higher up the winding mountain road and surrounded by trees. Only a small area enough to park a few vehicles had been cleared and it was as if the forest was slowly reclaiming the land. Kane scanned the area. It had been recently cleared of snow and a snowplow attachment like his own sat in a woodshed beside the cabin. A thin line of smoke curled from a chimney and on the front porch sat an ancient rocking chair.

"There's a meat locker." Jenna walked toward it pulling on gloves. "If I wanted to freeze a body, I'd put it in there."

Kane pulled on surgical gloves and grabbed a forensics kit from the back of his truck. He looked around. "For a single guy living alone, he takes the time to clear the snow. Most would just make a path in and out."

"Same in here." Jenna peered into the meat locker. "This has been cleaned recently and there's ice on the bottom."

Kane pulled out a test kit. "I'll swab it just in case but I guess he was making it ready for the bison meat he's getting today."

"Yeah, that makes sense." Jenna turned to look at the house. "It would be lonely out here."

Kane took the swabs then straightened. "No lonelier than your ranch. You're miles from town too."

"Yeah but I have conveniences." She chuckled. "Not to mention you living close by." She headed toward the cabin.

Inside, the cabin was neat, clean, and warm. Kane checked the kitchen and found what he'd expected for a man living alone. A ton of canned goods in a pantry, beer in the refrigerator along with stale milk. A half empty mug of cold coffee sat on the sink beside a warm coffee maker. "Well, it looks like he lives here."

"Yeah, I found clothes, the bed is made and there's toiletries in the bathroom. I can't find a cellar." Jenna walked down a narrow hallway. "Ah, this has to be it." She tried the door. "It's locked. Can you open it?"

"Oh, yeah." Kane pulled out his lockpicks and had the satisfying feeling when the tumblers moved. He tried the door and it opened with a whine. "This hasn't been opened for some time and the hinges are rusty."

"We'll go down and look around." Jenna took out her Maglite

Inside dusty cobwebs thick like lace curtains filled the entrance and old air escaped in a musty cloud. He aimed his Maglite down the old wooden steps. It was a small room, maybe five yards square, just a root cellar at best. "I don't think those steps will take my weight. It's empty apart from the spiders. It hasn't been used in decades."

"Okay, it's getting late. Let's go or we'll miss the snowplow." Jenna pushed the door shut and tried the handle. "It's locked again. I think I'd keep it locked too. It's dangerous."

Glad to be heading back to town, Kane followed her outside into the cold. The snow had stopped for a few minutes and the mountainside was so still, it was as if they'd walked out into a photograph. He slid an arm over Jenna's shoulder and pointed through the trees to the snowscape far below. From here, he could see for miles. "Look at that view. Summer here is glorious but even in winter this is a beautiful place to live. Why do crazy people have to spoil it by going and killing someone?"

"I don't know, Dave." Jenna let out a sigh making a cloud of steam around them. "Lately, I'm starting to believe I'm living in someone else's nightmare."

CHAPTER FIFTY-THREE

The promise Preacher made to allow Ava to walk free didn't eventuate. Preacher had lied to her. After returning from Aunt Betty's Café, Ava had been shoved in her room and left alone for hours. She was hungry and thirsty. By the time Preacher arrived home, she was ready to scream but had to be nice and go along with his craziness or she'd be the next one shoved in the meat locker. When the door finally opened, and he looked at her with excitement dancing in his eyes, her stomach dropped and fear dried her throat. What had he been doing? She stood in the middle of the room and curled her lips into a smile. "Oh, there you are. Would you like me to help with dinner?"

"I'm not hungry." Preacher gave her an appreciative look. "But I can make you some grilled cheese sandwiches."

Stomach growling, Ava nodded. He was being very charming, as if trying to impress her. In fact, if Preacher wasn't a crazy psychopath, she might like this side of him, but she refused to be lulled into a false sense of security. "I can help out." She frowned. "What about Isabella, she'd be hungry too?"

"Isabella is on a cleansing diet." Preacher smiled at her. "You'll understand later but right now, I need you sitting at the kitchen table. This is your last test. If you pass then I'll allow you to come hunting with me."

Cleansing diet? Trying to keep her expression neutral as a ton of possibilities raged through her mind, she sat down and allowed him to cuff one wrist to the table. As he meticulously washed his hands and then set about cooking for her, she wanted to say, "Hunting what?" But she guessed it wasn't animals. He wanted more girls, more people to murder. Instead she gathered her thoughts and forced herself to sound interested. "That would be nice."

"I've never hunted Delores with anyone before, I need to know I can trust you." He looked at her over one shoulder.

His scheme fell into place in a jolt of reality. She had to play along or become a victim. "You'll find it easier to hunt down Delores with me. She'll get into your truck, when she sees me inside."

"Most do anyway but you may be right." Preacher slid a pile of grilled cheese sandwiches across the table to her. "Can I trust you with a cup of coffee? I won't be happy if you get ugly and throw it in my face."

Ava gave him her best aghast expression. "I'd never do such a thing." She frowned. "Why do you think that?"

"They all get ugly." He poured her coffee and added cream and sugar. "Delores never smiles at me. I care for her and feed her but you should hear the names she calls me. It makes my head throb and I want to hurt her. When she's quiet, I can make her smile at me and I feel good again."

Goosebumps prickled over Ava's legs and arms. Preacher sounded like a little boy who'd been bullied for a very long time. *Heavens, I'm feeling sorry for him.* Giving herself a mental shake, she ate slowly. "How long ago did this start?"

"A long time but I finished it in high school." Preacher avoided her gaze. "I was small for my age with zits. I'm a different person now."

Ava tried to look interested but her knees shook in terror. "Was she cruel to you, Preacher?"

"Cruel?" Preacher turned his head slowly toward her and the evil expression in his eyes chilled her to the bone. "She figured I wasn't good enough to walk in her shadow but when my hands closed around her neck, she looked at me, I mean really looked at me for the first time. She pleaded with me and even offered me her body. It was too late for her then but that night everything changed. I became a man." He hadn't blinked once and seemed to have fallen into a trancelike state.

With only the sound of the kitchen clock ticking, Ava finished her meal and sipped her scalding coffee, although the sandwiches had formed a solid lump in her gut, starving wasn't an option. The hints he'd given her, of Delores always coming back, made sense now. In his deluded mind, every woman of a certain type reminded him of Delores and triggered a need to kill her over and over again. This Delores must have been some badass bully to have pushed him to murder.

"More coffee?" Preacher stood and walked to the counter. "I'll be busy for a time and if you need to use the bathroom, you'd better go now."

Ava eased the cup toward him. "Yes, please to the coffee and no to the bathroom." She smiled at him. If he wanted smiles, she would give him as many as he needed to keep her breathing. "The meal was delicious, thank you. I'm so lucky to have someone like you caring for me."

"We'll see." Preacher placed a cup in front of her and then turned on the TV. "This is your last test. Watch the screen. You can talk to me if you like." He looked at her and a sinister chuckle rumbled through him. "This is going to be so much fun, you'll see." He pushed the Glock into the back of his waistband and strolled out the room.

Ava could hear his voice clearly. He must be using the intercom in another room. She listened intently as his voice drifted out to her as smooth as silk.

"Delores, it's time to take a shower. Do it now."

A wave of foreboding hit Ava as she turned in her seat to face the screen. It had split into two, one showing the cellar and the other a small room covered in plastic with a bench set in the middle. *This can't be good.*

Nerves shattered, she sipped her coffee and waited for what seemed like an eternity. Nothing was happening and then she heard a rattle of keys, the creaking of a door opening and slow footsteps leading away. She stared at the screen. Preacher was in the cellar and heading for the bathroom door. He'd changed his clothes. He'd replaced the jeans and T-shirt with a plastic wraparound apron and wore rubber boots. She could hear his footsteps squelching on the cement floor.

She held her breath as the door to the bathroom was wrenched open, Preacher walked inside and she heard Isabella scream. Panic shook her as the girl was dragged out dripping wet, with her hands secured behind her back. Isabella's screams stopped when Preacher held a gun to her head. He ordered her to walk across the room to an empty bookcase and made her wait as he slid the bookcase to one side. Behind it was a door she'd never seen before. The next moment Preacher pushed Isabella into the second room and when she started to sob, tears filled Ava's eyes but she couldn't take her attention off the screen.

Preacher was talking in a low soothing voice, as if trying to convince Isabella everything was alright. The next moment he turned away from her and aimed a remote at the camera. The screen flickered and then became a full screen close-up of the plastic room. Bile filled Ava's mouth. Whatever he had planned, he wanted her to see it in detail. When he spun the terrified Isabella around and enclosed her neck with his large hands, Ava bit back a scream. She stared in horror as he grinned into the camera, lifted the wriggling girl into the air and squeezed. Vomit threatened to rise in her throat. He was testing her, waiting for her to protest. He'd stop when she didn't react—wouldn't he?

She heard him chuckle and her heart sank. He wasn't going to stop. She had to do something, say something to help her friend. "What game is this, Preacher?"

"Game?" Preacher stared into the camera and gave Isabella a little shake. "I don't play games, Ava."

Too shocked for words, she gripped the edge of the table so hard her nails shattered. Unable to believe the horror unfolding before her eyes, she held her breath willing him to stop. The room moved in and out of focus and panic gripped her. She had to stay conscious and show no reaction. She gasped air into her lungs and trembled. *He's killing her and he's doing it for me.*

CHAPTER FIFTY-FOUR

Before dawn, Thursday, Week 2

As warm as toast, Jenna ran along a sun-drenched beach, splashing through the waves. Her body was weightless and the sand went on forever snaking away in the distance against an azure ocean. Seagulls swooped around her and then one of them made a strange buzzing sound. She stopped running and gaped as it turned into Dave Kane. "What?"

"Jenna, wake up." A hand tousled her hair and she blinked at the sight of him bending over her. "You fell asleep."

Jenna sat up dropping her feet to the floor and unseating Pumpkin, who was curled on her lap. She blinked and looked around. The fire in her hearth crackled as a fresh load of pinecones burst into flames. "Oh, I'm sorry. I was dreaming I was on the beach. What time is it?"

"A little after midnight." Kane's expression was deadly serious. "Rowley just called. There's another body."

Instantly awake, she stared at him. "Where?"

"Under the 'Welcome to Black Rock Falls' signpost, the one on the northside of town." Kane straightened and went to his laptop on the coffee table and closed it. "He is on scene with the truck driver who called it in. He has the crime scene secure and Colt Webber is with him. Wolfe is in transit."

She looked at him. He looked exhausted and his hair was disheveled as if he'd been holding his head in his hands. "Webber? How did he get there so fast?"

"He's living a few minutes away from Rowley now." Kane glanced at the door to the kitchen. "I've just made a fresh pot of coffee. I'll fill the Thermos flasks. It's going to be a long night."

Jenna pushed both hands through her hair and stood. "Okay, I'll grab my gear."

She dashed into the bathroom and splashed cold water on her face. Another murder and they had two possible suspects, and only circumstantial evidence. She needed to think outside the box. After scrubbing a towel over her face, she dashed into her bedroom to retrieve her duty belt. She checked the load in her Glock and slid her backup weapon into an ankle holster. A killer would expect her to go straight to the murder scene, but she didn't intend to play The Sculptor's game this time. She peered out the window and her heart sank. During the two hours or so she'd been asleep, the snow had increased and the roads would be dangerous. She considered dragging the snowplow guy out of bed to clear the way as she headed for the family room.

Duke lay on the rug before the fire and Pumpkin was playing with his long floppy ears. She looked down at them. They had become a small piece of normality in her unsettled life. Sighing, she headed for the mudroom. Kane had already bundled up against the cold and was pulling on his boots. She looked at him. "You should've gone home hours ago. What have you been hunting down?"

"Similar cases across the country." Kane shrugged. "Jo sent a ton of unsolved cases with similar victims and cause of death. I was looking for a pattern, something we could use to catch the killer."

Trust Kane to work into the night. She wished he'd had a few hours' sleep. Even her short nap had refreshed her. "Find anything?"

"Not anything new." Kane indicated out the window. "The snow has set in again. It will be slow going. I'll go and fit the snowplow attachment to my truck. I don't plan on getting stuck in a snowdrift any time soon."

Jenna nodded. "I'll help you. I think you should leave Duke here. He'll be fine. He can get outside if needs be through the doggy door."

"Duke won't move until daylight." Kane smiled at her. "Are we good to go?"

"Yeah." Jenna disabled the house alarm and as Kane walked down the front steps, she reset it and pulled on her gloves.

Snow smacked her in the face sending icy trickles down her cheeks. She blinked away snowflakes attacking her eyelashes and stomped through the snow to the garage beside Kane's cottage. Under the floodlights the ranch seemed to shrink into a small patch of light surrounded by a black wall of shadows. The door of the garage creaked open and a light went on inside. She hurried to where Kane was dragging the snowplow attachment to the front of his truck.

"Wait! I'll start the truck first." Kane slid inside and the Beast rumbled into life. "It will save time if it warms up first."

A few moments later they were heading down the driveway, snow flying out beside them in a steady stream. It took some time to negotiate the road from her ranch but when they turned onto the main highway into Black Rock Falls, it was evident that Mayor Petersham had the snowplows and brine spreaders working around the clock. She pulled out her phone to access the file on her two main suspects. "Forget about the crime scene. It will still be there later. We'll chase down the whereabouts of the suspects. They won't be expecting us at this time of night."

"Then we'll need our vests." Kane shot her a glance and then returned his gaze to the road. "I don't want to come across a killer who is on a high from murdering some poor woman." He cleared his throat. "Rowley said this one is real bad. He said the killer went crazy. You'll need to release another statement and warn people we have a serial killer on the loose."

"Yeah, but if I say we have another crazy in town, I'll be ostracized. Maybe they'd prefer me to call him a sick SOB. Maybe that sounds more professional." Jenna sighed. "Although mutilating people and killing for fun fits the stereotypical definition of crazy."

"You shouldn't allow the press to get under your skin. Sometimes they act like it's our fault that serial killers end up here. They don't seem to understand it's in a psychopath's nature to believe they can outsmart law enforcement." Kane snorted. "The reporters are looking for any excuse to sensationalize a story and poke holes in our investigative process. I'd say the reporter has a hidden agenda, maybe a relative who plans to go against you in the next election." He chuckled. "They can't win. The townsfolk trust you to keep them safe and right now, you're batting a thousand."

Jenna stared ahead as snowflakes splattered on the windshield. "I don't believe the killers figure they can outwit me. They choose Black Rock Falls because there are so many places to hide. The county is so vast with over two million acres of forest and then there's the lowlands. If people don't want to be found, it's pretty easy to drop off the grid here." She glanced at the GPS. "Our first suspect is Axel Reed, the biker. It's not far. He lives on the corner of Stanton and Aspen. Pull up some ways away and we can suit up. I'll call Wolfe and explain our delay."

"Okay." Kane headed into town.

Jenna made the call. "Hi, Wolfe, it's Jenna. We're hunting down suspects. I'm hoping to catch them before they have time to destroy evidence."

"Sure. It's pretty messy on scene." Wolfe paused a beat. *"I'll be here for a while. I tested the samples Kane collected from Josiah Brock's cabin. There's no sign of any human blood or DNA on the swabs."*

She glanced at Kane and pulled a sad face. "Okay thanks. We'll be there as soon as possible." She disconnected. "Nothing on the swabs at Brock's cabin."

"At least we have two other, more promising suspects." Kane pulled the truck into the curb. "That's Reed's place. The redbrick two doors down and his truck is out front." He looked at her. "How do you want to play this?"

Jenna peered through the gloom at the house. Not one light shone from the windows and no smoke came from the chimney. Outside a streetlight sent an orange glow over the truck parked in the driveway. It appeared the occupant had gone to bed. "There's not much snow on his truck, he's not been home long. You go to the front and I'll watch the back." She eased out the truck closing the door gently and met Kane round back.

They pulled on their Kevlar vests and struck out across the slippery road and along the snow-covered sidewalk. When Kane opened the gate, it swung open without a sound and Jenna was through and heading around back. She ducked under low hanging branches and entered a void of blackness. Halted by the unknown, she pulled out her Maglite and shone it on the white ground. The yard was piled with snow and she doubted the back door had been opened for weeks. A drift had blown in up to the windowsills. If anyone attempted to escape from this side of the house they'd be in trouble. She heard Kane bang hard on the front door but inside nothing stirred.

After hearing Kane's four attempts to wake Reed with no response, Jenna edged her way across the back of the house and froze, heart pounding at the sound of muffled footsteps coming from the fence line. She doused the light and pulled her weapon. Temporarily blinded by the darkness, she pressed against the freezing wall and waited. Could the house have a side door? If Reed planned to escape, she'd hit him with the beam of her Maglite but for now, she'd blend into the night. Footsteps came closer, crunching almost silently in the ice-covered snow. Pulse pounding in her ears, she took a deep breath and aimed her weapon.

CHAPTER FIFTY-FIVE

"Jenna, where are you?" Kane's voice came out of the night and the beam of a flashlight pierced the darkness and swung back and forth.

Heaving a sigh of relief, Jenna stepped out into the beam of light. "I'm here. I thought you might be Reed."

"He's not home." Kane walked to her side. "I'm not sure why he left his truck outside in the weather. There's a garage on the other side of the house. I looked inside and his motorcycle is missing."

Following Kane back around the house, she looked inside the garage. "It's unusual to leave it unlocked as well." She glanced at the pickup. "Maybe he had to leave in a hurry." She walked over to the truck and peered into the back. A good coating of ice covered the bottom and icicles hung all around. "It looks as if it's been hosed down and left."

"Yeah." Kane moved his flashlight to a trashcan outside the garage. He walked over and lifted the lid. "Hmm, empty bleach bottles. He's been cleaning something but then he did use this truck to transport the bison."

Jenna shook her head. "No, he said he called in friends and they used an old pickup to transport it. No doubt one with a hook and a winch on the back." She shot him a glance. "I mean how many men does it take to lift a bison?"

"It wasn't a calf so might have weighed over a thousand pounds at least." Kane scratched his cheek. "Field dressed and without the head." He looked at her. "The truck would do all the lifting but

I'd want a guy each side to guide it into the bed of the truck. So, I'd say three. He'd need one to operate the winch." He stared into space. "There's not much space up there to drive a truck, Jenna. Most people would bring it out of the forest in pieces, unless he has a cleared area somewhere inside his property. It would make sense a bison would go there to look for food, especially if he lured it with hay."

"Okay." Jenna stomped away in the snow. "Enough about butchering bison. Reed could be anywhere. He's probably hightailed it over to visit Morgan, we'll worry about him later if needs be. We need to drop by Claude Grady's home." She reached the truck and pulled open the door. "He lives on Stanton."

They climbed inside and drove back to Stanton arriving at Grady's home a few minutes later. Jenna made her way to the side gate when she heard growling. The next second a huge mixed breed dog threw itself at the fence, snarling and barking. She stepped back and looked at Kane. "So much for surprising him."

"No matter." Kane hammered on the door making it shake in its frame. "Sheriff's department. Open up."

Lights came on in the house and a few long minutes later, Claude Grady opened the door. Dressed in day clothes, he stared at Kane and then slid his gaze to Jenna. She remained beside Kane. "When did you get home, Mr. Grady?"

"Why? Did you drop by earlier?" Grady seemed to fold into himself, recover, and then straighten.

"Just answer the question." Kane took a step closer.

"I went out." Grady looked at Jenna. "You know I help out at the shelter. Well, when I'd finished, I managed to grab a meal at Aunt Betty's before they closed. That's not against the law, is it?"

Jenna pulled out her notebook. "Okay, who did you speak to tonight?"

"Father Derry and ah, sorry, I don't know the homeless people's names but I spoke to them. Ask at the office, I made a pot of fresh coffee for the receptionist but she's new and I don't recall her name."

"And in Aunt Betty's?" Jenna stared at him. "What did you eat? Did you pay by card or cash?"

"I had the chili and paid in cash. I didn't speak to anyone special. I ordered at the counter and sat down. They were busy cleaning up." He shrugged. "They're always busy."

He'd become more confident as if he was certain she'd believe his story without checking him out. Jenna nodded. "So you wouldn't mind if we take a look around your house?"

"My house? Why would you want to search my house?" Grady looked appalled.

"Not search." Kane leaned one hand against the doorframe. "We're looking for a homeless woman. She was seen in town earlier and someone is hiding her." He smiled. "If she's not here, you'll be taken off our list."

Adopting a casual pose, Jenna smiled at him. "It's late and we want to get home to bed. You are the last person on our list who works at the shelter and may have come in contact with her."

"What has she done? Is she dangerous?" Grady eyed them with suspicion.

"She may be ill." Kane shrugged. "We're not sure but we have to find her first. You must understand we can't take everyone's word for gospel."

"I don't have anyone staying here." Grady stood to one side. "Come in and see for yourselves."

Jenna gave Kane a nod and he hustled along a hallway to hunt down the cellar. She wrinkled her nose. The house smelled of death. Not strong but the smell was one she'd never forget. The walls had lines of trophy heads, including deer and elk. An old sofa and a couple of easy chairs surrounded the fireplace and above the mantlepiece sat a flatscreen TV. Keeping Grady in sight, she glanced in all directions. "Show me around. Deputy Kane is going to look at your cellar."

"Sure." Grady frowned. "Nothing down there apart from the furnace and some old furniture." He led the way from the family room along a hallway to the kitchen. "Laundry through there, dining on the right."

Keeping her back to the wall, she peered into each room. The kitchen was old with dishes piled up in the sink. Coffee cups lined the counter, stained with the remains of coffee in various amounts. "Did you have a party?"

"Nope." My dishwasher died and I can't afford to buy a new one." Grady's attention kept lifting upward.

After clearing the rooms, she turned to him. "Best you get the dishes in some hot water before the rats smell them. Calling pest control costs a lot too." She caught him flicking his eyes upward again. "Okay, let's go upstairs."

As they headed toward the stairs, Kane came down the hallway and gave her a shake of his head. They followed Grady and inspected the bathroom and three bedrooms that led off the hallway. Two empty rooms with boxes and one messy bedroom with a double bed and a closet. Clothes littered the floor and the smell had gotten stronger. She glanced at Kane and screwed up her nose. When he pointed upward, Jenna examined the damp patch on the ceiling. She turned to Grady. "What's in your loft?"

"Nothing much, just a few things I use for my hobby." Grady folded his arms across his chest in a defensive manner. "You don't want to go up there, Sheriff."

Jenna smiled at him. "Oh, but I do. Show me."

As Grady led the way back into the hall, Jenna felt a tug on her arm. She looked at Kane. "What?"

"If we go up there first, he'll have an advantage. If we follow him up there, he will still have the drop on us." Kane bent close and whispered in her ear. "His body language tells me he's hiding something."

"Okay." Jenna nodded. "You go up and I'll watch your back."

"Watch him, not me." Kane narrowed his gaze. "He might attack while your attention is elsewhere."

Jenna lifted her chin. "It's not my first rodeo, Kane." She waved him into the hallway and waited for Grady to pull down the stairs to the loft. A waft of stink seemed to ooze out of the opening. Something dead lay in his attic and the killer could be an arm's length away. She moved to turn Grady around and away from Kane. "Thanks. How long have you been living here?"

"All my life." Grady smiled. "This house belonged to my parents. They passed last year."

Behind Grady, Kane pulled on gloves and a face mask and moved up the steps in silence. Jenna kept Grady's attention on her. "Oh, I'm sorry for your loss. Both at the same time?"

"Nope, within a few weeks." Grady shrugged. "They got sick last winter and died."

Above, Kane coughed and the creak of the steps told her he was on his way back down. She rested her hand on her weapon—one wrong move and she'd draw down on Grady. "Anything to report?"

"Yeah." Kane pulled off his face mask. "He's got a bison head up there." He looked at Grady. "Going rotten and stinking the place out."

"I'm going to mount it." Grady looked crushed.

"Do you have a current taxidermist license?" Kane shook his head. "You should've prepared the head by now."

"Yeah, I know." Grady glared at Kane. "The head is mine. It was given to me and I have a license."

"Then I want to see your records." Kane stared at him. "Who was the owner?"

"I haven't gotten time to fill in my book." Grady looked at him, alarm filling his eyes. "It was Axel Reed. I went up and helped him field dress the beast and he gave me the head."

"Small world." Jenna looked from one to the other. "We spoke to him earlier and he didn't mention you."

"He gives me all my heads." Grady looked at her. "I heard about him from Josiah."

Jenna closed her notebook. "Okay. I want you to drop by my office in the morning and show your license and record book at the front counter." She looked at Kane. "Let's go."

CHAPTER FIFTY-SIX

Hoping the cold night air would rid him of the stink permeating his clothes, Kane walked to his truck. Another possible suspect but again they'd found no sign of a girl or a freezer large enough to store a body and he'd searched every possible hiding place in Grady's home. He headed to the crime scene and turned to Jenna. "I'm wondering if he has a cabin in the forest. Anyone could build one and unless it's on one of the regular trails we'd never know."

"Maybe. There's something about Grady that disturbs me." Jenna poured two cups of coffee and handed him one. "He has strange views on women. Like if they're raped, they asked for it. I don't trust him."

When they hit the straightaway, Kane sipped his coffee, eyes front on the icy road. "His body language makes me think he's hiding something. Maybe it was the bison head dripping through his ceiling." He snorted. "I mean you don't need to be Einstein to put a bucket under it, do you?"

"My first thought was how he got it up there." Jenna glanced at him. "It would have been difficult on his own."

Kane shook his head. "He has a pulley system in the roof. It's electric and has a swinging arm, so he hauls it up and can set it down where he wants it." He placed his cup in the console. "Grady must have had help getting it inside the house but that's not our problem." He turned onto the highway. "I figure we need to find out if he sneaks off to a cabin in the forest. Then there is Reed. Where is he? For all we know they could be taking shifts watching the missing girl." He cut her a glance. "Maybe we should resort to something illegal before someone else is murdered."

"And that is?" Jenna didn't sound amused.

"A tracker on their vehicles." Kane slowed to negotiate a pile of snow spilling from a drift at the side of the road. "It won't hold up in court but it might save lives. We're running out of options. It has to be one of our suspects and we need to pinpoint their whereabouts." He glanced ahead at the wig-wag lights on Rowley's SUV blinking out of unison with the blue and red perimeter flashers. Crime scene tape fluttered in his headlights. Inside the taped area, a circle of lamps illuminated the scene. Wolfe and Webber bent over body parts taking samples and Rowley was to one side spewing. "I'll drive past and park behind Wolfe's van."

"Okay." Jenna pulled on latex gloves and shivered. "I'll think on the trackers. I don't want anything compromising the evidence when we catch this guy. Surveillance would be the better option."

With their limited manpower stretched to the limit, surveillance wasn't the best option. Kane shook his head. "We don't have the time or the resources to watch two men, Jenna."

"Okay, fine, use trackers." Her eyes flashed and her mouth turned down. "But if a killer walks free because of it, I won't be too happy." She slid from the seat and walked away without a backward glance.

He watched her go to Wolfe and then followed, stopping in shock at the scene before him. The strong smell of vomit rose from a steaming pile beside the road and Rowley walked to meet him, his face sheet white. Kane nodded at him. "Walk me through it."

"Ah… the body is female and the killer used a chainsaw to dismember her. She wasn't frozen this time." Rowley shook his head and his eyes held deep sorrow. "Wolfe said he believes she was restrained and alive at the time. He used the same display techniques as before, most of her is on the bench." He took a deep breath and let it out slowly. "I questioned the truck driver, took a statement, and let him go. He spotted the body and called it in is all. I have his details including the license plate of the truck." He coughed and heaved. "Sorry."

Compassion and horror rolled over Kane and he dropped into his special zone. In situations like this, he used a mental technique to regard the remains of the young woman without expression. Having the ability to shut down his emotions at will had its advantages. Rowley didn't have his years of training behind him and he noticed a slight tremble in his hands. He slapped him on the shoulder. "There's hot coffee in my truck. Go and take five."

"Thanks." Rowley gave him a curt nod and slipped and slid through the slush to the Beast.

Kane picked his way around the evidence markers and went to Jenna's side. She had her mask of professionalism firmly locked in place as well and was asking Wolfe questions.

"This is different, brutal, like he is trying to make a point." Jenna dropped into a crouch. "What's this?" She indicated to an indent in the blood-spattered snow.

"I'd say the indent is from where he placed the chainsaw on the ground." Wolfe moved around the corpse. "See here and here." He pointed to indents in the snow. "These resemble boot marks but he's smart, he used a tree branch to disguise them. He took his time with this one." He turned to Webber. "Start bagging the body parts. I'll be back soon." Wolfe turned back to them. "Come with me." He walked to a line of trees and ducked behind and then held out a hand to prevent them getting closer. "What do you see?"

The image of the girl's open staring eyes and hideous smile had fixed in Kane's head and he lifted his face into the falling snow for a few seconds before examining the crime scene. He scanned the area taking in the scuff marks and large pools of blood. He moved to Wolfe's side.

"From the amount of blood spatter, this is where the young woman met her death. Far enough from the highway to remain hidden but not so far to prevent the killer from carrying her body parts to the bench to display them." He glanced at Jenna. "He'd be covered in blood."

"Why has he changed his MO?" Jenna looked at him. "This is all wrong. Everything before was neat, clean, and no blood. It was as if he liked to present his art, like marble statues. This is carnage. It has to be a different killer."

After taking his time to examine the evidence, Kane shook his head. "I think it's the same man. There are too many similarities and none of them we've released to the press." He walked back to her. "The eyes are wide open, the smile. He used a chainsaw. It's the same guy, he's escalating."

"Okay. I've seen enough and Wolfe wants to get her back to the morgue before she's frozen solid." Jenna turned to Wolfe. "When you email the crime scene images, could you send a copy to Jo? I'd like her take on this sudden change of MO."

"Sure, but Kane's right." Wolfe narrowed his gaze at her. "There are many similarities but he was in a hurry this time." He exchanged a knowing glance with Kane. "I'll conduct an autopsy in the morning and give you my findings."

"I want to be there." Jenna's gaze moved over the gruesome scene. "This isn't cool and calculated, this is a frenzy kill. People out of control make mistakes. We need to sift through everything and find a clue to his identity, some shred of evidence to catch this killer."

Until they found the murderer, as sheriff, Jenna would shoulder the blame, and Kane could see the burden weighing heavy on her shoulders. He touched her arm. "We'll catch him, Jenna." He nodded toward his truck. "Rowley is shaken up, maybe you should have a quiet word with him."

When Jenna walked away, Kane turned to Wolfe. "I need a couple of trackers, suitable for off-road conditions. I figure at least one of our suspects has a secluded cabin in the forest, and I intend to find out where it is."

"Roger that." Wolfe grinned at him. "Jenna is cracking the whip on this case. She is not happy." He cleared his throat. "I'll do the autopsy at ten and we'll go through the evidence with a fine-tooth comb."

Kane stared into the darkness. "I'll talk to her on the way home. I think a video conference at the autopsy with Jo and Carter will give us a different perspective on the case. They have information at hand from the other murders and we need all the help we can get." He sighed. "I'll ask Jenna and if she agrees, I'll organize it in the morning. Is there anything else you need me to do?"

"No, we're finished here." Wolfe's attention moved over to the Beast as Rowley climbed out. "Although, you should send Rowley home and maybe follow him into town. He doesn't look so good." He blew out a cloud of steam. "It would've been gruesome for him out here all alone. Trees are cracking off like gunshots and the forest moans at night. Webber said he was a little jumpy when he arrived."

He had to admit no amount of experience prevented a person being spooked when alone at a crime scene, on the edge of a forest with a psychopath running riot. Kane nodded. "Sure, but we'll wait until you're finished. After seeing what this killer is capable of, we're not leaving anyone out here alone."

As he hustled to his truck, he heard a sound almost like laughter coming from deep in the forest. He turned, hand on his weapon, and aimed his Maglite into the trees. The beam highlighted dark trunks and deep shadows but nothing moved. The hair on the back of his neck stood in a warning and he had the uncanny feeling someone was watching them.

CHAPTER FIFTY-SEVEN

Thursday morning, Week 2

It had been the longest night in Ava's life, spent wide awake in the fetal position under a pile of blankets. She hadn't dared close her eyes. Staring in disbelief, she'd watched in horror as Preacher strangled Isabella and then waited for her to recover before rendering her unconscious again. The cruelness he displayed with obvious glee, going by the smile he aimed at the camera for her benefit, had made her sick to the stomach. Helpless to do anything, she'd stared in morbid fascination as he bundled Isabella in a blanket and carried her away to be butchered. Handcuffed to the kitchen table, she'd sat in shock, numb and unable to rationalize what had happened. She couldn't cry, tears refused to fall. It had been surreal, and she'd had difficulty thinking straight.

The fire was only cinders by the time he returned. He'd laughed as he'd described his hideous night's work. In his deluded mind he figured she'd enjoy watching him. Unable to speak, she'd pasted the required smile on her lips and tried to block out his voice by humming inside her head. If she'd given him one shred of doubt, she'd be next. Only self-preservation had kept her on her toes.

He was outside now. She'd heard him in the bathroom and the smell of coffee was leaking under the bedroom door. Her only chance of survival was to play along with his delusion. He wanted a partner in crime but was she strong enough to keep up the act? The door creaked open and her eyes moved to Preacher standing in the doorway staring at her. She lifted her head, noting his Glock was missing from his belt and forced her mouth into a smile. "Morning, Preacher."

"Coffee is on. Use the bathroom and come out for breakfast. We have work to do this morning. We're going into town. I need to find another Delores and you're going to help me." Preacher met her gaze with a raised eyebrow. "You look tired. An adrenalin rush is a bitch, isn't it, when you want to sleep?"

Ava swallowed the acid creeping up from her stomach and nodded. "It sure is." She stood on trembling legs and headed for the bathroom.

As usual, he'd laid out a set of clean clothes for her. Now she understood where they all came from; she'd been wearing the garments from any number of dead women, women he'd slaughtered. It took all her effort to push the graphic images of the previous night from her mind. If she wanted to live, she had to act normal. She smothered a sob and shaking, hurried through her shower, dressed, and headed back to the kitchen. Her mind swum with ideas of how to escape but first she needed to keep up the charade. Making him believe his murders interested her would be difficult but she'd been homeless for a time and had soon learned the ability to talk to people to get a handout or a bed for the night. With men, showing interest in their lives made them easier to manipulate but Preacher was smart and would likely catch on if she wasn't careful. He wasn't the kind of man anyone could deceive. When she sat at the table, a strong smell of bleach wafted from Preacher. "Have you been cleaning?"

"Yeah." Preacher didn't restrain her and filled a cup with coffee and placed it on the table before the cream and sugar. "When I complete a work of art, I clean the cellar with bleach and then my truck. I like to make sure no trace of them remains."

Trying to keep it all together but with her heart pounding so fast, she thought she might have a stroke, she nodded. "That's a good idea. But you keep the clothes, wouldn't that be a problem?"

"No, I wash them and they're generic. Anything unusual I burn. I burn my coveralls and boots as well. That's the stink outside, those rubber boots smell something awful when they burn." Preacher served up ham and eggs. "Eat before it gets cold." He took a plate and sat opposite, examining her face. "We'll leave the next one for a few days. You look a little pale. It's the excitement, I guess." He frowned. "Maybe we shouldn't go out today."

What and lose the chance to escape you? I'm not the crazy one here. Ava wasn't hungry, her head was spinning and her stomach was trying to turn itself inside out. She sipped her coffee. Not eating would be a mistake, a big mistake. "I'm fine. I can't wait to hunt down another Delores but first tell me about you. I want to know everything." She forced the corners of her mouth up. If smiling kept her alive, she'd smile at him until her jaw ached. "You've had such an interesting life. How many Delores artworks are there?"

"Many, maybe a hundred." Preacher ate slowly watching her mouth. "All slightly different. It wasn't like that at first. It took some time to work out how to make them smile and then it was easy."

Ava nodded feigning interest. "So why homeless girls like me?" She met his dead eyes. "Or is it the ink that attracts you?"

"Both. The color of hair, size and ink but I take the homeless ones because they're waste. Nobody wants them and I'm doing a service removing them from the welfare system." He looked at her. "You're smart like me and we want the same things." He chuckled. "I've changed since meeting you. For the first time in my life, I craved a blonde the other day. I wanted to bring her home and encase her in ice. I had it all planned. I'd seen a glass front freezer for sale. It had come out of a store and I could picture this blonde girl, Emily, inside. I could keep her here and look at her all the time."

The eggs in Ava's mouth turned to sand and she kept her eyes on her plate to keep him from seeing her disgust. She could smell him, scrubbed clean with aftershave. Her attention drifted to his bare forearms visible beneath the pushed-up arms of his sweater. He didn't have a hair on him. She lifted her gaze. "Like a living portrait, although she'd be dead." She smiled. "That sounds interesting and less messy than last night."

"I guess I went a little crazy." Preacher chuckled. "I wanted to impress you and rushed my work. I usually like to freeze them. It makes their skin look smooth. Ice is a wonderful medium to work with, it's not floppy like flesh." He inclined his head as if waiting for a reaction. "Last night, there wasn't time and Delores was a screamer." He suddenly burst into laughter. "She's out on the bench under the 'Welcome to Black Rock Falls' sign. She'll be frozen by now and for sure, I'll be on the news tonight."

Insides turning and threatening to return her breakfast, Ava made herself smile. She hadn't been able to prevent Isabella's death but with a little persuasion, she could turn Preacher's boasting to her advantage. Her life hung in the balance, he would kill her without mercy if he caught her escaping, but with luck cops would be out everywhere, hunting for Isabella's killer. Cops she could run to for help. She looked at him over the rim of her cup and tried to sound convincing. "I want to see her. Just from a distance and then next time, I want to try some artwork of my own."

"Well, finish up here and we'll go now before someone finds her." Preacher ran a hand over her head and then cupped her chin. "I knew I was right about you."

*

Mist hung over the mountain and swirled around Ava's feet as she climbed into the truck. Her gaze set on a hunting rifle on a mount at the back of the cab and she hadn't missed the Glock Preacher carried in a holster under the back of his shirt. She fixed her face into a smile. If he restrained her now, she'd have no hope of escaping. She needed a plan. Something she could do to get away from him but the torture of uncertainty crushed down on her. One false move, one small mistake, and he'd kill her in an instant. An idea sprang into her mind and her teeth chattered more from fear than cold as the truck moved down the mountain. Preacher had cleared his road before daylight and the main highway had a liberal coating of brine. As they turned onto Stanton Road, way in the distance she made out flashing lights. A wave of hope washed over her. She had to escape now. "Is that the cops?"

"Maybe." Preacher stared ahead. "We are close to Delores. They'd be there to control the press."

It was now or never. Driven by shuddering fear, Ava turned to him. "I need to use the bathroom, right now. I can't wait, pull over. I'll duck into the forest."

"I'll stop at the park. You can use the bathroom there and I'll show you where I left the snowman." Preacher grinned at her.

Heart pounding, Ava wrapped her arms around her stomach, rocked back and forth, and then let out a moan. "Later. I have to go now. I can't wait."

"Okay." Preacher frowned at her but drove off-road and followed a snow-covered track some ways into the forest. He opened the glovebox and pulled out a pack of wipes and handed them to her. "Best I wait here." He slid the Glock from his waistband and pressed the muzzle against her forehead. "Don't make me come after you. Next time you run I'll kill you where you stand."

Ava grabbed the wipes and shot him a glance. "I won't run."

"You know I'll enjoy killing you if you do? Get a move on. I'll turn the truck around." He waved her away. "Don't freeze your butt off out there."

The moment she shut the door behind her, the truck moved away, making a turn. Paralyzed with fear, Ava hesitated. Indecision crawled up her spine. He'd kill her for sure if she didn't reach the cops in time. Panic had her by the throat as she aimed for the thickest part of the forest. She didn't look back and bolted deep into the trees weaving around tall pines. The cold air cut into her lungs with each stride. It was maybe four hundred yards to the police vehicle, maybe more. Ahead, the forest loomed dark and foreboding. She must go deep and then turn parallel to the road before heading back to the lights and safety. Counting as each yard went by, was her only option. If she came out the forest too far away from the cops, as sure as her name was Ava, Preacher would spot her and she'd be dead.

Ice patches cracked under her boots and low branches grabbed at her clothes as if trying to slow her down. Breathing heavily, she chanced a glance behind her and spotted Preacher's truck. He was crawling along the track keeping her in sight. If she could see him, he could see her. He was toying with her and it had just become a game she couldn't win.

In sheer panic she zig-zagged through the trees, leaving the winding animal trails to push deeper into the forest. Fallen logs slowed her down and exposed roots tangled around her feet. Blowing out huge clouds of steam, she forced one leg in front of the other. Chest aching and heart pounding, she urged her aching legs forward. She tried to push down the rising panic as the tall pines closed in around her, like prison bars. Chunks of heavy snow fell from the branches sounding like footsteps behind her. She gasped in terror. *I must keep running.*

Two hundred yards from Preacher, she turned, panting, to get her bearings but everything looked the same. Trees and more trees for miles in every direction standing like sentries in the gloom. She let out a sob. Which way back to the road? Had she gone around in circles? She stared at her footprints in the snow. All Preacher had to do was follow her trail but surely by now, she had two hundred yards on him. Heaving with exhaustion, she sagged against a tree and bent over to get her breath. Freezing air burned her lungs and warm tears spilled down her cheeks.

The rumble of an eighteen-wheeler cut through the silence and using the hum of the motor as a guide, she took off again, leaping over dead bushes. After another three hundred yards over the rough terrain and with only adrenalin keeping her going, she staggered back onto a trail. The snow was thicker but she plowed on, her feet heavy and limbs cramping. At four hundred yards, she turned and headed back to the road. Through the gloom, blue and red lights flashed like a beacon to guide her to safety. Bursting through the perimeter of the trees, she stopped and gaped in astonishment. Not a police vehicle, or a crowd of cops waiting to help her. Nothing but a few lights guarding an area surrounded by crime scene tape. The highway was empty in both directions. Terrified, and alone, she slumped against a tree and pressed her head in her hands. "I'm dead."

Boom! A shot rang out. Branches splintered in the place her head had been moments before showering her with splinters and pine needles. Ava screamed and fell to her knees covering her head.

"I'm coming for you, Delores." Preacher's voice penetrated the stillness. "I'm going to hunt you down, girl."

Boom! Boom! Two more shots followed in rapid succession, slicing off tree limbs like butter. The gunshots echoed through the forest sending birds squawking into the sky. Ava's stomach turned to ice. She had no chance against him. Boom! Boom! Boom! Gasping in terror, she ducked and weaved slipping and sliding on the uneven icy ground. Behind her she could hear him crashing through the forest and getting closer by the second. She dragged up her last ounce of energy and ran for her life.

CHAPTER FIFTY-EIGHT

Head buzzing with information, Jenna listened to Wolfe detail every minute of Isabella's horrendous last moments. The prints matched, it was her, there was no doubt. Isabella had been in trouble with the law, small time, possession and obstruction, but she didn't deserve to be murdered—no, mutilated—and left out for the wildlife to eat. The majority of Wolfe's findings matched the other victims, the drug used, the method of dismemberment and the face to face strangulation. He was almost through and with Agents Jo Wells and Ty Carter watching via a video link, Jenna was anxious to hear their conclusions.

"There are two significant differences in this murder." Wolfe glanced up at her. "I have reason to believe he strangled her to the point of unconsciousness at least twice. The various marks on her neck are an indication." He walked to the screen. "More importantly, this." He pointed to an X-ray of the victim's neck. "In laymen's terms, her neck is broken. From the marks on the flesh, I'd say from sharp downward pressure from a boot to the back of her neck. I've seen this injury before; it's typically used in the military, a fast and lethal way to kill someone. I figure she woke up when he started to cut her. He had to stop her screaming and finished her quickly."

"I knew it! The killer's made a crucial mistake. He might as well have left us a calling card." Mind reeling with possibilities, Jenna turned to the screen. "Carter, didn't you figure the killer might have been in the military? Did you have time to hunt down any suspects?"

"Nothing specific, but Kalo is on it. Now we have names it will be easier." Carter stared into the screen. *"We did compile a list of men living in or around Black Rock Falls who served in the military and there are many."*

Jenna nodded. "Jo, why do you believe the killer has changed his MO. Kane believes it's because he was in a hurry and now, he's escalating."

"Yeah, I agree with Kane. He needed a quick fix and wanted to be noticed. By leaving the body beside the sign, he's thumbing his nose at the sheriff's department. He believes he's invincible and this makes him very dangerous. If he's cornered, he'll kill without any thought or reason. Don't try and talk him down, Jenna. There's no reasoning with a psychopath when his psychosis reaches this level." She turned to talk to someone and then turned back and smiled. *"We've got something for you. Two of your persons of interest are ex-military, Axel Reed and Josiah Brock. This information would remove Claude Grady out of the equation, nothing in his background suggests military or unarmed combat experience. Do you have eyes on the other two?"*

"One of them has vanished." Jenna frowned. "Axel Reed still hasn't returned home. Rowley drove up to his cabin at first light, he's not there either. Josiah Brock was home, Rowley checked on his cabin as well. The killer must be using another cabin. Somewhere close by."

"I don't recall passing any cabins on the way up the mountain to Brock's place." Kane stared at his boots, hands on hips in deep thought. "If we could get a bird up, we'd be able to search. Right now, it's hopeless." He lifted his gaze to Jenna. "A cabin must have access to the highway. We've probably driven past it a million times."

An idea came to Jenna and she headed for the door removing her mask and gloves. "I need to make a call."

She called the office. Old Deputy Walters was on duty. He liked to come in a few times a week and help on the front counter. "Hey,

I have a suspect who lives on the west side of the mountain, out on the backroad that goes way up top. He's out of Snowberry Way. We visited one cabin high up and another cabin lower, maybe ten minutes' drive away. Do you recall any old disused cabins out on that backroad between those two or beyond maybe?"

"There was one, out of Snowberry Way but it's been a while since the rockslide." Walters paused for a beat. *"I'm not sure if it's still there or if anyone would risk living there. The road is closed. There was a bad rockslide some ten years ago after a melt. The entire rockface just slid down. The town council posted warning signs and nobody goes near the place. That's the only deserted one I recall. There is one up higher, a small place owned by a trucker, I believe, and then there's another one further down with a mess of land around it."*

Exhilaration rushed through Jenna. He'd described both cabins she'd visited and she remembered seeing the danger signs. So, there was a cabin hidden up there. "Thanks. Tell Rowley to head out to the ME's office and pack for bear."

"Sure thing." Deputy Walters disconnected.

Everything was sliding into place. She hurried back into the morgue. "I know where to find the cabin and hopefully the killer. It's one of two men. Reed or Brock. Reed is my main suspect but I'm not discounting Josiah Brock either. He seems over cooperative to me and it wouldn't surprise me in the least if he is trying to slip under our radar. They both live in the same area and either one of them could be using the deserted cabin to keep the girls prisoner. If the killer is as unstable as Jo believes, we'll need backup. Rowley is meeting us here."

"I'll come." Wolfe pulled of his mask and gloves. "Emily, log the samples and Webber, get the body back into storage." He looked at Jenna. "I'll grab my gear." He headed out the door.

Jenna smiled at him. "Thanks." She turned to the screen. "We'll call you when we get back."

"Jenna." Carter looked at her, his expression serious. *"He's got nothing to lose. Don't take any chances."*

Jenna nodded. "I won't and my team will watch my back. We'll talk later."

As Jenna hustled beside Kane to his truck, she turned to him. "We can't allow this killer to slip through our fingers. We may be lucky and he'll come in without a problem. Most psychopathic serial killers believe they'll never go to jail but if he comes out shooting like Jo believes, I want you to take him down." She walked to the back of his truck and stared him in the eye. "We can't take the risk of him getting away and killing again."

"I want it made perfectly clear, Jenna." Kane handed her a liquid Kevlar vest. "If he shoots at us, I'm to take the shot, without your direct order."

Jenna secured her vest and pulled on her coat. She attached her earbud and turned on the receiver. "Yes. I'm not risking my team or the life of another girl." She handed him the case containing his sniper rifle. "Lock and load."

CHAPTER FIFTY-NINE

Jenna cleared her head to concentrate on bringing down a dangerous man. She looked at the three men before her, all willing to put their lives on the line to protect Black Rock Falls. Proud didn't come close to how she felt about her team but being sentimental wouldn't help in this situation. She'd play to her strengths and each member of her team was an asset. "We'll park some ways from the cabin and go in silent. If the killer is there, we call him out and play it by ear." She turned to Kane. "When we get there, get into position and then give me the go-ahead. Rowley you're with me. Wolfe you take the opposite side to Kane and watch our backs." She looked from one to the other. "We have two men as persons of interest at this stage and we don't have proof either is The Sculptor, but right now both are sending up red flags. Don't take chances. I don't want any dead heroes."

She instantly regretted deciding on a plan of action because deep down inside, she just knew something would go wrong. Predicting the actions of a psychopath was like crossing Niagara Falls on a tightrope, blindfolded. They headed toward Stanton Forest. Jenna rode with Kane and Wolfe was riding shotgun with Rowley. Snow built up on the windshield wipers and gathered around the windows as visibility decreased into a wall of white. As they traveled down Main, the vehicles ahead of them slowed to handle the rapidly changing conditions. She chewed on her bottom lip and looked at Kane. "We won't make it up the mountain if this weather sets in."

"We have to." Kane's hands tightened on the wheel. "If this is our killer, he is escalating fast and he won't care about the weather, in fact I believe he'd welcome a blizzard to cover his tracks."

By the time they reached Stanton, and the road opened onto a highway winding its way through the mountain, they'd left the local vehicles way behind. Jenna shivered as the crime scene flashers and tape came into view on the edge of town, she looked away in time to see someone bounding through the forest. "Slow down. I see someone."

When Kane pulled off the road, she turned and looked behind her. "Back there. It could've been a woman but she was moving fast."

Boom! Boom!

Jenna hit her mic on her com pack. "Shots fired! There's a woman running through the forest about two hundred yards away, heading toward town." She glanced wildly around. "Go back, there's a fire break two hundred yards or so away on the left. It runs into The Devil's Boulder. We can park there and take cover, if we can get through the snow."

"We'll get through." Kane spun the wheel and headed back toward town.

Jenna hit her mic. "Follow us. We'll go past the woman and take cover behind The Devil's Boulder."

Boom!

"I hope he's not aiming this way." Kane's expression was grim. "I don't take too kindly to people shooting up my truck."

Jenna gripped the edge of her seat. "There on the left. Dammit, the snow looks deep."

"If it's a fire break, it will be maintained regular. We'll be fine." Kane turned the Beast into the snow-covered road and slowed to a crawl. "We're good, the tires are gripping just fine. I see the boulder." He maneuvered the truck in close beside it and scanned the area. "Where's the shooter?"

Boom! Boom!

Jenna stared into the dark forest and caught sight of a flash of red. "There's someone coming this way." She pointed into the forest and then turned to him. "You'll need a vantage point."

"I'll be on your left." Kane grabbed his sniper rifle and slid silently from the truck.

By the time, Jenna had opened her door, Kane had disappeared into the trees. She turned as Rowley and Wolfe came to her side. "The woman is running this way. Fan out. We'll wait until she comes to us. Kane is positioned on the left. He'll handle the shooter."

"Copy that." Wolfe moved out vanishing like a mist into the forest.

"I'm watching your back." Rowley gave her a determined stare.

"I said fan out. The shooter might slip through our net." Jenna searched the forest. It was so dark and gloomy, she had to strain her eyes but movement ahead, caught her attention and then in the distance a young woman stumbled into an opening.

She opened her mic. "Here she comes."

Boom!

Branches shattered and the girl cried out and took off in a different direction. The young woman was over one hundred yards away. Jenna waved her hands. "This way, run this way."

She caught sight of the girl's wide frightened eyes as she tripped and fell, sliding over the icy ground. Terrified the gunman had a clear shot, Jenna broke cover and zig-zagged through the forest, to draw fire. It worked.

Boom!

A branch crashed down so close to her that lumps of snow prickly with pine needles bombarded her. She ducked behind a thick tree to catch her breath and drew her weapon but the girl was bounding away from her.

Boom!

The pine tree beside Jenna shattered, peppering her cheek with splinters. She peeked around the tree and then dashed through the forest, chasing the girl.

"Jenna, I'm coming in on your right." Wolfe's voice came through Jenna's earpiece. *"Wait for me. I'd be able to take him down from here but you're in my line of fire."*

"Sorry, Shane. If you miss, he'll kill her. Hold your fire. If I can get to her position, with any luck, he'll be distracted and break cover. Kane will have a clear shot." Jenna took off in the girl's direction putting her body between herself and the gunman. She hit her mic again as she ran. "He's not killing another girl on my watch. Jenna out."

CHAPTER SIXTY

Sobbing with fear, Ava crawled into the bushes. She'd seen a woman, waving her arms but at first, her brain had failed to register the bright yellow sheriff's logo on the woman's shirt. She'd been yelling something but the pounding in her ears had blocked out everything. Panting, she peered through the leaves. The sheriff was zig-zagging through the trees toward her, her shirt like a bright target in the dim forest. Ava wanted to scream out a warning but fear had closed her throat. Preacher was fifty yards from her and had stopped moving, his attention fixed on the sheriff. She watched in horror as he raised his rifle and aimed.

Boom! The tree where the sheriff had been standing exploded and woodchips flew out in a cloud of sawdust and pine needles. The sound of footsteps crunched on the snow, and she caught sight of Preacher moving with purpose but in no hurry through the trees like a hunter stalking his prey. Bushes moved and the sheriff darted toward her.

"This is the sheriff. Put down your weapon. We have you surrounded." The sheriff poked her head around the tree.

Boom!

The sound came like the roar of a dragon and the pine tree beside the sheriff blew apart but the brave woman kept on moving closer to her. Terror held Ava in a vicelike grip as she crawled on hands and knees toward her. If she could get ten yards farther, she'd get to her. "Help me! He's trying to kill me." She pushed her voice out of her parched throat. "He killed my friend. He's killed tons of women. I've been his prisoner. Help me... Pleeeeease."

"Stay down." The sheriff stared at her and then flattened her back against a pine, her weapon held chest high. "Take cover. I'll try and get closer, hang on." She dashed from tree to tree.

Boom! Boom!

Ava rolled away seconds before a bush exploded beside her sending a plume of ice and dead twigs high in the air. She poked her head around the trunk and caught sight of movement in the trees. She gasped in terror as Preacher advanced on the sheriff.

Boom!

Branches shattered all around the sheriff and the smell of gun smoke filled the air. Ava wanted to cover her ears to block the relentless crunch, crunch, crunch of footsteps as Preacher kept on coming. He was so close and wouldn't miss next time. Teeth chattering with fear, Ava watched in horror as the sheriff dashed between an opening and slid to her side. The woman stood over her like a bear protecting its cub.

"Stay down." The sheriff glanced at her. "I won't let him hurt you. Keep nice and quiet."

Panic gripped Ava as she took in the determined woman. It was hopeless. Preacher would kill them without mercy. "God help us, he's coming."

CHAPTER SIXTY-ONE

Pressing a finger to her lips, Jenna indicated to the girl to be quiet. She made out a man moving through the trees. He was being cautious but had the rifle aimed at her. She pressed her mic. "Shooter in sight. He's in the cover of trees. Do you copy, Kane?"

"Roger that." Kane's voice came through her earpiece. *"Waiting for a clear shot."*

Jenna bit her bottom lip. "I'll try and get him into the clearing."

Boom! Boom!

A massive chunk of wood vanished from the tree in a hail of woodchips. Sharp pain pierced Jenna's thigh. She glanced down at the blood oozing from her leg onto the pristine white ground. Lightheaded, she swayed a little and tightened her grip on her Glock as the shooter came through the trees and stopped just before a small clearing. At her feet the girl sobbed but Jenna lifted her chin. "Sheriff's department. Lower your weapon, put your hands on your head."

"I don't think so." Keeping in the cover of the trees, the man pressed his back to a tall pine and a smile crossed his lips. "Bleeding pretty bad there, huh sheriff?' He chuckled. "Head dizzy? You're bleeding out and won't last more than a minute or so. All I have to do is wait you out." He slowly pulled a Glock from under his jacket and rested the rifle against the tree. "Then I'll take Delores and skin her alive and maybe hang her in a tree close by for people to admire." He pulled down his scarf and wiped the sweat from his brow.

Astonished, Jenna recognized him at once. "You didn't fool me, Josiah." In an effort to make him step into the clearing and give Kane a clear shot, she moved from behind the safety of the tree. "That's why I'm here. I know about the second cabin at Snowberry Way. I know you're The Sculptor."

Ignoring the agony in her thigh, she held her Glock in trembling fingers aiming for him. Dizzy and bleeding heavily, she could feel the warmth of her own life's blood running into her boot. If she took the shot and missed, they'd both die. She needed to hang on for a few more seconds. Her team had him surrounded and all Kane needed was Josiah to take one more step. *Come on, move out of the trees.*

"Finding it hard to focus, Sheriff?" Josiah Brock dropped his Glock to his side and straightened. "You couldn't hit me if you tried. Your hands are shaking. You remind me of a sick dog, maybe I'll put you out of your misery." He raised the Glock and moved toward her out of the cover of the trees.

"Noooooo!" Ava's voice split the silence.

The second before Jenna squeezed the trigger, she heard the zing of a bullet. Her discharging weapon sounded loud in the still forest but her attention was fixed on Josiah. His smile had faded into a puzzled expression as the Glock slipped from his fingers and he staggered a few steps. Kane's bullet had gone through his neck and a crimson patch bloomed on his chest from her own shot. In an almost graceful collapse, The Sculptor fell face down in the snow and didn't move. He hadn't made a sound. Unable to stand a second longer, Jenna slid down the trunk of the tree and sat in the snow beside the trembling girl. Blood soaked Jenna's jeans and cold seeped through her clothes. Lightheaded, she swayed a little and tightened her grip on her Glock keeping it aimed at Josiah Brock. The girl beside her had covered her face and cried silently. Shivering, she pressed her mic. "Kane, the target is down."

"Do we have an ID?" She could hear Kane crunching through the forest.

Jenna winced at the pain. "Yeah, it's Josiah Brock"

"Copy, Kane out."

Jenna swallowed the lump in her throat. Combat mode Kane was front and center. She understood, after so many missions as a sniper Kane preferred to use his skill to disable rather than kill, but he'd carried out her orders and she'd have to carry the guilt of taking a life with him. She shook her head to remain conscious and hit her mic again. "Wolfe, I'm hit."

"On my way." Wolfe sounded unfazed and calm. *"I have you in sight."*

She gave the girl a little shake. "You're safe. He can't hurt anyone now. What's your name?"

"Ava Price." Ava sat up warily looking around. Her teeth chattered like castanets. "Is he dead?"

Jenna nodded. "Very."

"You're hurt. What can I do?" Ava's eyes rounded in panic.

Jenna smiled at her. "I'll be fine and help is on the way. "Are you okay?"

"Yeah, just a few scratches." Ava searched her face. "He didn't hurt me."

Relived, Jenna tried to keep her occupied. "Tell me about the shooter."

"You called him Josiah but his name is Preacher. He strangled Isabella in front of me. He likes to cut people up with chainsaws." She looked around wildly at the sound of footsteps and shrank back when Wolfe burst through the trees.

Jenna gripped her arm. "It's okay, he's with me."

"What was that crazy stunt?" Wolfe flicked his attention over Josiah's body and then dropped to his knees beside her dragging off his backpack.

Only Wolfe could speak to her like that. He'd become like a big brother and never pulled his punches. Jenna shrugged. "I needed to draw his fire and get him out into the open. He was going to kill Ava. I had to do something." She glanced at the body. "Ava said he called himself 'Preacher.' If I'd known that before, I'd have been convinced it was Axel Reed."

"Well, it looks like you both had a hand in taking him down. Personally, I wouldn't have waited until he drew down on me. The shooting was more than enough intent to kill." Wolfe cut away a section of her pants and examined her leg. "Well, darn. A chunk of wood went straight through your flesh. It will sting some when I clean it. You'll need to go to the ER to have the splinters removed, and they'll give you antibiotics. I'm insisting this time, Jenna."

"Okay, fine, I'll go. Just do it. I'm starting to freeze my butt off." She glanced up as Rowley pushed through the branches. "Rowley, this is Ava Price. Take her to my office, call Doc Brown to tend her injuries. Keep her warm. I'll be there shortly."

"Are you okay?" Rowley scanned her face. "A bullet?"

"Nope." Wolfe looked at him. "A nice chunk of pine but she is going to the ER."

Jenna smiled at him. "I'll be fine." She winced as Wolfe poured alcohol over her wound. "Ouch!"

It seemed forever before Kane walked to her position. When he crouched down beside her. She looked at him. "What took so long?"

"I called Carter to get Brock's details. He was dishonorably discharged from the military, we can run his prints for a positive ID, we have them on file." He looked at her. "You picked the sleeper, Jenna." He gave her a slow smile. "With you and Jo profiling, I'll soon be out of a job."

"Never. I need you, Dave." Jenna tried to ignore the pain in her leg. "I was thinking outside the box. I had two potential suspects and yes, Reed seemed to be the killer but I couldn't dismiss Brock. Apart from being a long-haul trucker, Brock didn't seem dangerous at all. He was polite and cooperative—too cooperative." She sighed. "I wonder why he used the name, 'Preacher'?"

"That I know. Once I had his name, Bobby Kalo dug up info about him in seconds." Kane frowned. "It was a name given to him at school. In his yearbook under his photograph he is listed as most likely to become a minister. In later books, he's listed as Josiah 'Preacher' Brock."

She shook her head, finding it hard to believe the polite Josiah capable of so many murders. "This is the problem we face every time a murder happens in our town. Violent psychopaths blend in, they could be a neighbor or the friendly old man at the store, the woman cutting hair at the beauty parlor. They don't look or act differently to anyone else. It seems the boogeyman comes in many flavors."

"Yeah." Kane stared into the dark forest. "And the moment we catch one, another comes along to take his place. I'm wondering more than ever if this town is cursed? I mean, look at Kim Strickland, who'd have thought an infatuation could've escalated into attempted murder?" He stared at her. "If we hadn't gotten to you in time—"

"But you did. You always have my back. The town isn't cursed, Dave." Jenna shook her head. "It would be cursed if we allowed killers to roam the streets but we've brought down every one who dared to set foot on our turf. Like you said, we're batting a thousand." She smiled at Wolfe as he finished bandaging her leg and then turned her attention back to Kane. "I say, bring it on."

CHAPTER SIXTY-TWO

Saturday, Week 2

After suffering through another painful night on Friday, Jenna decided to remain in her office for the day. The time after the shooting had been a blur. Kane had taken her to the ER where she'd spent a couple of hours having the splinters removed and the nasty puncture wound cleaned. According to the ER doctor, she'd had half the forest embedded in the wound. She never made it back to the office that day. Doc Brown had insisted Ava spend the night under observation, so the interview had to be held late on Friday.

When Jenna conducted the interview with Ava, the mystery around Josiah Brock came to light. The horrific tale of murder, kidnapping, drugs, escape, and capture had stunned everyone. Jenna had spoken to her alone but Kane, Wolfe, and Rowley had been watching along with Jo and Carter via a video link. It had been wonderful to have Jo whispering in her ear and guiding her through a very difficult interview. Jo's knowledge of framing a question to take a person back in their mind to remember a certain event was impressive. She'd seen Kane work his magic on traumatized witnesses but this time, with Jo's assistance, she'd taken the lead.

Ava revealed what Josiah told her about his past, and the way he'd been ridiculed and bullied throughout adolescence. The information had supplied a reason for his psychosis. This had been validated when Ava described his obsession with a girl named Delores and his need for her to smile and look at him. Jo had been correct: Delores Garcia, the high-school student found murdered and buried in a shallow grave eighteen years ago, had been Josiah's first victim and he'd regarded every victim since as a reenactment of her murder. The four-year gap between her murder and the next one fitted perfectly with his tour of duty. When Jenna discovered he'd been dishonorably discharged for attacking a female officer, everything fell into place. He was almost a textbook case. An already psychotic child, submitted to endless abuse during adolescence became the killer of his tormentor and each time he met anyone who resembled Delores, the need to killed became uncontrollable. Having the FBI at hand had been invaluable. Delores Garcia's cold case file had been reopened. Now with fresh evidence and DNA samples, the case would be laid to rest.

Waiting in her office for Kane and Wolfe to return from searching Josiah's house and his eighteen-wheeler truck, Jenna tried unsuccessfully to ignore the throbbing in her leg and spent the time updating case files. After reading the report from the DA on the Kim Strickland case, she'd been relived to discover the woman had pleaded guilty and had a court date coming up for sentencing. One thing was for sure, she'd be spending a long time behind bars.

It had been a lonely morning but she'd had Duke to keep her company—well, at least his snores and running in his sleep had kept her amused until Rowley dropped by to give her a report on a minor road accident. She had read his case notes and nodded. "Send the people involved a report for their insurance and then you can go to lunch." She heard voices. "Is that Kane calling you?"

"Yeah." Rowley poked his head around the door. "It looks like he dropped by Aunt Betty's to grab takeout. I'll go help him." He smiled at her and hurried out the room.

Jenna opened her notebook and selected a pen from the chipped mug on her desk, ready to take notes.

Kane had been gone for a long time, longer than she expected for a forensic search of a house and truck. When he eventually led the way into the room with Rowley close behind, Duke woke with a start, waddled around her desk, and did his happy dance, as if Kane had been missing for a week. She smiled at the display of affection. "He's missed you."

"More like he can smell hotdog sausage, Susie Hartwig put them by for him. They were left over from the Friday special." Kane dropped bags on the table and unpacked a six pack of to-go cups. "I picked up double the coffee, I figured it's going to take time to unravel everything we discovered about Josiah Brock." He opened a paper bag and emptied a pile of sausages into Duke's plate. "Wolfe has left the explaining to me, he has a ton of evidence he needs to analyze." He dropped into a seat, sighed, and reached for a bag of takeout. "We had to drive to Brock's employer out at Blackwater and collect his truck. Wolfe drove it back to the morgue and set Emily and Webber to work on it."

Jenna sipped her coffee. "So was the cabin as Ava described?"

"Yeah." Kane pulled out his phone and tapped the screen. He looked up at her. "I've transferred all the images I took at the house to the files. It will be easier to explain, if we go through them one at a time."

After setting down her cup, Jenna accessed the file and turned her computer screen so everyone could view it. "Okay, the first series seems to be a kitchen."

"Yeah. Everything we found verifies Ava's account of what happened there." Kane motioned with a sandwich to the image. "The kitchen table with the TV opposite, where Brock made her watch as he strangled Isabella. Can you make out the metal rings on the table where he handcuffed her? If you flick through, you'll see the ones he has on the floor too. Moving on to the next frame, there's the dumbwaiter and if you scan the images, you'll see the gap inside the wall, where Ava escaped only to be caught and taken back. It's all as she detailed."

Dumfounded Jenna stared at the hundred or so images as Kane explained. She looked at him. "And the truck?"

"Before I go onto the truck, open the file marked, 'physical evidence.'" Kane narrowed his gaze. "Our killer took trophies. There's over fifty. Wolfe will examine them all but they tally with the images we found on his computer and phone."

Jenna stared at the strands of hair carefully arranged and labeled on coat hangers. "Fifty?"

"At least." Kane pointed to the screen. "They're not labels, they're IDs of one sort or another and the hair was pulled out, not cut. This is the reason we took so long, every strand of hair had to be processed separately. I've sent a list of the names on the IDs to Carter. The FBI will take it from here and track down the victims' families. He'll send you a full report when it's done but it may take months."

Astonished, Jenna sat back in her chair trying to grasp the enormity of the crimes the quiet, helpful, Josiah Brock had committed. She shook her head. "How did he do this under our noses?"

"Beats me." Kane flicked through his phone. "Before I forget, he kept their clothes as well and shoes. Ava's story checks out. He kept women prisoner in his cellar. It's impossible to know how long this went on. He was very smart and chose hitchhikers from other states, brought them here and stored them until he needed to kill them. Ava mentioned three of them at once, so he was collecting women to kill."

Jenna pushed her sandwich away, no longer hungry. "If he was keeping the women holed up in his cabin and dispersing them in other states why suddenly start leaving bodies all over town?"

"Ah, I have a theory. Well, Wolfe and me came up with a theory after examining his truck. I'll explain." Kane took a bite of pie, chewed, and swallowed. "Brock has a refrigerated section in his truck, it was well hidden behind a blocked off section with a door. I guess he made it look like an extra sleeping area in case he was pulled over and inspected. We also found body bags and Carter has been running his credit card purchases and Brock regularly purchased dry ice. We figure he picked up women on the road, killed some, and stored them in his truck. He used the dry ice to quick freeze them. He dumped them in other states, weeks and sometimes years after." He sipped his drink. "Those he killed here, he transported to another state and left the bodies in unusual places, all posed and eyes wide open."

"He must have had a place to keep them frozen here?" Jenna swallowed hard. Her head ached with all the information. "We know about the meat locker but that would only work in winter."

"He had that covered." Kane eyed her over his cup. "In the basement, he had the section where he kept the women and what could only be described as a kill room. Plastic draped walls and a row of industrial sized freezers. He had five or six chainsaws, a bench for dismembering them, knives, everything." He frowned. "There's more. We found a hard drive, packed with video footage of him strangling and dismembering his victims in that room."

Jenna stared at him dumbfounded. "Are you saying he kept his victims frozen until he had a delivery in another state, and as the women were from all over and homeless, nothing tied him to Black Rock Falls?"

"Exactly." Kane finished his pie.

Jenna frowned at him. "That doesn't explain why he started dumping bodies here?"

"We figured after he'd collected three girls, he needed the space, and the urge to kill was escalating, so he had to dispose of the bodies fast." Kane shrugged. "His usual disposal methods included waiting until the temperature dropped to freezing. His victims were always found at the beginning of winter. This way, he avoided any chance of decomposition and the accompanying smell." He cleared his throat. "We might have found a trigger."

Jenna sighed. "Do tell."

"Carter discovered Brock had a problem with intimacy all his life. He'd seen many doctors about being impotent. Jo figures this is the reason he never raped any of his victims. It's obvious by the images he took of them in a drugged state, he was attracted to them. If Delores discovered his condition and used it to taunt him after being bullied for so long at school it could have pushed him over the edge."

An overwhelming sorrow flooded Jenna, both for the victims and Josiah Brock. After the cruel bullying he'd endured, he had lashed out to remove all the Deloreses from existence. The poor women, murdered for no fault other than resembling his tormenter. She looked at Kane, confusion tearing her apart. "If we hadn't taken him down, could he have ever been rehabilitated?"

"After fifty murders? Jenna, rehabilitation would have been off the table at once and if he'd gone to trial, states would be lining up to execute him." Kane leaned back in his chair and regarded her for long minutes. "Brock told everyone his name was Preacher. Do you recall Emily's flat tire, the one Wolfe was convinced was slashed? The guy who offered to give her a ride said he was a minister. I'd bet my last dollar that was him. Would you be feeling so compassionate toward him if he'd murdered Emily?"

Cold tingled down Jenna's spine at the thought. "No, I guess not."

"I'm glad after dealing with so many murderers, you still have compassion but having doubts about killing Josiah Brock is unfounded. You were under fire and it came down to *you* or him. I don't know what went through your mind, when you pulled the trigger but as I lined up my shot, all I could think of was how much Isabella Bennet suffered before she died by his hand. We gave him the best possible option. Unlike his victims, he didn't feel a thing."

EPILOGUE

Monday, Week 3

A knock came at Jenna's office door and Rowley appeared.

"Do you have a minute?"

She waved him inside. "I do. Problem?"

"No." Rowley grinned broadly and pulled Sandy into the room. His girlfriend's cheeks had flushed an attractive shade of pink and she looked embarrassed. "We have an announcement. We're engaged." He swung Sandy around and then placed her carefully back on her feet.

"He asked me over lunch." Sandy grinned at her and wiggled her fingers displaying a beautiful engagement ring. "It was his great-grandma's ring and it fits like a glove."

Jenna smiled at them. "Congratulations! Have you set a date?"

"Yeah the first Saturday after Christmas." Sandy grinned. "It will be a very small wedding, parents and close friends. I hope you and Kane will come?" She was radiant. "Do you think Shane would allow Julie and Anna to be my bridesmaids? All my relatives are boys."

Jenna laughed. It was good to see happy faces. "I'm sure he'd be delighted and we wouldn't miss it."

"That's great!" Sandy gave Rowley a peck on the cheek. "I have to get back to work. You don't need to walk me out. You're needed here." She gave a wave and practically danced down the hallway.

Jenna leaned back in her chair. "I thought you'd planned to ask her at Christmas?"

"Well, I did but we've had so many killers in town, I realized life is too short to wait and I didn't want to waste a single second." Rowley looked abashed. "Does that sound stupid?"

After a couple of weeks Jenna would never forget, at last a ray of sunshine. "No, it sounds like you're in love."

When Kane ducked into the room and looked at them with a bemused expression, Jenna stood and walked to his side. "Jake has proposed to Sandy. Isn't that neat?"

"It's wonderful news." Instead of shaking Rowley's hand, Kane gave him a bearhug. "About time."

"We must throw a party." Jenna stared at Rowley. "Unless your family is planning one, I'd love to hold one at my ranch?" She grinned. "You know, as a kid, I always wanted to be an event organizer. I love throwing a party. It's so much easier than fighting crime."

"That would be great." Rowley was grinning and his eyes were wet. "I can't believe she accepted." He shook his head. "I thought she'd want a big wedding but she said, straight up, she'd rather elope than waste our savings. We both want a ranch and have the deposit saved up already." He looked at Kane. "We need to talk. Got a minute?"

"Sure." Kane winked at Jenna and turned to Rowley. "You know the sheriff might be able to sweet talk the mayor into giving you the use of the town hall for the reception. There's not any events scheduled early January on the calendar."

Jenna watched them walk out the door and sat down. With nothing happening in town, she'd start organizing a party. She'd made a few notes when her phone rang. She didn't recognize the number. "Sheriff Alton."

"Hi, this is Ava Price. You saved me in the forest."

"Hello, Ava. How are you?"

"I'm home with my folks. I just called to say thank you. If you and your deputies hadn't dropped by, I'd be dead. It's changed my life. I've had a second chance and I'm going back to school."

Overwhelmed by emotion, Jenna wiped a tear from her cheek. "That's wonderful. I'm so proud of you and I bet your folks are too."

"Thanks, and please thank Deputy Kane for me. It couldn't have been easy for him. I hope he's okay."

Jenna stared out the door. "He's a fine man and would do the same for anyone in trouble."

"That's good to know. I'll be going now. Bye." The line went dead.

After making a list of what she needed for the engagement party, Jenna spent some time ordering what she needed. When Kane's shadow filled the door, she looked up to see him grinning. He'd been down to Aunt Betty's again from the delicious smell of hot peach pie wafting around him. "Okay, what have you done?"

"Me? I haven't done anything." Kane placed the takeout on the desk and slid a large slab of her favorite chocolate toward her. "Although, I might want to sweeten you up."

Jenna leaned forward in her chair and met his amused gaze. "Spill it, Dave."

"Sandy was in Aunt Betty's and we had a chat. Her folks don't have too much spare cash for the wedding and all." Kane remained standing. He wouldn't look at her and one finger traced the pattern on her leather-topped desk. He raised his head slowly. "As it's such a small wedding and you're so good at organizing parties, I volunteered you as their wedding planner."

Trying to hold back the rush of delight at the news, she met his gaze and allowed her smile to break through. "Really? Wow! I'd love to. I'll go and have a chat with Sandy after work. Thanks for putting my name forward." She laughed. "And the chocolate."

"Great." Kane let out a long sigh and sank into one of the chairs in front of her desk. Instead of eating he busied himself with his phone.

What could come between Kane and food? She eyed him with suspicion. "The pie is getting cold."

"Ah… yeah. Just a minute. I have some organizing to do as well." He tapped away on his phone and then grinned at her. "Great, I've ordered a private room at the Cattleman's Hotel and eight beds for the night."

Jenna blinked not understanding. "That's my job and they'll need more than eight rooms."

"Nah." Kane grinned at her. "For the buck's party, Jenna. I'm the best man."

Jenna burst out laughing. "You sure are."

A LETTER FROM D.K. HOOD

Thanks so much for choosing my novel and coming with me on another thrilling adventure with Kane and Alton in *Her Shallow Grave*.

We've all been through a historic event this year, many of us isolated from family and friends. I do hope *Her Shallow Grave* will offer a few days of escapism for you.

If you'd like to keep up to date with all my latest releases, just sign up at the website link below. Your details will never be shared and you can unsubscribe at any point.

www.bookouture.com/dk-hood

If you enjoyed my story, I would be very grateful if you could leave a review and recommend my book to your friends and family. I really enjoy hearing from readers, so feel free to ask me questions at any time. You can get in touch on my Facebook page or Twitter or through my blog.

Thank you so much for your support.
D.K. Hood

@DKHood_Author

dkhoodauthor

www.dkhood.com

dkhood-author.blogspot.com.au

ACKNOWLEDGMENTS

This year we have faced incredible challenges. All of us involved with bringing this book to publication have worked from home. I can only imagine how difficult it has been for Bookouture to carry on as usual to produce an amazing lineup of books for you to read, but they have succeeded under the leadership of CEO Oliver Rhodes and Publisher Jenny Geras.

Special thanks to Superwoman, Helen Jenner, Associate Publisher, my guiding light and her outstanding team, including thanks to Managing Editor, Alexandra Holmes, Leodora Darlington who helps with my audio books and my talented narrator Patricia Rodriguez, who brings my characters to life. Thanks to Alex Crow, Head of Digital Marketing, and to Kim Nash, Noelle Holten and Sarah Hardy who form the hardworking and truly remarkable promotions team. And thanks to Peta Nightingale, Head of Talent, Contracts and Rights, and to my gifted cover designer, James Macey.

There are so many more people behind the scenes to acknowledge and my thanks goes out to all of you.

Last but by no means least, the wonderful readers and bloggers who post reviews for my books, and join me on Facebook for a chat. I really appreciate your kind words and support.

Lightning Source UK Ltd.
Milton Keynes UK
UKHW040745250321
380971UK00001B/108